PENDRAGON

JOURNAL OF AN ADVENTURE THROUGH TIME AND SPACE

Book Nine:
Raven Rise

PENDRAGON

JOURNAL OF AN ADVENTURE THROUGH TIME AND SPACE

Book One: The Merchant of Death
Book Two: The Lost City of Faar
Book Three: The Never War
Book Four: The Reality Bug
Book Five: Black Water
Book Six: The Rivers of Zadaa
Book Seven: The Quillan Games
Book Eight: The Pilgrims of Rayne
Book Nine: Raven Rise
Book Ten: To Be Announced

PENDRAGON

JOURNAL OF AN ADVENTURE THROUGH TIME AND SPACE

Book Nine: Raven Rise

D. J. MacHale

Simon & Schuster Books for Young Readers
New York London Toronto Sydney

SIMON & SCHUSTER BOOKS FOR YOUNG READERS
An imprint of Simon & Schuster Children's Publishing Division
1230 Avenue of the Americas, New York, New York 10020

The text for this book is set in Apollo MT.
Manufactured in the United States of America
2 4 6 8 10 9 7 5 3 1
Library of Congress Cataloging-in-Publication Data
MacHale, D. J.
Raven rise / D. J. MacHale.—1st ed.
p. cm.—(Pendragon ; bk. 9)
"Journal of an adventure through time and space."
Summary: While Pendragon is trapped on Ibara, Alder returns to Denduron and reluctantly goes into battle again, and other Travelers face obstacles of various sorts, Saint Dane gains the power he seeks on Second Earth and makes his push toward destroying and rebuilding Halla.
ISBN-13: 978-1-4169-1418-1 (hardcover : alk. paper)
ISBN-10: 1-4169-1418-8 (hardcover : alk. paper)
[1. Adventure and adventurers—Fiction. 2. Space and time—Fiction. 3. Diaries—Fiction. 4. Fantasy.] I. Title.
PZ7.M177535Rav 2008
[Fic]—dc22
2007046886

For Gene & Theresa Gregory

PREFACE

The penultimate Pendragon.

Has a nice ring to it, no? In case you don't know what penultimate means, find a dictionary and look it up. Right now. Go. I'm serious. The book will still be here when you get back. Promise.

For those of you who already know what it means, bravo!

For those of you who actually ran off and looked it up, well done.

For those of you slackers who didn't know and didn't look it up either (cough *lazy* cough) I'll just tell you.

Penultimate: Second to last in a series or sequence.

Yup. This is it. The second to last chapter in the story of Bobby Pendragon and the Travelers. It's hard to believe. When I began writing *The Merchant of Death* so long ago, reaching the end of the story seemed like a distant, unattainable goal. Now we are on the verge of bringing it all to a close. I can actually see light at the end of the tunnel. Of course the tunnel happens to be a flume and the light is a force that was sent from the far reaches of Halla to come grab hold and launch us on the next-to-final leg of our journey.

So we may be close, but we're not done just yet.

You may think that getting a Pendragon book on the shelf is all about me. It isn't. Not even close. As always, I'd like to write a few words of thanks to those who have helped give life to the Pendragon saga. Many have been there from the very beginning. Some are new to the adventure. All have been instrumental in bringing this story to you.

All my friends at Simon & Schuster Children's Publishing

have continued to be great supporters. My sincere gratitude goes out to Rick Richter, Rubin Pfeffer, Justin Chanda, Ellen Krieger, Paul Crichton, and so many more wonderful, talented people in marketing, promotion, and sales. I thank you all.

There's a new editor in town. Liesa Abrams. She has taken hold of the Pendragon reins with such joy and enthusiasm that I'm confident the story will be in very good hands until the last chapter of the final book is written. Thank you, Liesa.

A special note of thanks goes to Matt Schwartz, who is principally responsible for dusting off the cobwebs and spiffing up the Pendragon website. Great job, Matt.

We have a new cover designer and artist. They are Lucy Cummins and Dawn Austin. When I first saw their vision for *Raven Rise*, my jaw dropped. *In a good way.* I think it perfectly captures the next step in the evolution of Bobby's story and character. Very cool, guys.

Heidi Hellmich, ace copyeditor, has once again done a masterful job of correcting my improper English. Heidi has used her laserlike green pencil on every word of every book from the very beginning. If she gets hit by a bus before #10 is complete, we'll all be in trouble. Thanks so much, Heidi. Please be sure to always look both ways before crossing the street.

My good friend Richard Curtis has, as always, provided the kind of wisdom and sage guidance that allows me to muddle through the task of disassembling the universe without having to concern myself too much with real life. Thank you, Richard.

Peter Nelson has always been a great friend. He and Mark Wetzstein defy logic by being terrific lawyers while simultaneously being great guys. Incredible. I guess anything is possible in Halla.

Thank you again to Danny Baror, who continues to work to spread the Pendragon saga throughout the world. Also to Eileen Hutton, the talented Bill Dufris, and all the folks at Brilliance Audio who produce the awesome Pendragon audio books. And I owe a debt of gratitude to all the foreign language publishers of the Pendragon journals. I love seeing all the different versions of the books on my bookshelf. Of course I can't read a single one of them, but the covers sure do look great!

One of my favorite experiences when writing a Pendragon book is handing over the pages I'd written that day to my wife, Evangeline. She's the first critic to get a crack at the story and her insight is invaluable. She points out things that don't make sense or that feel wrong or are just plain bad. The first thing I do the next day is fine-tune the previous day's writing based on her thoughts. It's a great system. Though I have to admit my favorite comment I get from her is when she finishes the pages, drops them, looks at me, and says: "I want more." That's when I know I did something right. Thanks, babe.

I still haven't introduced my daughter, Keaton, to Bobby Pendragon. After all, she's only four and a half. She's way more interested in princesses and magic. Every night she asks me to make up a story for her, starring her. Usually it's about a princess. Or magic. Duh. But a while back she said: "Daddy, tell me a scary story." I raised an eyebrow in surprise and said, "Really? You sure?" She nodded. "Okay." I shrugged and proceeded to make up a story that I think freaked her out so much that she's going to need serious therapy some time down the road. Oops. The story wasn't even that intense but for a minute I was afraid I had warped her for life. That is until shortly after when she started telling me her own stories that had to do with monsters and running around in dark caves and yellow snakes that disguise themselves as spaghetti. That's my girl. Just like her old man. I'll be writing scary stories for her for a long time to come . . . and enjoying hers. What a team!

I'm deeply grateful to all the booksellers, librarians, teachers, and parents who have recommended my books. There are a lot of great books to choose from and I'm honored that so many have chosen mine as one that is worthy of bringing to their young readers. Thanks!

Of course Pendragon wouldn't be Pendragon without you, my friends. To those of you who have been there since the beginning, a special thanks for sticking around to see how it will all come out. To everyone who has written to me, thanks for your thoughts, comments, and questions. It's a great feeling to know that my story has such an impact on you. I can't tell you how much I appreciate it. Or maybe I can. I appreciate it. A lot. There.

I think that about covers it, right? No? Oh, right. This is supposed to be about *Raven Rise*, isn't it? Almost forgot. Now where were we? Oh yeah…

Convergence.

You could look that one up in the dictionary too but I'll do it myself and save you the trouble. (Cough *still lazy* cough)

Convergence: a coming together from different directions, especially a uniting or merging of groups or tendencies that were originally opposed or very different.

When we were last with Bobby, he made an incredible sacrifice that he thought would end the war with Saint Dane for good. He destroyed the entrance to the flume on Ibara, trapping himself and the demon on that territory. Though he knew the bold move meant he would never see his friends or his home again, he felt it was necessary because he was putting an end to Saint Dane's evil quest. There was only one problem.

The Convergence had already begun.

The war wasn't over. The story didn't end there. Not for Bobby. Not for Saint Dane.

And not for us.

Did you seriously think it would be any other way?

Like I said, we're not done yet.

This is the penultimate Pendragon.

Hobey ho, let's go.

—D. J. MacHale

PENDRAGON

JOURNAL OF AN ADVENTURE THROUGH
TIME AND SPACE

Book Nine:
Raven Rise

❖ DENDURON ❖

"Ibara!"

The tunnel remained silent. The only sign of life was the hollow sound of the command as it echoed through the dark void.

"Ibara!" the tall knight cried again, louder, as if that might make a difference. He knew it wouldn't. The tunnel to infinity ignored his plea. He hadn't expected this, though he'd feared something was wrong long before the flume went deaf. It struck him the last time he'd spoken with Bobby Pendragon.

Alder, the Traveler from Denduron, stood alone in the mouth of the flume on the territory of Quillan, wondering what had happened. Why wasn't the flume working? What had his friend done? When Alder left Pendragon on Ibara, he sensed that the lead Traveler was keeping something from him. Pendragon had a plan. Pendragon always had a plan. For some reason he hadn't wanted to share it. Alder sensed it at the time, but didn't question. Now he wished he had. He knew in his heart that Bobby Pendragon had done something to prevent him from returning to Ibara. But why? Only Pendragon had that answer, and Pendragon was on Ibara. Isolated. Unreachable.

"What have you done, my friend?" Alder muttered to no one.

The knight felt as if there was only one thing he could do. Go home. That's where Pendragon would look for him when he was needed. If he was needed.

"Denduron!" Alder shouted into the tunnel. He held his breath, fearful that the flume would continue to ignore his commands and leave him stranded on an alien territory.

It didn't. The flume growled to life. The tunnel began to writhe like a monstrous snake working out the kinks after a long nap. Alder heard the comforting sound of the rocks cracking and grinding against one another. The flume still worked. It was only the route to Ibara that was closed. A pin spot of light appeared in the distance, transforming the dull gray rocks into clear crystal as it came to sweep him up for his journey home. Alder braced himself. The light grew bright. The jumble of musical notes that always accompanied a Traveler's journey grew louder. Alder felt the gentle tug of energy that would pull him in and send him on his way.

He had come to Quillan on a simple mission: to return four weapons to their original territory. They were six-foot-long metal rods. Dado killers. Bobby didn't want them on Ibara. He wanted to purge that territory of all technology from other territories. Alder got the weapons back with no problem.

If somebody asked him why he'd changed his mind at that moment, he wouldn't know how to answer. Maybe it was the instinct of a warrior. Maybe it was the fear of the unknown. Maybe it was confusion over the fact that once again things weren't happening the way he expected them to. Maybe it was all of the above. No matter. The instant before he was swept into the flume, Alder had bent down and grabbed back the four dado-killing weapons. He wanted them on Denduron. Just in case.

A moment later he was on his way.

As he traveled through the flume he gazed out of the crystal tunnel to the star field beyond. The ghostly images of Halla that had been appearing in space had become so dense it was difficult to make out any single one. Alder caught glimpses of screaming rockets, marching armies, and crumbling buildings. Enormous toothy sharks soared through a pack of vicious snarling animals that were imposed over massive, sand-swept pyramids. Alder didn't recognize or understand most of the stunning images. He was a simple knight from a small farming village. But he understood chaos. Seeing the spectacular fury of these impressions in space made him fear that in spite of their many victories, the Travelers' battle to save Halla was not over. Not even close.

They had taken a bold chance on Ibara. They knew that mingling the territories went against the laws of what was meant to be, but they saw no other way to save Ibara. Saint Dane had amassed an enormous army of dados from Quillan to attack the village of Rayne. Without the help of the Travelers, it would have been a slaughter. Ibara would have been crushed and any hope of salvaging Veelox would have been destroyed along with it. Pendragon and the Travelers chose to take a stand. There was no weapon or resource that existed on Ibara that could have stopped Saint Dane's army. For that they looked to Denduron. Alder's home.

They called it tak. It was a reddish, claylike mineral found deep underground. It was deadly. It was explosive. Pendragon, Alder, and the Traveler from Ibara, named Siry, unearthed enough of the volatile material to use as a weapon against the dados. The result was as effective as it was frightening. The army of dados was obliterated along with most of the village of Rayne. Still, the Travelers had won. Ibara was saved. Saint Dane had been turned back once again. Pendragon and the Travelers felt certain the decision to use tak was the right one, for Saint Dane's quest to control Halla had been crushed.

Yet the images in space remained. Halla was still in turmoil. Seeing the chaotic images among the stars made Alder wonder if they had done the right thing after all. Did they truly win on Ibara? If so, how steep was the price? He tried to force those dark thoughts from his head. Alder took pride in being a problem solver. Worrying didn't solve problems. He knew he had to move on and be ready to do battle if the time came again. *When* the time came again. It was what he did best. He turned his thoughts toward home. Denduron. It was the first territory where Pendragon and the Travelers had battled Saint Dane. It was their first victory. After the horror of the war on Ibara, he looked forward to returning to the now peaceful territory.

The sweet musical notes grew louder, warning him that he was almost home. He twisted himself upright as he flew on the warm cushion of air, ready to be deposited at the gate on Denduron. Alder smiled. He needed a rest and hoped that his duties as a Bedoowan knight would allow for a little downtime.

It was at that moment that he caught one last image floating in the sea of space. It was a fleeting image of a large group of dark-skinned men holding up spears, waving them angrily. The image caught his eye because it was familiar. The men were tall and thin. Each one was as bald as the next. They wore thick leather armor that was distinctly purple. Alder recognized them. They were a primitive tribe that lived on the far side of the mountain from where his village lay on Denduron. They were a peaceful people. Seeing them waving spears, wearing armor, and chanting angrily was disturbing. What could it mean? The image was gone as quickly as he registered it, swallowed up by the vision of a silver dygo machine from Zadaa. In Alder's mind, the image of the angry armed tribe remained. He knew it wasn't a good omen.

Seconds later Alder was standing in the familiar cave that was the gate to the flume on Denduron. His teeth began to chatter. He was freezing. No big surprise. The gate on Denduron was near the peak of a snowy mountain, and Alder still wore the lightweight, tropical clothing from Ibara. He quickly dropped the dado rods and changed into the warm, leather uniform of a Bedoowan knight. It felt good to be home. At the mouth of the cave was the small sled he would ride down the snow-covered mountain to his village below. He pulled the vehicle out of the cave and onto the snow, squinting against the bright light from the three suns of Denduron. He waited a few seconds to let his eyes adjust. He filled his lungs with cold air. It felt good. Ibara was much too warm for his taste. After a few blissful seconds his eyes adjusted enough for him to make out detail.

He wished they hadn't. What he saw made his blood run cold, and it had nothing to do with the temperature. A field of untracked snow spread out before him. Jutting from the snow were several yellow spikes. They looked like gnarly, pointed rocks that were thick at the base and came to sharp points. Alder knew they weren't rocks.

"No," he gasped.

The quigs were back, lying beneath the snow, guarding the flumes. The rocky points were spikes that ran along their spines. Alder wasn't afraid of dealing with a quig-bear. He had battled them before. What terrified him was that they were there at all. Quigs existed on territories where Saint Dane was active. On Denduron the Travelers had beaten the demon, and the quigs had not been seen since.

Until then.

Alder didn't stop to wonder what it might mean. He wanted to be out of there. Without a moment more of hesitation, he picked up his sled and dashed across the snow. He picked a route that was clear of quig spines, threw the sled down, and jumped aboard. Belly down. Head first. The small sled was primitive, but fast. It was made from carved wood, with slick runners that slipped across the snow like skis. In no time he was gathering speed, heading down the steep field of snow. He risked a quick glance back to see if he had disturbed any quigs. None of them moved. It was small consolation.

Why had they come back? What was happening on Denduron?

Alder negotiated the snow field expertly, flying down the mountainside while steering past towering boulders of ice. The lower he dropped, the more patchy the snow became. He was soon skirting stretches of dirt and grass. He stayed on the snow as long as possible before his runners scraped rock, forcing him to give up his ride. He sat up and dug his feet in to stop, climbed off the sled, and stood to look down the mountain toward the village below.

What he saw made him fall to his knees. He couldn't help himself. It was as if his legs had turned to rubber. Down below, on the vast grassy field that stretched between the Milago village and the seaside ruins of the Bedoowan castle, Alder saw an army of Bedoowan knights, dressed in full armor, lined up in tight formation.

Battle formation.

The Bedoowan knights were preparing for war.

The territory had changed.

"What has happened?" he gasped to nobody.

As much as he needed it, there would be no rest for the Traveler from Denduron.

He wanted Pendragon to be there. He *needed* Pendragon to be there. But Bobby Pendragon was still on the territory of Ibara.

Alone. Isolated.

Unreachable.

THIRD EARTH

Patrick Mac knew something was wrong.

He knew it before he opened his eyes on that May morning in the Earth year of 5014. It was the smell. He couldn't place it, mostly because he had rarely smelled anything like it before. It seemed to him like a mixture of foul chemicals and rotted garbage—two smells that weren't often present on clean, green Third Earth. Whatever it was, it wasn't good. It wasn't natural. He opened his eyes to scan the bedroom of his small apartment. Nothing seemed out of place, other than the alien odor.

Patrick lived in the underground village of New York City known as Chelsea. It was the first subterranean complex built below Manhattan and served as a model for the others that had transformed the surface of New York from a crowded, environmental disaster area into a beautiful parklike community. Chelsea was made up of fifty levels of apartments, shops, museums, theaters, and just about every convenience needed to live belowground. There was even a large lake at its bottom level that was open most of the year for swimming and sailing. From November through January it was intentionally frozen for skating and ice hockey. Many thousands of people made their homes in the small community. Most of them worked there too. There was no reason to ever venture aboveground, unless you wanted to enjoy the beautiful, open countryside and feel the warmth of the sun.

Patrick thought that everything about Chelsea was perfect, except of course for this strange new smell that had so rudely forced him awake. He rolled out of bed, every sense on alert. Was he in danger? Was there a fire? No. It didn't smell like that. He had received no warning through the communication system that ran throughout the underground village. If there was an emergency, people were notified immediately. Patrick had lived in Chelsea for most of his thirty years. He had only experienced one emergency. A water pipe had burst on the fifteenth level near his apartment. Everyone within three sectors was evacuated in minutes. The pipe was repaired and he returned home within the hour. Chelsea was an efficient place. If there were any real danger, Patrick felt certain he would know about it.

But what was the foul smell?

It was a Tuesday. Patrick had to be at work by eight. He was a teacher and the librarian at Chelsea High, five levels down from his apartment. He could make it from dead asleep to his classroom in fifteen minutes. Ten if he pushed. It was early. He didn't need to push. He needed to find out what the putrid smell was. He sat up in bed, took a good whiff, and hacked out a cough. The smell tickled the back of his throat. He ran his hands through his long brown hair and scowled. The odd smell gave him a bad feeling that went beyond the throat tickle.

Patrick was the Traveler from Third Earth. He had already experienced the shock of seeing his territory change once; he didn't want to go through it again. Events in the past had been altered, creating a ripple of events through time that led to the creation of a race of humanlike automatons called "dados." One day all was normal; the next day Patrick woke to find these robots were suddenly part of the normal fabric of Third Earth life. They functioned as efficient worker bees who served the people of the territory. The dados may have been handy, but they were wrong. It wasn't the way things were meant to be. Bobby Pendragon and his acolyte Courtney Chetwynde went back in time to First Earth to try and prevent the events that would lead to their creation. Had they succeeded? Did this odd smell have something to do with the past having been changed yet again? Was this foul odor a good sign? It sure didn't smell like it.

"Hello?" Patrick called out nervously.

He lived alone, but on the "new" Third Earth, he had a dado servant who made him breakfast and washed his clothes. Patrick thought it was creepy and cool at the same time. As much as the dados shouldn't have existed, he had to admit that it was pretty nice to have a machine handle the more mundane chores around the apartment.

There was no answer. Were the dados no more?

Patrick decided to call his school to see if anybody knew what the strange smell was all about. He reached to his bedside table for his telemonitor, but his hand hung in the air. The device wasn't there. Patrick quickly looked to the floor. Had he knocked it over in his sleep? No. It was just . . . gone. The hairs went up on the back of his neck. His pulse quickened. Something was definitely wrong.

It was then that he noticed a faint sound. It wasn't distinct or specific enough for him to guess what it could be. It was more like a distant rumble of white noise. Harmless, except for the fact that the sound in Chelsea was totally controlled. Nothing as intrusive or annoying as white noise existed in his home, or anywhere else on Third Earth for that matter. The only place he'd heard anything remotely like it was on a recorded bit of history that was stored in the massive computer data files of 5014.

Patrick forced himself to stand up. He shuffled slowly toward his bedroom door, fearing what he might find on the other side. He reached for the silver-handled doorknob, grasped it tightly, took a breath, and pulled the door open to see . . .

It wasn't his apartment. At least it wasn't the apartment he used to have. There was nothing unusual or sinister about the place, other than the fact that it wasn't his. The furniture was different. The paintings on the walls were different. The appliances in the kitchen were different. For a moment he wondered if he had accidentally entered the wrong apartment the night before, but quickly dismissed that as being idiotic. There was less chance of that happening than all of history being transformed by Pendragon and the other Travelers. That's how strange the reality of his life had become.

Patrick fought panic. It wasn't easy waking up to discover your life had been turned inside out. Again. Still, panic would only make things worse. He was an orderly guy. He knew what he had to do. He had to determine exactly what had changed. After that, he would contact Pendragon to let him know about the changes and find out what had happened in the past to cause them. Yes. That's what he had to do. One step at a time. As long as he didn't let his mind shoot forward to all the unknown possibilities, he'd be okay. At least that's what he told himself. He was the Traveler from Third Earth, a territory that up until then had not been targeted by Saint Dane. He realized it might very well be his turn. Running and hiding in the closet might have been tempting, but it wouldn't change things. It was time for him to step into the show.

On the outer wall of his living room were two large windows covered by white horizontal blinds. They weren't much different from the windows he had in his normal apartment, except that his regular blinds were vertical. No big deal. Vertical? Horizontal? Who cared? If this was the worst he'd see, he figured he could handle it. Normally the windows looked out onto the center atrium of Chelsea. He had a balcony outside where he spent many an afternoon reading and enjoying the happy sounds of people splashing and playing in the warm waters of the lake far below. He desperately wanted to open those blinds and see the familiar sites of his underground home.

The alien sounds and smells told him not to get his hopes up.

He walked slowly toward the windows. His bare feet felt cold on the tiled floor. No big deal, except that Patrick normally had carpet. The white tiles beneath his feet were cracked and grimy. He wondered why the broken tiles hadn't been replaced. Or cleaned. Had he become a lazy load on the new Third Earth? In some ways that was more disturbing than knowing the whole world had changed.

He stopped at the window, his nose inches from the closed blinds. He knew in his heart that when he opened them he would see a changed world. The question was, how changed would it be? He already knew that it smelled bad. Maybe that would be the only difference.

He didn't believe that any more than he believed the vertical blinds would be the only change.

Patrick found the string that ran down the side of the window. He grasped it, ready to pull. He took a second to catch his breath. As much as things had already changed, he figured he could handle the differences he'd seen so far. He didn't know if the same would be said after he'd seen what lay beyond. He savored the last few seconds of his old life. He knew that once he pulled those blinds, it would all begin. Or end.

He thought of letting go of the string, leaving the blinds closed, and contacting Pendragon to find out what had happened in the past. Yes. Good idea. It might help him prepare for what was out there. He looked at his hand as he was about to let go of the string. On his finger was his Traveler ring. He heard all the stories of what Pendragon had been through in the battle against Saint Dane. He knew the sacrifices the Travelers had to make. Many had died trying to stop the demon from controlling Halla. He knew that he had had a relatively easy time of it. He suddenly felt guilty and a little ashamed for being so uncertain. For being afraid. It was his turn now. It was time.

He pulled the string.

The blinds twisted open, revealing a sight that made Patrick stumble backward, as if being repulsed by the impossible vision before him. He screamed. He couldn't help it. It just came out.

Staring back at him was an eye. A giant sideways eye. His brain couldn't compute what he was seeing. Did giants now roam Earth? Or did he somehow pull an "Alice in Wonderland" and shrink to action-figure size? He couldn't catch his breath. His heart raced. What was this giant going to do? Eat him? How did it get underground in the first place?

The eye didn't move. It stared in at Patrick, unblinking. Patrick had to force himself to look back. His terror slowly gave way to confusion. The eye was green. Completely green. The white, the pupil, even the skin around it was the same dull green color. It took Patrick a few seconds to realize that it wasn't a living creature and never had been. It was a sculpture. It was so immense that he couldn't see it all, but it seemed to be a statue of a head lying on its side, staring in at him.

Patrick stood on shaky legs. Though he no longer feared being eaten by a gargantuan one-eyed monster, he was still left breathless at the idea that such an immense sculpture could be right outside his window in the atrium of Chelsea.

Unless . . .

A sickening thought hit. His mind had trouble accepting the idea, but it seemed like the only logical explanation. He knew how to find out for sure. He had to go outside. He had to face the face. It didn't matter that he was still in bare feet and pajamas. He had to go outside because he couldn't see it all through the windows. Patrick moved toward the front door. It was the portal that led out onto the balcony on the fifteenth level of the underground village of Chelsea beneath New York City in the year 5014. With every bit of courage he could conjure, Patrick reached for the doorknob and pulled. The white noise grew louder. The strange odor grew stronger. Being inside the apartment had kept the worst of it away. Patrick now understood why. He didn't need his eyes to tell him what his nose and ears already understood.

He no longer lived underground. He was hearing sounds that he had only experienced before through the holographic images stored in the data drives of the computers in the library. He was smelling the smells of a city above the ground. A city that hadn't solved the problems of pollution. Of housing. Of overpopulation. The scientific advances that the people of Earth had made in order to save their planet never happened. Patrick stood there stunned. This was the new Earth of 5014. He had only caught a small glimpse, but he knew what he would find. No, he *feared* what he would find. He would have to explore this city. He would have to try and figure out what went wrong. What had changed. What Saint Dane had done to win Third Earth without ever having set foot on the territory.

A foul wind blew down the street, ruffling his hair and kicking up a cloud of filthy papers that swirled around him. He was standing on a fourth-floor balcony on the surface of a city that had been transformed. He understood that the foul odor wasn't anything unusual in this new environment. It was simply what the city smelled like. Same with the white noise—this was the new, normal sound of the city. The tranquility was gone. The faint citrus aroma was gone. The grassy meadows were gone. The sky was gray. Was it cloudy? Or something more sinister? Maybe that looming gray ceiling was what he was sucking into his lungs as it tickled the back of his throat.

Almost nothing was familiar. Almost. Patrick could have convinced himself that he had been transported to an alien city anywhere in Halla, except for an undeniable reality that was staring him right in the face. It was the green sculpture. Now that he was outside he saw it for what it really was. He saw that he'd been right—the eye was actually sideways and the face was on its side. The sculpture was so huge that the uppermost eye was on the level of his fourth-floor balcony. The rest of the statue stretched down the cracked pavement of the wide street in front of his new home. He was almost close enough to reach out and touch its nose. He saw through the dull green patina that there were signs of rust and corrosion spread over its surface. This sculpture was made of metal.

Patrick was in shock. Maybe that was a good thing. If not, he surely would have crumbled under the weight of the reality he was faced with. Literally. He was having trouble breathing. He wasn't sure if that was due to the foul air, or because the sight in front of him had taken his breath away. He felt weak. He had to lean against the building or he would have fallen down.

He tried to swallow. He couldn't. His mouth was too dry.

"So?" he croaked hoarsely at the lifeless statue. "What happened?"

The statue didn't answer, of course. It wasn't alive. It had never been alive, though it could not have looked more dead. As much as Patrick wanted to deny it, he was definitely in a *new* New York City, staring into the eye of the Statue of Liberty.

FIRST EARTH

"You must realize this enterprise will make you and your partner quite wealthy," the tall man with the large teeth said with a knowing smile.

"Andy Mitchell is *not* my partner," Mark Dimond shot back quickly. He wanted to leap out of the cushy leather chair and shake the guy to emphasize the point. He actually leaned forward, ready to pounce, but a strong hand held him back.

"Easy there, big fella," Courtney Chetwynde said soothingly. For a change Courtney was the voice of reason, while Mark was the voice of butt kicking. "He gets it."

"I am afraid I do not 'get it' at all," the man corrected, lifting the corner of one lip. Mark wasn't sure if it was a half smile, or a full sneer, or if he had just smelled something foul. The man held up a piece of paper that, unfortunately, Mark recognized. "This is your signature, is it not?"

Mark dropped back in his chair. Beaten.

"Yeah."

"Then whatever unpleasantness has transpired between you and Mr. Mitchell is immaterial. You both signed this contract, therefore you are forever joined together as principals in the . . . " He looked at the paper through half-glasses. "What is it you call yourselves? Ah yes, the Dimond Alpha Digital Organization." He looked up at Mark over the paper and continued, "I have no idea what that signifies, nor do I care. What I do know is that between having signed this letter of intent and receiving our advance payment, your company has given Keaton Electrical Marvels the sole right to develop the technology you have created and named 'Forge.'"

Mark wanted to scream, but he knew it wouldn't do anything more than make him look silly. He and Courtney were in the large London office of Mr. Iain Paterson, president of KEM Limited. The company that was going to bring about the ruin of Halla. Of course, Mr. Paterson had no idea of that. As far as he knew, all he had done was license an impossible new technology from two teenage American kids that he hoped would revolutionize the electronics industry. He had no way of knowing that one of those kids was actually a demon who had manipulated Mark into igniting an explosion of technology that would change the future of Earth, Quillan, and Ibara. It was not the way things were meant to be. But Mr. Paterson couldn't know that. Mark wished that somehow he could explain it to him. Maybe then he'd destroy Forge. More likely, Mark thought, he'd have him sent to an asylum for the impossibly strange.

"I must admit, I do not understand your position," Paterson continued. Mark thought the guy was pretty arrogant. He wore a dark tweed suit with a vest that had a gold watch chain dangling from the right pocket. He held his head high and pointed his chin at whoever he was speaking to. "Why the sudden reluctance? Don't you relish the opportunity to change the future of the world?"

Mark shot Courtney a glance. Paterson had no idea how true those words were.

"Or four worlds," Mark muttered.

"Pardon me?"

"Look . . . lain . . . pal," Courtney interjected. Paterson visibly stiffened. He wasn't used to having a young girl treat him so informally. "If you develop Mark's technology, he'll sue you. Simple as that. Do you really want to go through all that? Hmm?"

Paterson snickered. It was Courtney's turn to stiffen. Snickering irked Courtney, especially if it was at her expense.

"It is most unfortunate that Mr. Dimond feels that way, but rest assured we are confidant in our legal position. A letter of intent was signed. Monies have changed hands."

"We'll give you back the money!" Mark exclaimed.

Paterson snickered. Again. Courtney stiffened. Again.

"We don't want your money," he said flatly. "We want Forge."

Mark took a desperate gamble and said, "Well, too bad. You have the plans, but I'm the one who made it. I destroyed the prototype, and I don't think you can duplicate it. You don't have the know-how." Mark looked at Courtney with renewed hope. "It's true," he exclaimed to her. "They won't figure out how to build it!"

Another snicker from Paterson.

"Stop that!" Courtney demanded.

"Please, come with me," Paterson commanded as he got up from behind his immense mahogany desk. He strode quickly across the stuffy office, opened the heavy wooden door, and gestured for Mark and Courtney to follow.

Courtney whispered to Mark, "Why do I think we're not going to like this?"

They both got up and followed Paterson along the wide hallway of the headquarters of KEM Limited. Along either side of the corridor were glass cases filled with odd-looking devices that were on display as if in a museum.

"These are some of the projects we're developing here at KEM," Paterson explained.

One case held a series of six colorful cups.

"Plastic," Paterson explained. "Durable, lightweight, inexpensive. Someday the majority of simple, everyday items will be molded out of plastic. Incredible, no?"

Mark and Courtney exchanged looks. They continued on until they saw a case that contained a round glass screen that looked like an ancient TV set. On the screen was an animated character that looked to Mark like a black-and-white version of Bugs Bunny.

Paterson commented, "Someday moving images will be broadcast into homes the way radio is today."

Courtney sniffed. "Not exactly plasma quality."

"Plasma?" Paterson asked, intrigued.

Mark winced. He feared that Courtney had just given Paterson another idea that was way ahead of 1937. He changed the subject by asking, "What's that?"

In the next case was a small machine that looked like a tiny, old-fashioned record player complete with a small black three-inch vinyl record.

Paterson explained, "We feel that miniaturization will be key in developing future technologies. This small phonograph can be easily packed into a suitcase and transported anywhere. In the future, entertainment will no longer be restricted to the home or theater."

Courtney laughed. "Nice. Put that thing on a chain around your neck, and you could run with it."

"Why on earth would anyone want to listen to music while running?" Paterson asked, again intrigued.

"What do you want to show us?" Mark interrupted, changing the subject again.

"You have theorized that we would be unable to read your schematics and duplicate your work. Observe."

Paterson pointed to the next case in line. What Mark and Courtney saw inside made them deflate. Lined up on a purple velvet pillow were six small items that looked like identical blue eggs.

"Are those what I think they are?" Mark asked, though he was pretty sure he already knew.

"Try it for yourself," Paterson answered.

Mark called out in a clear voice, "Square."

Instantly all six "eggs" writhed and morphed into six perfect squares. There was no mistake. It was Forge. Six times over. The people at KEM had succeeded in re-creating Mark's prototype, proving they had the know-how.

The early dados had been born.

"You see, young sir," Paterson said, proud of himself, "we are quite capable of reading and duplicating your plans. My suggestion to you is sit back and enjoy the spoils of your incredible invention. You are the father of a technology that will revolutionize our lives. You should be proud."

Mark felt a lot of things. Fear, anger, embarrassment, frustration, confusion, and above all, nausea. There was a lot of nausea going on. Nowhere on that list was the feeling of pride.

Mark and Courtney left Mr. Paterson and took "the lift" (as they called the elevators in London) down to the lobby of the small office building. Waiting for them when they stepped off were Mark's parents and Douglas "Dodger" Curtis, the feisty bellhop from the Manhattan Tower Hotel in New York City who had helped Courtney track down Mark. Dodger had become their guide to the territory, helping the aliens from Second Earth maneuver through the strange world of 1937.

"Well?" Dodger asked enthusiastically as soon as he saw Mark and Courtney.

The look on Mark's and Courtney's faces was all the answer they needed.

"I shouldn't be surprised," Mark said, defeated. "We knew destroying the prototype didn't change anything. It was dumb to think we could have talked them out of developing Forge. I've been doing a lot of dumb things lately."

"Stop," Mrs. Dimond said. "You couldn't have known any of this would happen."

"I got played, Mom," Mark shot back. "I did everything Saint Dane wanted."

"And it backfired on him," Mr. Dimond added. "The Travelers beat his army on Ibara, and now he's trapped there."

"Yeah," Mark said, sounding even more depressed. "Along with Bobby."

The group fell silent.

"So what do we do now?" Courtney asked.

Nobody was sure of what to say, until Mark finally spoke. "I think we go home. Back to New York. That's where the flume is."

Dodger offered, "The *Queen Mary* sails back in a couple days. I can book us return passage if I get a move on."

"Can't we just fly?" Courtney asked.

"How?" Dodger countered. "You got wings?"

Mr. Dimond observed, "I don't think there's regular air service across the Atlantic in 1937."

"You mean people fly across the ocean on Second Earth?" Dodger asked. "Like taking the train?"

"Yeah," Courtney said. "You get free pretzels, too."

Dodger whistled. Courtney wasn't sure if he was impressed by the idea of regular air service or free snacks.

"Do it," Mark said confidently. "We should get back."

"I'm on it," Dodger declared, headed for the door. "Meet you all back at the hotel." The little bellhop tipped his hat and was gone.

"We're all tired," Mrs. Dimond declared, always the mother hen. "We should get some rest."

"You guys go," Mark said. "I want to walk a little."

"I'm coming with you," Courtney declared.

A few minutes later Mark and Courtney were strolling along the southern border of Hyde Park, the massive expanse of green grass in central London. They looked like any other couple from 1937. Mark wore a dark gray suit with a fedora cap and a wool overcoat to ward off the November chill. Courtney wore a dress and a cream-colored overcoat. She even wore high heels and stockings. To her it was a costume for their meeting with Paterson. She didn't think a stiff British businessman would take her seriously if she wore the pants and floppy wool hat she'd bought at Macy's in New York. Turned out it didn't matter.

The two had grown up since their adventure began when Bobby Pendragon left home to travel through the territories. They were now both seventeen . . . and felt around a hundred. They walked together along the sidewalk, their minds a million miles away from their bodies. For the longest time neither said a word. They walked past Buckingham Palace, Westminster Abbey, and on to the Houses of Parliament, where the famous Clock Tower with the bell known as Big Ben rose into the sky. Both stopped to look up at the immense tower in awe.

"Wow," Courtney declared. "I had no idea. They should call it '*Really* Big Ben.'"

They continued along the river Thames until they reached Westminster Bridge. But their walk wasn't about sightseeing—it was about taking time to think. Finally, on their way back toward Hyde Park, Courtney broke the ice.

"You know, maybe it's a good thing we couldn't stop KEM," she offered. "At least now we know how things are going to play out. Technology on Earth is going to change. The dados are going to be created, but Bobby is going to beat them on Ibara. That's all good, right? Who knows what might have happened if we'd stopped Paterson and his KEM geeks? We might have started a whole nother chain of events and Saint Dane might still be in business."

"And Bobby might not be trapped on Ibara with him," Mark muttered.

"Yeah, that," Courtney whispered softly. "But it was his choice, Mark. He ended the war. Halla is safe from Saint Dane. Who knows? Maybe that's the way it was supposed to be."

"This is my fault," Mark said.

"Stop!" Courtney shouted quickly. "You had no idea you were being manipulated. It's not like you set out to invent something that was going to change the course of Halla. Come on!"

"I should have seen him coming," Mark muttered.

"But you didn't! Just like a whole lot of people all over Halla. What about me? I was fooled too, remember? Whitney Wilcox? Hello?"

"Except when you got fooled, it didn't start a chain of events that changed the future of a bunch of territories and created a war."

"Details," Courtney said quickly.

"Really bad details."

"Okay, so it led to a war, but it was a war that Saint Dane lost! Look at it this way, maybe he blew it. The way things have worked out, by getting you to invent Forge, Saint Dane set up his own defeat on Ibara. Now he's trapped there. It backfired on him, Mark. Maybe you're the hero in this whole thing!"

Mark stopped walking and looked directly at Courtney. "Do you really believe that?"

Courtney wanted to shout out, "Yes!"

She didn't. "I don't know," she admitted. "But it's possible, right?"

"Let's go home," Mark said. "We'll have plenty of time to figure things out on the boat."

"I can't believe we've gotta get on that tub again," Courtney complained. "It's nice and all, but it's still just a floating hotel. Talk about claustrophobia."

They had reached the Royal Albert Hall, the large round brick concert hall. Behind it was the small hotel where Dodger had found them all rooms.

"I want to walk a little more," Mark said. "On my own."

Courtney nodded. "Don't be long. The sun'll be down soon, and it's getting cold."

The two of them hugged.

"We did okay, Mark," Courtney added. "Bobby would be proud."

Mark didn't respond. He wasn't so sure he agreed. Courtney left him, headed for the hotel. Mark turned the opposite way and entered Hyde Park in the area known as Kensington Gardens. The trees were alive with autumn colors. Kids played pickup games of soccer. The air was turning colder, and Mark had to button up his coat to fight the chill. It was a beautiful day. Mark stood in the middle of a wide, grassy area and did a three-sixty to take it all in.

He had a moment. A brief moment. In spite of the fact that his best friend had sacrificed himself by destroying the flume so he couldn't leave Ibara, and in spite of the fact that he felt embarrassed by having been duped by Saint Dane, Mark allowed himself a moment to think that the sacrifices might actually have been worth it. Saint Dane's evil quest might be over. Halla might be safe. He even had the hope that they might have the chance to recapture some semblance of a normal life.

It was a great moment.

It didn't last long.

"Hello, Mark," came a familiar voice.

Mark spun quickly to see a woman standing near a thick oak tree, her hands shoved into the pockets of her long wool coat, her feet set apart defiantly.

Mark froze. The moment of bliss passed as quickly as it had arrived.

"You don't seem all that surprised to see me," Nevva Winter said.

Truth be told, Mark wasn't.

In his heart, he knew he had been kidding himself.

He knew it wasn't over.

FIRST EARTH

(CONTINUED)

The two stood facing each other. Mark didn't want to talk to Nevva. She was a traitor. She was the enemy. What he wanted was to turn and run away. He didn't. He didn't want to show weakness.

"It's over, Nevva," Mark said, trying to sound as if he meant it.

"Is it?" Nevva asked while raising an eyebrow.

Mark thought that Nevva was beautiful. She had dark hair and flawless skin. Mark didn't know how old she was. Maybe in her early twenties. Like Courtney, she wore a dress and overcoat that were stylish for 1937. When he first met her, she'd taken his breath away. Mark wasn't used to dealing with beautiful women, especially women who were trying to bring about the destruction of all that existed.

"Where's Saint Dane?" Mark asked, though he knew exactly where the demon was. On Ibara. Trapped with Bobby. Mark didn't know if Nevva knew. He wanted to be cagey.

"You don't know?" Nevva asked as she slowly approached him. "He's trapped on Ibara."

So much for being cagey.

"You must have heard," Nevva continued while glancing at

Mark's Traveler ring. "Surely Bobby told you that he buried the flume on Ibara under tons of volcanic rock."

"He might have mentioned something about that, yeah," Mark said, trying to sound casual. He had given up on cagey.

"Walk with me, Mark," Nevva said with a small smile. She turned and took a few steps. Mark didn't budge. Nevva stopped and looked back at him. "We need to talk."

"Why should I talk to you?" Mark barked angrily. Casual wasn't working for him either. "All you've done is manipulate me and cause us all grief."

"I understand," Nevva replied with sympathy. "But if you don't, your grief will only reach new depths."

Mark got a chill. The woman was heartless.

"Shall we?" Nevva said with a smile as she continued walking.

The last thing Mark wanted to do was follow the woman, but he willed his feet to move. The two strolled through the park, looking every bit like a normal couple enjoying the chilly autumn afternoon. Mark wondered if anybody could tell that every muscle in his body was so tense he felt as if he might snap in two.

"It's a beautiful park, don't you think?" Nevva asked.

"Do you really want to talk about the p-park?" Mark shot back. He winced when the stutter came out.

"Nervous?" Nevva asked with a chuckle.

Mark hated it when his stutter betrayed him. He thought he had it beaten, but it still snuck back at the worst possible times.

"No," Mark said adamantly.

"Really? You should be."

Mark tried not to react. He wanted to be cool. He wanted to be in control. He wanted to be able to handle anything Nevva had to throw at him. Or at least give that impression. He didn't think he was doing such a hot job.

"Go home, Mark," Nevva commanded. "Enjoy your life. You

can't do anything else for Pendragon. He chose to stay on Ibara. He wants nothing more to do with the plight of Halla, and neither should you."

"That's it?" Mark asked sarcastically. "That's all you wanted to say? You want me to go home and pretend none of this ever happened?"

"Yes."

"Why don't I believe you?"

Nevva smiled, but Mark saw no warmth. He knew she wasn't concerned about his peace of mind.

"There is one other small thing," she said slyly.

"I figured," Mark shot back quickly.

"I want your ring."

Without thinking, Mark grabbed his Traveler ring with the opposite hand. He had only parted with the ring once, when he gave it to Courtney to continue on as an acolyte while he traveled with Nevva to First Earth to try to save his parents. Once they were reunited, Courtney had given it back. She knew the ring belonged on Mark's finger. The idea of giving it up again made Mark wince.

"What? No! Why?" he exclaimed.

"To give Pendragon exactly what he wants."

Mark stared at her, uncomprehending. "Uh, what?" he muttered.

"Pendragon destroyed the flume on Ibara," Nevva said coldly. "He wanted to be cut off from the rest of Halla. I want to oblige him and make it a full break."

"What for? Revenge?"

"Call it that if you'd like."

Mark twisted the ring on his finger. "Forget it!" he snapped. "This is the only link I have with my best friend. Why the heck would I give it up?"

Nevva looked deep into Mark's eyes, as if trying to read his thoughts. It unnerved him. If he had said anything at that moment, it would surely have come out as a stutter. He knew she had to have an agenda that went beyond trying to isolate Bobby.

"Saint Dane has taught me many things," Nevva explained. "He's working on an entirely higher plane than the other Travelers and he's shared some of his unique abilities with me."

"Good for you," Mark said sarcastically. "Why should I care?"

"Because unlike the other Travelers, I know how to control the flumes," Nevva answered quickly. "I can not only travel between territories, I have the ability to control the time when I arrive."

Mark felt his throat clench. He knew this couldn't be good.

"So what?" Mark commented coolly.

"I prevented your parents from boarding the airplane that crashed, Mark," she said coldly. "You know that. What if I told you I could travel back to Second Earth to a time before their plane took off and this time watch silently as they handed over their tickets and boarded?"

Mark felt as if the park were spinning. He had lost his parents once . . . or thought he had. It was the whole reason he'd agreed to come to First Earth. Nevva told him that by traveling to the past he could change the future and save his parents from dying in that plane crash. But she was lying. Nevva had already saved his parents. That wasn't why Saint Dane wanted him on First Earth. It was all about getting him to sell Forge to KEM and start the chain of events that would lead to the creation of the dados. It wasn't about his parents. It had never been about his parents.

Until now.

"Wh-Why?" Marked croaked. He didn't care anymore that he sounded nervous. "Why would you do that?"

"I don't want to," she said, trying to sound sincere. It didn't work. Nevva Winter was cold, efficient, and calculating. "I like your parents. I don't want to see them die."

"Then why?" Mark cried. "I did what you wanted. KEM has Forge. What else do you want from my life?"

Nevva looked at Mark's ring and coolly answered, "I want your ring."

Mark quickly put his hand in his pocket. "This can't just be about Bobby."

"It isn't," Nevva answered. "Call it a test."

"Test? Of what?"

"Of you. Of people. Of Earth," Nevva replied. "Saint Dane and I have the same vision. Our goal is to create a perfect Halla."

"Yeah, by destroying it," Mark spat.

"No, by breaking it down in order to rebuild," Nevva said passionately. "Halla must be purged of all impurity before it can thrive. Unfortunately, the Travelers don't share that vision. That's what the struggle has been about, Mark. Saint Dane's vision of a perfect Halla, versus the flawed existence that the Travelers insist on trying to protect."

"So what is the test?"

"I'm giving you a choice," Nevva said dispassionately. "Give me the ring and I'll never bother you again."

"I don't believe you," Mark cried. "If you want the ring so badly, it must be because it will help you in some way. And helping you is helping Saint Dane."

"That's where the test comes in. How firm are you in your convictions? How important is it for you to continue helping the Travelers? Helping Pendragon? Which is more important? The futile quest to stop Saint Dane . . . or your parents? Think, Mark. Think hard and make the right choice, because if you choose the Travelers, I promise you, your parents will die."

Mark's knees buckled. They actually buckled. He fell down to the ground and sat on his feet, trying to catch his breath. His head spun. What was this about? Why was his ring so important to Nevva? To Saint Dane? Mark couldn't breathe. As badly as he felt about being duped into inventing Forge, he'd had no idea that he was doing exactly what Saint Dane wanted. Now he was faced with a much more difficult choice. His parents were in danger again. To save them, he had to agree to help the demon. There would be no excuses this time.

"That's the test?" Mark asked, numb. "Halla or my parents?"

"Something like that," Nevva said without compassion.

"Why does it matter? What's the point of a test like that?"

"It's everything, Mark. If you choose your parents, you'd be proving once again how selfish and corrupt the people of Halla are."

"You think it's selfish to protect people you love?"

"It's selfish to put your personal concerns ahead of millions, no, billions of others."

Mark looked up into her steely eyes. He had never felt hatred before. He was a forgiving kind of guy who never held a grudge and always saw the good in people. As much as Andy Mitchell had made his life a living hell, he'd never felt actual hatred for him.

At that moment Mark hated Nevva Winter.

"You're as bad as Saint Dane," he seethed.

"Thank you," Nevva answered with a self-satisfied smile.

Mark wanted to hit her. He forced himself to look away to allow the rage to pass. He had to think. The choice was impossible. He needed to buy some time. Hopefully an answer would jump out.

"How can I believe you?" he asked. "I could give you my ring, and you might hurt my parents anyway. What proof do you have that they'd be safe?"

"None," Nevva answered abruptly. "You only have my word. But you also have my word that if you *don't* give me the ring, they will die."

Mark felt as if he had been hit in the stomach. He needed help. He needed to talk to Courtney. He couldn't make this huge of a decision on his own.

It was at that moment that an idea came to him. It was a simple idea, but it offered a glimmer of hope.

"This is about isolating Bobby, right? You don't want him to be able to contact me anymore?"

Nevva's answer was to stare back at him silently. Mark felt the rush of hope. He got to his feet.

"You really think that by keeping Bobby from sending journals to me, it'll help Saint Dane?"

Again Nevva didn't answer.

Mark didn't need an answer. He had already convinced himself that it was the truth. What he was beginning to realize, to hope, was that giving up his ring would mean nothing. There were other rings spread throughout Halla. Dodger was Gunny's acolyte. He had his own ring! If Bobby wanted to contact him, or they wanted to contact Bobby, he could use Dodger's ring. Was Nevva that dumb? He needed to talk to Dodger to make sure the little bellhop still had his Traveler ring.

"Can I give you my answer tomorrow?" Mark asked.

"No, you can give me your ring right now" was Nevva's curt response.

Mark convinced himself. Giving up the ring would be inconvenient, but not disastrous. He clutched the heavy ring and yanked it off his finger. He held it, feeling its weight. Holding it with two fingers he took a close look. He hadn't examined it for the longest time. In the center of the silver ring was a dark gray stone. Etched in the silver, circling the stone, were ten symbols. Each represented one of the territories of Halla. His mind flashed back to the time several years before, when he'd been awakened in the middle of the night by Osa, Loor's mother. She handed Mark the ring, saying it was from Bobby. He had given it up only once since then. Other than that, he had worn it every minute for nearly four years. He knew that if he gave it to Nevva, he'd never see it again. But he convinced himself that it was okay. There were other rings he could use to contact Bobby. Saving this one ring wasn't worth risking his parents' lives, no matter what kind of test it represented. If it meant saving his parents, he wouldn't mind failing.

He took a deep breath and held the ring out. "If you're lying," he warned, "I swear you'll regret it."

Nevva didn't take it right away. Instead, she looked into Mark's eyes. For a moment she seemed to soften. Mark thought she actually seemed disappointed.

"Saint Dane was right," she said softly. "You are all selfish and shortsighted."

Mark almost took the ring back. Before he could make a move, Nevva pulled it out of his grasp.

"Promise me," he said. "Promise me my parents will be safe."

"They won't die in that plane crash, Mark," Nevva said. "You have my word. You can trust me, which is more than I can say for you."

Mark winced. What did she mean by that?

"Now go home," she commanded. "Or do whatever you'd like. Go!"

Mark turned to head for the hotel. He didn't want to have to look at Nevva anymore, but he was confused. Nevva's reaction made no sense. He took a few steps, then stopped and turned back quickly. "I don't get it. Isn't this what you wanted?"

Nevva was gone. He heard a screeching *caw* and looked to the sky. Overhead he saw a large black bird rising up—a raven. He watched it circle once, then with a quick flap of its wings, it shot off. As it moved, the sun reflected off something near its head.

In its beak, the raven clutched a ring.

FIRST EARTH

(CONTINUED)

Dodger had arranged for three rooms in a small, out-of-the-way hotel on Brompton Place, near the large department store known as Harrods. Not that that mattered. Nobody felt much like shopping. The Dimonds were in one room, Courtney had her own, while Dodger and Mark shared a third. It was expensive, but Mark was paying and didn't care.

"Why not?" he exclaimed when they first checked in. "I'm a rich inventor now, right? If I'm being paid the big bucks to alter the course of humanity, we might as well be comfortable."

Nobody thought that was funny. Including Mark. The money truly meant nothing to him. He'd give it all back in a second if it meant he could reclaim Forge.

They had been in London for a little more than twenty-four hours and were already making plans to return to New York, having failed to convince KEM to give up Forge. The five sat together in the lounge of the hotel, drinking tea and eating scones. It was five o'clock. Tea time. That's what people did in England at five o'clock. Mark wasn't a tea guy. He wasn't a scone guy either. What he really wanted was a Mountain Dew and some Garden Poultry fries.

"This is like eatin' sawdust," Dodger exclaimed as he chewed on the flaky pastry. He puckered his lips and tried to whistle. All that came out was a spray of dry crumbs. "Now I know why they drink so much tea. You gotta wash this stuff down or you'll choke." He took a big gulp of tea and added, "Gimme a good ol' greasy doughnut anytime."

Mr. and Mrs. Dimond chuckled. They seemed to actually enjoy the snack. Courtney did too. She was so hungry she'd eat anything, but that was Courtney. Mark simply stared out the window, lost in thought.

"Drink your tea before it gets cold," Mrs. Dimond said to him.

Mark grabbed his teacup, took a gulp, then quickly tossed the cup back down onto the saucer with a loud clatter, knocking his spoon onto the floor.

"Whoa, easy there, partner," Dodger warned.

To everyone else it seemed that Mark was being clumsy. To everyone else but Courtney, that is. She stared at her friend uneasily.

"You okay?" she asked with trepidation.

"Yeah, sure," Mark answered quickly. He avoided making eye contact with her to try not to give away the fact that he wasn't even close to okay. He kept his right hand buried in his pocket. He didn't want anybody to notice that something was missing.

"All right, folks. Here's the plan," Dodger announced while clapping the crumbs off his hands. He reached into his jacket pocket and pulled out three black and red paper folders. "We've got three berths in cabin class for the voyage back, day after tomorrow. It ain't a cheap haul, let me tell you, but since DADO is payin' for it—"

"Don't say that," Mark snapped.

Everyone shot a look at Mark. They weren't used to him being so opinionated. About anything.

"Sorry, chum," Dodger apologized. "I didn't mean nothin' by it."

Mark looked at his shoes. Courtney looked at Mark, frowning.

"We sail at noon, so we should get an early start to the docks," Dodger continued. "So if you want to do any sightseeing, tomorrow's the day."

Nobody said a word.

"Though I guess nobody's really in the mood for that," Dodger added.

The awkward silence continued.

"This is what you wanted, right?" Dodger asked, confused. "I mean, did I mess up or something?"

"You did fine," Courtney offered. "I think we're all just a little bit tired. Thanks for getting the tickets."

"Things'll look better once we get home," Dodger offered hopefully. "You know, back to familiar surroundings."

"I'm not exactly sure what home is anymore," Mark said softly.

Mrs. Dimond looked to her son, pained. He had grown a lifetime in the past four years.

Dodger stood, trying to break the gloom. "There's a little restaurant next door that looks good for dinner. Okay if I make reservations?"

"Good idea," Mr. Dimond replied.

Dodger nodded. He didn't know what else to say, so he ducked out. Courtney and the Dimonds kept looking to Mark, waiting for him to say something. Finally Mark took a breath and looked back at them.

"He's right," Mark exclaimed. "Things'll look better once we get back. Let's not sit around feeling sorry for ourselves. I'm hungry, and not for one of those dry little turd balls."

Everyone laughed, in spite of the heavy atmosphere. An hour later they all sat in the Wild Boar restaurant next to the hotel, feasting on shepherd's pie, haddock cakes, and roast beef. Though it was actually on the menu, nobody took a chance on ordering the wild boar. They talked about England . . . about what they'd seen and what they might catch a glimpse of the next day. They talked about the *Queen Mary* and what they looked forward to on the voyage back to New York. They even talked about the weather. The weather! To anybody who may have been eavesdropping they sounded exactly like a normal, everyday family from America on holiday. Truth was, there was nothing normal about them, other than the fact that for a few hours they tried to pretend like everything was okay. It was pretty clear that nobody wanted to talk about anything that had to do with Forge, KEM, or Saint Dane. It was like a short holiday. Very short. By ten o'clock everyone was in his or her room, sound asleep.

Everyone but Mark. He lay awake, staring at the ceiling, listening to Dodger's grinding snore. For hours. At times it got so loud he was surprised the windows didn't rattle. It wasn't the snoring that kept him awake though. Mark couldn't stop thinking about his meeting with Nevva. He had convinced himself that she told him the truth. She only wanted the ring so that Bobby would be truly isolated, with no contact from the rest of Halla. Did he believe her? Surely she must have known that there were other rings floating around. Or had she made deals for those as well?

Mark twisted his head to look over at the next bed. "Dodger?" he whispered.

Dodger's answer was an even deeper snore. The guy was long gone. Mark had only known him for a short time, but liked the feisty acolyte. And why not? If Gunny trusted him, he had to be a great guy. He definitely proved useful in getting them around on First Earth. He was going to be a huge asset once they got back to New York and had to figure out what their next move would be. Dodger was definitely a friend.

Dodger also possessed the key to knowing if Mark had made the mistake of a lifetime. Sitting on the night table between the two beds was a lamp, a phone, a roll of British pound notes . . . and Dodger's Traveler ring. It was right there, a few feet from his head. Mark sat up slowly. The old bedsprings let out a groaning creak. He froze and took another look at Dodger. Would this wake him? Dodger rolled over and mumbled something in his sleep that sounded to Mark like, "Fur bell gone girl." Mark didn't think it required a response. He took a breath and stood up quickly. The bed creaked. Dodger didn't. Mark swept Dodger's ring off the table and hurried for the door. With the stealth of a cat burglar trying to break *out* of a house, he left the room and closed the door without disturbing the dreams of his new friend.

A grandfather clock at the end of the corridor chimed twice. Two in the morning. Normal people were asleep. Mark crept down the carpeted stairs to the small sitting room where they all had shared tea. The place was empty. The only sound came from several different clocks that echoed multiple ticks and tocks throughout the small hotel. A single table lamp was lit. There was enough light to see, if not to read. Mark desperately hoped that soon there would be a lot more light filling the room.

He placed the ring down reverently on the thick rug, knelt down, and leaned over so that his nose wasn't more than a foot away from the ring.

"Ibara," Mark whispered.

The ring didn't move. Didn't twitch. Didn't grow.

"Ibara," Mark said again, this time in a normal voice.

The response was the same, which is to say, there was no response. The ring lay dormant.

"Ibara!" Mark called, this time in a voice very near a shout.

It didn't matter. The ring wasn't listening.

Somebody else was.

"Mark! What the hell?" came a voice from the doorway.

Mark spun quickly, landing on his butt. Standing in the doorway was Courtney.

"It doesn't w-work," Mark stuttered nervously. "The ring doesn't work."

Courtney hurried into the room. She wore the white dress-shirt that she'd bought in New York, and nothing else. It worked perfectly as a nightgown. "What doesn't work?" she yawned.

"The Traveler ring. It's dead."

"Are you trying to send something?" Courtney asked.

"No."

"Maybe that's why," she said hopefully. "It might only work when there's something to send."

"How would the ring know if I had something to send or not?" Mark countered.

"How should I know?" Courtney said in a harsh whisper. "I don't know how it does anything!"

"I'm telling you, it doesn't work."

Courtney looked at the ring on the rug, cleared her throat and called out, *"Ibara!"*

Nothing happened.

"Zadaa!" Courtney called.

Instantly the ring twitched and began to grow. Mark and Courtney shot each other looks. Flashing light spewed from the growing circle. Courtney sprinted back toward the door of the sitting room and swung it shut to avoid disturbing anyone in the hotel. She hurried back to Mark and sat down to watch the ring grow to Frisbee size, opening up the narrow passageway between territories. Sparkling light flashed through the room. The jumble of musical notes grew louder, coming to First Earth to retrieve whatever message was being sent. But there was no message. It was a false alarm. Nothing would be dropped into the opening.

The ring stayed open for what seemed like a few seconds longer than usual, waiting for its cargo. It then snapped shut quickly, as if piqued that its efforts were for naught. The music subsided. The light died. Mark and Courtney were alone once again, with only the steady ticktock of ancient clocks for company. The two stared at the innocent-looking ring lying on the carpet for several seconds.

"Your ring works, Mark," Courtney declared.

"It's not my ring."

Courtney gave him a curious look. Mark jumped to his feet and paced nervously.

"You've been squirrelly all night," Courtney scolded. "Something's going on and you're not sharing."

Mark shared. He told Courtney what had happened. He told her that Nevva was on First Earth and about how she wanted his ring or she'd go back to Second Earth to make sure his parents got on the doomed airliner. He told her everything.

When he was finished, Courtney shrugged. "I saw you didn't have your ring on. I thought you took it off because you were angry at Bobby for having quit."

"I wish," Mark said wistfully.

"Yeah, me too."

"What could I do, Courtney?" Mark cried. "I couldn't sacrifice my parents! I figured if she wanted to cut Bobby off by taking my ring, so what? There are other rings. But now . . . " He let that thought trail.

Courtney picked up Dodger's ring and stared at it closely, as if it would reveal something.

"Now none of the rings connect to Ibara," Courtney said, finishing his thought. "It can't be because the flume is buried. Bobby sent us a journal after the explosion. Something must have happened since he sent that last journal. Question is, *what*?"

Mark gave a heavy sigh. "I'm afraid that's not the only question."

Courtney looked at him. She saw the tears in his eyes.

His voice quivered. "If Bobby was already cut off, why did Nevva really want my ring?"

FIRST EARTH

(CONTINUED)

The young boy was dying.

Nobody doubted that. Not the nurses. Not the doctors. Not any of the other young patients in the clinic who were kept safely away, in case the disease that was burning inside him could spread its deadly reach. The only issue left in doubt was when the curtain would fall on his young life. Nurses took care to wear masks when they wiped his forehead with cool, damp cloths to try to keep the fever down. Or at least to make him a little more comfortable. He was delirious. When he opened his eyes, the nurses saw that he focused on nothing. His eyes had the watery, vacant look they knew all too well. It pained them to know he was suffering. They liked the boy.

He was only seven years old, give or take a few weeks. His exact birthday could only be guessed at, since he was found as an infant on the doorstep of a foundling hospital in the town of Redhill, outside London. It could have been worse. He could have been abandoned somewhere in the city.

He was given the name Alexander, after the conquering Greek general, in the hopes he would battle the odds and survive to create a sound life for himself. Though always smaller than his peers and often sickly, it looked as if he would do exactly that. Alexander was fearless. Better, he was smart. While the other boys dominated him physically, Alexander was able to talk his way out of most situations. He never threw a punch in anger, nor was one thrown at him. Ever. While boys fought around him and bloody noses were as common as pollen on the breeze, Alexander was never touched. He never insulted, nor was bothered by insults hurled his way. Boys much older than he would seek his guidance. The masters and mistresses who cared for the orphans were amazed at Alexander's wisdom and self-confidence. They had high hopes for their young conquering hero.

Until the fall of 1937, when he became sick. The diagnosis wasn't certain. It started as a simple cold, but rather than run its course, it ran roughshod over the frail Alexander. The doctors at the hospital's clinic feared it was pneumonia. Or worse, influenza. They remembered the influenza epidemic of 1918. It was a global disaster that killed somewhere between twenty and forty million people. Twenty years later there was still no vaccination against the dread disease. The doctors at the foundling hospital feared for Alexander's life, but the fear of what might happen should his illness spread was worse. They kept the young boy comfortable, but isolated. Their ability to battle his illness was limited. They knew that Alexander's body would have to heal itself.

Alexander's body was losing.

His fever rarely dropped below a hundred. He lost weight. The nurses would clutch their arms around their waists when they heard his horrible coughing, as if each hack were just as painful to them as to the poor, sick boy. Everyone agreed that if he had been physically strong to begin with, he might have had a chance to beat the illness. But Alexander was a waif. He looked sickly even when his health was perfect.

After three weeks of decline, the best they could hope for was that the end would come quickly and painlessly. They didn't want to see their favorite young charge suffer any longer.

It was past midnight that November. Alexander lay in his hospital bed, surrounded by a white sheet that had been erected as a screen to keep any questionable airborne particles from finding their way to other, healthier lungs. This was being overly cautious. The rest of the children had been moved out and made to double up in the ward next door. Alexander was alone. He was frightened. He wanted one of the nurses to come and sit with him, but he never asked. He hoped they would have come on their own. They didn't. He knew why. They were afraid of what he had inside.

Alexander was also angry. He didn't understand why the doctors couldn't help him. He hated that the nurses left him alone. It didn't make sense to him that with all their knowledge and complicated talk and fascinating, shiny instruments, they couldn't do something as simple as fix what was wrong with him. He wanted them to be smarter. He desperately needed them to be smarter. They weren't.

He managed to push one of the drapes aside so that he got a view through the window up near the ceiling. Through the glass he saw stars. He wanted to be outside. He wanted to take a deep breath of fresh, cold air. The thought alone made him cough. The coughing hurt. He wanted the hurt to stop. He didn't care how. Not anymore. He was tired of fighting.

He saw a shadow flash quickly past the window. It got his attention, if only because it was something different to think about. He wondered what it might have been. A bird? A tree branch? A passing airplane? The angel of death? He kept looking, hoping to see it again. It was something to do. The shadow didn't return and Alexander gave up waiting. He wanted to sleep. His chest hurt. He knew his fever was spiking again because he had the shivers. He tensed to fight it, which made his muscles ache all the more.

He called out, "Hello?" which made him cough again. The pain tore through his chest and stomach. He stopped calling. He wasn't so sure he wanted help anyway. Whenever his fever spiked, the nurses dunked him in a cold tub of water. He never understood why, if his body temperature was so high, he felt cold. Being dunked into cold water when you were already freezing was a nightmare. He didn't want any more nightmares. He wanted to sleep in peace. He clutched his thin blanket around him and concentrated. He willed himself to relax and clear his mind. He didn't want to be awake. He didn't want to be tortured anymore. He wanted to sleep . . . and not wake up. Mercifully, sleep came.

When he thought back on that night, which he did many times, Alexander didn't remember if he had any dreams. He remembered the feeling of being totally relaxed. It was such a welcome relief, it was worth remembering. He remembered not shivering anymore. He remembered not feeling pain. He had the vivid memory of thinking that he must have died. It was the only logical explanation for feeling well again. It had been so long, he had almost forgotten what it was like to be pain free. He remembered feeling warmth and light on his face. Was he in heaven? He had to see. Alexander cautiously opened his eyes, expecting to see the pearly gates.

What he saw instead were the same windows of the hospital ward. The only difference was that it was morning. Bright sun shone in, warming his face. He was at peace. He felt . . . good. But that didn't make sense. He actually wondered if he were still asleep and living inside a dream. There was nothing out of the ordinary happening, other than the fact that he felt so good. Alexander decided that if this was a dream, he was going to take advantage of it. He closed his eyes and took a long, slow inhale through his nose. His lungs expanded. He braced his body, ready to be racked by the horrid coughs.

They didn't come. Alexander let his breath out and took another, this time through his mouth. He filled his lungs with air until they felt ready to burst. He blew the air out and took another so quickly it made him light-headed. It wasn't the dizziness that came from fever, either. It was the result of too much oxygen being sent through a system that wasn't used to getting much at all.

Alexander laughed. He couldn't help himself. It was the best dream he'd ever had. Either that, or he'd died and gone to heaven. He didn't care which. All that mattered was that his head and his lungs were clear.

"Alexander?" came the concerned call of a nurse. "Alexander lad, why're you laughing like that?"

The nurse poked her head in tentatively through the curtain, as if not wanting to expose the rest of her body to the germ-infested enclosure. She had a thick white mask over her mouth and nose. Her eyes went wide with wonder when she looked upon Alexander, who lifted his head off the pillow to greet her.

"Morning, mum," he called cheerily. "Might there be some toast about for brekkie? I'm famished."

The nurse's eyes grew even wider. She drifted through the curtains, her eyes trained on Alexander. She approached the bed, hesitated, then lifted her hand to touch his forehead. She instantly pulled her hand back, as if Alexander were electrified.

"Alexander," she whispered in astonishment. "Your fever's broken."

Alexander answered, "I didn't break it, mum. I promise."

The nurse didn't remove her mask, but Alexander could tell she was smiling. "Well, maybe you did and maybe you didn't, but there's one thing for sure . . . it's a miracle." She backed away from the boy, finally pulling off her mask. Her smile was as big and broad as Alexander thought. It made him smile as well. "It's a miracle!" she repeated and ran off through the curtains, calling, "Doctor! Doctor! Come quickly!"

Alexander lay there smiling. He wasn't sure why. He felt good, that was for certain, but after all, it was only a dream. He thought he would wake up soon enough, to be right back where he'd started, shivering and in pain. His only hope was that this glorious dream would last a while longer.

He shifted his weight to get a better view of the window overhead. That's when he felt it. There was something in his hand. He hadn't noticed up until then because he hadn't moved much. But when he went to pivot his body, he realized that something was in his right hand. He squeezed it. It was hard, like a small stone. Or a marble. A shooter marble. But he didn't remember bringing a marble to bed with him, and the nurses definitely wouldn't have allowed it. With more than a little curiosity, Alexander used his left hand to pull the thin blanket away. He didn't need it anymore. He was plenty warm enough. Once the covering was gone, Alexander lifted his hand to see what the mysterious object was.

His first thought was that it was beautiful. He had never seen anything like it. It wasn't a stone, or a marble. Not even close. There was some fine workmanship involved in making this treasure. It had to be valuable. No doubt about that. Did it belong to one of the doctors? Why would they give it to him? Alexander raised the object up to his face to give it a closer look.

It was a silver ring with a large gray stone set in the center. Surrounding the stone were markings—ten in all. They were like no letters Alexander had ever seen. They were more like ancient characters from some unknown language. He turned the ring over in his hand and stared at the gray stone. It didn't look like a valuable jewel. It was definitely cut and polished, but the stone itself was gray and drab.

Though not for long. As he looked at it, the stone began to sparkle. This didn't frighten Alexander, or even surprise him. The stone transformed from opaque gray to brilliant crystal. The light that flickered inside it seemed alive. Alexander looked deep into this magical gem, and smiled.

"Maybe it is a miracle," he said to himself.

He would have continued staring into the flickering light if something else hadn't grabbed his attention. Another shadow flashed by the window overhead. This time it didn't continue on. Alexander looked up to see that something had stopped to rest on a branch just outside the glass. It was a large black bird. A raven. Alexander couldn't tell for sure, but it felt to him as if the dark bird was looking down at him.

"This isn't a dream, is it?" he said softly in the general direction of the bird.

As if in answer, the raven let out a sharp *caw!* and flew off.

❖ DENDURON ❖

Alder made his way quickly toward the Milago village, trying not to be seen by anyone who might know him. He needed to understand what was happening before being swept up in the activity. Better yet, he wanted to avoid anything to do with this kind of activity. He was still a Bedoowan knight, and the knights were assembling for battle. He would be expected to join his troop. Worse, he might be punished for not being there already. He couldn't let that happen. He had to be on his own. Whatever was going on, he was absolutely certain that it had something to do with Saint Dane and the battle for Halla. The reappearance of the quigs on top of the mountain had told him that. He had to think like a Traveler now, not a Bedoowan knight. For that, he had to steer clear of his comrades.

Alder found a spot in a grove of trees not far from the edge of the forest that led up into the mountains. From there he had a clear view of the activities below. Hundreds of knights were assembling in the large area between the Milago village and the ruins of the Bedoowan castle. They marched in formation, forty at a time, locked in step. Some carried spears and shields. Others had bows, with quivers of arrows strapped to their backs. Two troops of knights on horseback appeared and took up positions on either side of the assembling army. They were followed by a long line of what looked to Alder like cannons being wheeled in and positioned to the rear. This last was the most disturbing image of all. There weren't supposed to be cannons on Denduron. The weapons they used were primitive. Spears, arrows, rocks, wooden staves—all were common to the Bedoowan knights of Denduron. Cannons were not.

What had happened since he'd left with Pendragon for Ibara? How long had he been gone? By his own clock, Alder had only been gone for a few days. But when he left, there weren't this many Bedoowan knights on Denduron. Now the number of armored knights looked to have tripled. Alder thought he saw some Milago farmers in uniform, as well as the white-skinned Novans, who seemed to have been pressed into service as well. And then there were the cannons. Weapons like that could not be developed from scratch in a few days. No, Alder was beginning to realize that he had returned to Denduron at a time far into the future. But how far? Why had the flume done that? Why were his people preparing for battle, and with whom?

He remembered the final image he saw floating in space before the flume set him down. He saw another army gathering. The primitive tribe that lived on the far side of the mountain from the Milago village were known as the Lowsee. There was never trouble between the Lowsee and the Bedoowan and Milago, yet seeing that image of the Lowsee in armor and waving spears made Alder fear the worst. Were they about to attack? Or were the Bedoowan knights preparing to march over the mountain and invade the Lowsee? There were so many questions, and only one answer as to why all these changes had occurred.

Alder felt certain he knew what that answer was.

Boom!

He jumped at the sound of a far-off explosion. Had the battle begun? He looked to the assembled knights. Nobody seemed to be concerned about the eruption. They kept in line without moving. The first explosion was followed by another, and another. Alder realized the sounds were coming from the training ground, where the Milago had prepared to battle the Bedoowan so long ago. Whatever was happening there, it was only training. The explosions confirmed Alder's fears. He didn't know why the Bedoowan were preparing for war, but he knew what lit the fuse.

Tak.

He had helped Pendragon and Siry use the incredible digging device from Zadaa to find a new vein of the explosive compound beneath the surface of Denduron. It was the only way to battle Saint Dane's army of dados—the only way to save Ibara. The gamble had worked. Ibara was saved. But what of Denduron? Tak was as tempting as it was powerful. When the Milago miners originally discovered it, they had planned to use it against the Bedoowan to win their freedom. But that wouldn't have been the end of it. Rellin, the leader of the miners, spoke of tak as being the tool that would create a powerful empire. The Milago had lived for generations as slaves. They were angry, and justifiably so. Their anger was not going to dissipate once they had defeated the Bedoowan. They planned to march on the rest of Denduron, conquering tribes and putting them under the rule of the Milago. But they never got the chance, for the Travelers realized that the discovery of tak was the turning point for Denduron. Saint Dane wanted the Milago to use tak. The Travelers didn't.

The Travelers won. Pendragon exploded the tak mine in such spectacular fashion that it not only destroyed the Bedoowan castle, it shattered the Milago village as well. With both their worlds in shambles, the Milago and the Bedoowan were forced to end their rivalry and rebuild, together. Most important, the eruption buried the vein of tak so deep that it ended any temptation to create an army that could use its destructive power. The explosive tak was unreachable by any tools or methods known to Denduron.

Until Pendragon and Siry showed up with a dygo from Zadaa.

Was it possible that the unearthing of the tak had created another turning point for Denduron? Had all that was accomplished, all that was risked to end the bitter dispute between the two tribes been for naught? Did Saint Dane get a second chance? From where Alder stood, it looked sickeningly possible.

He crept cautiously closer to the parade ground, keeping to the safe shadows of the trees. As he grew closer, he saw two people arrive on horseback to address the knights. One he recognized instantly as Rellin, the chief miner of the Milago who had led the revolution against the Bedoowan. For his strong leadership, Rellin was elected to lead the Milago during the rebuilding process. Alder's heart sank when he saw that Rellin wore the armor of a Bedoowan knight. Worse. His armor was decorated with bright yellow stripes on each arm. Under his left arm he held a leather helmet that had a bright yellow plume of feathers attached to the back. Rellin looked as rugged as Alder remembered, but now his hair was combed back and neat. His horse was beautiful, with its own leather armor gleaming in the sun. Rellin looked every bit like a proud general who wore armor for show, rather than for protection.

On the horse next to him was a woman Alder didn't recognize. He moved a few yards closer to get a better look and stopped short, unbelieving. The woman wore a flowing white dress, with a ring of yellow flowers in her hair. The flowers surrounded a simple silver crown. It was Kagan, queen of the Bedoowan. What surprised Alder was how she looked. The Kagan that Alder knew was, by all accounts, grotesque. Everything about her was huge. Her eyes, her nose, her hands and feet—all freakishly immense. Not anymore. This queen had lost a lot of weight. By Alder's estimation, Kagan had lost an entire Kagan. She wasn't pretty by any means, but she was no longer beastly. Just the fact that her clothes were no longer covered by greasy food stains helped her to look more human. It also helped that she wasn't constantly stuffing her face with various meat products. She sat on her horse with a serene expression as she watched Rellin address the troops.

Alder got his feet moving again and saw one more surprise: Rellin held his helmet under his arm for a reason. On his head was a small crown. What? Had he married Kagan? Was he now the king of the Bedoowan as well as the leader of the Milago? There was nothing good about what Alder was seeing. He was still too far away to hear what Rellin was saying to the knights, but every so often a raucous cheer erupted from the troops. Whatever Rellin was saying, he was firing them up.

"Alder!" came a surprised shout.

Alder bent his knees, ready to be attacked. He turned to see a Bedoowan knight jogging toward him along the treeline. Alder wished he had thought about the possibility of there being guards in the woods. He would have been more careful. Now it was too late. He crouched, ready to fight, until he saw that the knight wasn't in attack mode. If anything, he looked happy to see Alder. The guy had a big smile on his face. Alder relaxed. Slightly.

"Where have you been?" the knight called to him excitedly.

Alder recognized the man. It was Graviot, one of the knights from Alder's troop. Graviot was a friend, though he knew nothing of Alder's calling as a Traveler. Graviot reminded Alder of himself . . . or at least of the knight Alder used to be. Graviot was younger by a few years. He was also big and clumsy and absolutely honest to a fault, just as Alder had been so long ago. It pained Alder to think that he himself was no longer as honest and naive. He had seen too much of Halla to be able to hold on to the person he once was. He had a moment of sadness for the loss of his own simple life, but shook it off quickly. Alder knew he had to be careful with the knight, friend or not. Too much had happened since he'd been gone to assume anything.

"I traveled with Pendragon and the boy Siry," Alder answered. "Remember? We unearthed the tak to help a tribe far from here."

"Of course I remember," Graviot answered. "We did not think you would be gone for so long. Many things have happened. We will soon be at war."

"Why is that?" Alder asked. "What has happened? Have we been attacked?"

"In a way, yes," Graviot answered.

"The Lowsee attacked us?" Alder asked, surprised.

Graviot's eyes narrowed. "How would you know of the Lowsee problem if you have been away?"

Alder couldn't admit that he'd seen images of the Lowsee preparing for battle as he flumed through time and space. He had to come up with a plausible response to keep Graviot on his side.

"I never trusted the Lowsee," Alder answered quickly. "It was only a guess." It was also a total lie, but Alder was getting used to being less than honest.

"You were wise not to trust them," Graviot continued. He bought it.

"Yet I did not expect them to attack us," Alder added. "They are a peaceful tribe."

"They did not attack us with weapons," Graviot continued. "But they are trying to crush us just the same."

"How?"

"By withholding their triptyte" was Graviot's answer.

Alder knew about triptyte. It was a mineral the Bedoowan had used to create light within their castle. Before the castle was destroyed there was an elaborate system of tubes that snaked across every ceiling. When darkness fell, triptyte glowed brightly. It was a clean source of light that was much safer than fire. It was also a cause for shame, because the Bedoowan had not shared the technology with the Milago. They kept the Milago in the dark. Literally. When the Bedoowan castle crumbled and the Milago village was rebuilt, that changed. Triptyte lights were erected throughout the village. It was an incredible step forward, allowing the Milago village to continue operating into the night without the fear of an accident caused by fire. Many said that triptyte was what helped create a modern Milago.

Alder also knew that the triptyte came from mines on land that was controlled by the Lowsee.

"Why would they withhold the triptyte from us?" Alder asked.

"Because we are no longer mining glaze," was his answer. "The triptyte was paid for by glaze. Once the Milago stopped mining, we could no longer trade with the Lowsee and—"

"And now we are going to war to *take* what we need," Alder said gravely, finishing Graviot's thought.

"It is a wonderful opportunity!" Graviot said enthusiastically.

"How can war be wonderful?" Alder asked, incredulous.

"Once we defeat the Lowsee, we will not stop there. Glaze has been discovered in the lands beyond the Lowsee. Once we control those lands, the glaze will be ours."

Alder shot a harsh glance at Graviot. "You are saying that we plan on mining glaze again? How can that be? It is deadly to mine that mineral. Have you forgotten?"

"Of course not," Graviot scoffed. "But we will not be mining it. That will be the task of the Lowsee . . . once they have been conquered."

"And whose plan was this?"

"King Rellin's of course!" Graviot answered, as if it were a ridiculous question to ask.

Alder winced. It was coming full circle. Rellin once began a revolution to fight the barbaric practice of forcing his people to dig and die in the toxic glaze mines. Now that he had achieved power, he was willing to go to war to force another group of unfortunates to do the exact same thing.

Alder looked at Graviot and said sadly, "So dying for glaze is acceptable, as long as it is somebody else who is dying?"

Graviot shrugged. "The strong survive, Alder."

Alder wanted to scream. All they had been fighting for on Denduron, all they had achieved was about to be wiped out.

"Why do you look pained?" Graviot asked. "You should be proud! None of this would have been possible if not for you and Pendragon."

Alder gave Graviot a steely glare.

"Do not be modest," Graviot chided. "You and Pendragon brought that wondrous machine to unearth the tak. If not for the tak, none of this would be happening. Besides, it may save your life."

"Save my life?" Alder asked, stunned.

"We are about to go to war," Graviot announced. "You have been branded a deserter. I fear you will be tried for treason, old friend. It is very possible that you will be executed. Or perhaps sent to the new glaze mines. You should hope that Rellin has mercy, because without you, we never would have recovered the tak."

Alder struck without thinking. He uncorked a punch that Graviot never saw coming. The unsuspecting knight probably didn't even know he had been hit. He was unconscious before he hit the ground. Alder felt a twinge of regret. Not that he had decked Graviot, but that the attack had come from an outburst of emotion. It wasn't professional. Alder was a professional. He wouldn't let emotions rule his actions again. There was too much at stake. He had work to do.

He dragged the unconscious knight back into the trees, away from curious eyes. There he stripped the knight of his new, modern armor. He took off his own armor and lashed on Graviot's. It was good that they were the same size. Now Alder could walk among the Bedoowan without attracting unwanted stares. Remaining hidden was suddenly more important than he had realized. He had been gone a long time . . . too long. Enough time to be charged with desertion and treason. He couldn't be arrested. That would be disaster, because he had a mission and he could not fail.

The Traveler knight stopped for a moment and took a breath. He was tired. He had just fought a war against an army of dados. There was nothing he wanted more than to sit down, sleep, and heal. Alder was strong. He knew he could keep going physically. It was his mental state he was more concerned with. Would he be able to bring himself to do what needed to be done to save his territory? The tak mine had to be destroyed. If he was successful, the Milago village might be destroyed along with it. Could he bring himself to do that?

He didn't have a choice. The future of Denduron was at stake. The future of Halla was at stake. He had to go into battle once again. He picked up the long wooden stave that was the weapon of choice for Bedoowan knights, spun it once, and held it close to his side. He was on familiar turf. He left the trees and headed for the village, prepared to destroy all that was left of his former life.

He wished Pendragon were with him.

❖ DENDURON ❖

(CONTINUED)

The first part of Alder's plan was simple. He had to make his way into the new tak mine. He had no doubt there would be guards. Guards didn't worry him. He had the element of surprise on his side. They wouldn't expect an attack to come from a Bedoowan knight.

The second part of his plan wasn't as simple. He had to destroy the mine. Igniting the tak wouldn't be the problem. Being somewhere else when it erupted would. He didn't have much time. That fact was made all too clear when he moved past the rows of knights who were listening to King Rellin's speech. Now that he was closer, he heard some of what Rellin was saying. Rellin was pontificating, using words like "glorious victory," "spreading the empire," and "triumph of the superior tribe."

Empire? When did the little world of the Milago and the Bedoowan become an empire? It chilled Alder to hear how the power of tak had completely corrupted Rellin. He was once a good man. He had fought for his people and against injustice. Now he was about to fight for power and glory.

Alder shuddered when he realized that Saint Dane's prophecy

was about to come true: The first domino of Halla to fall would be Denduron, just as he had predicted several years before. It may not have played out exactly as Saint Dane wanted, but what did that matter? Or maybe this *was* exactly what Saint Dane wanted. Maybe this was how he'd planned for his grand scheme to unfold all along, and the Travelers were only going along for the ride. There was no way to know. There was only the mission. Alder had to stop the war. To do that, he needed to destroy the tak.

As he hurried past the assembled knights, he could feel tension radiating from the masses. They had their game faces on. They were ready for battle. He knew the feeling. It was bloodlust. This wasn't an exercise. They were about to march on the Lowsee. From what Alder remembered, he guessed it would take the rest of the day and into the night to move the army of knights up and over the mountain and into attack position. Just moving the cannons would take most of the night. His guess was that they would take up positions under cover of night and attack at first light. Alder knew he didn't have much time. If he was going to stop this war, he would have to destroy the tak before the army left. He not only had to seal the mines, he had to find a way to destroy whatever they had already dug out of the ground.

Alder's journey brought him through the Milago village, past farmland and toward the field where the Bedoowan knights were training with tak. He wanted to see how they were using the explosive. What he saw didn't calm his fears.

He peered over a tall berm of dirt built up to contain flying shrapnel. It was definitely needed, because there was a lot of shrapnel flying around. Alder saw several cannons to his right. Each were manned by three Bedoowan knights. They seemed to be practicing. One knight packed a small amount of the red-clay tak and gently lowered it into the muzzle of the six-foot-long black cannon barrel. The second knight loaded a round cannonball on top of that. The third knight aimed the cannon. Their target was a wall of hay bales set up nearly fifty yards in front of them. At least, it used to be a wall of hay bales. It was now a mass of burning debris, surrounded by huge crater holes from the cannonballs. The tak was very effective.

Once all was ready, the third knight scratched a small metal device that Alder realized was making a spark. The knight held it next to a thin rope that dangled from the rear end of the cannon. A fuse. After two flicks, the rope was set on fire. While the three knights stood back and covered their ears, the fuse burned quickly until it reached the back end of the cannon. An instant later . . . *boom!* A cloud of smoke blew out of the barrel, and two seconds later the cannonball hit the pile of burning hay dead on. When the projectile landed, it exploded as well, sending up another cloud of smoke. This second explosion rocked the ground, nearly knocking Alder down. The sound was deafening. Alder figured the cannonball must have had more tak inside it. No chunk of metal alone would have exploded like that.

The tak cannons were deadly . . . and deadly accurate. Alder knew that the Lowsee wouldn't stand a chance, and neither would Denduron. He had seen all he needed to see. He skirted the training ground, headed for the remote area where he and Siry and Pendragon had used the dygo to find the new vein of tak. They had deliberately dug far from the Milago village for safety. Alder was happy about that. Perhaps, he thought, when the mine exploded, it wouldn't damage the village. Much. It all depended on which way the underground vein of tak ran. He hurried through the woods, trying not to think too far beyond the next step. *One thing at a time. Just keep going. Don't get caught. Don't stop.* When he reached the end of the woods near the clearing with the tak mine . . .

He stopped. He didn't expect to see what was there before him. When he left Denduron only a few days before, the mine was nothing more than a hole in the ground. Now there was a building. A huge building. It was made entirely of wood, with a flat roof. The structure stood higher than any other building in the Milago village and took up many times as much ground. It looked like a giant storage building. Alder feared what might be stored inside.

There were two large doors in front. They were closed and guarded by two Bedoowan knights. If Alder was getting into that building, it would have to be past those knights. The show was about to begin. Everyone would soon know that Alder was back. He straightened up, held the wooden stave at his side, and walked boldly toward the building. As he drew closer, the guards stiffened.

"What is your business?" one of them growled.

Alder didn't break stride. "I have news from King Rellin," he said with authority. "We must all assemble on the field for his final instructions."

The knights gave each other a quick, confused glance.

"Those are not our orders," the first knight responded. "We are not to leave our posts."

Alder didn't recognize either of the knights. He was relieved about that. He didn't like hurting his friends.

"Your orders have been changed," Alder said as he drew closer to the guards. "You are to move immediately to—" He didn't finish the sentence. He quickly brought his stave up and jammed it into the gut of the first knight. The second knight was so surprised he hesitated before reacting. It cost him. Alder flicked his stave, catching him under the chin. The knight's head flew back and his feet flipped up into the air. The knight landed square on his back with a sickening thud. Before he hit, Alder had already flashed his stave back toward the first knight, catching him on the side of his head. The knight crashed against the building. At the same time, Alder spun backward with his body and the stave, catching the second knight square on the jaw. Within four seconds both knights lay unconscious at Alder's feet.

Alder stood over them as casually as if he had just swatted

two flies. After defeating an entire army of dados, getting past two Bedoowan knights was somewhat less of a challenge. Alder stepped over his fallen comrades and pushed open the large wooden door that led into the building. The sudden darkness inside made it difficult to see. He stood with his back to the door, on full alert. Though he couldn't make out detail at first, it was clear to him that the entire building was one room. There were windows near the ceiling that glowed with the light from the suns of Denduron. Alder waited impatiently for his eyes to adjust. After a few seconds he began to make out shapes.

His heart sank. The room was an arsenal. Most of the floor was taken up with rows of brand-new, gleaming cannons. To the rear was a cache of what looked like thousands of tak-filled cannonballs. The giant room was ringed with balconies that were laden with tak arrows, bows and crossbows. Another balcony was filled with what looked like small bricks of tak. They weren't fancy, but if one of those tak bombs exploded, it could destroy a house. Or eight. Alder's fears had become reality. The people of Denduron had been busy. They were ready for war. The tak mine had provided tons of explosives. With weaponry like this, Alder had no doubt that the Bedoowan army could overrun the Lowsee, and any other tribe they set their sights on. The conquest of Denduron was about to begin, along with the fall of Halla.

Alder walked forward in a daze, staring at the tools of death and destruction that loomed over him. He almost didn't see that he was about to step into a hole. He pulled up short at its edge and peered down into the darkness.

"The mine," he whispered to himself.

It was the same hole that he and Pendragon had dug with the dygo. Only now there were ore-car tracks leading down into it. The shaft was steep, but not straight down. It was walkable. This was a working mine. From the looks of the arsenal, it was a productive one.

Alder knew what he had to do. That realization led him to a sobering truth. He didn't have time to figure out a way to explode the tak from afar.

This was a suicide mission.

It wasn't a truth he welcomed, but he felt that if Pendragon was willing to give up his own life on Ibara to destroy the dado army, then perhaps he should be willing to do the same to save his own territory. His only consolation was that Pendragon felt certain a Traveler's existence wouldn't end with death. Was that possible? Were the Travelers actually illusions, as Saint Dane told Pendragon? As Alder stood in that vast arsenal, there was only one thing he could be certain of: He was going to find out the truth about the Travelers.

He dropped his stave, ran to the side wall of the structure, and grabbed two of the tak bricks. He ran back to the mine shaft and was about to descend when his eye caught something else. Hanging along the opposite wall from the tak bricks were coils of rope. Fuses. There were hundreds of them, all wound neatly, ready for use. Alder's heart leaped. He had an idea. After gently placing one of the small tak bombs on the floor, he ran and grabbed one of the coils of rope. Looking around quickly, he spotted one of the small metal devices he'd seen the knights using to ignite the rope. It looked like a narrow loop made of two thick wires. On one end was a flat piece of metal, against which the other end of the loop rested. Alder grabbed it and squeezed. As one end of the loop scratched against the metal plate, sparks flew.

He knew how to ignite the fuses.

He jammed the device into his pocket, ran back to the mine opening, where he picked up the second tak brick, and descended into the mine. He didn't have to go far. Triptyte illuminated the length of the tunnel, lighting up a frightening and awesome sight. Thousands of reddish-brown tak bricks were stacked along both walls of the tunnel. Thousands. The amount of explosive that had been pulled out of the mine was mind numbing. Alder carefully put down the two small tak bricks he had carried in. He wouldn't be needing them. All he needed was the fuse. He even let himself believe that he had a chance to not only destroy the mine, but stay alive. As much as he didn't fear death, he didn't exactly welcome it either. Besides, Pendragon had to know what had happened on Denduron. So did the other Travelers. Saint Dane wasn't close to done. If they were to know what was happening on Denduron, Alder had to survive.

He quickly set to work, kneeling down and unreeling the coil. The rope was dry, which was why it burned so easily. It also made it easy to snap off a length. Alder measured out four six-foot lengths. He had no idea how long it would take for six feet of fuse to burn. He wanted enough time to get out and away from the mine, but didn't want the fuses to burn for so long that somebody might find them and put them out.

Even with the fuses, Alder wasn't entirely convinced that this tactic would ensure his safety. Sure, he felt confident that he could get out of the mine and the armory building before the boom, but how far would he have to run in order not to be killed when the vast stores of tak exploded? Which direction should he go? He could easily be running to a spot that was directly over a thick, underground vein of tak.

He decided not to worry about it. What else could he do? He took three of the lengths of rope and buried one end of each in the soft tak stacked along the walls. He put two across from each other in the tunnel, and the third a few yards deeper into the dark. The last he saved for the mine car that was sitting on the track in front of him. The car was loaded with newly mined tak, ready to be molded into bricks. He jammed one end of the fuse into the clay. He was ready. He took one quick look around and actually chuckled.

"This will be dramatic," he said to himself.

Without hesitating for another second, he took the metal loop, held it against the other end of the rope leading to the tak in the mine car, and squeezed. Sparks sprayed, igniting the fuse. The clock was ticking. He gave the mine car a shove, sending it rolling deeper into the shaft. Turning quickly, he ran back to the other three fuses, igniting each. Soon, all four ropes were burning. It was time to be somewhere else.

Alder sprinted back toward the mouth of the mine tunnel while calculating his best route of escape. Where would it be safe? He had no idea. All he could do was get as far away from the mine as possible and hope the vein of tak didn't spread too far. He feared that miners might still be down in the tunnel. He feared that the explosion would do serious damage to the Milago village. He feared for the potential loss of life. But his fear for what Denduron had become, and its future, was greater. He knew he had done the right thing. The only thing. His next challenge was to survive long enough to warn the other Travelers that Saint Dane was back in the hunt. He was nearly at the end of the tunnel . . .

When he saw that he wasn't alone. Graviot stood at the mouth of the mine, along with four other Bedoowan knights. Alder pulled up short, his hope of survival quickly evaporating.

"What has happened to you, Alder?" Graviot asked sadly. "Have you lost your senses?"

Alder didn't answer. He had to buy time. Did the knights know that fuses were burning a hundred yards into the tunnel?

"You are right," Alder said, trying to sound troubled. "I do not know what has come over me. Perhaps I fear war more than I ever imagined. I believe I should throw myself on the mercy of King Rellin."

"What is that smell?" Graviot asked quizzically.

All five knights went on alert. If they didn't realize a fuse was burning, they would soon. Alder didn't make the first move. He would leave that to the other knights.

"There is a fire in the mine!" one of the knights shouted, horrified.

"What have you done?" Graviot exclaimed.

All five knights took off running into the mine. Alder had a brief thought that these were good men. Their first thought wasn't to save themselves, it was to put out the fire. He respected them for that.

But it didn't stop him from taking them apart. The knights weren't as experienced as Alder. Alder flung himself sideways at the first two, knocking them back. He kept moving, rolling off them and unleashing a barrage of punches and kicks to keep the others back. Graviot struggled to crawl deeper into the mine, but Alder was on him before he could stand. He lifted the young knight into the air, spun, and flung him toward the others. His strength was impossible. He was possessed. He knew the future of Halla might be decided by this one, brutal fight. There was no way he could keep all five back for long; he could only hope that it would be long enough.

One of the knights charged him. Alder turned his back to the knight and drove his arms forward, making an impossible target. The knight bounced off him as Alder spun and nailed him with a roundhouse kick to the jaw. It was the last kick he would throw.

He felt a sharp blow to the back of his head and fell forward. The world began to spin. He knew he had been hit by something harder than a fist or a foot. Where had the weapon come from? The knights weren't armed. Alder hit the dirt floor and rolled onto his back. He was losing consciousness. He looked up to see if the knights were sprinting into the tunnel. They weren't. He hoped to see a white flash that would signal the beginning of the end of the tak mine. He didn't. What he saw instead was a sixth man standing in the center of the tunnel—a miner. In one hand he held a pickax used for digging through rock. At least Alder knew what had hit him. It was what the miner had in his other hand that crushed Alder.

The miner held four three-foot lengths of partially burned rope. There would be no explosion. The tak was safe.

The war would begin.

Alder's eyes opened cautiously. Where was he? His head hurt, no big surprise. Getting hit with a pickax will do that. He squinted against a bright light that shone directly into his eyes. Though it hurt to move, he held his hand up to shield the light. As his focus sharpened, he saw that the light was blasting in through a small window halfway up the wall. A closer look told him the truth. Across the window were bars. Prison bars. He was being held captive. He wasn't surprised. He tried to destroy the mine, the village, and Rellin's aspirations for conquering Denduron. Of course they threw him in jail. The only surprise was that they hadn't executed him before he had the chance to wake up.

He was alone in the cell, lying on the floor. He took a breath and coughed. It was a dirt floor and he had sucked in a lungful. He wiped his mouth . . . and saw his ring. His Traveler ring. Alder brightened. There was still a chance. He could contact Pendragon through the ring. Why hadn't he thought of that before? If he could get a message to Pendragon and let him know what was going on, the lead Traveler might take up the fight. He could come back to Denduron. With Siry. And Loor. They could take up the fight for Denduron once again, but that couldn't be unless they knew what had happened. But how? He had no paper to write a message and didn't think the guards would give him any. No, he had to send a sign. Something. Anything that would make Pendragon think. He stared at the ring, desperate for an idea.

The answer was right in front of his eyes. Literally. Alder's sleeve was covered with blood. He wasn't sure if it was his own blood, or from one of the other knights. It didn't matter. His sleeve was soaked. The blood was already drying and turning brown. It looked as if someone had been seriously injured. It was exactly what he needed.

Alder was dizzy. He had to force himself to focus. He reached out, grabbed his sleeve with his other hand, and pulled, trying to rip off a bloody piece of fabric. He didn't have the strength. He brought the bloody sleeve to his mouth and bit, gnawing at the fabric, tasting the blood. After several minutes of chewing on the grisly material, he finally tore a small hole. It was plenty. Once the tear started, he was able to rip it farther and eventually pull off a piece of fabric about six inches long. It was perfect. Alder rolled the gruesome swatch of fabric into a tube, took off his ring, and placed it on the ground next to his face. He didn't care if a guard saw what was about to happen. There was nothing he could do to hide the show of light and music.

"Ibara," Alder called.

The ring didn't move.

"Ibara!" he called again, louder.

It didn't matter. The ring didn't respond.

Alder remembered the silent flume when he'd tried to rejoin Bobby on Ibara. For the first time in his life, he cried. Tears of frustration ran down his dirty cheek, stinging his open cuts. His warning would not find its way to the lead Traveler.

"What has happened to you, Pendragon?" he sobbed. "What has happened?"

THIRD EARTH

Patrick Mac desperately needed to see something familiar. Something he could wrap his mind around that would allow him to start rebuilding his sanity. He chose to go to the library—his refuge. His fortress of solitude. Things always made sense to him when he was in a library. Libraries were orderly and structured and filled with the knowledge of the ages. He always found answers in the library. He hoped that would happen again on the new Third Earth.

He hoped the library still existed.

He walked through the destroyed streets of New York City in a daze. There were plenty of people, but to Patrick they seemed more like rats. They scurried in and around the derelict buildings, grubbing through garbage cans for food or crouching down on all fours to slurp water that dripped from rusted, leaking pipes. It was like walking through a dream. Or a nightmare. The world he knew was gone. He wasn't so sure he wanted to get to know this new one.

Nothing looked familiar and he quickly got lost. Where was the library? He knew that his beloved refuge was built on the same spot where the library had always been, as far back as the nineteenth century. Where was that? On the old Third Earth it was a short walk across a grassy plain, over a footbridge that spanned a clean brook, and a few hundred yards along a pathway made of sparkling, crushed quartz.

Now he was faced with a sea of crumbling buildings. He wasn't even sure where he was starting from. Did he still live in Chelsea even if Chelsea was no longer underground? He desperately looked around for something that would give him his bearings. This was still New York City. Obviously something had changed in the past that sent it on a very different path from the history he knew, but it was the same city. There had to be something he would recognize. He was a historian, after all.

He passed several storefronts. Most were shuttered, but a few were open for business, selling cans of food or bottled water. To Patrick it seemed as if this were a city trying to recover from the ravages of a war. The thought made him shudder.

He stumbled a few more steps, rounded the corner of a building, and smiled. The sight was so obvious it actually made him laugh. Why hadn't he thought of it before? Looming over him was a huge skyscraper. On his old Third Earth it had a shiny silver skin. On this transformed territory it looked more like the ancient, historical version he had seen in holograms. It was the Empire State Building. This huge, majestic structure was one of the few historical buildings that had been retained when the move underground began. However, this didn't look much like the building he remembered. Instead of the gleaming steel tower, this ancient structure was pitted and sad. Giant holes were peppered through its walls, as if monster moths had eaten their fill. The majestic antenna that topped off the structure was long gone. Patrick feared that a strong wind would topple the once-mighty building like a rotted tree. As sad as this sight was, it lifted his spirits. He had his bearings. His beloved library wasn't far away.

The closer he walked toward the Empire State Building, the more crowded the streets became. Some people actually seemed to be walking with purpose, as if they had places to be and people to meet. This was once a center of business for the city. Patrick wondered if these were people on their way to or from work. Most wore nondescript clothing that looked old and worn. Still others had on old-fashioned business suits, complete with neckties. The clothing looked tired though. And dirty. And sad. Still, the people walked with their heads up. Whatever had happened to them, they were resilient. It actually made him smile.

"Typical New Yorkers," he said to himself.

As he walked, he kept glancing up at the skyscraper to judge where the library might be. It wasn't easy. The sidewalk was full of gaping holes. Many streets were closed off altogether because of buildings that had either collapsed or were about to. It was frustrating. As soon as he felt he might be getting close, he would have to detour around debris that sent him in the wrong direction. Finally Patrick saw a sight that brought tears to his eyes. It was a stone statue of a lion. This lion and his matching partner still guarded the front steps of the library, both on his Third Earth as well as in its past. He was home.

It wasn't the home he remembered though. The other lion lay on the ground near the first one, crushed. Only its face was recognizable. The stone steps led up to an austere building that in Patrick's time was only a facade. The interior of the old library had been torn down to make room for the high-tech structure that housed the powerful computers containing the history of Earth. What Patrick saw when he climbed these familiar steps was that the old library building was still there. It gave him mixed feelings. He was glad to see the library, but he had held out hope that he would be able to access the computers that would tell him what had happened to Earth. Seeing the ancient, crumbling building told him that there would be no computers inside. He hoped there would still be books.

Entering through the front door, Patrick was faced with an alien sight. This was the library. The *old* library. He stepped into a grand hall with large windows that were rounded on top. This was only an entryway. There wasn't a book in sight. He walked to his left, down a wide corridor that led him into a large room, the sight of which made him smile. Patrick was a teacher, a librarian, and a historian. What he saw in that room was like stepping into Earth's past. Not a hologram depiction. The real deal. Patrick saw with his own eyes what an old-time library was like.

Long wooden benches stood haphazardly in front of shelf after shelf of books. Old-fashioned books. Patrick had never seen so many books. He had barely seen *any* books. On his Third Earth the accumulated knowledge of the ages was stored on computers. Books were more likely to be found in a museum than in a library. He had the brief thought that if he weren't out of his mind, he might actually have enjoyed this trip into the past. The only problem was, it wasn't the past. It was the present. Things weren't right.

Another reality struck the Traveler. The library was empty. Had people given up reading? Patrick was both fascinated and horrified. He didn't know where to begin. How would he learn of what had happened to Earth?

"Can I help you?" came a thin voice from deep in the shadows.

Patrick turned quickly to see an elderly man shuffle into the room from the corridor he had just left. As he moved, he kicked up pools of dust that swirled through the filtered light. He was bent at the waist, as if the weight of his years had proved to be too much for him. The man was stick thin, with gray hair and even grayer skin. He wore thick glasses that made his eyes look twice their size.

"I said, 'Can I help you?'" the man said earnestly.

Patrick had to keep his wits about him. He needed answers, and it wouldn't help if he started blathering about how horrified he was that Earth had changed.

"Where is everyone?" Patrick asked.

"Who?" the man asked back.

"Readers. You know. People using the library. Nobody's here."

The old man chuckled. "You are my first visitor today. Why does that surprise you?"

Patrick wasn't sure of how to answer. "I don't know. This is a big library in a big city. You'd think a couple of people would drop by."

The old man shrugged the kind of resigned shrug that could only come from an old guy who had seen it all. "Life is short," he said with a sigh. "Nobody wants to read about why."

"My name's Patrick. I'm a teacher." Patrick held out his hand to shake. The old man took it. Patrick felt as if he were holding the limb of a fragile bird.

"My name is Richard. I'm a dinosaur."

Patrick laughed. The old guy had a sense of humor.

"I guess you're a librarian."

"I am *the* librarian," was Richard's quick answer. "For the entire city. Possibly the whole state. As libraries close, the books are sent here. This is the last stop. Once this place turns to dust . . . " He shrugged, and didn't finish the sad sentence.

"Can you help me do some research?" Patrick asked. "I'm not familiar with how the library works."

Richard's eyes lit up, as if this were the first time somebody needed his expertise in a long, long time. Patrick sensed that the man stood up a little straighter.

"Are you preparing a lesson?" Richard asked with professional authority. "Or is this for your own interest?"

"A lesson," Patrick answered quickly, jumping on the idea. "I need to fill in some details about a period in history, and I want to be accurate."

Richard shuffled off, heading deeper into the room full of books and waving for Patrick to follow. "What period would that be?"

Patrick wasn't sure of how to answer. He wanted to find out when things had gone wrong. What was it that had changed Earth's destiny? Where had it begun? When had it begun? He wished he had given a little more thought to that before talking to the old man. What should he say? Once he turned his mind to it, the answer was obvious.

"Early twenty-first century," he declared. He then took the chance and added, "I want to know what went wrong."

The old man stopped and glared at Patrick. "What do you mean?"

Patrick wanted to say that he felt sure that whatever had happened, it was on Second Earth. Third Earth had fallen into decay, and that decline hadn't happened overnight. It had to have been a gradual process. From what Patrick knew about Saint Dane's quest to control Halla, it might very well have begun on Second Earth. All the territories had a turning point. Patrick realized that there was a good chance that Second Earth had reached its turning point and things had gone horribly wrong. It was as good a guess as any. Of course, he couldn't say any of that.

Instead he shrugged and answered, "Just a hunch."

Richard glared at Patrick. Patrick sensed a change in the old man. A wall had gone up. Had he said the wrong thing?

"Is there a problem?" Patrick finally asked.

"I don't know," Richard answered coldly. "You tell me. Am I being observed?"

"I don't know what you mean," Patrick answered, puzzled.

Richard snapped, "You're testing me again, aren't you? I'm tired of you people suspecting me of mischief just because I'm a librarian. I'm too old to put up with it anymore."

"What are you talking about?" Patrick asked, genuinely confused.

"Show me your arm," Richard barked.

"Excuse me?"

"You heard me. Show me your arm!"

Patrick had no idea what the old man was fired up about. Before he could ask again, Richard reached out and grabbed Patrick's right wrist. The fragile old man wasn't so fragile anymore. He held Patrick's arm with one hand and shoved his shirtsleeve up to the elbow with the other, revealing his forearm. Richard yanked Patrick's arm closer, scrutinizing the skin. Patrick didn't resist. He was too confused to do anything but stare at the old man who was staring at his arm.

"What are you looking for?" was all he could manage to mumble.

"Don't insult me," Richard snarled. "You know as well as I do."

"Actually, I don't," Patrick shot back.

"Scars," Richard barked. "I can tell when it's been removed. You can't fool me."

Patrick pulled his arm away. He had had enough of being manhandled.

"I'm not trying to fool you. What do you think's been removed?"

Richard squinted through his thick glasses at Patrick, sizing him up. "You know that all records from that period were destroyed. Did you think you could trip me up by asking for them? How stupid do you think I am?"

"Look, Richard," Patrick began patiently, "I don't know who you think I am, but I am not spying on you or trying to trip you up. All I wanted was to see some records that had to do with that time in history. That's all. There's nothing sinister about it."

Richard seemed to soften. "Let me see your arm again." He added, "Please."

Patrick rolled his eyes and shoved his arm out. The old man took another close look while rubbing his thumb over the skin, feeling for scars.

"I believe you, son," Patrick finally said. "There's nothing here. Never was."

Patrick took his arm back and rolled his sleeve down. "What did you expect to find?"

Richard gave Patrick another curious look. "You really don't know, do you?"

"I'm sorry," Patrick said. "Maybe I should, but I don't."

"Maybe you don't want to," Richard added.

Patrick agreed completely. Maybe he didn't want to know. But he had to. "Is it true?" Patrick asked. "Have all the records from the early twenty-first century been destroyed?"

Richard took a tired breath. "You'll forgive me for being cautious, but to hold any pertinent records from that time is a crime punishable by death. They have spies everywhere, rooting out anything that remains. They've been here before, asking the same questions. But they had the mark. It's part of them. They usually don't try to hide it, unless they're looking for trouble."

"What kind of mark?"

Richard rubbed his eyes beneath his glasses. He looked tired. "Come on," he said, and walked off.

Patrick noticed that the old man was once again stooped over. The momentary hope that he could use his skills to assist someone with a legitimate research project was gone. Richard led him along the rows of musty books, stopping at a wooden door that he used an ancient key to unlock. Patrick decided not to ask him any more questions until they reached their destination. He was too busy trying to get his mind around the fact that all records from Second Earth had been destroyed. Why? By whom? Who were the mysterious people whose arms were marked and who spied on people to make sure they weren't harboring secrets? Or the truth.

The door moved with a creak that told Patrick it hadn't been opened in a long time. Inside the dimly lit room were tables loaded with ancient papers. It was all pretty haphazard. The walls were lined with books. With all that he'd seen that strange morning, the sight of so many books was still jarring.

"Close the door," Richard commanded as he shuffled to a bookcase and ran his hands along the volumes. "I shouldn't worry so much anymore. I'm tired. Nobody cares. Why should I?" The old man found what he was looking for. He pulled a heavy leather volume out from between the others and placed it on the table. Patrick expected him to open it. He didn't. Instead he reached into the empty space the book had occupied. Patrick watched with fascination as the old man opened a hidden panel in the wall behind the bookcase and took out a flat object wrapped in red cloth.

"This is all that's left," Richard explained. "At least, it's all that I know about. I suppose there are other bits here and there, but this is all that I'm aware of." The old man walked toward Patrick, carrying the mysterious parcel. "I don't know who you are or why you're looking for answers. Maybe it's time more people tried." Patrick pulled the red covering away to reveal what looked like the cover of a book. Just the cover. One edge was shredded, as if torn from the binding.

"They've destroyed all the evidence," Richard continued. "They've destroyed history. It's been so long that people now question if it ever happened at all. There are a few who try to keep the memory alive, if only to stop the insanity from happening again. But it's too late for that. It's still happening. It never stopped. That's why I'm afraid. That's why I checked your arm. I needed to see if you had the mark that made you one of them."

"Who are they?" Patrick asked, numb.

Richard's answer was to show him the book cover. "Take this," Richard ordered. "It's not doing any good hidden away here."

It was definitely the cover from some ancient volume. How old, Patrick couldn't begin to guess. It was made of cracked brown leather and had two faded gold imprints. Running vertically down one side was a single word in ornate one-inch-high letters.

"Ravinia," Patrick whispered, reading.

The word meant nothing to him, but it wasn't the word that held his attention. It was the symbol next to it. The symbol was familiar. The symbol made his head spin.

"Beware of people who are marked with that symbol, Teacher," Richard warned. "After all these years, they aren't finished. They haven't given up. I don't know what their goal is, but it isn't good. If they knew this book cover existed, they'd destroy it. And then they'd destroy you."

The large symbol was five inches across. At one time it must have been embossed with shiny bright gold. All that was left of the color were small flecks. Patrick ran his hand over the imprint, hoping to gather insight. He didn't. He was more confused than ever.

The symbol was a five-pointed star. It was the symbol that marked the gates to the flumes.

Shortly after, Patrick sat alone in the overgrown park behind the library. At one time it was called "Bryant Park," but would now more aptly be called "Junky Messed-Up Park." Benches were broken, garbage was strewn, weeds choked everything they could grab on to. Patrick held the book cover inside his shirt, against his chest. He looked up at the gloomy gray sky. He wanted to cry. What had happened to his home? What had gone so terribly wrong? He was alone. He needed help. He needed to get a grip.

He needed to be a Traveler.

He pulled off his ring and laid it on the ground. He didn't worry about being seen. Not a soul was around. His plan was to send the book cover to Bobby Pendragon. Pendragon would know what to do.

"Ibara," he called out.

The ring didn't move. Patrick stomped on it, as if trying to wake it up.

"Ibara!" he called again.

The ring didn't respond. Patrick was reeling. In desperation he said, *"First Earth."*

The ring didn't respond. Patrick's world was closing in on him and it wasn't even his world. Not anymore. He had never felt more alone.

"What have you done, Pendragon?" he whispered, choking back emotion. "Where are you?"

FIRST EARTH

The voyage back to New York on the *Queen Mary* took six days. To Mark it felt like six weeks. He rarely left the cabin he shared with Dodger. The personable acolyte continually tried to cajole him into getting some air. Or exercise. Or anything. Mark wasn't interested. He spent most of the day in bed or staring out at the never-ending Atlantic.

Dodger had better luck with Courtney and the Dimonds, convincing them to make the best of their situation. They played tennis and swam in the pool and enjoyed some fine meals. It was mostly because they didn't know what else to do. There wasn't much joy involved. They were passing time. It was better than going crazy.

Looming over everyone's head was the concern over what their next move would be. Courtney promised Mark she wouldn't let on to his parents about what had happened with Nevva Winter and his Traveler ring. It would be up to Mark to tell them when he felt ready. The few times she asked Mark what was going through his head, she was answered with a shrug and a grunt. Courtney feared that Mark was sinking into a depression and she didn't know how to shake him out of it. Courtney wasn't a stranger to depression. She knew that no amount of cajoling or discussion would help. He would have to work things through on his own. All she could do was be there for him when he needed support. A few times she had to stop Dodger from barging into the stateroom to try to sweep Mark up and out. Up and out was the last thing Mark needed. What he needed was time. And answers.

It wasn't until the last evening of the voyage that Mark came out of seclusion and knocked on the door to his parents' stateroom.

"I'm sorry," Mark said, hanging his head when he saw his mom and dad. "For everything."

Mrs. Dimond hugged her son, squeezing him as if she never wanted to let him go.

Mr. Dimond said, "Mark, there isn't a whole lot I understand about what's been happening, but the one thing I know for certain is that you have nothing to be sorry about."

"We're proud of you," Mrs. Dimond said, sniffling back tears. "To think of what you've had to deal with. It's unfathomable. My little boy. When did you grow up?"

Mark wasn't so sure when that happened. He kind of wished it hadn't. He liked his old life just fine. At first the idea of Bobby fluming around to other worlds to battle evil sounded romantic and exciting. If he were being totally honest, he'd have to admit that back in the early days, he longed to be part of the adventure. As much as he feared the possibility of Saint Dane setting his sights on Second Earth, some part of him couldn't wait for it to happen. He wanted to be part of the action. But those days were long gone. Saint Dane was evil. There was nothing romantic or adventurous about evil. It destroyed his life and nearly killed Courtney and his parents . . . not to mention the fact that his invention helped Saint Dane create the mechanism for mayhem on multiple territories. Almost four years had passed since he received Bobby's first journal. He had become a different person. He missed the old person.

Mark hugged his mom back then pulled away. He wasn't there only to apologize. He had business. It was time for a family conference.

"We're worried about you," Mrs. Dimond began.

"I'm worried about everything," Mark countered.

"That's why we're worried," Mr. Dimond added. "You can't solve the problems of Halla yourself, nor can you be blamed for them."

This made Mark look up at his dad. He wasn't so sure he agreed.

"I don't know how else to say this, so I'll just say it flat out," Mark said, changing the subject. "You guys can't go home."

The Dimonds exchanged confused looks.

Mark added, "To Second Earth I mean. I'm afraid if you do, you'll die."

"You mean because we have to use the flume with a Traveler?" Mr. Dimond asked.

"That," Mark answered. "And because Nevva threatened your life."

The Dimonds stared at their son for a long moment. A small "Oh" was all that Mrs. Dimond could get out. They watched Mark with wide eyes as he explained the deal he'd made with Nevva. His ring for their life. When they heard that, both the Dimonds winced.

"I didn't want to tell you," Mark added quickly. "But that would be wrong. I made a decision, and we're going to have to live with it."

"You shouldn't have done that," Mr. Dimond said flatly.

"What else could I do?" Mark cried. "I thought Nevva made a mistake. She said she wanted to cut off Bobby, but since Dodger had a ring, I thought it wouldn't matter. I was wrong."

"Then why else would she want it?" Mrs. Dimond asked.

"I don't know and it's killing me," Mark shot back. "I've already messed up once with Forge; I think I just did it again."

"She's barbaric," Mrs. Dimond hissed.

"Yeah, that's one word to use," Mark said with resignation. "I can think of a bunch of others."

Mr. Dimond stood and paced. "We have to go back," he announced with authority. "We can't let her use us against you. Against Halla."

"It's too late," Mark said softly.

"Mark!" his dad shouted. "This is about the future of humanity, not just your mother and me."

"I know that, Dad," Mark said patiently. "But the damage is done."

The three stood staring at one another. Mark was right. The damage was done. Nevva had the ring.

A soft knock came on the door.

"Come in," Mr. Dimond called.

Courtney poked her head inside to see the tense standoff. "Oops, sorry. Family stuff," she said, and started to close the door.

"No," Mark called out. "Come in. You're part of this too."

Courtney sheepishly entered the stateroom and looked at the Dimonds, saying, "I guess tennis is out of the question?" She gave them a big, hopeful smile, trying to lighten the mood. All three Dimonds stared back at her blankly. "Got it," she added. "I'll just slink off."

"I told them," Mark said. "They know about Nevva and the ring."

Courtney relaxed, happy that the truth was out. She plopped down in an easy chair. "Sucks, doesn't it? Now what do we do?"

Mark walked to the porthole. It was obvious he had something to say, so the others didn't offer their own opinions. Not that they had any.

"I've been thinking about this a lot," he began. "It's pretty much all I've been doing since I gave up the ring. After we read Bobby's last journal from Ibara, we thought it was all over. It wasn't. Bobby's trapped. Saint Dane is trapped. Nevva isn't, obviously. She's on the loose, and whatever she wants to do with that ring, it can't be good."

Courtney blurted out, "You think maybe she can use the ring to get Saint Dane off Ibara?"

"Maybe," Mark answered. "I don't know."

"How would that work?" Mrs. Dimond asked.

"Mom," Mark said with a touch of impatience. "You ask that like we know how *any* of this works."

"You're right," she said quickly. "Sorry. Sorry."

Mark continued, "I'm pretty sure what we should do. We've got to stay on First Earth. All of us."

"We couldn't travel if we wanted to," Courtney added. "No Travelers here, remember? I doubt Nevva will let us hitch a ride with her."

"Even if we could travel, I think it's better that we stay here."

Mr. Dimond entered the conversation, saying, "I told you not to worry about us."

"But I do," Mark shot back. "As long as you're here, I think you're safe. I don't believe Nevva. If you go back home, all bets will be off."

"But why?" Courtney asked. "She's not Saint Dane. She wouldn't do something horrible just for fun. Would she?"

"I don't want to take the chance," Mark said with finality.

"But, Mark—," Mr. Dimond complained.

"Dad!" barked Mark. "We have to stay here. This is where we belong now."

Mr. Dimond looked at his wife. They had never heard Mark speak to them like that. He wasn't a sheepish little boy anymore.

"All right, son," Mr. Dimond said calmly. "This is your show."

"What are we supposed to do in 1937?" Mrs. Dimond asked. "Start a new life?"

"If we have to," Mark said. "We can get by. The money from KEM will help with that. It's the other reason I think we should stay. As much as it hurts to admit, I'm in business with KEM. Dado is a real thing. Maybe if we accept it and become part of the process, we can find a way to sabotage Forge. It's still First Earth. It's still 1937. We might be able to change history yet."

"It's true," Courtney chimed in brightly. "We're not done here. We could still scuttle the dados!"

"And don't forget Nevva," Mark added. "We need to find out why she wanted my ring. If she finds out we're creating trouble for KEM, she'll be back. I want to be waiting for her."

"I like that," Courtney said with an evil gleam in her eye. "Let's make her come to us."

Everyone exchanged glances and nods. Mark's words rang true. Better, they contained hope. That had been in short supply.

"I guess that's it then," Mrs. Dimond said. "We're going to be living in the past."

"I wasn't much for cell phones anyway," Mr. Dimond said with a smile. "Or microwaves or computers or sushi."

"I kind of liked the microwave," Mrs. Dimond said wistfully.

It actually gave them all a chuckle. This was a family, including Courtney. There was a bond between them that they knew would help get them through, or even better, help them start doing damage control.

Another knock came at the door. Without being asked, Dodger poked his head in. "Hey hey! The gang's all here! It's our last night on board. I made dinner reservations. Who's with me?"

Everyone looked to Mark, who shrugged and exclaimed, "Why not? Let's celebrate the beginning of our new lives."

It was a wonderful evening. They ate in the same opulent dining room where Dodger and Courtney had cornered Mark on their voyage to England. This time, there was no pressure. Dodger acted as host, ordering for everyone. Mrs. Dimond danced with her husband to the music of the swing orchestra. She even coaxed Mark onto the dance floor. Courtney and Mr. Dimond shared a dance, but Dodger cut in and spun Courtney around the floor expertly. Since the age of twelve, Courtney had taken dozens of ballroom dance classes, all under protest, thinking it was a dork skill she would never have to use. It never occurred to her that one day she'd travel to the past, where an orchestra would play swing music for her dancing pleasure on an ocean liner.

The group did their best to forget their troubles for a while and enjoy their last few hours on the most elegant ocean liner of its time. They spent hours in the restaurant. There was no hurry. They weren't going anywhere. At one point Courtney grabbed Mark by the hand. Before he had a chance to complain, she pulled him onto the dance floor. The song was slow—a ballad.

"I'm actually starting to recognize this music," Courtney said with a laugh.

"Yeah, I'm kind of starting to like it too," Mark added.

"I wouldn't go that far," Courtney groused.

The two swayed back and forth in time to the orchestra. Mark stepped away, took Courtney's hand and spun her around with surprising grace. Seconds later she was back in his arms.

"Where the heck did you learn that?" she asked in surprise.

"We were in the same ballroom class for two years, Courtney," Mark said flatly.

"Oh. Really?"

"You didn't know I existed."

"I wouldn't say that! I just thought, I mean, I really kind of . . .

Okay, you're right. I didn't know you existed. Did we ever dance together?"

"No. I was afraid of you."

"That was a long time ago," Courtney said with a touch of sadness.

"So much has happened."

"Really."

"At least I'm not scared of you anymore."

Courtney laughed and held Mark closer.

"You're my best friend, you know that?" Courtney said.

"I'm your only friend," Mark replied with a smirk. "It's kind of hard to maintain a social life when you're bouncing around Halla. I haven't been to many parties lately."

"True." Courtney sighed. "Then again, you didn't go to many before, either."

"Gee, thanks for that." Mark chuckled.

Courtney added, "For what it's worth, I think you're great."

Mark had never had a girl tell him he was great before. He barely spoke to girls at all. This was alien territory. He didn't know what to say.

Courtney answered for him. "You're supposed to say, 'Thanks. I think you're great too.'"

"I do."

They danced for a few more moments, then Courtney asked somberly, "Do you think we're going to spend the rest of our lives in the past?"

"I don't know. But if we do, I'm glad we're together."

The two held each other even closer and let the music become their world, if only for a few minutes longer. For that one short magical moment, Courtney liked the music too.

The next day was filled with a whirlwind of activity. The *Queen Mary* had docked in New York, and the romance of being on board had worn off for the nearly twenty-five hundred passengers. They were all about getting packed up and off the great liner. It was organized bedlam.

Courtney, Dodger, and the Dimonds gathered in the Dimonds' stateroom, waiting for the crowds to thin. Their luggage had already been sent ahead to the Manhattan Tower Hotel. Dodger saw to that.

"I got rooms for all of you," Dodger said. "Good rate, too. You can stay at the hotel for as long as it takes to find someplace to settle in permanent. Courtney can bunk in Gunny's apartment. The Dimonds have adjoining suites. It's all very cush."

"Who died and made you manager?" Courtney asked.

"I told you, we bellhops run the place. We know where all the skeletons are buried."

Courtney quipped, "From what I've heard of that hotel, that's no figure of speech."

"Yeah, real funny. Everybody ready?"

Everyone exchanged glances. Mark broke the silence. "Let's go home."

They made their way along the passageway and up to the Promenade Deck, where the gangway off the ship was waiting for them. As a group they stepped onto the bridge and off the deck of the ship that had been their home, more or less, for many days. Nobody was sorry to say good-bye. Dodger hailed them a cab, and they all crowded in the back together.

"Manhattan Tower Hotel," Dodger announced. Then added, "Wait." He reached through the partition that separated the front seat from the back, grabbed the cabbie's chin, and turned him to face the group.

"Hey!" the cabbie protested.

"Relax, pal," Dodger ordered, and faced the others. "This guy look familiar to anybody?"

Everyone shook their heads. Dodger let go of the cabbie and said, "Good. Let's go."

Courtney laughed. She knew exactly what Dodger was thinking. The last time they were in a cab together, the driver turned out to be Saint Dane, and they were both nearly killed. Dodger wasn't taking any chances.

Traffic was light, and they made it uptown to the posh Manhattan Tower Hotel in no time. The cabbie rolled off Park Avenue, into the circular driveway, and up to the wide stairs that led to the front door.

"All ashore!" Dodger announced. He paid the cabbie and said, "Thanks, pal. There's a little something extra for your trouble."

The cabbie took the cash while glaring at Dodger. He didn't like the cocky bellhop, but he didn't mind taking his money.

As everyone piled out of the cab, Dodger said, "I'll check on the bags. Meet you all in the lobby." He didn't wait for an acknowledgment and bounded up the stairs, throwing greetings to all his pals. Dodger was back on familiar turf. Mr. and Mrs. Dimond followed close behind, with Mrs. Dimond mumbling something about needing to use the ladies' room.

The cab charged off, leaving Mark and Courtney alone at the curb. Mark looked up at the tall, pink-colored hotel in awe.

"Just like Bobby described, isn't it?" Courtney asked.

"It's like stepping into the pages of a book," Mark said softly. "Or a journal."

"It's pretty cool. Old, but cool. I'll show you around."

The two were about to walk up the steps when they heard a man's voice call from behind them.

"Courtney?"

They both heard it, but neither thought it involved them. Nobody knew Courtney in 1937. It had to be a different Courtney. They kept walking.

"Courtney Chetwynde?" the voice called, more adamantly.

Mark and Courtney froze, then slowly turned. Apparently someone *did* know her.

The man stood in the garden that was beyond the far edge of the circular driveway, across from the front door of the hotel. The first thought that came to Mark's mind was *haunted.* The guy looked haunted. He stood stock still. His clothes were a mess, like he'd been in a fight. His face didn't look much better. He had a scratch on his cheek, with dried blood caked beneath it. Stranger still, his clothes didn't look like they belonged on First Earth. He wore a simple, black long-sleeved shirt and jeans. His dark hair straggled over his ears. His eyes were sunken in their sockets, as if he hadn't slept in years.

Neither Mark nor Courtney knew who he was.

"I didn't know where else to go," the guy stammered without moving. He seemed on the verge of breaking down. He was definitely on edge. "I waited here, hoping you'd come back. I'm sorry, I didn't know who else to talk to."

Though the guy gave Courtney the creeps, she walked slowly toward him. Mark grabbed her arm.

"Whoa, wait," he cautioned.

"It's okay," Courtney said calmly.

She walked closer to the man. Mark was right with her.

"I'm sorry," she said soothingly to the stranger. "I don't think I know you."

The man chuckled, though not because he thought anything was funny. "I'm not surprised," he said. "I haven't been myself. I'm not so sure I'd recognize me either."

"Who are you?" Mark asked.

"It's all changed, Courtney," the man said. "Nothing is as it was. We have to find out why."

Courtney and Mark didn't know what to say.

"Maybe this will jog your memory," he said, lifting up his right hand. On his third finger was a ring—a Traveler ring.

For Courtney, it clicked. She looked at the guy's face, stunned.

"Patrick?" she gasped.

Patrick smiled. He'd made contact. They knew who he was. The rush of relief was too much for him, and the Traveler from Third Earth passed out cold, right in front of the Manhattan Tower Hotel.

FIRST EARTH

(CONTINUED)

Patrick slowly opened his eyes. It was dark—too dark to understand where he was. For a moment he wondered if all that had happened to him had been a dream. Was he in his own bed far below the grassy plains of Manhattan? Was there no longer a giant green statue outside the window, peering in at him? Was everything back to normal?

No.

"Hey, you okay?" Courtney asked him.

Reality quickly flooded back for Patrick. "I was until I heard your voice."

"Gee, thanks," she said sarcastically. "Maybe you don't want the water I brought you."

Patrick struggled to sit up. He was dizzy. His head hurt. Nothing was right. "No, I'm thirsty."

Courtney helped him sit up and offered him a tall glass of ice water. "Drink slowly."

Patrick took a sip. The water tasted good. Patrick thought it was the only good thing that had happened to him since the horrible day began.

"You're in Gunny Van Dyke's apartment in the Manhattan Tower Hotel," Mark Dimond offered.

Patrick focused and saw that Mark was sitting in the cushy easy chair across from the bed in the one-room, basement apartment that belonged to the Traveler from First Earth. "I'm Mark Dimond, one of Bobby's acolytes."

Patrick did a double take. "The dados really do look just like you."

"What?" Mark shouted, aghast.

"It's cool," Courtney said with a chuckle. "The dados on Third Earth were made to look like you. You're their daddy, after all."

Mark frowned. "There's nothing even remotely cool about that."

"You're right. Sorry," Courtney added quickly. "But the resemblance really is amazing."

"Stop!" Mark scolded.

"Good to meet you, Mark," Patrick said warmly. "I've heard a lot about you. I'm glad you're not dead."

"That's pretty okay with me, too," Mark agreed.

Patrick took another sip of water and surveyed the room, scrutinizing every ancient touch of Gunny's life on First Earth.

"Weird, huh?" Courtney said, reading his thoughts. "You ever been away from Third Earth before?"

Patrick nodded. "I've been here before. With Gunny. It's still disconcerting."

"That's one way of putting it," Courtney added.

Mark and Courtney watched Patrick with curiosity. Mark thought the guy looked dazed. He'd obviously been through something traumatic. They didn't press him for details. They wanted him to get his head back on straight first. Finally, Patrick took one last gulp of water, wiped his mouth with his sleeve, and looked at Mark and Courtney.

"The future isn't what it used to be," he declared solemnly.

Courtney and Mark exchanged glances.

"I have no idea what that means," Mark replied.

"It means Third Earth has changed."

"Yeah, I told him about the Mark-looking dados," Courtney said.

Patrick laughed ironically. "I wish that were the biggest change."

He went on to explain in detail what had happened to him since he woke up on a different Third Earth. From inside his shirt he pulled out the mysterious, torn book cover with the star symbol. He had been holding it next to his heart, protecting it. Mark and Courtney examined the cover with awe.

"It's the symbol that marks the gates." Mark gasped.

Patrick nodded. "When I couldn't contact Pendragon, I went back inside the library. I needed to learn more. Richard, the librarian, was my only link to reality, if that's what you can call it."

Patrick wiped his eyes nervously. It was clear to both Mark and Courtney that what happened next wasn't good.

"I heard shouting coming from the room where Richard had given me the book cover. I ran down the corridor and stopped short of the door when I heard a crash come from inside. It sounded like something had been knocked over."

Patrick stopped talking, as if the memory choked him up. Mark and Courtney waited patiently. They knew Patrick would tell the tale as best he could.

"When I looked inside I saw that most of the books had been pulled down from the shelves. The floor was littered with them. There were four men wearing dark red clothes. I can't tell you what any of them looked like other than they all had their hair cut very short. They were"—Patrick stopped again and took a gulp of water before continuing—"they were pushing Richard around, taking turns throwing him against the bookshelves. He was an old man. He couldn't defend himself. I was about to jump in to help him when one of them got in Richard's face and shouted, 'Where is it?'"

Mark held up the book cover. "This what they were looking for?"

Patrick nodded. "The hidden panel where Richard kept the cover was open. I don't know how they knew it existed, but they knew. What they didn't know was that it was gone. Richard had given it to me. He wouldn't tell them either. For that he took a horrible beating. I'd never seen anything like it. He was so frail. One of the men lashed out and hit him with the back of his hand. Richard's glasses flew off and his nose bled, but he didn't say a word. I—I wanted to help him but—"

"But they would have gotten the cover," Courtney said, finishing Patrick's thought.

"That's what I thought, honestly," Patrick concurred. "That cover was the only physical link to the past. I couldn't let them have it. I hope I was right, because that brave man paid a terrible price."

"So you took off?" Mark asked.

"No!" Patrick answered, anguished. "I couldn't even do that! I stood there, paralyzed. I didn't know what to do. I'm not a coward. I'm not. But I'd never seen anything like that before. I was just . . . stunned."

"We get it," Courtney said reassuringly.

"Do you? It was horrible! They threw Richard against the wall. The poor man crumpled like a rag doll. When he hit the floor, he looked up and saw me. One of the men noticed and followed his look. He saw me standing there like an idiot, but he didn't react. The others turned to look at me too. None of them reacted. It was chilling."

"Were they dados?" Courtney asked.

"I don't think so. They weren't identical. The one who spotted me pointed to Richard and said, 'This man is a criminal. It is forbidden to possess banned documents.'"

Patrick swallowed hard and continued. "When he pointed to

Richard, I saw something on his forearm. It looked like a green tattoo about two inches across."

"A tattoo of what?" Courtney asked, her eyes wide.

Patrick pointed to the book cover on Mark's lap.

"The star?" Mark gasped. "He had a tattoo of this star on his arm? The star from the g-gates?"

Patrick nodded.

Courtney exclaimed, "That must have been what Richard was looking for when he inspected your arm. He wanted to know if you were one of them . . . whoever *they* are."

"He knew they were watching him, and he wanted to protect this book cover," Patrick answered. "To protect history. Whoever these thugs are, they're trying to erase that history. I couldn't let that happen. So I ran."

"To where?" Courtney demanded.

"Anywhere. Away. It didn't matter so long as they didn't get the cover. I ran deeper into the library, dodging broken tables and scattered books. I had no idea where I was going, but I couldn't stop because they were right behind me. I jumped down a stairwell and ran through an emergency exit that led to the derelict park behind the library. I skirted decaying statues and huge chunks of fallen walls, playing cat and mouse with my pursuers. They weren't smart. They didn't divide up to chase me. I eventually lost them in the maze and hid under a slab of crumbling cement. I stayed there for at least an hour. I think I'd still be there if not for what happened next."

"What was it?" Mark asked.

"When I finally got the nerve to peer out from my hiding place, I saw black smoke billowing from the library."

"Fire." Courtney gasped.

"It was coming from the same area where I'd left Richard. Seeing that put me over the edge. I didn't care about the book cover anymore. I had to go back. I retraced my steps into the building and found the central corridor, thick with smoke. I could barely see, but I found the room. The four men were gone. Richard wasn't. He lay there unconscious, surrounded by burning books. They'd left him to die. I dragged him out of the burning room and pulled him up onto my shoulder. It wasn't hard. He was so light. I made my way back to the front entrance of the library and out onto the steps. A crowd of people had gathered, but nobody made a move to help me. They were far more interested in the burning building. I expected a fire truck to come and battle the blaze. It didn't. I'm not even sure if fire trucks exist on Third Earth anymore."

"What about Richard?" Mark asked with trepidation.

"He was battered, but alive. I sat beneath the stone lion, holding his head in my lap. He looked up at me with cloudy eyes and smiled. He actually smiled and said, 'Find the truth, Teacher. It's what they fear.'"

Patrick was doing all he could to control his emotions as he added, "He looked back at the library. Flames were leaping from every window. Richard looked pained, and it wasn't because of the beating he took. He turned away, not wanting to see any more, and said, 'Our history is all we have left. Don't let them destroy it.'"

Patrick fell silent, letting the horror of his story sink in. Or maybe it was to take a break from having to relive it.

"Some people finally showed up who said they would take Richard to a hospital, but I didn't have much confidence in that. Who knows what hospitals are like now on Third Earth? But I had to trust them, because I couldn't take Richard with me. Not with what I had to do."

"What was that?" Courtney asked.

Patrick sat up in bed and looked straight at her. "I had to find Pendragon. He had to know what happened. He still does. The last I heard he had gone to Ibara, but when I tried to contact him through my ring, it wouldn't work. I left Richard and found my way to the flume and tried to travel to Ibara myself, but the flume wouldn't let me. My only other choice was to come here." Patrick was getting worked up. "This is where the two of you came when you left Third Earth. It was the only place I could think of coming. What is wrong with the flume? Why can't we contact Ibara? Where is Pendragon?"

Courtney took a deep breath. She knew that what she was about to tell Patrick wouldn't make him feel any better, but he had to know. She filled him in quickly about what happened on Ibara and the dado battle for Rayne. For Veelox. She told him about the origin of dados on First Earth and Mark's Forge technology. She ended the story by telling him how Bobby had destroyed the flume on Ibara, trapping himself and Saint Dane . . . which was probably why Ibara was cut off.

Mark listened without adding anything until the end, when he told Patrick how he had given his Traveler ring to Nevva Winter in exchange for his parents' life. He said he thought it wouldn't matter because he would still be able to communicate with Bobby through Dodger's ring, but Dodger's ring didn't work—just as Patrick's ring didn't work.

Patrick listened to it all, his shoulders growing heavier with each new revelation. "Why won't the rings work?" he asked.

"They *do* work," Courtney corrected. "They just won't let us contact Bobby on Ibara."

Mark said, "The real mystery is why Nevva wanted the ring. I can't help but think it has something to do with the events that led up to those changes on Third Earth."

"Gee, you think?" Courtney asked with a trace of sarcasm.

"I'll tell you what I think," Mark announced, standing up. "I think it's finally time."

"For what?" Courtney asked.

"For the event we've been fearing from the very beginning. Everything points to it."

"To what?" Patrick asked, confused.

"Third Earth has changed. Again. Patrick, you ran into some guys who were trying to destroy all evidence of specific events that happened during the first part of the twenty-first century. Second Earth. That can't be a coincidence."

"My god . . . ," Courtney whispered, the realization hitting her.

"Yeah," Mark said. "Whatever happened on Second Earth must have led to the horrible changes on Third Earth."

"So it's finally here," Courtney gasped.

"Yeah," Mark agreed. "The battle for Second Earth."

"It's on, Courtney," Mark said with finality. "We've got to go home."

"But we can't use the flume without a Traveler," Courtney countered.

Mark looked at Patrick. "Good thing we've got one."

Mark called another family meeting in his parents' suite at the hotel. That family included Dodger and Courtney. He and Courtney laid out all that Patrick had told them. Every last disturbing detail. He said how he still wanted his parents to stay on First Earth, not only because of the danger with Nevva, but to stay in touch with KEM. There was still the hope of scuttling the dados. Dodger would be their guide to the past. Mark added that they would all get a good night's sleep, if possible, and then leave first thing in the morning for the flume. Mark had it all figured out, except for one thing: In spite of all that he had been through, in his mother's eyes he was still her little boy. Hearing what he was about to jump back into, no matter how logical it might seem, was too much for her. She started to cry.

"Why?" she asked. "Why is this happening and why are you the ones responsible for stopping it? Can't we just call the police? Or the president? Or . . . or . . . somebody!"

Mark sat down next to his mom and put his arm around her. It was the kind of loving gesture his mom had offered him countless times in the past. Things were different now. It was Mark's turn to be strong.

"I don't know, Mom," he answered sincerely. "I don't know anything, except that we've been given the job to help the Travelers stop Saint Dane. We don't have a whole lot of choices here."

Mark's dad added, "I still want to go with you."

"I know, Dad," Mark replied. "You can't."

Mr. Dimond nodded. He knew.

Nobody slept much that night. Patrick bunked in with Mark in Gunny's room, resting fitfully on the easy chair. He and Mark shared stories, mostly about Bobby Pendragon. By the time they nodded off, Patrick felt as if he had a much better picture of the lead Traveler. Mark felt as if he had made another friend and ally. He knew that he and Courtney were going to need all the friends they could get.

The next morning everyone went to the Dimonds' suite to enjoy a feast of a breakfast that Dodger had ordered from the hotel's kitchen. There were heaping trays of scrambled eggs, pastries, bacon, potatoes, pancakes, and fruit. "Can't jump through time on an empty stomach" was his reasoning. Mark knew he was right. He had no idea what they would find on Second Earth and when they might eat again. In spite of the fact that nobody had much of an appetite, they ate. It wasn't a celebratory feast like the one they had enjoyed on their final night aboard the *Queen Mary*. To Courtney it felt more like a pregame meal. Butterflies were flying wild. Nobody said much. Their minds were elsewhere.

When they were finished, Dodger excused himself, saying, "I'll let you all say your good-byes." He shook Patrick's hand, and then Mark's, promising, "I'll take good care of your folks." Mark replied with a nod.

Dodger then stood in front of Courtney and gave her a mischievous smile, holding out his arms for a hug. "You know something?" he quipped. "For a skirt, you ain't too shabby."

Courtney replied, "That's *dame* to you, pal."

They both laughed and hugged. "Thanks, Dodge," Courtney whispered in his ear. "Gunny chose well. You were spectacular."

"I was, wasn't I?" Dodger quipped. He pulled away from Courtney, quickly pushing aside a tear. "Take care of yourself now, would you, sister? If you ever get back here again, you know where to find me."

"I'm sure you'll be running the hotel by then," Courtney said with a smile.

"Hey, I run it now!" The bellhop tipped his cap, backed away, and left after giving them all one final, "Good luck."

"We should go," Mark announced.

Patrick shook hands with the Dimonds, saying, "Someday you'll know how much those two kids have been through."

"I'm not so sure I want to," Mrs. Dimond replied.

Courtney hugged both the Dimonds. "Don't worry about us. Worry about messing up KEM."

Mark stood in front of his parents. Nobody quite knew what to say.

"Shouldn't you pack something?" Mrs. Dimond asked.

"No, Mom. We can't bring things between territories, remember?"

Mrs. Dimond nodded quickly. She hadn't.

Mr. Dimond said, "I feel as if I'm sending my only son off to war."

Mark shrugged, but said nothing. The truth was, that's exactly what was happening.

"We'll be in touch if we can. Try not to worry. And watch your backs. We still don't know what Nevva is up to."

"We will, son." Mr. Dimond hugged Mark.

Mark then gave his mother a big hug. She was crying.

"I want to see you again" was all she could get out.

"You will," Mark answered with authority. "I promise."

They traveled to the flume in silence, taking a cab north to the subway station that held the gate. They descended the stairs to the station and walked quickly to the far end of the platform. Luckily, it wasn't busy, so they wouldn't have to worry about being seen when they climbed down onto the tracks to make their way to the flume. Before they descended, Patrick stopped and looked around at the First Earth subway stop.

"There was something strange," he declared. "On Third Earth."

"More strange than what you've already told us?" Courtney asked.

Patrick looked around, his mind trying to grasp a fleeting idea. "It was at the gate. I knew it would be different from what I was used to, since all Third Earth was different. But the changes to the gate were just . . . odd."

"How so?" Mark asked.

"I took me nearly a day to find it," Patrick explained. "I just had my memory of being on Second and First Earth to go on. I figured the gate looked something like this, only derelict, like the rest of Third Earth."

"It didn't?" Courtney asked.

"No. If it weren't for my ring glowing, I never would have found it. The flume was under a collapsed building. It wasn't underground."

"You mean it was out in the open?" Courtney asked, incredulous.

"No, but it seemed as if at some point it had been unearthed, and the only thing covering it was the wreck of the building."

"What do you think that means?" Mark asked.

Patrick shrugged. "I don't know. But I think we're going to have to find out."

A few minutes later Mark, Courtney, and Patrick stood in front of the flume beneath the streets of the Bronx. They stood shoulder to shoulder, staring into the dark tunnel.

"Last thoughts?" Mark asked.

He looked at Courtney. Courtney gave a shrug and said, "This has been coming for a long time. At least the wait is over."

Mark looked to Patrick, who was staring into the depths of the flume. Mark thought that he looked pale.

"You okay?" Mark asked.

"I may be the Traveler here," Patrick said with a shaky voice, "but you two have been through a heck of a lot more than I have."

Courtney gave him a friendly punch in the arm. "Don't worry, we'll get you through this."

Mark added, "And who's gonna get *us* through this?"

"Still working on that one," Courtney said. "Let's go home."

Patrick stood up straight and called out, *"Second Earth!"*

The flume came to life. The three didn't budge as they waited to be swept away.

"I wish Bobby were here," Courtney whispered to Mark.

And they were off.

JOURNAL #33

IBARA

I hope you'll read this one day, Mark.

Courtney too.

I know that's probably impossible. Still, I'm going to continue writing these journals as if I'm writing them to you. It helps me feel that we're not so far apart. Even if I'm pretending. It's hard to accept that we may never see one another again, though it's even harder to imagine how we ever could. The gate to the flume is buried under a mountain of volcanic rock. The second gate in Rubic City is just as inaccessible under the wreckage of the destroyed buildings. Bottom line? I'm not leaving this territory.

Then again, neither is Saint Dane.

I don't know if that's the way it was meant to be, but that's the way it is. Halla is safe, and for that I don't regret anything I've done.

But don't get all "poor Bobby" on me. I'm okay. Seriously. I'm happy. Maybe happier than I've been since I left home with Uncle Press. Let me fill you in on some of the major things that have happened since I sealed the flume. I have to tell you, it's all good.

Well, mostly good. There is one significant problem that I'll tell you about. In time. I first want to tell you how great things have become.

As I wrote before, the village of Rayne was devastated by the dado battle. Or maybe I should say it was destroyed by the tak. Surveying the carnage, it really gave me second thoughts as to whether it was all worth it or not. Most of the village was devastated. Homes were lost. Common structures were leveled. Food supplies were obliterated. People had to sleep out in the open. There were a few tropical storms that came through, making it all the more miserable. It wasn't a fun time.

Still, the village survived. Ibara survived. That's the most important thing. No, the most important thing is that Saint Dane lost this territory. He threw everything he had at us, and we stopped him. His plan for creating the dados that began with weaseling his way into your life, Mark, was for naught. I'm not proud of what we had to do to stop him. Mixing the territories the way we did was a risk, but I didn't see any other way. I think the results proved it was the right move. Not only did we stop his attack on Ibara, I was able to trap him here. Saint Dane has been shut down. End of story. End of his quest to control Halla. If the price for that was the destruction of Rayne, I don't think it was such a bad deal.

Of course the people of Rayne didn't know the grander importance of their victory. All they had was a village left in ruins and a big job ahead. No, a huge job. It wasn't just about the rebuilding of Rayne, but the re-creation of a culture and, hopefully, an entire world. For me it was also about the rebuilding of a territory. Of Veelox. Yup, my plan is to complete Aja Killian's vision. When Saint Dane influenced the Flighters into destroying the pilgrim ships, he thought he was finishing off this world for good. He was wrong. The spirit to restore life here is greater than ever. I'm proud to say that I'm part of it.

Rebuilding an entire world can't happen overnight. One step at a time, and that first step was to begin the reclamation of Ibara and the village of Rayne. After the dust (and the sand) settled from the battle, there was jubilation. I guess that'll happen when you defeat an army against all odds. There was a moment of absolute euphoria. Or maybe it was just relief. Whatever. There were a lot of smiles and shouting and hugging. It got even better once the older people and the very young returned from the far side of the island, where they had been taken to ride out the battle.

It wasn't all happy happy, joy joy though. Many people died to defend Rayne. Once the rush of victory subsided, reality crept in. The burial of the dead began the slow process of dealing with it. Remember, until the sinking of the pilgrim ships, most of these people didn't know about Ibara's history. They didn't know about Rubic City and Lifelight and the fact that their island world began as a secluded outpost, protected from the technology that had decimated the larger world. Veelox. It was a lot to get their heads around in a pretty short time. The joy of having survived the attack was soon replaced by a numbing fear of the unknown. What would happen next?

It was up to the tribunal, the leaders of the village of Rayne, to guide the healing process. I'm honored to say that Genj, the chief minister of the Rayne tribunal, asked me to help them. Me. Can you believe it? I guess it's not so far fetched. Between Alder and Siry and myself, we led the village to victory. To be honest, it was more Alder than myself, but afterward Alder wasn't around. Neither was Siry.

That took a little bit of explaining. I couldn't exactly tell the tribunal that I had sent Alder to Quillan to return some dado-killing weapons and Siry to Zadaa to return the dygo digger and then I sealed the flume by exploding the final bit of tak to make sure two more Travelers weren't trapped on this territory. That wouldn't have gone over so well. I decided to pretend I didn't know what happened to them. They became casualties of war. Heroes. Especially Siry, since he was the son of Remudi, a former member of the tribunal. The idea that Siry had grown up as a rebellious outlaw, but turned it all around to help save his home, made him a legend. It's too bad he couldn't be around to appreciate it, but it's better that two more Travelers weren't trapped. I hope someday he'll forgive me.

If you remember, the tribunal was made up of Genj, the older guy with the short graying hair, who was so tan he reminded me of a sea captain; Moman, a serious, dark-skinned woman who chose her words carefully and always spoke with wisdom; and Drea, who was full of enthusiasm and joy. She was probably older than my mother, but her light skin, freckles, and long curly red hair made her seem like a kid. These were the people who had the task of putting Rayne back together.

Them . . . and me. A stranger to the island who tried all that he could not to reveal his true past. These people had enough to deal with. They didn't need to hear about Travelers and Saint Dane and the battle for Halla. Still, questions were asked. People wanted to know about Rubic City and Lifelight. I more or less played dumb. It was up to the tribunal to educate them about their history. When questions came up about the dados, I planted the idea that the robots were simply another manifestation of how technology had gone awry. Their attack was seen as the last gasp of the old order trying to bring down Veelox. The people of Ibara had so much to grasp that a simple explanation like that was plenty. I don't think they really wanted to know much more.

The first task at hand was to clean up the village. They had no earth-moving equipment. It had to be done by hand. It was backbreaking. I was put in charge of a group of thirty men and women whose task it was to clear out every last piece of debris. There was a lot. We sifted through tons of splintered bamboo and wood, saving anything that could be reused and piling the rest on the beach. The fallen trees were rough. I had no idea that palm trees were so heavy. I do now. It took several strong backs to move a single tree onto the beach. They weren't the biggest challenge either.

There were millions of pieces of exploded dado everywhere. We picked up countless arms, hands, legs, heads—everything. It was gruesome at first, but we all quickly realized that these were machines. They may have looked like body parts, but they were actually chunks of metal and plastic. Soon a giant mound of dado pieces grew on the beach.

We also had to deal with the thousands of skimmers that the dados had used to travel from Rubic City. That was an interesting dilemma. Many skimmers were intact. They were great little water vehicles that could have come in really handy. But they were from Cloral. They represented technology from a different territory. They didn't belong here. Of course, I didn't mention that to anybody. I'm happy to say that the tribunal made a decision to discard them. It was totally in keeping with the spirit of Ibara. In their minds the skimmers represented technology from a time long past. It was that technology that brought about Veelox's downfall, and they didn't want to repeat history. It was all about starting with a clean slate.

The fishing fleet was pressed into service. As the dado and skimmer debris was piled on the beach, the fishermen began the laborious process of piling the junk onto their ships, taking it out beyond the breakwater that enclosed the bay of Rayne, and sinking the junk out at sea.

My job was to organize the workers. It wasn't hard. The people respected me. They knew how I had helped them. To be honest, I enjoyed it. I liked the simple process of organizing groups of workers, giving out assignments, creating schedules, and also doing a lot of the physical work myself. There was something about it that felt so—I don't know—healing. I don't mean to get all cosmic on you, but you might have sensed from my last few journals that my head wasn't in the greatest place. The battle with Saint Dane changed me. It was all feeling so . . . futile. It didn't help that in order to beat him, I had to go against everything that Uncle Press had taught me and mix items between the territories. As I look back on that now, I don't regret what I did. There was no other way. Still, it was wrong. That wasn't the way things were supposed to be. I had sunk to Saint Dane's level and disrupted that natural order.

It was time to end the battle. I did it by destroying the flume.

Since then, I've thought less and less about the troubles of Halla because it was all I could do to concentrate on digging up dado parts and dumping them on the beach. It was simple, mindless work. It was also really satisfying, because it was all about rebuilding. I don't know how long it took to clean up Rayne because I have no way of judging time here, but I'd guess it took months. That was okay. With each passing day, the beauty of Rayne was restored a little more. I think I know what a sculptor must feel when he's faced with a giant block of granite that he chips away at gradually to reveal the masterpiece hidden within. That's what it felt like to clean up Rayne. What began as a devastated war zone was slowly being transformed back into a wonderful tropical beach. It was all done by hand. I can't begin to tell you how satisfying that felt.

A schedule was made for sleeping inside Tribunal Mountain. Families with small children and the elderly got priority. When every square inch of sleeping space was taken, the rest of the village slept outside in makeshift huts. Or under the stars. I didn't spend a single night inside the mountain. I preferred to see the sky. Why not? It was warm. The rains were nasty but didn't come too often. It gave me the chance to look up and wonder at what might be happening in the rest of Halla. It was a great feeling to know that on Ibara, things were good. An entire village was working together to bring back their home. It was a positive thing. It was about building a future. It was exactly what I needed to be part of.

You guys have to know how much I miss you, and my old life. There's no getting around that. But don't feel sorry for me, because I'm not alone here. The villagers have adopted me as one of their own. In some ways so has Genj. He has been like a father to me. It's nice to have an adult around to tell me what to do for a change. I know that sounds strange, but after being the lead Traveler and having everyone look to me for the answers for so long, it is a relief to let somebody else make the decisions.

Four of the surviving Jakills were with me. There was the girl named Twig and the guy I always referred to as "rat boy." I finally found out his name. It was Krayven. I think I like rat boy better. I wouldn't tell him that though. He'd been through enough already. So many of the Jakills died in Rubic City. It was a tragedy, especially because all they were doing was looking for the truth. Unfortunately, they found it. I tried my best to convince the survivors that it was their sacrifice that helped save Rayne. I think it helped them deal, but not a lot. They worked beside me tirelessly to help salvage their home. It was like they were doing it for all their fallen friends. In some ways I was too.

The most important person in my life, by far, is Telleo, Genj's daughter. She has become my best friend here. You should have seen her after the battle. She cared for more of the wounded than I could count. I don't think she slept for days. It was incredible. She seemed to be in so many places at once. With all that responsibility, she still took time to find me and ask how I was doing. Those amazing green eyes never seemed to lose their sparkle. She has become my guide to this territory. You might even call her my acolyte. Of course, since I'm no longer in the Traveler business, I don't need an acolyte, but under other circumstances I'd consider her a perfect candidate. She has strong opinions, but she listens to others. People are drawn to her. They trust her and I can see why. It's almost as if her touch is healing.

We've spent many nights together, sitting on a secret ledge high up on Tribunal Mountain. During the day she'd tie up her long, deep red hair in a practical knot as she went about caring for the sick and wounded. At night she'd let down her hair, literally. It was a time to relax. Nobody knew we were there. It was like floating on our own private cloud high above Rayne. There was no pressure, only possibility. We'd look out onto the sea and the stars, imagining a new future for Ibara. Not that we had any real say in the matter, but it was an amazing feeling to be in a place that was more or less starting from scratch. Everyone here has complete control of their own destiny. It's a very bright future, and Telleo and I are going to help shape it. How great is that?

She seems perfect in so many ways that I feel bad for writing this next part, but since these journals are about documenting everything that I experience, I'd be remiss if I didn't. Telleo is as bright and open and friendly as you can imagine, except when it comes to one topic: her mother. The first time I brought up the subject was when we were sitting up on that ledge on a warm, clear night. Her father, Genj, had been working pretty hard, and I was worried about him. He wasn't a young guy and he was pushing himself. Maybe a little too hard.

"How's your dad?" I asked, trying to sound casual and not cause her any real worry.

"Happy" was her answer. "I think he's finally seeing past the loss of the pilgrims. He thinks you're wonderful, by the way."

That made me feel pretty good. "He's working kind of hard."

"He wouldn't have it any other way," she replied confidently. "Do you think that's wrong?"

"No," I said quickly. "I just thought that since he's kind of older, he should take it easy."

Telleo gave it some thought, then nodded. "I'll visit him in the morning. If I think he's too stressed, I'll tell him to lighten his load."

"Will he?"

Telleo smiled slyly. "He can't say no to me. I'm his only daughter."

I chuckled. "Right. Hey, you haven't told me anything about your mom."

As soon as I said the words, I realized it was a mistake. Telleo's bright eyes turned dark. It was weird. She suddenly got all vacant. Up until that moment neither of us had talked about anything personal. I mean, about our backgrounds. It was a subject I wanted to dodge at all costs for obvious reasons. The few times I thought about asking Telleo about her family, I stopped myself because I didn't want the same questions coming back at me. That night I asked without thinking. It just came out. I realized my mistake too late and shut the heck up. Telleo was silent for a long time. It was pretty clear that her thoughts had gone to a troubling place. I didn't know whether she was going to ignore the question or was working to find the right words to answer me. When she finally spoke, it was as though the words were coming from a different person. A darker person. Someone with secrets.

"I don't talk about her," she said, so softly I could barely hear. The words "Why not?" almost flew out of my mouth, but I swallowed them.

"I'm sorry," she said, softening. "It's just . . . difficult. My mother and I had problems. I want to let it go at that, okay?"

"Yeah, sure, sorry," I said, trying to do damage control.

"Don't be sorry. Just don't mention that woman anymore. To anyone."

That woman. Yikes. Whatever had gone down between Telleo and her mother, it wasn't good. My curiosity was running wild, but I had to respect her wishes and made a pact with myself to forget all about Telleo's mother. It was a smart thing to do for lots of reasons.

As time passed and Rayne healed, my thoughts returned to the bigger picture. I guess that was inevitable. My main goal in destroying the gate was to trap Saint Dane here on Ibara. I could only hope that it had worked; I had no proof. Since the battle, not a single Flighter had been seen on Ibara. Sentries were positioned all over the island. That was one of the big changes that was made after the dado attack. There were no reports of Flighters trying to land. In some ways that worried me. Since Saint Dane was stuck here, you would think he'd try to rally them for another shot at Ibara. Why not? There was nothing else for him to spend his time on. What was he doing? Hanging out in Rubic City watching the buildings crumble? In some weird way the fact that there were no Flighters hanging around made me nervous.

A few times I went down to the rocky rubble on the beach to see if there was any way to get to the flume. There wasn't. I suppose a dygo could dig down to it, but there was nothing on Ibara that could tunnel that deep through so much rock. I tried myself once, for about a minute. I threw a couple of boulders aside and quickly realized it was a waste. The flume was buried. Still, I didn't have proof that Saint Dane was trapped.

That is, until one afternoon that I don't think I'll ever forget.

I was working with Twig and Krayven, carrying what felt like the one-millionth dado part down to the junk pile on the beach. No sooner had I lobbed the foot (yes, foot) onto the pile, when I heard something overhead. Nobody else would have given it a second thought. In fact, Twig and

Krayven didn't. But I did. The sound was the single, loud *caw!* of a crow. A big crow. A raven. I looked up to see the huge bird circling the pile. I froze. Could it be?

"Big bird," Twig commented.

That made me think of the big goofy yellow dude from *Sesame Street*. I should have laughed at that. I didn't. The black bird circled once more, then flew off along the beach . . . in the direction of the buried gate. It didn't seem like a random move. It felt more like it was waiting for me to see it before shooting off.

I wanted to puke.

"I'll meet you back at the village," I told the others. "I want to check something out."

"What?" Krayven asked. "I'll help."

"No!" I snapped, a little too quickly. They both jumped in surprise. "I mean, it's not important. I'll be right back."

I didn't stick around to debate and walked quickly along the beach. My heart raced. What did this mean? Was it a random bird that I was following? Was my paranoia meter set a little too low? Or was something else going on? I knew where I'd find that answer.

It was the fifth time I had gone to the tomb of the gate. Each time I came away with the same conclusion. The flume was buried. It was inaccessible. No problem. Then time would go by; I'd get itchy and go down to make sure. Again. What can I say? I'm paranoid. This time was different. My paranoia was justified. I followed the shore until I reached the huge mound of volcanic rock, turned inland and began to climb. Normally when I'd reach the pinnacle, which was around three hundred feet high, I'd look to see if there was any possible way to get to the flume. This trip would be different.

As I climbed the mound of rocks, I didn't know what I hoped to find. I didn't want to face Saint Dane. I really didn't. Who would? I'd just as soon never lay eyes on the demon again. But seeing him there might have confirmed that my plan had worked. I wanted to know for sure that I wasn't the only one trapped on Ibara. His presence would confirm that. When I reached the top, I threw my leg over, hoisted myself up, got to my feet, and had my answer.

"Good morning, Pendragon," Saint Dane said with a casual smile. "Lovely day to enjoy the beach, don't you think?"

JOURNAL #33

(CONTINUED)

IBARA

He sat on a flat boulder, looking all sorts of casual, with his feet propped up on a smaller rock. If I didn't know better, I'd say he looked like some guy who was just hanging out, catching some sun.

I knew better.

He was in his normal form, wearing the dark suit that buttoned up to his chin. His bald head was so white in the gleaming daylight it made the jagged red scars seem like streaks of blood. The word "vampire" came to mind. Actually, a lot of words came to mind. None of them were good. I stood staring at him. This was his show. He'd lured me there. I wanted him to speak first. He didn't. He stared at me with those creepy blue-white eyes. What was going through that twisted brain? I knew this couldn't be a social call. Saint Dane always had an agenda.

I finally couldn't take it anymore and said, "I hope you used sunblock on that skeleton head of yours. You're gonna fry."

He chuckled and asked, "Do you really care?"

"Nope."

Saint Dane stood up to his full height, which was several inches taller than mine. I thought back to a time when he towered over me like some ominous giant. I'd grown up since then. Now he was just an ominous regular-height guy. He strolled around the peak, kicking at random stones.

"Quite the dramatic choice you made here," he began. "I have to admit, I was surprised. Not that you used tak from Denduron, mind you. I predicted that. But I didn't think you would do something so drastic as sealing the flume. Bravo. It was a selfless act. Desperate, but selfless."

"Desperate?" I said, scoffing. "I kicked your ass."

"It *was* quite the battle, wasn't it?" he said with glee, as if enjoying the memory. "The dados didn't know what hit them. Literally. Then again, they didn't think about anything at all. They were mindless automatons."

"Now they're trash."

"Don't gloat, Pendragon. It's unbecoming."

"Hey, I earned it," I shot back. "I didn't start this. But I finished it. And I finished you."

Saint Dane threw me a look with those cold eyes.

"What do you want?" I snarled.

"I want to congratulate you," he announced jovially. "I must say, events did not play out exactly as I expected. You have proven to be a formidable adversary. I thought this conflict would have ended long ago, and that is to your credit." He bowed deeply and added, "For that, I commend you."

"That's it? That's why you came here? You got so bored hanging out in the rubble of Rubic City that you flew all the way over here just to tell me what a great job I did? Talk about desperate."

"There's more," he said flatly.

Oh. There always was. The guy sat down again. He

looked out over the ocean, then back to the island, as if soaking up the beauty of the tropical territory. He seemed almost human. Almost.

He continued, "We've come a long way, you and I. I'd like to think we've both learned from each other. I now understand the resilience and fortitude the people of the territories possess. They are a passionate people, and for that, I've developed a certain . . . respect for them."

"But not enough respect to leave us alone," I added.

"Ah!" he exclaimed. "That is exactly my point. You see, my friend, we are—"

"I'm not your friend."

"Yes, of course. I hope that by now you understand exactly where our differences lie."

"I do. I'm trying to protect the territories, and you're trying to kill everyone. I've had that one down for a while now."

He smiled and shook his head, as if I were an annoying child who didn't understand his obvious lesson. It made me want to hit him.

"You speak of methods," he said patiently. "I speak of philosophy."

"Methods!" I shouted. "You use genocide like some kind of . . . of . . . garden tool, and I'm supposed to ignore that?"

"Are you any different? Didn't you condone the destruction of the dirigible *Hindenburg*? People died, Pendragon, but since it was for the greater good, you accepted it. Why are your tools any better or more righteous than mine?"

I wanted to argue, but I realized there was more going on here than debating about the past.

"Please," he continued calmly. "For once in your futile

existence, open your narrow mind to the larger issues."

I turned around to look out on the ocean and take a deep breath. I had to calm down. Saint Dane may not have been human, but he had human emotions. I'd gotten to him more than once. I definitely had learned a few things over the past several years, and one of them was that I was better off letting Saint Dane spew than baiting him into an argument. It didn't help if I got all emotional, either. I forced myself to relax.

"I'm listening," I said through gritted teeth.

"Thank you. I was speaking about our differences. If I may be so bold as to speak for you, I would say that you hold the opinion that free will is the right of every being in Halla. It is up to the individual to choose his or her own path, good or bad, wherever it may lead. That's putting it simply, but am I correct?"

I turned back to him. "And it's your opinion that the people of Halla can't be trusted with their own destiny and need a guiding hand to help them live the kind of life you think is correct."

Saint Dane's eyebrow went up. It actually went up. "Indeed," he declared with a touch of surprise. "Again, an oversimplification, but in essence, correct. Perhaps you *have* been paying attention."

"It wasn't hard," I snarled.

"You see, Pendragon," Saint Dane continued, "that difference in philosophy has been the very core of our dispute. The people of the territories are egocentric, shortsighted children. You say they should control their own destiny, but time and again they have proven themselves incapable. You accuse me of practicing genocide. Believe me, the strife I have caused is but a mere drop of blood against the turmoil that the people of the territories have created for themselves. In spite of what you might think, I am not responsible for every war that has ever been fought. I cannot be blamed for hatred, bigotry, crime, religious conflicts, turf wars—the list goes on to infinity. You know enough of the history of your own world to know I'm right. It's no different with the other worlds. Veelox, Cloral, Quillan—it's all the same. History is written in the blood of its people. I want to put an end to that."

I took a few seconds to let his words sink in. I didn't want to speak out of emotion. "Put it that way and it sounds great," I said, measuring my words. "You're like some concerned parent who wants his children to stop fighting. I like that. The end of all human conflict. Sounds pretty good. There's only one problem."

"Please. Enlighten me."

"You think you should be the sole voice of reason. Judge, jury, executioner. You are the only one who knows what's best for everyone. If what you've told me in the past is still true, your plan is to pit the people of the territories against one another until all of Halla falls into turmoil. Then when all seems lost, you'll come riding in like some kind of savior to put everybody straight. Is that how it's supposed to work?"

Saint Dane chuckled. I hate chuckling. I've mentioned that, right?

"Something like that," he answered.

"Who's to say you have all the answers? Who's to say *any* one person has all the answers?"

"Leaders are chosen all the time—"

"Exactly! That's *my* point! Leaders are chosen. *Chosen*. It's about free will. People can choose who to put their trust in, whether it's the Council of Faar or the viceroy of Leeandra. It's up to the people. And if that leader fails, they won't be leading for long. History has proven that. Nobody can have ultimate power because nobody is infallible, especially not a leader who rises to power by manipulating the very people he claims to care so much about. Dictators don't stay in power long, and you want to be the dictator of all there ever was or will be. You expect me to think that's a good thing? Give me a break! You don't care about the people of Halla. That's just an excuse. You only care about the power."

"I can guide Halla to heights you can't even imagine," he said, his temper flaring.

"How? By playing on people's worst instincts? That's what you're obsessed with—the worst side of people. Your power comes from bringing that out. What kind of leader is that? Halla isn't perfect and never will be. But it's right. That's the way it was meant to be. People have the right to choose their own destiny, right or wrong."

"And that is where we disagree."

"Who are you?" I screamed.

Yes, I was losing it. Wasn't it about time?

"Where did you come from? How can you do what you do? Why is this all happening? How is any of this possible? You told me the Travelers were illusions. What the hell does that mean? You keep saying the battle is between us, but I'm at a total disadvantage. You know it all and I know nothing. Who *are* you? Who . . . am . . . I!"

Saint Dane stepped back from me. It was strange. It was as if he had deflated. His energy was gone.

"That is the one thing I cannot tell you, Pendragon," he said. "If I did, this would all have been for nothing."

"What?" I screamed in total frustration. "What does that mean?"

"You'll understand soon enough, when this is over."

"It's over now!"

"Soon enough, Pendragon," he repeated. "You won't have to wait much longer for your answers. I am sorry that you didn't allow yourself to open your mind to see things from my perspective. This was your last chance."

"I did open my mind," I snarled at the demon. "Forgive me if I'm not buying it. I don't care how you spin it, Saint Dane, you are evil. Everything you've done is evil. You can't make me believe for a second that anything you've done is justified because it will create some greater good."

"Yet *you've* made choices you knew were wrong," he argued.

"Not like you," I countered. "Not even close."

"Keep telling yourself that," he said calmly. "Your self-righteousness is all you have left."

He took one step backward and jumped off the cliff. It didn't even surprise me. I didn't budge, because I knew what I'd see next. A moment later the jet-black raven flew up and sped off across the ocean, headed toward Rubic City. I screamed at it in anger and frustration. I couldn't help myself. What was he trying to tell me? Why didn't he just come out and say it? How could this guy possibly believe that all the misery and destruction he caused were justified? And why was he keeping the ultimate truth a secret? It was like we were playing some cosmic game of chess, and if I knew all the rules, it wouldn't count. I'd been on this quest going on four years now, and I knew barely more about what it all meant than I did when I first left home with Uncle Press.

I screamed again. That's how frustrated I was. This wasn't how things were supposed to play out. I had made my choice. I ended the battle. I wasn't a Traveler anymore. I'd stopped Saint Dane. Why was he messing with my head? Was he just trying to torture me because I'd stopped him cold? Was he as frustrated as I was? Maybe he was just better at hiding it. I had a brief thought that the two of us would be locked in this mind game for the rest of my life, here on this island. I wasn't sure which was worse: battling Saint Dane across Halla or being trapped with him in the cage of Ibara.

I had to force myself to let it go. The war was over. I had won. Or at least I had forced a draw. We were stuck here. Both of us. That's the best thing that came out of my encounter with the demon. It was official. He was just as trapped as I was. That was good. I was going to have to take comfort in that and not let him get to me. I promised myself that the next time I saw him, I'd be ready. In fact, I'd welcome it. The debate between free will and forced destiny would continue.

I sat down on that mound of rock and laughed. I had this vision of the two of us having a philosophical debate that raged for decades. Like two old war veterans who fought on opposite sides of a long-ago battle, we'd argue our sides. That would be okay. Nobody ever died over a debate. Or over a game of checkers. At least, not yet.

That meeting with Saint Dane happened weeks ago. I think. I've tried to put it out of my head, but it hasn't been easy. I'm not only haunted by his words, but by the fact that he wouldn't admit the battle was over. He said that the end was *almost* here. Almost. Did that mean he had one last play I wasn't aware of? As much as I did my best to put that idea out of my head, it kept me awake at night.

Before I finish this journal, there's one more thing I have to write about. I mentioned at the beginning that in spite of how great things have become here on Ibara, there is one serious problem. Besides my disturbing confrontation with Saint Dane, that is. It's the single worst thing that's happened to me since the dado battle. Worse than sparring with the demon. Worse than learning of Telleo's problems with her mother. Worse than the backbreaking work or vicious storms. I don't know how to set this up, so I'll just write it.

I've lost my Traveler ring.

I don't know when it happened, or where. My big fear is that it slipped off my finger while I was working, got jumbled up with some dado parts, and is now lying on the bottom of the ocean. I haven't given up hope of finding it. I'm always on the lookout and have asked everyone to keep an eye out for it. Losing that ring has made my exile here on Ibara all the more final. It's why I'm not able to send this journal to you, Mark and Courtney. You may never read these words. When I made the decision to seal the flume, I knew that as much as it would trap me here, I would still be able to communicate with you. Now that I can't, I still don't regret what I did, but it's made the experience way more lonely.

Until I find it, and I will find it, I'll continue to write these journals and hope that one day you will read them. The rest of my life here will continue as it has. Now that the village has been cleared, the next step is to rebuild the homes. I'm looking forward to that. Who knows? Maybe once that's under way, we'll begin to construct new ships to send more pilgrims off to repopulate the rest of Veelox, just as Aja envisioned.

Beyond that, I have one other goal, which may be as important as anything else I've done here. I want to rid Ibara of anything that came from other territories. Maybe that's kind of like closing the barn door after the horse has gotten out, but in spite of what we had to do to protect this island, mixing the territories and their destinies was wrong. My hope is now that Saint Dane is out of the picture, the same can happen on all the territories. That is the way it was meant to be. That's the way Uncle Press said it was meant to be. I'm going to do all I can to make sure Ibara gets back on the right track.

And so we go.

Or maybe I should say, "And so I go."

END OF JOURNAL #33

SECOND EARTH

Mark, Courtney, and Patrick stepped out of the mouth of the flume into the root cellar beneath the abandoned Sherwood house in Stony Brook.

Connecticut.

Second Earth.

The carpet of light and music quickly receded back into the flume, leaving them alone.

At home.

In the dark.

Courtney was the first to notice that something was wrong. "There's nothing here," she announced.

"Of course not. We're underground," Mark replied.

"I mean there are no Second Earth clothes. When Bobby and I left, we brought a bunch of things from home. Shoes, shirts, pants. They're gone."

All three scanned the small, dark cellar but found nothing.

"Maybe somebody discovered this place," Patrick suggested.

"Not likely," Courtney replied. "We're in the basement of a mansion that's been empty for decades. This isn't right."

"It's okay," Mark said. "If wearing First Earth clothes is the worst thing we have to do, we're lucky."

"I don't like it," Courtney groused. "It's not a good way to start."

"What should we do?" Patrick asked tentatively. He was nervous. Both Mark and Courtney sensed it.

"It's okay, Patrick," Mark said calmly. "Relax."

"Relax?" Patrick echoed. "You didn't go through what I did."

Mark and Courtney exchanged looks.

"Yeah, we've all been on a picnic," Courtney said sarcastically.

Patrick immediately realized his mistake. "I'm sorry. I didn't mean to suggest that it's been easy for any of us."

"We'll be fine," Mark interjected. "We're all a little stressed. Let's just get out of here and back to my house. We can figure out our next move from there."

Courtney went first, walking the few steps across the dirt floor to the ancient wooden door that protected the long-abandoned root cellar. She pushed it open slowly. There was a loud creek of rusted hinges that echoed throughout the cellar.

"Gotta oil that," she said casually, and stepped into a pitch-dark basement.

Mark followed right behind her. "Looks like it's nighttime," he observed.

Patrick was right behind him, staying close. When they had all passed through, Courtney closed the creaky old door behind them.

"Check this out," she said to Patrick while running her hand across the door's wooden surface. "We watched this being burned into the door by the ring. It was incredible."

The darkness made it difficult for Patrick to make out detail. He ran his hand across the wood to feel the scar of the five-inch star that marked the gate to the flume.

"What does it mean?" he whispered.

"It means it's a gate," Courtney answered. "Duh."

"No, I mean the book cover. Ravinia. And the tattoos those men had on their arms. What's the connection?"

Mark stood between the two and answered, "That's what we're going to have to find out."

The three turned to face the empty basement.

"Wait for our eyes to adjust," Mark suggested. "It won't take long. Light from the street comes in through the windows over there and—"

The words caught in Mark's throat. He stared straight ahead into the pitch-black empty basement . . . that wasn't empty anymore.

"Uh-oh," Courtney gasped.

"What?" Patrick asked nervously.

As their eyes adjusted, they were able to make out the forms of boxes stacked everywhere.

"What's the problem?" Patrick asked, his panic growing. "What are they?"

"Doesn't matter," Mark answered. "They aren't supposed to be here. The house is empty."

"Not anymore," Courtney stated.

Grrrrr.

The sound came from upstairs. Mark and Courtney stiffened.

"Oh hell," Courtney muttered.

"Did you hear that?" Patrick asked. "This place doesn't sound empty."

Courtney whispered, "Did anybody see a small silver canister back by the flume? About three inches long?"

"No," Patrick whined. "What is it?"

Grrrrrr. The growl was louder.

"A weapon," Courtney answered.

"A weapon!" Patrick echoed loudly.

"Shhhh!" Mark scolded.

"Weapon?" Patrick whispered. "For what?"

Courtney's answer was simple and direct. "For quigs."

Bang! The basement door at the top of the stairs flew open, followed by the sounds of vicious barking and claws scrambling on steps.

"The d-door!" Mark yelled.

He took off across the basement, headed for the door he knew led up and outside. He remembered the door from long ago. He had never needed to use it. Until then.

"Ow!" Mark screamed as he ran headfirst into a stack of boxes and fell backward. Boxes tumbled over, scattering onto the floor, tripping up Patrick. Courtney grabbed the Traveler before he could fall.

"Don't stop," she commanded.

"Find the door!" Mark ordered as he scrambled to his feet.

The animal continued barking and growling as it charged down the stairs. Mark caught a glimpse of the black beast. It looked big, but at least there was only one. Courtney reached the wall first and was faced with a barrier of boxes stacked up high, blocking off their only means of escape. The door was buried.

The barking echoed through the huge basement as the vicious dog hit the floor, heading for its prey.

"Is there another way out?" Patrick yelled desperately.

"Up those stairs," Courtney answered. "On the other side of the quig."

The three turned their backs to the wall of boxes and faced the charging black animal. They all knew there was no way to fight a bloodthirsty quig. At least Mark and Courtney knew. Patrick would soon find out.

Mark shouted, "Whichever one it goes for, the other two have to get out."

He took a subtle step forward. Mark wanted to be the one the quig hit first. Courtney realized it, grabbed his jacket, and pulled him back, saying, "I don't think so."

The dog was almost on them. The barking was deafening. Nobody knew who it would attack first. The animal chose Mark. It leaped at him, hit his shoulders with both paws, and knocked him back into the cardboard boxes. Mark fell, the boxes fell, the dog was on top of him dripping slobber onto his face.

"Run!" Mark shouted. He held the dog off as best he could, waiting for the pain to come when its teeth ripped into his face.

Patrick and Courtney froze, not knowing what to do. They both looked down to see . . .

A big black Labrador retriever was standing on Mark's chest, licking his face.

"That's a quig?" Patrick uttered, stunned.

"Uh, I, uh" was all Courtney could say.

"Get him off!" Mark yelled.

Courtney grabbed the big dog and pulled him back. The dog spun and licked her right on the mouth.

"Eeyew, stop!" she complained. "Sit!"

The dog obeyed. It sat down, eager to please. The barking was finished. He lifted his paw, expecting somebody to take it. Mark sat up, looked at the big goofy dog, patted him on the chest, and said, "Uh, good boy."

"I—I don't understand," Patrick stammered.

Mark willed his heart to stop racing. The fear of a sudden, painful death had gotten him a little worked up. "This isn't a quig," he gasped.

"Obviously. He's not much of a watch dog, either," Courtney said, hugging the big, friendly fur ball. "What if we were here to rob the place?"

All three tensed up again. Their fear of the quig was replaced with another.

"Somebody lives here," Mark announced, stunned.

"We're trespassing," Courtney added.

"Does that mean things have changed again on Second Earth?" Patrick asked.

"We gotta get outta here," Mark ordered.

He turned to the wall, pushing aside some of the cardboard boxes to try to get to the door. What he found instead was a solid wall.

"They cemented over the door," he declared.

"I don't get it. How long have we been gone?" Courtney asked in wonder.

"Long enough. We've got to go up through the house," Mark announced, heading for the stairs.

The others followed. The dog trailed behind, wagging his tail happily.

"Let's hope they're asleep," Mark whispered.

"Let's hope they don't have guns," Courtney added.

"Yeah, that too."

They crept quickly and quietly up the wooden stairs. Both Courtney and Mark had been through the house many times before, yet they had no idea what to expect when they entered the living area this time. Patrick had no idea about anything. The dog probably knew something, but he wasn't talking. The door on top of the stairs was still open, thanks to the black Lab. Mark reached the top step first, and he stopped to look back.

"If the barking didn't wake anybody up, maybe the house is empty," he whispered hopefully.

"Or maybe the police are up there waiting for us," Courtney countered.

Mark gave her a sour look. He glanced down at Patrick. Patrick looked as if he were going to faint. Mark gave him a smile of assurance. He wished that somebody would give him one too. He turned forward and quietly stepped into the house. It was exactly as Mark and Courtney remembered it . . .

Except that it was fully furnished. The basement door led up into the grand foyer. From there a circular staircase led to the second floor. Mark gazed around in wonder at the opulent surroundings. He looked to Courtney and opened his eyes wide as if to say, "Wow."

The place definitely deserved a "wow." Mark thought that whoever now lived there had some serious money. A soft glow from the living room gave them enough light to see detail. A huge, ornate crystal chandelier hung overhead. Rich Oriental rugs graced the highly polished wooden floors. Oil paintings of idealized countrysides hung everywhere. Mark glanced into one room to see fancy, expensive-looking furniture, along with enough sculptures to make it appear more like a museum than a household. The wall paint was no longer chipped and scarred. Intricate wooden trim traced every corner. The stairs leading to the second floor looked like highly polished marble. It was a showplace.

The only detail that truly mattered just then was the front door on the far side of the foyer. Freedom was only a few yards away. The dog pushed past Mark and scampered deeper into the house, passing through an archway that led into the living room. Mark motioned for the others to follow him toward the front door. All three moved quickly and quietly across the floor, until Courtney stopped so suddenly that Patrick bumped into her from behind. Nobody said a word, nobody complained. Though Patrick did throw her an impatient look. Courtney didn't notice. She was too busy staring through the archway where the dog had just gone.

Mark tugged on her sleeve to keep her moving. Courtney ignored him. She kept staring into the next room. Mark tugged again. Courtney's silent answer was to point into the room. Patrick and Mark followed her gaze. Patrick gasped. Mark stared in wonder.

Beyond the archway, in the living room, a fireplace blazed. The fire in the hearth was the source of the warm, flickering light that was guiding their way. That wasn't what they were staring at. Nor was it the dog, that had curled up in front of the fire to keep warm. What got their attention was hanging over the fireplace. In the dim light it wasn't clear if it was a painting or a sculpture or even a photograph. It didn't matter.

Looming over the fireplace, measuring about five feet across, was a huge, five-pointed star. It was the symbol that marked the gates. It hung in a place of honor, like a revered icon.

Mark's knees went weak. He was getting too much information to assimilate in such a short time. There was no doubt anymore. Things had changed, and it wasn't just that somebody had moved into the Sherwood house. The star symbol was now known here on Second Earth. It was out in the open. Did that mean the flumes had been discovered too? Mark forced himself to look away. He had to focus. They were in a bad place. They wouldn't find the answers if they were stuck in jail for breaking and entering. That realization snapped Mark back to his senses. He pulled Courtney's arm again, this time more forcefully. They had to get out of there.

The three moved quickly to the front door. A thick, dead-bolt lock sat just above the door handle. Mark put one hand on the handle, the other on the bolt's turn key. He glanced back at the others and whispered, "We'll go for the wall where we always climb over. Stay close to the house, in the shadows."

Mark twisted the lock. They didn't have to be quiet anymore.

The moment the lock was thrown, an alarm shrieked. The horn cut through the silence of the big house as loudly as if a fire truck were barreling through the living room. The dog started barking again. A red light on a keypad next to the door started flashing. It was the alarm control.

Courtney looked at Mark with wide eyes and said the only thing that made sense under the circumstances. "Run."

The three bolted out of the door, ran across the wide porch, and jumped down the stairs to the gravel drive below. Floodlights burst on, lighting up the yard like a football field. Or a prison yard where a break was under way. Courtney and Mark took a sharp right and ran for the cement wall that surrounded the property. They knew there was a tree on the other side they could climb down. The trick was scaling the wall from this side. They'd done it enough times to know how. No words were needed.

The harsh alarm sound was even louder outside. Speakers were hidden in trees. Floodlights followed them as if powered by motion detectors. The once-deserted home of a chicken farmer named Sherwood was now equipped with some serious security.

"We're okay," Mark panted as they ran. "We'll be long gone before the police show up."

Bang!

A bullet whistled by. They weren't alone anymore.

"I think they're already here," Patrick whined.

"No way," Courtney gasped. "The police don't shoot at you, even if you *are* trespassing."

"Then who is?"

Two more flat cracks sounded. *Bang! Bang!* Grass and dirt kicked up around them.

"I'm on the bottom!" Mark shouted. They were at the wall. Courtney didn't argue. She knew what he meant. Mark put his shoulder to the wall and cupped his hands for Courtney to step into an "alley-oop" up. Courtney barely broke stride. She leaped into Mark's hands, right foot first. Her momentum kept her going. Mark launched her upward as she pushed off her foot. She was airborne. Like a flying trapeze artist she grabbed the top of the cement wall and hoisted herself up, all in one smooth movement.

"Let's go!" she called down before she was even settled.

Mark cupped his hands again, looking to Patrick. "C'mon!"

Patrick was unsure. "I can't do that."

Patrick needed inspiration. He got it. The sound of machine-gun fire cut through the alarm. To their right, the cement wall began to explode from rounds being pumped into it. Splinters of cement flew everywhere. The attack was getting closer. It was all the convincing Patrick needed. He jumped into Mark's waiting hands, leaped up, and grabbed Courtney's down-stretched hand. Mark pushed and Courtney pulled. Adrenaline helped. Patrick was up on the wall.

"Climb down the tree," Courtney barked at Patrick.

Patrick didn't need to be told twice this time. He scrambled for the tree. As the cement wall was torn apart by gunfire, Courtney leaned down and reached for Mark. Mark looked up to see that she was actually smiling.

"Welcome home," she said with a wink.

Mark bent his legs and leaped straight up, grabbing both Courtney's hands. Courtney leaned back, pulled hard, and a moment later Mark was on top of the wall. Without another word Courtney followed Patrick down the tree.

As Mark waited for her to climb down, he looked back at the Sherwood mansion. The clattering machine-gun fire stopped. Whoever was shooting must have realized that the intruders were gone. Mark allowed himself a few seconds to inspect the old house and wonder what had changed. Who lived there now, and why did they have the gate symbol over their fireplace? Mark couldn't help but feel that whatever change in history had happened on Second Earth, the people in this house were part of it. The coincidence was too much. They lived on top of a flume.

He threw his legs over the side, and was about to slip onto the tree when his eyes caught movement inside the house. He glanced up to the second floor. A large window overlooked the front yard across which they had just made their escape. A lone figure stood in the window. It looked to Mark like a man. An old man. Maybe wearing a bathrobe. The light was on behind him, creating a silhouette. If the guy was upset about his house being broken into, he didn't show it.

He stood at the window, looking out at the yard as calmly as if he were looking for deer. In the window next to him, with its front paws up on the window frame, was the black retriever. The old man had one hand on its head, patting the animal as they both gazed outside. To Mark it seemed as if they were looking at him. A cold shiver shot up his spine.

"Stop right there!" came a shouted command.

Mark looked down to the ground to see four people wearing dark clothes that could have been uniforms, sprinting along the front lawn toward him. One of them held the machine gun. Mark didn't need to see any more. He jumped off the wall and climbed down the tree, landing by the other two.

"Let's disappear," he said, and the three ran into the neighborhood. Mark and Courtney's neighborhood.

They were home.

SECOND EARTH

(CONTINUED)

The suburban street was dark. And cold. No leaves were on the trees. It felt to Mark like early spring. The dirty, melting snowbanks along the sides of the road completed the picture. The houses were dark. That was good. It was late at night. The town was asleep. There was little chance of anyone spotting three people walking around who looked as if they had just stepped out of a time machine. With any luck, Mark figured they'd get to his house without a problem.

Better, the neighborhood didn't look any different to Mark from when he'd left. For a moment he could almost pretend as if things were normal. He knew he was kidding himself.

"When did you leave home?" Mark asked Courtney as they walked along the sidewalk.

"A couple of days after you did" was her answer. "I don't remember the exact date. Some time in December."

"This isn't December," Mark thought out loud. "Not cold enough. No Christmas lights. Feels more like late February or March."

"How far is your house?" Patrick asked. "The police are sure to show up after all that ruckus."

"Ruckus?" Courtney said with a grin. "You really are a geek teacher, aren't you?"

"Not a problem," Mark answered. "We're here."

Mark's house looked exactly as it did the day he left for First Earth with Nevva Winter. As he stood in front, he had trouble understanding his own conflicting emotions. He was happy to be home, but sad that his parents weren't there. He was encouraged that things looked normal, but knew they really weren't. Most of all, he was nervous about going inside and finding things that would tell him that his familiar life had changed.

Mark decided to stop thinking.

"Let's go around back," he suggested.

He led them across the front lawn, around the side of the house, and up the stairs of a redwood deck that led to his back door. A heavy plastic container near the door was where the Dimonds kept a garden hose and a spare house key. Mark opened the container and let out a relieved breath when he saw the key was there.

"Lots of things haven't changed at all," he said, relaxing a little.

They entered the house and quickly closed the door behind them.

"Pull all the shades," Mark suggested. "It wouldn't be good if somebody saw us walking around. They might think we're prowlers."

"Yeah, we'd *never* go inside a house where we didn't belong," Courtney said, joking.

Nobody laughed.

"C'mon people!" she cajoled. "Just trying to lighten things up!"

Mark looked at the kitchen clock. "Three in the morning. Let's get the shades down before the world wakes up."

"What are shades?" Patrick asked.

"Sit down," Courtney said, pointing to the kitchen table. "We got it."

Patrick sat at the table, but he didn't look comfortable. He sat straight up, looking at his hands, afraid to see anything more on Second Earth. He had been jumping from one alien environment to the next, and his nerves were jangled.

"We'll be right back," Mark said to him kindly as he and Courtney left the kitchen.

"I'm worried about him," Courtney said to Mark softly, so Patrick wouldn't hear. "He's a mess."

"He's been through a lot," Mark offered.

"Like we haven't?"

"Yeah, but we're used to it."

The two looked at each other and laughed. "It's true," Courtney said, shaking her head in amazement.

"Patrick will be fine," Mark assured her.

"He better be. He's the Traveler of this trio."

They quickly walked through the house to see that most of the shades were already drawn. They only needed to pull down a few on the second floor. Mark thought that was good. If somebody looked at the house the next day there wouldn't be any obvious, suspicious changes. Mark went into his bedroom and stopped short when he saw a few touchstones from his former life. The anime posters, the stacks of books, the pictures of him and Bobby when they were younger. He felt a lump rise in his throat. He missed his old life. He missed being geeky Mark. He didn't want to know about Travelers and Halla, and most of all, he didn't want to know anything about Forge.

One thing caught his eye that was different. It was the computer screen on his desk. Mark had been using an old-fashioned tube monitor for the longest time. Now sitting on his desk, the desk he recognized so well, was a high-tech-looking flat screen like he had never seen before.

Courtney stepped into the room to see Mark staring at the alien computer.

"Strange, huh? When you brought computer technology back to First Earth, it jump-started the whole computer revolution by sixty years. No wonder you're a legend."

"How is it different?"

Mark had barely gotten the words out of his mouth when the computer screen blinked to life. A 3-D geometric pattern appeared, making Mark and Courtney take a step backward in surprise.

"Hello, Mark," a pleasant, female voice said from the computer. "It is three fifteen in the morning. How may I help you?"

Mark and Courtney stared at the screen for several seconds. Finally Courtney uttered, "Well, there's that."

"It recognized my voice," Mark said with dismay.

"Ask it something," Courtney suggested.

Mark thought, then said, "Uh, what's today's date?"

The computer answered, "It is March the eleventh."

"Bobby's birthday," Courtney said with a smile. "He's eighteen today."

Mark ran his finger across the top of the computer screen, wiping off a thin layer of dust. "Three months," he said thoughtfully. "That means a whole lot of things."

The computer said, "What exactly does that mean?"

Courtney shot a look at the screen and barked, "Hey, mind your own business."

"Turn off," Mark said to the computer.

"Good-bye," the computer responded as the screen winked to black.

Mark looked at Courtney with surprise. "Wow, that was easy."

Courtney plopped down onto Mark's bed, thinking. "This is bad," she said. "Being gone for so long, I mean. If the flume sent us back to when we'd left, like it did when we went to Eelong, we could just pick up like nothing happened. But now we're going to have to answer questions. Everybody here still thinks your parents were killed when that plane crashed. You'd have to deal with that."

"It's true," Mark said, rubbing his eyes. "My relatives would be all over me. They'd probably make me go live with my aunt in Maryland. I can't go to Maryland."

"And I can't go home. What would I tell my parents?"

"And how do we explain Patrick?"

"As wrong as this sounds, we can't go back to our regular lives," Courtney concluded, glum.

"Agreed. It'll prevent us from figuring out how things have changed and what Saint Dane is up to."

The two fell silent. Then, "Mark?"

"Yeah?"

"How exactly are we going to do that?"

"I have no idea."

They decided that whatever they were going to do, it wouldn't be that night. They had to get their internal clocks set to local time. They each found a bed and settled in for a few hours of sleep. Mark was in his own bed, Patrick took the Dimonds' room, and Courtney claimed the couch downstairs. All three of them lay awake, staring at the ceiling, unable to nod off.

Finally, at nearly six, Courtney poked her head into Mark's bedroom and announced, "Stop pretending like you're asleep. I'm hungry."

When they hit the kitchen, they discovered that Patrick was already there, sitting at the kitchen table, staring at the torn book cover he'd brought from Third Earth.

"Hey, you all right?" Courtney asked.

"I don't know what I am anymore," Patrick answered wearily.

Courtney gave Mark a nervous look.

Mark went for the refrigerator to find it mostly empty. "Cupboard's bare," he announced.

"Check the freezer," Courtney suggested.

In the freezer Mark found orange juice and Eggo waffles. He tossed the frozen juice to Courtney and grabbed the box of waffles.

"Better than nothing," he declared, and walked to the counter. There he stopped and looked around with confusion. "Uh, the toaster's gone."

"Put 'em in the oven," Courtney suggested.

Mark opened the oven and put a layer of frozen waffles on the top rack, but when he tried to turn the oven on, he was lost.

"There aren't any buttons," he said with dismay. "This isn't our oven."

"Sure it is," Courtney said patiently. "It's just improved, remember? Try telling it what to do."

"Yeah, right," Mark scoffed. He looked at the oven and said, "Cook the waffles."

Instantly, the oven light went on and the coil began to heat.

"Whoa" was all Mark could gasp.

Patrick asked, "That isn't normal?"

"Uh, no," Mark answered.

"But it is," Courtney interjected. "At least the new normal after Mark brought Forge to First Earth. Mostly things look the same, but there are small differences with technology. Just be lucky you don't have any pets. That would really make your head spin."

Patrick added, "What about that house over the flume?"

Courtney frowned. "That's different. No way somebody moved in and made all those changes so fast."

"That means even more things have changed since we left," Mark added. "Which means something else must have happened in the past besides Forge."

"We've got to figure out what that was," Courtney said.

Patrick lifted the torn book cover from the table and added, "And find out why people seem to know about this."

Mark and Courtney looked at the cover.

"Ravinia," Mark whispered, reading the cracked word on the cover.

"Maybe it's a good thing," Courtney offered hopefully as she mixed the orange juice in a pitcher.

Patrick winced. "You wouldn't think that if you saw what happened to Third Earth."

"Oh. Right," Courtney said, embarrassed. "That."

"I think our first step is to look around and see what things are different," Mark declared. "We might find something we can trace back to First Earth."

"How?" Courtney asked.

Mark pointed to Patrick's Traveler ring. "We've got a hotline to the past. If we find anything suspicious, we can send a message to Dodger."

"You sure?" Courtney asked.

Mark grabbed a piece of paper and scribbled something. "Put the ring on the table," he said to Patrick as he folded the note in half.

Patrick took off his ring and placed it next to the pitcher of orange juice.

"Let's give it a shot," Mark said. He cleared his throat and spoke distinctly to the ring. *"First Earth."*

The ring came alive. The relief in everyone's face was obvious. They may not have been able to communicate with Bobby, but at least the rings still worked. The circle opened up, spewing light and music. When it reached its full size, Mark dropped the note into the hole, after which the ring immediately shrank back, ending the event.

Courtney picked up the ring and examined it. "Do you think we're ever going to figure out how this works?"

"How do we know it worked?" Patrick asked.

"Oh, it worked," Courtney answered for Mark. "But did it go to

Dodger, or Nevva?" Mark shot a surprised look at Courtney. "She has your ring, Mark. And if she's still on First Earth . . . " She didn't have to complete the thought.

"We'll know in a couple of hours" was Mark's answer. "When the bank opens."

Patrick frowned and looked to Courtney. Courtney shrugged. Neither knew what Mark was talking about. Then it hit Courtney and she brightened.

"Hey, you asked them to put something in the safe-deposit box!" she declared.

"No," Mark answered, pouring orange juice. "I want them to open an account and make a deposit at the bank. If we're going to be here awhile, we're going to need money. They've got the KEM money from Forge."

"Will that work?" Patrick asked. "They can deposit money back on First Earth and it will be in the account today?"

"Should," Mark answered. "I gave them the number of our safe-deposit box and told them to put the deposit slip inside."

"Amazing," Patrick gasped.

"It's ironic," Mark said thoughtfully. "We're going to try to stop Saint Dane by using money from the company he got me to sell Forge to, and that we tried to stop from giving me that money in the first place, so they wouldn't create the dados and change the future of Halla."

"Excuse me?" Patrick said, totally lost.

Courtney laughed. "I actually understood that."

"Then please explain it to me," Patrick pleaded.

"No problem," Courtney answered. "If you're going to be part of this, you're going to have to get up to speed fast."

A voice called to them from across the room, saying, "Your waffles are ready."

Everyone looked at the oven.

Mark said, "I'm not going to get used to this."

The plan was for Courtney and Patrick to stay at the house while Mark went to the bank. Courtney's job was to fill Patrick in on all that had happened with KEM and DADO and Forge, while searching the house for clothes that would help them blend in on Second Earth. Mark put on some of his own clothes. He chose jeans, a T-shirt, and a pair of old running shoes. Mark never went running. He just liked the way they felt. He decided to leave his hair combed back in the style from First Earth in case anybody might recognize him. It helped that he wore a pair of gold wire-rimmed glasses he got on First Earth and put on a navy blue, short golf jacket of his father's. That completed the transformation from Mark, to not-Mark. He looked in the mirror and barely recognized himself.

Courtney's comment was, "You look like some old-dude banker from the 'burbs. Perfect."

Mark was afraid that an "old-dude banker" would look odd riding a bike, so he chose to make his way to the bank on Stony Brook Avenue on foot. It was only a few miles, and he wanted to take the opportunity to observe any other changes that might have occurred on Second Earth.

Most of the walk was through suburban streets that didn't look any different from what he remembered. The houses looked exactly the same. The lawns. The sidewalks. The cars. Pretty much everything. Though something did feel different to him, and it took him a mile of walking before he realized what it was. All the telephone poles were gone. Every last one. His neighborhood used to be full of overhead lines that carried power, telephone, and cable TV. Not anymore. He was surprised that he didn't realize it right away, but figured he was looking for something new, not something that wasn't there. Once it clicked, it was obvious. He wondered what had replaced them. Was everything underground? Or was it all sent through signals in the air? Since the main changes on Second Earth were about technology, he figured that anything was possible.

Though he did wonder where the birds were going to hang out.

Stony Brook Avenue looked pretty much the same as well. It was the closest thing that Stony Brook, Connecticut, had to a "main street." It was lined with shops and restaurants. The cool kids used to hang out there, which was why Mark didn't. He'd go to the Garden Poultry Deli, get his daily dose of fries and Mountain Dew, and eat as he walked home. He was never a "hanging around" kind of guy.

Mark was also pleased to see that his old friend Ms. Jane Jansen still worked at the bank. Every time he saw something that hadn't changed about Second Earth, it gave him hope that things weren't really as bad as he feared. He was a little nervous though that the woman might recognize him and start asking difficult questions about where he'd been so he made a point of going to another bank officer to get the key to his safe-deposit box.

The bank had just opened for business for the day and was next to empty. In no time Mark was in the vault, peering at the journals that he and Courtney had put there for safekeeping. There were two items of note that he hadn't seen before. One was a journal from Bobby: #28. Courtney had placed it there on First Earth. He was tempted to read it right then and there, but was sure that Courtney had already filled him in on everything Bobby had written. The other item was what he had come for. It was a deposit slip. An old one. It had been sitting in the vault for so long, it had turned yellow. It didn't matter. All Mark needed was the account number. His dad had deposited twenty thousand dollars. Back then it was a fortune. It wasn't so bad on Second Earth either. It would be plenty.

Attached to the slip was a handwritten note. It said, "We love you. Good luck. Mom and Dad." Mark smiled and slipped the note into his pocket. He closed up the box and walked back to the lobby to fill out a withdrawal slip. He didn't want to raise suspicion, so he decided not to take out a big amount. He figured that four hundred dollars would be enough to start. He could always come back for more. Mark filled out the slip and went to a bank teller he didn't know. He picked a pretty blond girl wearing a turtleneck. She looked as though she might go to Davis Gregory High, but Mark never hung out with pretty blond girls in turtlenecks, so he figured she wouldn't recognize him.

"G'morning!" the girl greeted with a bright smile.

"Hi. Just making a withdrawal. Not a lot. Just four hundred. No biggie, right?" Mark realized he was jabbering.

"No problem," the girl said. "Can I see your ID?"

Uh-oh. Mark had his wallet with his student ID. He'd taken it from his desk at the last second, but he didn't want to have to flash it. He was the Mark Dimond that people must have been talking about. His parents were killed, and he disappeared three months earlier. Stony Brook was a small town. If she recognized him, it would be all over.

"Y-You sure you need it?" he asked.

The girl gave him an innocent smile. "Yeah, sorry. Policy."

Mark fumbled through his wallet. "I'm n-not sure what I have." Mark suddenly wished that the girl was not only cute, but more concerned with being cute and popular than watching news stories about local tragedies. The girl stared at him, the first hint of doubt creeping into her eyes. Mark realized he had to take the chance. He handed her the plastic ID and held his breath.

The girl looked at it and beamed. "Hey, you go to DG?"

"DG?"

"Davis Gregory! I just graduated. What year are you?"

"Uh, senior. I think. I haven't been around much. I've been, uh, traveling."

"Really? Where?"

Mark figured it was better not to lie. He wasn't a good liar. "New York, mostly. But I was in England." He left out the part about it being in 1937.

The girl looked at her computer and said clearly, "Mark Dimond."

Mark didn't get it. Why was she saying his name at the computer? He quickly realized it was the new technology. There was no keyboard. It was all about voice recognition. The girl looked at the screen and scowled. Something was wrong.

"Is there a problem?" Mark asked.

"No. But I have to clear this with my manager." She looked up and called out, "Ms. Jansen?"

Uh-oh. Mark heard her before he saw her. The sharp sound of quick, clicking heels on the marble floor meant the überefficient Ms. Jane Jansen was incoming. He put his hand up to his face in hopes that she wouldn't get too good a look at him. He figured that surely she must have heard what happened to him and his family. Ms. Jane Jansen was the picture of perfection. She wore a dark, conservative suit, and her hair was tied back so tightly into a bun that Mark wondered how she moved her lips. She looked over her half-glasses at the computer screen and frowned.

"There hasn't been activity on that account for quite some time," she said with clipped perfection. "Is there a reason for that?"

"It was opened a long time ago," Mark answered. "By my grandfather. It was kind of a legacy for his grandkids. I'm just starting to use it now."

Mark had no idea where that semi-made-up story came from, but he was grateful for it, because it seemed to do the trick.

"Very well," Ms. Jane Jansen said, then added in a loud voice to the computer, "Approved."

Mark could breathe again. Apparently Ms. Jane Jansen didn't

follow the news either. Maybe, he figured, she never left her desk at the bank. Mark didn't care. He was golden. Ms. Jane Jansen took Mark's ID from the cute girl as the teller counted out Mark's money. She eyed it quickly, then held it out for Mark. Mark reached for it, and froze. When Ms. Jane Jansen reached out with the ID, her jacket sleeve ran up her arm. There on her forearm, as plain as could be, was a green tattoo. It was the five-pointed star.

Mark stared at it without moving.

"Here you are, young man," Ms. Jane Jansen chirped.

"What does that mean?" Mark asked without thinking. "That mark. What does it signify?"

Ms. Jane Jansen looked at Mark coldly. The cute girl seemed to shrink away. Whatever Mark said, it was definitely a faux pas.

"Answering personal questions at a place of business is not part of my job description," she said coldly. "Good day."

The woman spun away and clicked off. She was ticked. Or insulted. Or something. Mark didn't know exactly what.

"Here you go," the cute teller said, handing Mark the money. "I gave you twenties and fifties, is that okay?"

Mark was in a daze, still watching Ms. Jane Jansen. He had to snap himself back to reality.

"Uh, yeah, sure. Thanks." He took the money and stuffed it into his wallet. Mark wanted to get out of there and get back home. He needed to talk to the others.

"Don't mind her," the girl whispered. "She's old school."

Mark took a chance and asked, "Why was she so ticked that I asked her about the star?"

The girl shrugged. "Who knows? Some people don't like to talk about it."

"About what? Tattoos?"

The girl gave Mark a strange stare, as if he had just asked the most ridiculous question in the world.

"You're kidding, right?" the girl asked. "I thought you were traveling, not living under a rock." The girl pulled up her sleeve to reveal that she, too, had the star tattoo on her arm.

Mark gasped. He couldn't help himself. The room was suddenly getting hot. He backed away, headed for the door.

"What about your receipt?" the girl called.

Mark didn't answer. He was too busy running away.

SECOND EARTH

(CONTINUED)

"Maybe it's a Dr. Seuss thing," Courtney said. "Remember *The Sneetches*? All the cool birds had 'stars upon thars' and wouldn't hang out with the regular-old Sneetches on the beaches."

Mark gave her a sour look.

"I was kidding," Courtney added.

She took a big bite from a carrot. Mark had stopped on the way home to pick up groceries and of course bought carrots. The two sat in the kitchen of Mark's home, eating and speculating. On the table in front of them was the mysterious book cover.

"Patrick's been sitting in the living room staring at the TV," Courtney commented. "He's like a couch potato from the future. All he needs are chips and dip, and he'll be set for weeks."

"Can you blame him?" Mark asked. "The guy's an academic. This is like the best research project possible. He's living his own history."

"Or maybe he's just too scared to get his butt off the couch," Courtney quipped, taking another bite of carrot. "I can't blame him for that, either."

"It's weird," Mark said thoughtfully. "The bank lady didn't want to talk about the star, and the girl made it seem like it was something everybody knows about."

"You don't think it's just some innocent thing?" Courtney asked. "Like a peace symbol or a yin yang?"

"It's the symbol that marks the gates, Courtney," Mark snapped.

"Yeah, but it's just a star," Courtney shot back. "It could be coincidence. I mean, stars exist in other places besides the gates."

"Sure," Mark said patiently. "Like on this book cover from Third Earth. And hanging over the fireplace in the Sherwood house on top of the flume. And suddenly on the arms of old ladies and young girls and thugs from the future who are willing to torch a library to destroy it and—"

"All right, I get it," Courtney said, holding up her hands in surrender.

Mark raised the book cover to the light, staring at it for the thousandth time, as if the simple word and symbols would suddenly reveal secrets they hadn't before. "Ravinia," he said thoughtfully.

Courtney added, "That sounds kinda like Dr. Seuss too."

"Stop!"

Courtney huffed and tossed the rest of her carrot into the sink. "I want to go back to my house and get some clothes. Your mom's stuff is a little too, oh, I don't know . . . wrong." She stood up to show Mark she was wearing a pair of jeans that were two inches above her ankles and a sweater that was so tight it made her look as if she were wearing doll's clothes. "If Bobby can wear his own boxers, I say I can wear my own things too."

Mark looked her over and laughed.

"That doesn't help," Courtney snarled.

Patrick started yelling from the other room. "Hey! Hey! Come here! Hurry!"

Mark and Courtney bolted from the table and sprinted into the living room. Patrick had sprung to his feet and was standing in front of the couch, staring at the television screen.

"What?" Courtney yelled.

"Look!" he shouted, pointing to the TV.

It was a huge, flat-screen monitor that the Dimonds did not have when Mark left Second Earth. On screen was a montage of happy, wide-eyed faces, all looking up at something while raising their hands. There were all kinds of people, all ages and races. Stirring music played. It seemed to Mark like some kind of inspirational film. The image became wider to reveal there were many people. Thousands. All looking up at the same thing.

"What is it?" Courtney asked, confused.

"Keep watching," Patrick ordered.

A smooth but authoritative man's voice cut through the music, saying, "It is yours. It is ours. It is everything."

More faces were seen. Multiple images, fading in and out, superimposed over one another. All seemed to be in awe of something. Close-ups were superimposed over wider shots of hundreds of people.

"Touch it," the voice offered. "Feel it. Become part of It."

"This is kind of creepy," Courtney grumbled.

"Shhh!" Mark implored.

The joyous faces were replaced by a close-up image of an old man. He looked to be in his seventies, with salt-and-pepper hair that was perfectly combed. The guy looked like a kind grandpa with strong eyes. He wasn't a doddering old man. He was sharp. He held a small, warm smile as he gazed out onto the sea of faces. It was the old man that all these people were looking at and holding up their hands to. The images became even wider to reveal that he was wearing a simple white robe and standing on a circular stage above the huge crowd of people. His arms were spread, as if he wanted to hug them all in his loving embrace.

"Yeah so?" Courtney said impatiently. "Looks like some kind of televangelist."

"Wait," Patrick cautioned.

The voice then said, "The Convergence is upon us."

"What?" Courtney shouted.

"Shhh!" Patrick chastised.

The voice continued, "March twelfth. Madison Square Garden. Touch the future and the past."

The old man stood on the stage in the center of a sea of arms and adoring faces. It looked like a sports arena. People on every level were reaching their arms out as if to touch him, but were too far away to make actual contact. The music reached a crescendo as a huge image appeared above the man for all to see.

Courtney gasped.

"Oh man," Mark whispered.

It was the star. The star from the gate. It exploded with light. The crowd cheered. Some seemed overcome with the image and fainted dead away. The eyes of the others sparkled with the light that glowed from the giant star. The image was replaced by a glowing, animated version of the star that filled the TV screen against a background of black. The music rang out and the voice said with passion, "Ravinia. Yesterday, today, and forever." The star faded out. The screen went black. A second later regular programming continued. A rerun of *Seinfeld*. Courtney, Mark, and Patrick stared at the screen, stunned.

It was Mark who was able to speak first. "Did he say the Convergence was upon us?"

"Yeah," Courtney confirmed. "And Ravinia."

"Who is he?" Patrick demanded.

Mark and Courtney shook their heads and shrugged. Neither had ever seen him before.

"What is a Madison Square Garden?" Patrick asked.

"Big indoor stadium in New York City," Courtney answered. "That was like a commercial to promote an event there."

"It was like a commercial to promote the Convergence!" Mark corrected. "Could that have been Saint Dane?"

Patrick nodded thoughtfully. "March twelfth. That's today."

Mark plopped down on the couch. The *Seinfeld* episode was loud. The characters were complaining about something, as usual. Mark looked around, annoyed. "Where is the remote?"

Patrick called out, "Turn off."

The TV turned off.

"Oh," Mark uttered, numb.

Patrick faced the others. "None of that was familiar to you?" he demanded to know. "The gray-haired man? The people? The sentiment?"

"No," Courtney said. Mark shook his head.

"What about the Convergence?" Patrick added. "Is it some definite event that can just . . . happen?"

Mark said, "You're assuming it's Saint Dane's Convergence."

"Like there could be two?" Courtney shouted back sarcastically. "Slight coincidence, don't you think?"

"I don't know what to think," Mark fretted.

Patrick paced, deep in thought. "We need to know who that man is," Patrick concluded.

"And if the Convergence is going to happen tonight," Courtney added.

"That too." Patrick paced more quickly, the tension rising in his voice. "Whoever that guy is, he's got a following. Those people looked at him as though he's some kind of . . . of . . . god. If he didn't exist on Second Earth before, there's a good chance that whatever he's doing, it's going to lead to the changes on Third Earth."

"We should go to that event at Madison Square Garden," Mark offered.

"I'd rather go see the Knicks play," Courtney complained.

"I need to get to a library," Patrick announced, ignoring her. "That man didn't just show up yesterday. We need to find out everything we can about him."

"Use the Internet," Mark offered. "My computer's upstairs. But it's not like on Third Earth. No holograms. No huge databases. You're going to think it's all pretty crude."

"If a guy has that kind of impact, I don't think the database will have to be all that deep to find him," Patrick said with authority. "We have to know how he got started. Where he came from. How he ended up having such a big following. That kind of information has to exist, and I can find it."

Mark smiled at Courtney. Courtney gave a little shrug.

"Glad you're with the program," Mark said to Patrick.

"It's what I do," Patrick replied with confidence.

"Do what you can," Mark said. "Then we'll head into the city."

Soon after, Patrick sat at Mark's computer doing his best to dig through the crude (to him) data that was available on the Internet. Mark and Courtney left him alone to work undisturbed and went to Courtney's house to get her clothes. It was within walking distance of Mark's, but through a neighborhood where people knew them. It would have been safer to make the trip at night, but Courtney's parents would have been home. They had to go during the day. They walked casually but quickly, so as not to draw any attention, and arrived without a problem. As with Mark's house, the extra key was hidden near the back door.

"We've got to do this fast," Mark cautioned. "If your parents come home, or if somebody spots us—"

"We'll be in and out in five minutes," Courtney assured him.

Courtney opened the back door and stepped inside. As much as she wanted the clothes, she worried that this visit would be difficult. She was wrong. It was worse than difficult. It hurt. She was prepared to see things that would make her lament the loss of her old life. She was prepared for that. What she didn't expect to have to deal with were the smells. Stepping into her kitchen, she was met with a wave of familiarity that had everything to do with the normal smells of her house. It immediately brought her back to the times she ran in the back door after playing ball, looking for her mom and the cookies she knew would be baking. Courtney thought she recognized the faint, familiar smells of those sweet cookies, and she was hit with a sad wave of nostalgia for a time that would never again exist. Once her head went there, it was tough to stay focused. What bothered her most was the notion that her parents must have thought she was dead. She had been gone for over three months. Were they still searching for her? Or had she become a "cold case"? It bothered Courtney to know that her parents were going through such grief. Her older brothers as well. She hoped her brothers had come home to spend some time with their mom and dad and deal with it all as a family.

Courtney's heart ached knowing that she would never be part of that family again. At that moment, she had a fleeting thought of calling it all off and staying at home. For good. It would have been so easy for her to walk up the stairs, throw open her bedroom door, and crawl into bed.

"It's tough," Mark said with sympathy. He knew.

All Courtney did was nod. She quickly wiped away a tear and declared, "Let's get this over with."

She led Mark through the kitchen and into the living room, making a beeline toward the stairs while trying not to focus on anything that might affect her again. She didn't want to see the family pictures. Or the artwork she did as a child that was still hanging in the living room. She *really* didn't want to see the dado cat or anything else that might stop her from completing her mission.

It didn't work out that way. When Courtney entered the living room, she froze. Mark stood still behind her, just as stunned. What she saw wasn't a fond memory of the past, it was something she feared was a taste of the future.

"Oh man," she gasped.

Hanging over the fireplace was a large star.

"I guess I don't have to ask if this was here when you left," Mark said.

"Whatever that is," Courtney said softly, "my family is part of it now."

Courtney stared at the star a moment, then turned away, headed back toward the kitchen.

"Forget it," she said abruptly. "I gotta get out of here. I'll find some other clothes."

Before she could take a second step, the front door of the house flew open, smashing against the wall. The sound was so loud it made them both jump in surprise. They spun to see five men enter quickly. They all wore dark red clothing and small-brimmed red caps.

One man, who seemed to be the leader, called out, "Don't move, please."

"Like hell!" Courtney shouted, and ran for the kitchen.

Mark was right behind her. They sprinted for the back door, but before Courtney could grab it, that door flew open as well.

"Ahh!" Courtney screamed.

More men poured in. They were dressed the same as the others, only these men were holding something over their faces, like masks. Courtney took a swing at the first guy. The man ducked it easily. She wound up for another punch, too late. The next man through the door held up a small canister.

"Look out!" Mark yelled to Courtney.

She didn't. The man sprayed something in her face, hitting her with a thick, wet mist. Courtney thought it smelled like lemons. A second later her world twisted. She glanced back to see Mark on his back. He had gotten an even bigger whiff of the lemons. Courtney fell to her knees, beginning to lose consciousness. She looked up at the intruders with the fleeting thought that her parents couldn't be involved with these monsters. How could they be?

She had one more thought before folding. The man who held up the canister had a star tattooed on his arm. She wondered if her parents were tattooed as well.

Her cheek hit the floor and she was gone.

JOURNAL #34

IBARA

It feels strange to write these words, but I have to because, well, they are the truth.

Mark, Courtney, I am having an amazingly great time. I guess I'm feeling kind of guilty about it, because I shouldn't be having so much fun when you consider that the reason I'm here is because of a brutal war and the near destruction of a territory. Maybe Saint Dane is right. You've got to break something down before you can rebuild.

Whoa. Did I just write that? Did I actually agree with something Saint Dane said? Oh great. There's something else to feel guilty about. But not really. This is different. Saint Dane's plan for the destruction of Ibara was intentional. He was trying to bring it about. I'm just dealing with the end result of events that were beyond my control. I'm coming from a completely different place. I guess you could say that I'm trying to make the best of it, and it's working out pretty well.

I suppose "fun" isn't the best word to describe what I'm doing. I've actually been working really hard. Cleaning up the wreckage of Rayne was grueling. I wrote all about that before. Every last person who lives in Rayne did their part, and we were left with a clean slate. The beach was clear. We saved many of the beautiful palm trees. Tribunal Mountain was intact. What followed was the rebuilding of a village.

I won't go into all the details of the work because it was extensive. Rayne may have been a simple fishing village built on a quiet tropical bay, but it was surprisingly sophisticated. As much as the tribunal didn't want to repeat the mistakes of the past and become slaves to technology, some of the more rudimentary elements of civilization were used once again. Pipes were replaced to bring running water back through the village. The simple power grid needed repair so that each new hut would have light. The communication system was intact because it was powered from Tribunal Mountain. There were engineers who maintained each of those systems, and oversaw their rebuilding.

My crew worked on rebuilding the huts. For me it was the best job, because the results were tangible. After a hard day's work we had an actual, physical structure to show for it. Simple as that. I guess it was symbolic as much as anything, but seeing these structures begin to dot the sand gave me the gratification of knowing I was working to make something real. Maybe guilt played in there a little bit as well. I was the one who brought the tak to Ibara that destroyed the village in the first place. Of course, it would have been worse if Saint Dane had his way, but still. I had a hand in leveling the place, and now I'm having a very big hand in rebuilding it. It's an awesome feeling to do something so positive. There are no downsides here. I'm feeling great.

Another good thing is that the people of Rayne seem to like me. I'm no longer considered a mysterious outsider. I'm one of them. They trust me and follow me. I'm in charge of many workers, and they could easily blow me off, but they haven't. I think I'm a good leader. I try to be fair and spread the workload, and I never ask somebody to do something I wouldn't do myself. I think they respect that. It's keeping me in great shape, too. I'm putting on some serious muscle. That'll happen when you're lugging around lengths of building materials all day.

Genj and the others on the tribunal are always asking my opinions on things too. Genj in particular. He's always telling me how glad he is that I'm there and what a great job I'm doing. More than once he's said that he doesn't know where they would be if I hadn't come to Ibara. I believe it was that feeling that led them to do something that took me by surprise. Even as I'm writing this, I'm having trouble believing what happened.

One evening, at the end of the workday, I was summoned from the job site to the mountain for an audience with the tribunal. That's what the security guy called it: "an audience." Up until that point my relationship with Genj and Moman and Drea had been pretty informal. Even though they were the big bosses, they always treated me as an equal. More or less. The fact that I was being summoned for an audience suddenly felt kind of official. Ominous even. As I walked toward that meeting, I kept racking my brain trying to figure out what I might have done wrong.

I entered the mountain and climbed the stone stairs that led to the vast cavern that was the tribunal's meeting place. The closer I got, the more nervous I became. What had I done? What had gone wrong? I reached the floor and saw the three members of the tribunal sitting behind their desk, looking seriously formal. They wore the same simple light green clothing with long sleeves and pants that they had worn the day I first met them. That was a surprise, because for the last few months they had been dressing exactly like everyone else in Rayne. They were working hard too, and they dressed for it in work clothes. Now they were looking all sorts of official. Gulp. I walked forward, uncertain. It was like a wall had descended between us. Just that morning we were talking and kidding like friends. Now I was being called to the principal's office. I stood in front of them without saying a word. Genj, Drea, and Moman stared back at me, expressionless. I wanted to break the tension and shout, "Guys? What the heck?" I didn't. I'm learning to keep my mouth shut.

Finally, after enough time had gone by so that my armpits were totally soaked with nervous sweat, Genj said, "Pendragon, do you know why you're here?"

Swell. A quiz. Did he mean did I know why I was standing in front of them feeling awkward and sweaty, or did I know why I was on Ibara? I didn't know the answer to the first question and didn't want to answer the second.

"No." Can't go wrong with that answer.

Drea continued, "We've been observing you closely since the day you arrived on Ibara and were attacked by the swarm of bees."

Right. The quig-bees. I'd almost forgotten about that. Or maybe I forced it out of my head.

"As you know, we do not welcome outsiders," Moman continued. "But you knew of our dear, lost Remudi. We originally decided to let you stay, on the chance you might help us learn what had happened to him."

I knew exactly what had happened to him. He was the Traveler from Ibara. Saint Dane killed him during a Tato match on Quillan. As much as they wanted to know what had become of their former tribunal member, they would never learn that particular truth.

"Unfortunately," Moman added, "we still do not know of his fate."

I nodded sympathetically and said, "I wish I could help you." It was the truth. I really did wish I could help. But I couldn't. Or wouldn't.

"At first you had us worried, Pendragon," Genj said. "Especially when you put in with Siry and his band of Jakills."

"If not for the Jakills," I interrupted, "we never would have known of the dado attack. We owe them all a debt of gratitude."

I shouldn't have said anything. This was their show, but I couldn't stand there and let them disrespect the Jakills. Ibara was still around because of them. I guess I hadn't learned to keep my mouth shut after all.

"Indeed," Drea said. "We never understood Siry and his friends. Perhaps we should have listened to them a bit more attentively. Sometimes we equate youth with ignorance. It is a failing that comes with age, and of that we are guilty."

Oh.

"Which brings us to the point of this audience," Genj interjected. "As much as we owe the Jakills a debt of gratitude, it is a debt we also owe you. You saved our home. You saved Veelox. We wish that Siry and your friend Alder could be here to hear this as well. Not only did you guide us in the battle, but since then you have proven to be a valuable ally in the rebuilding of Rayne. We don't know why you have adopted Ibara, but we are certainly glad that you did."

I had to smile. They had brought me there to thank me.

Though I wasn't sure why they were being so formal about it. All they had to do was say "thanks" and I'd be happy.

"What are your plans?" Moman asked. "Will you be leaving us?"

Huge question. They had no idea that I had come from another territory in another time. For all they knew, I was planning on taking a boat and sailing back to wherever it was I had come from in the first place. They didn't know I had nowhere to go and my boat was buried under a few thousand tons of rubble.

"I can't go back home," I told them honestly. "The reasons for that are too complicated to explain. Even if I could, I'm not so sure I'd go. Rayne is my home now. I want to do what I can to help rebuild it. But that won't take forever. I think that once the village is rebuilt, we can look to the future and start building another fleet of pilgrim ships. Veelox is still waiting. There's an entire world to bring back from the dead, not just a single island. I want to be around to see that."

All three tribunal members exchanged looks, and smiles.

"That is what we hoped to hear," Genj said. "Given how hard you've been working, we aren't surprised. Still, we needed to hear it. Seeing as this is the decision you have made, we'd like to inform you of a decision we have made, along with many other village leaders."

As if on cue, people started walking into the large chamber. They had been listening to this conversation from the tunnels surrounding the cavern. Everyone was dressed in the same formal clothing that the tribunal wore. I was suddenly feeling kind of cheesy in my sweaty work clothes. In all, there were around thirty people, many of whom I recognized as leaders of various groups within Rayne. There were engineers, musicians, doctors, architects, security people, and pretty much every leader of every important group on the island. Telleo was there too. She stepped behind her father with a broad grin. What the heck was going on?

Genj stood and looked me right in the eye.

"We have been discussing this for quite some time," he began. "The vote was unanimous. There has been a vacant chair on the tribunal of Rayne since Remudi left. It needs to be filled. We would be honored if you took that seat. You have earned it, Pendragon. Will you help lead Rayne and Ibara into the future?"

To say I was stunned would be an understatement. These people were asking me to become one of the four leaders of the village. Of Ibara. And for all practical purposes, of Veelox.

They had brought the idea up once before, but I didn't take it too seriously. It was right after the battle and everybody was caught up in the excitement of victory. I thought it was just one of those things that you say in the moment, but don't really mean. And since nobody had mentioned it since, I forgot all about it. Until then. There was no mistake. They were serious. They wanted me on the tribunal.

So many thoughts flashed through my head. Could I do this? I was only a kid. Eighteen years old, I think. Who knows? I haven't blown out a birthday candle in a bunch of years. Of course, I'd seen more things in those years than most people see in a lifetime, and that included the people who now sat on the tribunal.

I truly didn't know how to answer. I looked at Telleo. She smiled and gave me a nod of encouragement. She wanted me to accept the offer. I think it was seeing her that made things come clear for me. It suddenly seemed as if everything that had happened could very well have been leading to this. Maybe this was my destiny as a Traveler. I had battled Saint Dane on eight different territories. Maybe the battle for Ibara was actually the final battle for Halla. Saint Dane threw everything at the small island, and lost. Now he was trapped here. It made me think that I had done the exact right thing in burying the flume. I had ended Saint Dane's reign of terror. Now I was in a position to start picking up the pieces. Suddenly everything felt right. I was in the right place. This was the way it was meant to be.

"I would be honored," I said, bowing my head in respect.

A cheer went up from the crowd. Everyone applauded. Telleo ran around the desk and gave me a hug. While we were hugging, I shook Genj's hand, then Moman's, and Drea's. It was incredible. I was officially one of the leaders of a village. Of a territory. Its future was in my hands; I wasn't about to fail. It was the best feeling in the world.

What made it all the better was that life didn't change all that much once I had been elected to the tribunal. It wasn't like I suddenly had to get all serious and attend meetings and wear stiff clothes and give speeches or anything. Just the opposite. My relationship with the tribunal was pretty loose. They'd ask my advice and I'd offer my opinions. Sometimes we'd debate over things, like whether we should build another common celebration area before tackling the next ring of homes. Or if we should push deeper into the jungle with our construction, which would allow for larger huts. It was easy. I still got to lead my group of builders and got my satisfaction from that. The only real difference was that Twig and Krayven started kidding me about being on the tribunal and being one of "them," but it was all in fun.

No, it was more than that. In some ways this was the ultimate victory that the Jakills sought. They wanted the truth. They wanted their voices to be heard by the tribunal. Now their thoughts and concerns were very much on the tribunal's plate, through me. I wished that Siry could know that. I wished that all the Jakills who lost their lives could know.

Many of the debates I had with the tribunal were during meals. I had lots of dinners with Genj and Telleo. We'd talk about the day's work and the troubles and successes we were having. The conversation usually went to things like what we should do in the future. Rearming the water guns for the protection of Ibara was important. There was no telling if the Flighters would stage another attack. We talked about creating an additional security force to concentrate more on threats from off the island. It was exciting to know we were making decisions that would impact the future of an entire civilization.

There were problems, of course. It wasn't all perfect. The work was hard and there were many injuries. Telleo assembled a medical force and supervised the doctors to care for everyone as best as they could.

Like I said, I was pretty close to Genj and Telleo. They had become my second family. But it wasn't without a little weirdness. There were a few times when I got the feeling that Telleo wanted our relationship to be a little more than the brother-sister thing we had going on. It usually happened when we were sitting on our perch, high above the jungle. A few times she held my hand. That was okay. It was all innocent. But still, I didn't feel comfortable holding my sister's hand. A few times she looked up at me, right in the eyes, and I thought for sure she was going to lean in for a kiss. I usually coughed and changed the subject. I didn't want to embarrass her or anything. I really liked Telleo. But I didn't want things to get weird. There was too much going on to be thinking that way. You know, about having a girlfriend. Especially with a girl who was the daughter of the guy I sat on the tribunal with. There were too many things that could go sour.

Besides, I had already tried that once with Loor. I still have such strong feelings for Loor, but she made it very clear that as long as we were in the middle of this battle with Saint Dane, a serious romantic-type relationship was dumb. No, it was impossible. Of course, I couldn't help but wonder what would have happened between her and me now that the war was over. Would we ever see each other again? If we did, would we still have the same feelings? The main thing we had in common was the fight against Saint Dane. Now that that was over, would we have anything to talk about? I guess it doesn't really matter. We won't get the chance.

Telleo was a whole different issue. We *were* together. Though even with all the practical stuff aside, I just didn't feel "that way" about her. Problem is that I think she felt "that way" about me. The best I could hope for was that it wouldn't become too tricky. I didn't want to have to have one of those "we're just friends" conversations because the truth was that we were more than just friends. We were really close. But in a way different from what I think she wanted.

Another strange thing happened, and I'm not sure what it means. I was alone with Genj one night after a long day of work. I was beat. I mean, really beat. Genj was talking about the fishing fleet and how we should start moving some of the fishermen who had been building homes or dumping dado parts back onto the boats to start fishing again. He was right. It made sense. But I was too tired to care. My eyelids kept drooping. I mention that because I wasn't thinking and said something I regret. I blame it on the fact that I was too tired to think straight. Or that I'm an idiot.

Remember I told you how I've been avoiding any talk about the past, only because I didn't want to have to talk about mine? Well, Genj was talking about the fishing fleet and about how much his wife, whose name was Sharr by the way, loved a particular kind of fish that was rare because it didn't run that often. It was the first time I had heard Genj mention his wife. I knew from the other tribunal members that she had died years before. Some sort of illness that I didn't ask too much about. Telleo cared for her until the end. Moman told me it was Telleo's experience with her mother that had turned her into a healer. So I knew what happened to Sharr, but I never brought her up with Genj. I figured it was a tough subject, so I didn't go near it. Until that night. Without thinking, I asked, "How come Telleo didn't get along with her mother?"

Genj sat up straight. I did too. Suddenly I wasn't so sleepy anymore. What had I said? I wanted to grab the words out of the air and shove them back into my head. I didn't say anything. I had to prepare for damage control.

"Telleo and Sharr were as close as any mother and daughter could be," Genj said with authority. "They were more like sisters. When Sharr passed, Telleo was devastated. I didn't think she'd come around, but she's a strong girl. She loved her mother very much. Why would you think they didn't get along?"

There was no way I was going to tell him that Telleo said she and her mother had problems. It was pretty obvious that there had been more going on between those two than Genj realized. Maybe they kept it from him. Whatever. It wasn't my business, and I didn't want to spoil his memories, even if they weren't entirely accurate.

"I must be wrong," I said quickly. "Telleo doesn't like to talk about her mother, and I thought that was because they had problems. I see it's just because she misses her."

Genj nodded sadly. He bought my explanation. I wasn't so sure I bought it though. I was learning more about Genj's family than I wanted to know, and things didn't quite add up. I decided that it was best left alone. The subject didn't come up again.

I haven't added to my journal in a few weeks, mostly because nothing journal-worthy was happening. Work on Rayne continued. The village was slowly taking shape. All was well. I wish I could find the right words to describe how satisfying it all was, but I think you get it. It all felt so right. . . .

Until something very wrong happened. The irony is, it began with something wonderful. Amazing, in fact. No, impossible. I'm not completely sure what to make of it yet. It was an event that can be best described as "a miracle." I'm serious. But along with the joy came a dark cloud. As I write this now, I still don't know how dark it will get. But I will know, and soon.

We had been working really hard. My crew was exhausted. It was hot. Hotter than usual. It was midday and we had put the finishing touches on yet another hut. By that afternoon a family would be moving in. That was always cause for celebration. Since we had been working so hard, and there were only a few hours left in the day, I gave my guys the rest of the afternoon off. I told them to relax. Go for a swim. Take a nap. Anything. They had been doing a great job and deserved it.

There was another reason why I wanted the afternoon off. I wanted to go to the flume site. As I've written before, I'd been down there several times just to make sure it was definitely, positively out of reach. Each time, that was confirmed. Then days would pass and I'd begin to wonder again. On that particular afternoon the nagging little feeling started tickling my brain again. It was time to pay another visit to confirm what I already knew. What can I say? I'm obsessive. I'll probably be checking the flume for the rest of my life.

I walked to the beach alone. The new huts hadn't gotten close to the shore yet. It would be months before we broke ground on the outermost circle of Rayne. I had the beach to myself. I walked along the shore, feeling anxious. More so than anytime before. I looked up into the sky to see if there were any ravens circling. All I saw were puffy white clouds. I was alone. I got to the rocks that led up to the mound that covered the flume, and climbed. The last time I had done that, Saint Dane was waiting for me on top. I didn't want a repeat performance. I climbed anxiously and popped my head up over the edge to see . . .

Nothing. No evil demons in sight. Big relief. I climbed up onto the flat summit and kicked around a few rocks. I didn't know what I was looking for. A hole that might lead down to the flume? A crack that could be worked on and opened up? A staircase? An elevator? I had no idea, and ended up finding the exact same thing I'd found on every trip—nothing. The flume was sealed tight.

I turned to begin the climb back down and finally did see something that was out of the ordinary. It was floating about a hundred yards offshore. It had already made its way through the two fingers of land that nearly enclosed the Bay of Rayne, and it was headed toward the village. At first I thought it was a small boat that one of the fishermen had taken out, but it was too small for that. The shape was all wrong too. It wasn't a boat. It took a few seconds for me to realize what I was looking at.

It was a skimmer. The same kind of skimmer that Saint Dane had brought from Cloral by the thousands to transport the dados from Rubic City to attack Rayne. I stood staring at the craft, trying to understand why it was there. It wasn't under power, that much was clear. It was drifting in the current, moving closer to shore. I thought that it might have been one of the skimmers that we had scuttled out at sea when we dumped all the wreckage from the beach. Maybe it had somehow floated to the surface and was now a piece of loose debris that we would need to haul back out.

I was wrong. As the craft got closer, I saw that someone was on board. At least I thought it was someone. It was hard to tell. Skimmer pilots controlled the craft while standing up. Whoever was on that skimmer was definitely not standing. In fact, they looked as if they were lying out flat on the deck. Whoever or whatever it was, it wasn't controlling the skimmer.

I quickly scrambled down the rocks. The whole way down I feared what I might find. Was it another dado that had somehow gotten lost and was only now showing up for the battle? Was it a Flighter who was making an attempt to land on Ibara? Was this something we should be afraid of, or just another piece of carnage left over from the battle? I had to force myself to stop worrying and concentrate on climbing down the steep rocks. Falling would have been dumb. And painful.

I hit the sand and ran the rest of the way to the water. The craft was about fifty yards offshore. I could now see that there was a body on board, facedown. It didn't look like a dado. The hair was too long. Dados didn't have long hair. Robot hair didn't grow. I figured it must have been a Flighter. Whoever it was, the guy was in bad shape. Or dead. I was torn. Should I go out and drag the thing to shore? I didn't want to be helping anyone who might cause trouble. But there was only one person aboard. Flighters traveled in packs, like wolves. It might not have been a Flighter, but somebody from Rayne who somehow got cast adrift. One thing was sure: If the person was alive, they needed help. I decided to risk it. I ran into the water and did the crawl out to the craft, always keeping my head above water and my eyes on the skimmer. Junior Lifeguard training never leaves you.

The closer I got, the more detail I could make out, but I still couldn't tell if it was a guy or a girl. Whoever it was had long blond hair. Their clothes were in shreds. There was a definite Flighter vibe going on. I suddenly felt vulnerable. If this was a trick, the Flighter could easily jump up, gun the engine, and run me over. I stopped about five yards away and treaded water.

"Hello?" I called. "You okay?"

The body stirred.

"Can you talk?" I called.

The victim lifted his chin. The blond hair fell in front of his face. He twisted his head, as if trying to understand where my voice was coming from.

"Who are you?" I called.

The person on the skimmer yelled out a word that I can only describe as somewhere between a hoarse croak and a cry of agony.

"Help," he called.

I didn't hesitate a second more and swam for the craft. It may have been a trap, but so what? I grabbed on to the side rails and looked up at the horrible, sunburned face.

"Who are you?" I called.

The guy could barely move. He reached up a hand and pushed the blond hair away from one eye. A lifeless eye. He was blind. His face was blistered. It was a hideous sight. I had no idea who the poor guy was.

"Did I make it?" he asked hoarsely.

"I don't know," I said. "Where are you trying to go?"

The guy smiled. I think I had answered his question.

"Pendragon," he gasped with obvious relief.

I froze. He had recognized my voice. He knew me.

"Where else would I want to go but home to Ibara?" he croaked.

It was when he said the word "home" that the truth hit me. It was impossible. It couldn't be. But it was.

"Loque?" I asked in dismay.

The guy nodded. I couldn't move. Loque was dead. I saw him die in a crushing avalanche of shattered glass. Yet he was there, lying on the skimmer. Back home.

Alive.

I looked into his dead eye. He nodded. My heart hurt.

It actually hurt. There were so many emotions going on. I had to fight off both laughing and crying. He pulled himself over to the edge of the craft until his lips were right next to my ear and whispered the few words that I really didn't want to hear.

"They're coming."

It took every last bit of gas in his tank to say those words. Once the message was delivered, he passed out.

JOURNAL #34

(CONTINUED)

IBARA

Loque was alive. Barely. I wasn't sure if I should be happy or terrified. The idea of the Jakill making it all the way back to Ibara only to die within sight of shore was unthinkable. And what did he mean by "They're coming"? Who was coming? When? Why? It didn't sound like a good thing. I didn't think Loque would fight to stay alive just to deliver a casual message that some friendly folks were going to drop in for a visit.

"Loque!" I cried, shaking him. "Who's coming?"

He didn't budge. He was gone. With one hand I grabbed the edge of the skimmer. With the other I paddled furiously toward shore. Within minutes I hit the beach and dragged the craft onto the sand. A quick check for a pulse told me he was still with me. But for how long?

"Help!" I screamed, hoping somebody was within earshot. "Somebody!"

I was lucky. Or rather Loque was lucky. A young kid was wandering toward the beach to fish. I waved him over. When he got close enough to hear me, I yelled, "We need a doctor."

The kid stood staring at me, his eyes wide.

"Now!" I shouted, shocking him into action. He sprinted back toward the village.

I waited for help to come, not sure of what to do. His heart was beating, so he didn't need CPR. All I could do was make him comfortable. I thought back to what had happened with Loor in the caves below Zadaa. She was dead. A sword had been driven through her heart. But I held her in my arms and willed her to stay alive. It was a ridiculously desperate thing to do, except for the fact that it worked. Loor somehow survived with no injuries. To this day I don't know how that happened. Could I do it again? I put my hand over Loque's heart, but had no idea how to go about healing somebody. I closed my eyes and repeated to myself, "Don't die, don't die, don't die."

The good news is that he didn't die on that beach, but I don't think it had anything to do with me. There was no miraculous recovery. No instant healing. If anything, his heartbeat grew fainter. That meant that whatever happened with Loor, it wasn't because I had magical healing power. The mystery of why she came back to life would continue.

It wasn't long before several men and women came running toward us from the village. I recognized one as a doctor that Telleo worked with. Man, what a relief. Loque had a chance. An hour later he was lying in a cavern medical room in the base of Tribunal Mountain. I waited outside to get a report on how he was doing. Between the doctors and Telleo, I knew he was in good hands. If he had any chance of surviving, these were the guys who would pull him through. It was torture sitting alone, waiting for news. All the memories of that nightmare in Rubic City came back to me.

Loque was Siry's best friend. I guess you could call him

the second-in-command of the Jakills. Siry was the leader of the young rebels and didn't want anything to do with me, or with being a Traveler. It was Loque who calmed Siry down. He was the strong voice of reason to the tightly wound, angry Siry. If not for Loque, Siry might never have accepted his role as a Traveler, which led to the saving of Ibara. Loque was a hero, which made the memories of that horrible day all the more painful. Twig had been captured by the Flighters. Siry, Loque, and I were on the run. We hid in the ruins of a massive cathedral-like structure with Flighters swarming all around us. When we thought they were gone, it was Loque who took it upon himself to scout around, to see if it was safe for us to come out of hiding. I'll never forget seeing him standing in front of that massive wall of stained-glass and noticing the ominous shadow outside. The cannon. We realized what was happening, but too late. The Flighters shot the glass wall, shattering it into a billion pieces that rained down on Loque.

How could he have survived that? The only one who could answer that question was Loque, and he was barely clinging to life. The guy deserved to live. His sacrifice and vision helped save Ibara. He was a brave and loyal friend. For me, I wanted there to be one less victim of Saint Dane's vicious crusade.

I had been waiting around for a few hours, writing my journal, when Telleo finally came to talk to me.

"It doesn't look good," she said sadly. "He was in surgery for a long time. He's lost a lot of blood. Being exposed to the elements out on the water didn't help. He's totally burned."

"His eyes?" I asked.

"I don't know," Telleo said somberly. "Losing his vision may be the least of his troubles."

"When will we know?" I asked.

"Every moment he stays alive, his chances for survival increase" was Telleo's professional answer. "We'll see if he makes it through the night, and then reevaluate in the morning."

She sat down and put her arm around me. I didn't fight her. She clicked out of professional mode and into friend mode. "This is hard, especially with Siry gone," she said with compassion. "I know how much Loque meant to him."

"Loque helped save Ibara," I said.

"We'll do all we can to save him," Telleo assured me.

She held me tighter. I think she wanted me to hug her back, so I gave her a quick hug, but then pulled away and stood up. Telleo seemed a little surprised but didn't say anything.

"Can I see him?" I asked.

"He's sleeping. Better not disturb him."

I nodded. "Okay. I'll be back in the morning. I'm glad you're here for him, Telleo. Siry would be happy about that."

Telleo smiled. "I did all I could for the Jakills. You know that."

I nodded, and left Tribunal Mountain to find a quiet spot near the beach to lie down and sleep. There was nothing I could do to help Loque. Knowing that he was in good hands, my mind went to the two words he'd said to me.

"They're coming."

Two simple words. What did they mean? Should I be worried? Or should I dismiss them as the fevered ramblings of a very sick guy? It was yet another reason why I didn't want Loque to die. I had to know what he meant. I don't know how long I lay there under the stars, rolling the possibilities around in my head. At some point I know I fell asleep, but that's only because in the middle of the night I was suddenly shaken awake.

"Pendragon!" a frantic voice called. "Wake up! It's Loque!"

I forced myself back to reality and looked up into the wild eyes of Twig.

"What?" I mumbled. "Is he awake?"

"He's dying!" she shouted, and ran back toward Tribunal Mountain.

I was running before I was awake. I passed Twig and sprinted up the sand path toward the mountain. The village was asleep. Good thing. If anybody got in my way, I would have knocked 'em down. I ran into the cave at the base of the mountain and sprinted through the tunnels, directly to the medical area. People were hurrying in and out of the cavern room where Loque was staying. Something was happening. I didn't wait to get permission. I barged right in. Twig followed close behind.

Loque was surrounded by several medical people, including Telleo. He was leaning over the bed, being held up by two of the stronger-looking guys. I don't know how else to say this so I'll just say it straight out: He was puking. I mean seriously puking. Telleo had a hand on his forehead as his entire body shuddered with each heave.

"It's okay," Telleo said to him soothingly. "Let it go. You'll feel better."

Another doctor walked in. I grabbed him and said, "What happened?"

"Overdose" was the answer. "It's a good thing one of the nurses checked on him. He was convulsing. We've induced the vomiting to clear out what we can. This is the last thing he needed."

Overdose. How could that have happened? The poor guy was clinging to life. He relied on these doctors. To die because of getting too much medication was just . . . wrong.

After a few minutes Loque's puking turned into the dry heaves. His stomach was empty, but his mind didn't know it.

"Let's lay him down," Telleo instructed the others.

The medical personnel got him back onto the pillow. He lay on his back, breathing hard. Telleo looked across the room. We made eye contact. She shook her head gravely.

"Stay with him," she ordered another one of the nurses, and went for the door.

"You too," I said to Twig.

I followed Telleo and caught her outside.

"What happened?" I demanded.

Telleo looked as shaken as I felt. "I don't know," she said nervously. "Wrong dosage. Wrong medicine. It could have been anything."

"That's not good enough, Telleo!" I bellowed. "He deserves better than that."

"I know!" Telleo shouted in tears. "I'm going to stay with him. Nobody will touch him but me. I'll double-check everything the doctors do from now on."

"Will there be a 'from now on'?" I asked.

"We may have purged him in time. I can't say for sure."

This time I didn't leave the mountain. I sat outside of Loque's door and slept right there. If something was going to happen to him, I wanted to be close. I sent Twig home. There was no sense in both of us sleeping on rock. I was angry. Loque had been through hell. Mistakes can happen, but it didn't seem fair that after all that, he should die because somebody made a dumb mistake. I wished there was somebody I could yell at, but nobody knew who was responsible. They said that it could have been anybody, or a combination of people. Or or or—it didn't matter. Between Telleo and me, we were going to make sure that Loque was taken care of properly. Everything would be double-checked and second-guessed. How could they say no to me? I was on the tribunal!

I spent the rest of the night dozing in front of Loque's doorway. The floor was hard rock. The wall was hard rock. There was nothing comfortable about it, but I wasn't going to move. Whenever somebody tried to go into the room, I immediately woke up and asked what they were going to do. Some gave him medicine. Others were just checking to make sure he was okay. When morning came, I didn't know it. I was out cold. Literally. The rock floor was freezing. It didn't matter. I probably would have slept for a few more hours if one of the nurses hadn't gently shaken me awake.

"Huh?" I gurgled.

"He wants to talk to you," she said softly.

"What? Who?"

"Who do you think?" she said with a smile.

The smile gave it away. I took a deep breath, rubbed my face, and jumped up to go inside. Loque was lying flat on his back. He didn't look any more awake than he had on the beach. Had I just dreamed that the nurse asked me to come in?

"Pendragon?" came a hoarse whisper.

I ran to the side of the bed, my heart racing. "Don't talk," I said.

"I'm tired of not talking," Loque said. "Can you give me a drink of water?"

I looked to the nurse who stood at the foot of the bed.

She nodded. I thought she was going to cry. I wasn't sure if they were tears of joy, or grief that the guy was on his way out. I grabbed a small cup from the side of the bed and held it to his lips. Loque took a few small sips, coughed, but got most of it down.

"Thanks." The little bit of water helped to clear his voice.

Loque had bandages over his eyes. His skin looked just as nasty and red as I'd remembered. The blisters from the sunburn were gruesome and painful looking. But he was alive. For how long I didn't know. I struggled for words to say to him. There was so much I needed to know. All I got out was one simple question: "How?"

"You mean how come I'm not dead?"

I nodded, then realized he couldn't see me. Idiot. "Yes," I answered.

"Luck."

I glanced back to the nurse. She didn't need to hear any of this. "Can I talk to him alone?" I asked. The nurse hesitated, but she wasn't about to say no to a member of the tribunal. It's good to be a boss. She nodded and left.

I turned back to Loque. "The Flighters shot a cannon into the stained-glass wall," I said, bringing us both back to the moment of truth.

"I figured it was something like that," Loque whispered. "All I knew was that the whole world exploded. I looked up to see colors raining down on me. I wish I hadn't."

He slowly lifted his hand and touched one of his bandaged eyes. I winced. I couldn't even imagine what that must have felt like.

"Good morning!" came Telleo's bright greeting as she stepped into the room. "Glad to see you back with us." She joined me by the bedside and did a quick check of Loque's vital signs. "How do you feel?"

Loque growled, "Like I've been trampled by a herd of animals and left out in the sun for a week."

"That good?" I asked.

Telleo gave me a look that said I shouldn't be making jokes. "Let's not stress him," she said to me.

"We need to talk," I protested.

"We really need to talk," Loque echoed.

"There's plenty of time for that," Telleo scolded. "It looks like you're going to be with us for a while."

She took my arm and led me out of the room.

"But—"

"Let him sleep, Pendragon."

I looked over my shoulder and called, "Welcome home. I'll be back later."

"I'll be here," Loque said softly. I think he fell back to sleep. Telleo was right. He needed the rest.

Once we got outside the room, Telleo was all smiles.

"It's good, right?" I asked. "He made it through the night."

"It's a very good sign," she said. "No guarantees, but he's got a better chance than we thought. You should go somewhere and get some rest too. You're a mess."

I pulled away from her and sat down right in front of Loque's doorway. "No chance," I replied.

"Pendragon," she scolded. "You won't help him by staying here. The doctors will be by soon, and I'm perfectly capable of caring for him."

"And I'm perfectly capable of hanging around," I said. "Give up. I'm not leaving."

"Do what you want," she snapped, and walked off in a huff.

She was ticked. I wasn't sure why she should be so angry that I was staying there, but it didn't matter. I wasn't moving until I knew that Loque was definitely going to get well . . . and until he told me all that had happened back in Rubic City, and what he meant when he said, "They're coming."

I settled myself in to wait on that freakin' hard, rock floor for as long as it would take. Loque deserved nothing less.

JOURNAL #34

(CONTINUED)

IBARA

I knew I was dead," Loque said. "Or would be soon."

It wasn't until later that afternoon that the doctors allowed me to talk to Loque again. He'd slept most of that day, only waking up to eat a little and drink some juice. The food was helping him get strength back. He could sit up. Things were looking good. I think the doctors wanted to wait another day before letting him talk. I know Telleo wasn't happy about it. I guess they were afraid he'd get all worked up or something. But Loque insisted. He wanted to tell me what had happened, and I was all too happy to listen. Sort of. I sat next to his bed, alone. Telleo wanted to stay, but I wouldn't let her. I had no idea what Loque was going to talk about. We had seen things in Rubic City that most of the people of Rayne knew nothing about. It would be better to keep it that way.

"The shattered glass was coming down on top of me," he continued. "There was no place to run, so I just stood there, waiting for the end. I felt a rumble and suddenly I was falling. The floor had collapsed under my feet. I don't know how far I fell. Twenty feet? I landed hard and crumpled, but I still had focus. I knew that the glass was coming down, so I rolled. I didn't know how much of the floor had given way, but I hoped I could get under a section that hadn't collapsed. It was the right move, because the bulk of the glass didn't hit me. It landed on the section of floor above. For one brief second I thought I had escaped. Then the floor above me collapsed. The weight of the glass was too much."

"A section of floor fell on you?" I asked in horror.

"With the weight of the glass on top of that. It felt as if I were being crushed, but it was better than being shredded."

I laughed. I know, it was a weird thing to do, but hearing the truth of what happened in that moment helped wipe away the nightmare memory I'd carried with me since the moment I heard the stained-glass wall explode. My version was a lot more gruesome. Loque laughed too. I'm not sure why we both thought it was funny. I guess it was some kind of relief.

"This isn't funny, you know," I said.

"I'm sure you thought I was done," he wheezed. "There were a couple of times I wished I was."

I stopped laughing.

"I lay there for a long time," he continued. "My eyes were burning. I wanted to open them to see where I was, but the only time they felt even a little okay was when they were closed. Didn't matter. It was pitch dark anyway. For all I knew, I was bleeding to death. I probably lay there for a couple of hours before I got the courage to move. I think it was the pain in my legs that finally got me going."

"How badly were they hurt?"

"I think they were broken. Both of them. Moving them

was more painful than I can describe. I had to drag myself out from under the rotted piece of floor and across a sea of broken glass. I moved an inch at a time. Every time I put my weight down, I had to be careful that it wasn't on something sharp. Didn't matter how cautious I was. It happened. A lot. I don't know how long it took to crawl out of the wreckage. It could have been days. Eventually I got myself to a piece of floor that was clear of glass."

He hesitated; the memory was tough to relive.

"You want to rest?" I asked.

"No," he said quickly. "I want you to know what happened in case I . . . " His voice trailed off.

"You're not going to die," I assured him.

"I wanted to, Pendragon. I really did. The pain was horrible. I was bleeding everywhere. My eyes burned. My legs ached. I found myself wishing the fall had killed me, because I was looking at a long, agonizing death."

"But you didn't die," I said.

"No. The Flighters found me," Loque continued. "I thought for sure they would kill me, but they had other plans. They carried me out of the basement into the city. The pain was unbearable. I think I passed out a couple of times. One positive thing, I realized, was that I hadn't lost my sight entirely." He touched the bandage over his right eye and said, "I can see light and shapes through this eye. My left eye is useless, but I'm not blind. I guess that's one thing to be grateful for."

"You've got a lot to be grateful for," I said softly. "You're alive."

"Funny, huh? It's all because of the Flighters. But they didn't help me out of kindness. They needed me."

"For what?"

"I wouldn't find that out for a while. They took me to this big, black triangle-looking structure. It didn't look anything like the other buildings."

I knew exactly what it was. It was a Lifelight pyramid, but I didn't want to get sidetracked onto that particular story train, so I didn't say anything.

"The place smelled like animals," he continued. "I guess that's not far from the truth, because it's where the Flighters lived. They laid me down on the floor in a dark corner with a group of sick and injured. It was horrible. I was put between people who were crying out in pain or coughing with disease. The putrid smell of infection is something I'll never forget. The only thing that kept me from going out of my mind was the will to see Ibara again. To see someplace green and clean. I told myself that I'd do all I could to stay alive, just to get back home."

"And you did."

"Not for a while. They barely spoke to me. Whenever I asked for something, they'd grunt and ignore me. But they fed me. I don't know what I ate, but it kept me alive. Sometimes there were bits of foul-smelling meat. I didn't want to know where it came from. Mostly they fed me some goo that wasn't horrible and gave me energy."

"Gloid," I said.

"What?"

"Never mind. Keep going."

"There was no medical care. My legs ached, but they didn't have anything to give me for that. I think their theory was they'd feed me for as long as I stayed alive. If I survived, fine. If not, nobody cared. There were plenty who weren't as lucky as I. Sometimes it was somebody lying right next to me. The only way I'd know they were gone was that their bodies went stiff. And cold. That's how close we were to one another. I could tell when they got cold. The Flighters would drag them off and replace them with somebody else who didn't stand much of a chance either."

"What did they need you for?" I asked. I wanted to get off the subject of death.

"I got my first clue when we were visited by a man. My vision wasn't good, especially there in the dark, but I could tell that he was tall. And clean. Whatever he was, he wasn't a Flighter. I don't know why, but the guy frightened me."

"Saint Dane," I said.

Loque sat forward in surprise. "You know this man?"

"What did he do?" I asked, ducking the question.

"He spoke to us. To all the sick and injured. His voice was cold, Pendragon. That's the only way I can describe it. He was talking to people who were in agony . . . a step away from death. Yet he showed no compassion. Who is he?"

"Somebody you don't want to mess with. What did he say?"

"He told us the only reason we were being kept alive was to be used as workers for his project. He said it didn't matter to him if we lived or died, but if we lived, we were going to work. If we weren't prepared for that, he told us to die quickly and make room for others."

My heart started to race. *Project*. What could that mean? Saint Dane was up to something. I tried not to let on to Loque that I had just stepped onto a road leading toward panic. He was dealing with enough.

"Did he say what the project was?" I asked, trying not to let my dancing nerves show.

"Not right away. That was the last I saw of him for a long time. I survived, obviously . . . and healed. Every second was torture, but my strength slowly returned. It was a miracle I didn't contract something deadly, or become infected, or get sick from the garbage they fed us. The pain never went away, but it subsided. My eyes stopped burning, and I had partial vision. It was better than nothing. I think that if I were totally blind, they would have stopped feeding me, and I would have been finished. They didn't want blind workers."

"Did you find out what the project was?" I asked.

I wanted to hear about Loque's recovery, but the fact that he was lying there in front of me meant that he had survived. I was much more worried about what Saint Dane was up to.

"Eventually I could stand and walk," he said. "It was painful, and it took a long time for the stiffness to go away, but at least I was mobile. I didn't want anything to do with that heartless guy and his project, so my plan was to try and escape. I figured I wouldn't be put to work until I was fully healed, but I was wrong. As soon as they saw that I could get around, they pulled me out of there. At first I was relieved. I figured nothing could be worse than that hellhole. I was wrong."

Loque took another sip of water. It was tough being patient. I needed to know what was going on in Rubic City. I sat quietly, waiting for him to drink and get the energy to continue.

"It's a mine," Loque finally said. "I think they're looking for precious gems or minerals. It's the only thing I can think of. There were hundreds of Flighters underground, digging through rock and rubble. There was no air and little light. They pushed me into this hole and told me to dig. With my hands. There were no tools. No shovels. I took my place in line behind other Flighters who were in worse shape than I. There was barely enough room to move. If you backed away or tried to rest, one of the supervising Flighters would beat you with a heavy stick. It was grueling, mindless work. My hands bled. They didn't even tell me what I was looking for. None of us really knew. We were just told to dig. And dig. I got to the point where I wished I hadn't survived the crashing glass, because I felt sure I would die in that claustrophobic mine.

The only thing that kept me going was the hope of escape. I organized a group of Flighters. They may be savages, but they're not dumb. They knew they would die down there. Our chance came one evening during the rest period. There was always a short window when the guards changed shifts. It was the same every night. We weren't watched during those times. That's when we made our escape. There were six of us. We found our way to the surface of the city and ran, before the next shift of guards showed up. I told them I had a ship in the harbor, and if they could get me there, I'd help them get away."

My heart sank. "The ship wasn't there, was it?"

"No," Loque answered. "The Flighters helped me get through the dark streets to the harbor, but the pilgrim ship was gone. I guess I shouldn't have been surprised. You all thought I was dead. There was no reason for the Jakills to wait for a ghost."

I knew I was going to have to tell Loque the truth about how the Flighters attacked the ship and sank it, killing most of the Jakills. But that would have to wait for another time.

"The Flighters had another idea. They told me about these small, fast ships that had been sitting near shore since before they were born. Nobody knew where they came from or why they were there. They brought me to a long pier, under which these boats were supposed to be stored. They told me there were thousands of them. When we climbed below, we saw that only a few remained. But that was okay—we didn't need many. We boarded three, two of us on each. They seemed easy to control. I sat on the back of one ship, waiting to head out to sea and wondering if I should bring those Flighters to Ibara. Turned out I didn't need to worry. The attack took care of that."

"Attack?"

"The Flighter guards came after us," Loque answered. "I thought they would try to recapture us, but I was wrong. They didn't want us back. I think it was more about making an example of us, so none of the other slave workers would try to escape. I didn't even know they had found us until the shooting started. They blasted us with these guns, probably the same kind of gun that destroyed the stained-glass wall. Two of the Flighters were hit instantly. Their ship exploded. I never saw them again. The other ship started off and it too got hit. The Flighters dove off at the last second. They may have survived. I don't know."

"And your ship?"

"The Flighter at the controls nearly got away. A shot was fired." Loque fell silent. I knew he was remembering the moment, and I didn't think it was a happy one. "The guy took the blast head-on. It knocked him clear off the little ship as if he were made of paper. It was horrible."

"So you took the controls?"

"It was all I could do. Between the dark and my one good eye, I could barely see. But the instinct to survive is strong. I stood at the controls and did what the Flighter had done. The small craft lurched and took off. It was so fast. I wasn't sure what direction I was going, except that it was away from the city. All around me there was cannon fire churning up the water. The farther away I got, the less accurate their aim was. In a few minutes I felt confident that I had gotten away. I was the only one."

"Then you had to find your way back here," I said.

"I used my navigation skills from working the fishing boats. I thought I was going in the right direction toward Ibara, but I didn't know for sure. I was still weak, and after a few days of intense heat, I didn't have anything left. I couldn't stand up anymore, which meant I couldn't control the boat. All I could do was lie down and go to sleep. After all I had been through, I didn't have the energy left to keep going. When I closed my eyes, I was convinced it would be for the last time . . . until I heard your voice."

That was it. An incredible story of survival. But there was still a big fat unanswered question looming.

"Now," he said, "tell me what has happened since I last saw you."

I shook my head. "No, I want you to finish your story first. What did you mean when you said, 'They're coming'?"

"There are more of them, Pendragon. More than we imagined."

"More of who?" I asked.

"Flighters" was his answer. "They haven't given up. I've heard them talk, and plot. They haven't given up on trying to invade Ibara. They're organized, much more than we thought. I'm afraid that sinking the pilgrim ships was only the beginning. They're preparing for something else."

I was actually relieved. I was afraid he was going to say there were more dados gathering. After all my worrying,

Loque was actually delivering old news. We expected the Flighters to attack again. We were preparing for it. The biggest surprise was that it hadn't happened already.

"It's okay," I assured him. "They've already attacked once. Right after we returned from Rubic City. We won. There's nothing else they could throw at us now that we can't handle."

Loque frowned. "You don't understand. Their attack has something to do with the mineral we were digging for. From the little bit I heard, once they find this mineral, they're going to use it to attack Ibara. It sounds like some kind of weapon."

My blood pressure spiked. Was it possible? I didn't want to believe it. I had to force myself to stay calm. "Mineral? What did they call it? Tak?"

"No."

I let out a relieved breath. The idea of a vein of tak existing on Ibara would have been disastrous.

"It was a strange word. I'd never heard it before. The only person who used it was that tall, cold guy. He said we were digging for something called . . . flume."

My ears started to ring. I wasn't sure whether the room was spinning or my head was spinning. I should have put it together when Loque first mentioned digging in a mine. It wasn't a mine. They weren't looking for precious minerals. They weren't hunting for weapons. Saint Dane was digging for something all right, but it wasn't a mineral natural to Veelox.

He was trying to unearth the flume. He was trying to escape from Veelox.

I had to get out of that cavern room. I needed air.

"Rest," I told Loque, silencing him. "There's a lot I have to tell you, but not now."

"Where is Siry?" he asked.

Oh man. I didn't want to get into that yet. "He's fine," I answered.

He was, too. He was just on another territory with no chance of ever coming home. I didn't think Loque needed to hear that just yet. "Go to sleep. I'll tell you everything after you've had some rest."

"Thanks. I am pretty tired."

I started for the door when Loque called to me, "Pendragon? Is everything all right?"

How could I answer that?

"Yes," I said. "Go to sleep."

That seemed to be enough for him. His heavy breathing told me he had dropped off instantly. I was glad that somebody felt better, because I sure didn't. When I left the room, I ran into Twig, who had come to visit.

"He's going to be okay," I told her.

Twig squealed with delight and threw her arms around me. I wished I could have been that happy. I was, actually. I was thrilled that Loque was alive. But the other news he delivered kind of put a damper on that.

"He fell asleep," I added. "Stay by him."

I left Twig with Loque and walked out of Tribunal Mountain. I walked toward the beach on Ibara, but my mind was elsewhere. It was in Rubic City. Rather it was below Rubic City. Was it possible? Could Saint Dane unearth the flume by using Flighters to dig with their hands? No wonder we hadn't seen a single Flighter try to land on Ibara. They were busy. Busy digging. Busy trying to spring Saint Dane from the prison I'd created for him.

I arrived at the beach, sat down in the sand and looked out to sea. Ibara was truly paradise. I'd grown to consider it my home. I didn't want anything more to happen to it. The people had been through enough, dating back to Aja Killian's time. As I sat on that beach, smelling the sweet flowers that framed the bay, I made a decision. As much as I didn't want to, I had no choice.

I had to learn the truth.

I had to go back to Rubic City.

JOURNAL #34
(CONTINUED)

IBARA

"You can't leave us," Telleo commanded. "Not now."

We were alone on our perch, high above the growing village of Rayne. Telleo was the first person I told about leaving. She was the only person I fully trusted to take care of Loque. She had to know that she would be on her own.

"I don't want to go," I argued. "Believe me. I *really* don't want to go. But I have to."

"Why?" she demanded to know.

I didn't know how to explain this. No, I take that back. I knew exactly how to explain it, but not in a way that anyone from Rayne would understand. I decided to tell the truth, more or less.

"The guy who launched the attack on Ibara is still around," I said. "Loque saw him. He's organizing the Flighters. Who knows what he might try next? If we're in for another war, we need to know about it so we can be prepared."

"Send someone else," she insisted. "Haven't you done

enough? You're on the tribunal now. You can't just run off on some . . . some . . . spy mission. Send some men from the security force."

"It's more complicated than that," I explained patiently. "Trust me. It's *way* more complicated."

"That's exactly what Remudi said before he left to go on his mysterious mission. Look what happened. He was killed playing a foolish game and we lost a tribunal member. The people look up to you, Pendragon. You have become their guide into the future. If you're not worried about yourself, worry about your people. They love you. I love you."

Whoa. I hadn't expected that. Telleo stood close and took both my hands.

"Don't act all surprised," she said. "You know I love you. Please don't leave me."

Okay. Awkward. Telleo was putting herself on the line. How could I tell her I didn't feel the same way? Things were going badly enough as it was.

"You know how I feel about you, Telleo. I wish there was another way. There isn't. I'm going to go talk to your father now and let him know what I'm going to do."

Telleo looked down. I think she realized that she had lost the argument.

"When will you leave?" she asked softly.

"Tomorrow morning. First light."

She nodded. Accepting it.

"You can help," I added. "Take care of Loque."

"I've been doing all that I—"

"I know. I'm asking you to watch him. Don't leave him alone until he's well enough to take care of himself. Either you or Twig or Krayven should always be with him."

"Why? What are you worried about?"

"I'm worried there might be people around we can't trust."

"What?" she asked, stunned. "Like who?"

"Just take care of him, please?"

"Tell me who you think—"

"I don't think anything. I'm just worried about Loque. Promise me you'll protect him. He deserves that."

Telleo nodded. She didn't understand, but she nodded.

"Talk to my father," she said. "I'm going to stay here and look out on the beautiful village we've built and pretend that everything is going to be all right."

I let go of her hands and left her alone. It was sad. Things had been going so well. The future was bright for Ibara. I didn't want to believe that could change. I had made up my mind to do all I could to secure Ibara's future. At that moment, to do that, I had to go to Rubic City.

I found Genj alone in the tribunal cavern. I quickly explained to him about what Loque reported to me. The Flighters were still around. They were active. They were organized. I repeated what I'd said to Telleo about the man who was running the show. Of course, I didn't go into any real details about Saint Dane. Genj already knew of him. To Genj, he was the guy who launched the dado attack. That was enough.

"Can't we send others?" Genj asked. "You are on the tribunal now. The people need you."

"I know that," I said. "And by going, I'm doing exactly what I have to do to protect them. I can't do that from here."

"Have you told Telleo?" he asked.

"Yes. She wasn't happy about it."

"She loves you, you know."

I nodded.

Genj put his arm around me and said, "We owe you a debt that can never be fully repaid. All I can ask is that you come back to us. I don't want to lose two friends in such a short time."

"Two?" I asked.

He gave a tired sigh. "Have you forgotten about Remudi? He also went on a mysterious mission. He never returned."

Right. Of course. "I didn't forget," I said softly.

The two of us hugged. There was nothing more to say, so I started for the door. I got halfway across the cavern floor when a thought hit me. Something was wrong. It was something Genj said that triggered it. I turned back and asked, "What did I tell you about Remudi?"

"What do you mean?"

"What did I say happened to him?"

"You said he was killed by the man who destroyed the pilgrim ships and staged the attack on Ibara."

"Right. Did I tell you *how* he died?"

Genj frowned and shook his head. "No."

I walked back toward him. Alarms were starting to go off in my head.

"I never gave you any details?"

Genj shook his head.

"Are you sure?"

"Of course. Don't you think I'd remember something like that? If there's anything more you can tell me, please do."

I could feel my heart pound. I hadn't told anybody about how Remudi died. No way I would have. It would have meant explaining about Quillan. And the games. I never would have told anyone on Ibara about that.

But Telleo knew.

Only a few minutes before, she said how Remudi was killed playing a foolish game. That's what she said exactly. A foolish game. I heard it. I was there. How could she have known that? There had to be some explanation. Maybe Siry told her. Or Alder. My mind flew back to a million different moments. Things that were said. Comments that were made. Was I being paranoid?

Genj must have sensed my growing panic and asked, "What's wrong, Pendragon?"

"I'm sorry for asking this, I really am, but you told me Telleo and her mother had a great relationship. You said they were like sisters. Can you think of any reason why Telleo might say she had problems with her mother and would never talk about her?"

Genj straightened up, as if I had slapped him. "That's insanity," he barked. "The two were inseparable. Telleo held Sharr's hand until the moment she died. They couldn't have been closer. She would never say a harsh word about her mother."

"Unless she didn't know what kind of relationship they had," I muttered.

"Pardon me?"

I couldn't catch my breath. My head got light. I think I was hyperventilating as I backed out of the cavern room.

Genj called out, "Pendragon? What's wrong?"

"Close off the mountain," I ordered. "Send a security team to the medical section."

"What? Why?"

"To protect Loque."

I turned and sprinted out of the tribunal's cavern. I

desperately hoped that I was wrong. If I wasn't, Loque was in trouble. Suddenly the strange overdose made sense. Loque had information. He had seen things—things Saint Dane didn't want me to know. Was it possible? Could Telleo be Saint Dane? Had she tried to kill Loque? As I ran down the stone stairs, barely staying upright, I thought back to the time we had spent together. There wasn't a single moment that she and Saint Dane were together, but that alone didn't make her guilty. There had to be other clues.

I hoped that I was being paranoid. Maybe Telleo truly hated her mother and hid it from Genj. That was possible. Or maybe Telleo didn't really mean what she said about her mother. She might have been in a bad mood. It happens. It could all have been a misunderstanding.

Except there was no way she could have known that Remudi died playing a game. I had no explanation for that one. As I ran, I tried to convince myself that I was overreacting. I didn't want to believe that I had been fooled again. Unfortunately, I wasn't doing a very good job of convincing myself. In my heart I knew the truth.

Telleo was Saint Dane. Loque was in danger.

I hit the ground floor of the mountain, ran through the stone corridors, and finally arrived in the medical area. The place was empty. No doctors. No Twig. No security. I didn't hesitate and flew into Loque's room.

Telleo stood next to Loque, gently laying him back down on the bed. She had a brown cup in her hand.

"Stop!" I shouted.

Telleo jumped in surprise.

"Get away from him," I ordered.

"Quiet!" she said harshly. "He's asleep."

I leaped forward and grabbed the cup. It was empty.

"What did you give him?" I demanded.

"A sedative . . . to help him rest. What's wrong?"

"How did he get the overdose yesterday?"

"I told you. It could have been from a number of sources. Can we discuss this outside?"

There wasn't time to do this dance. If she had given him something lethal, time was critical. If she hadn't, then I was an idiot. I had to know which way this was going to go.

"Tell me how you knew Remudi died playing a game."

Telleo's eyes widened. She took a breath, ready to answer, then stopped. My gut clenched. I wanted her to keep talking. I wanted to hear the logical explanation. I wanted her to say that Siry told her all about the Quillan games. Or Alder. Instead, she exhaled and smiled.

"So close," she said calmly.

That's all I needed to hear. If I hadn't grabbed the end of the bed for support, I would have fallen over.

"A momentary lapse," she lamented. "A simple, foolish mistake. Slip of the tongue. I'm embarrassed."

I was hearing the words but didn't want to accept them.

"Don't worry, Pendragon," she said. "I didn't poison him. At least not this time. It was different before. He hadn't told you what he knew." She gently stroked the hair back from Loque's forehead. "His death now would be pointless."

"Don't touch him," I spat.

"I hadn't anticipated this," she said, pulling her hand away from Loque. "Without him you would have no idea what was happening in Rubic City. Or maybe you had suspicions and pretended not to care. After all, you took yourself out of the equation when you blew up the flume. You're finished with being a Traveler."

I wanted to leap across the bed and throttle her. Telleo had been my best friend since the moment I arrived on Ibara. We shared everything. The realization that she was Saint Dane all along made me want to scream.

"Telleo's dead," she said, as if reading my mind. "Since before you arrived. I didn't learn as much about her background as I should have. I'm surprised it took you this long to have suspicions."

I swallowed, trying to get my wits back. "I did actually. I just didn't put it together until now. That's not like you, Saint Dane. You usually don't make mistakes like that."

Telleo shot me a look and broke into a wide grin. It was an odd reaction. It threw me.

"Of course!" She laughed, as if realizing something she hadn't thought of. "That's exactly what you would assume."

"What are you talking about?" I asked with caution and more than a little confusion.

"It appears I'm better at this than I thought." With that, Telleo began to transform. Her image melted before my eyes. She became a moving mass of liquid smoke. I knew what was coming, or at least I thought I did. I was ready to see her become Saint Dane. She didn't. When the transformation was complete, I stood face-to-face with Nevva Winter. It was a good thing I was still holding on to the bed, or I would have gone over for sure.

"Surprise," said the beautiful, dark-haired woman from Quillan. "It was fun while it lasted, wasn't it?"

I opened my mouth, but no words came out.

Footsteps were heard outside, coming quickly. It was the security detail I had asked for.

Nevva walked quickly to the window, then turned back and added, "It's too late, Pendragon. While you were busily rebuilding this sandy village, the Convergence has begun. Unlike you, Saint Dane didn't quit. I suggest you continue to enjoy your oblivious little life here. At least what's left of it."

I ran for Nevva too late. She dove out the window, already transforming into the raven that quickly flew away. A second later the security team entered the room.

"Is everything all right?" the first guy to arrive asked.

I stood at the window, numb. I didn't even bother to look out. My entire world had collapsed. Nothing was what I had thought it was. I had been played as a fool for months.

"Yes," I said in a soft whisper. "Everything's fine. False alarm. I'm sorry."

"We'll wait outside," the guy said.

"Sure, whatever you want."

They gave me an odd look, as if I were acting strangely. Which I was. I didn't care.

"Go!" I shouted.

The security guys quickly backed out of the room, leaving me alone with Loque. I looked down at the sleeping Jakill. He was out of danger. He would live. But what kind of life had he come back to? What was Saint Dane's plan for Ibara? Was it possible that this Convergence was truly under way? Had Saint Dane unearthed the flume? Was Nevva lying, or was it really too late?

I sat down. I had to think. I felt like such an idiot. If Loque hadn't beaten the odds and pulled off an impossible escape, I'd still be clueless. But clueless to what? What was going on? There was only one way to find that out. Other than learning that I had been a total idiot, nothing had changed. I knew where I would find the answers.

Rubic City.

JOURNAL #34

(CONTINUED)

IBARA

I planned to leave before sunrise.

I wanted as much daylight as possible to navigate my way across the ocean, back to Rubic City. I would have left right then and there if I hadn't thought I'd get totally lost at sea. Besides, I needed sleep. There was no telling when I'd get another chance. It was going to be a long, grueling trip, and that would be the easy part. I had to be at my best. Or at least, I needed to be at my most awake.

I found an empty room with a bed near where Loque was staying. I lay down and proceeded to stare at the ceiling for the next several hours. So much for sleep. It's not easy to relax when so much is bouncing around inside. Things had changed so drastically, so quickly. When I destroyed the gate to the flume, I truly believed I would never have to deal with Saint Dane again. I had had enough. I thought I had done more than my part and deserved to let it go. Trapping us both here was the perfect solution. Or so I thought.

The thing is, once the pressure was off, I totally gave myself over to my new life. I think you probably got that from my earlier journals. For the first time in a long time, I was looking forward to the next challenge, as opposed to always looking over my shoulder, wondering when the next disaster would hit. I had put the battle with Saint Dane behind me. Rebuilding Rayne was like rebuilding my own life as well. I accepted the fact that I'd never see Second Earth again. Or my family. Or you guys. That was the only regret in an otherwise perfect plan.

But since Loque returned, I not only found out that Saint Dane might possibly find a way out of here, but the new life I had been building was with the enemy. Nevva Winter. A traitor to the Travelers. I may be slow, but I'm not dumb. Saint Dane must have sent her here to watch me. No, it was more than that. In the form of Telleo, she supported me. She made me love Rayne. She and her father took the place of the family I had lost. I can't help but think that my wanting to live the rest of my life in Rayne was exactly what Saint Dane wanted. I may have been done, but he wasn't. He wanted me out of the way while he worked to reopen the flume in Rubic City. He sent Nevva Winter to make sure I didn't leave.

Okay, maybe I *am* dumb.

How could I have kidded myself into thinking that Saint Dane would just lick his wounds and not cause any more trouble? Had I wanted out of this battle so badly that I would throw logic away? It was beginning to look that way. I figured I could beat myself up over it, or I could move forward. But what did that mean? I had totally checked out of this war. Other than writing these journals and examining the flume-grave on Ibara every once in a while, as far as I was concerned, the fight for Halla was over. I was done. Would I be able to jump back in?

The answer I came up with was yes . . . and no. When I wrote that my days as a Traveler were over, I meant it. Halla would have to take care of itself. Of course, that was an easier choice to make when I thought Saint Dane wouldn't be jumping around to cause trouble. Still, my feelings hadn't changed. I had done my part. I was finished. But I didn't plan on being a total load and hanging out eating pineapple. Part of the decision I made when I destroyed the gate was that I was going to do all I could to help rebuild Veelox. That's exactly what I've been doing, and I've loved every minute of it. At least every minute until I heard Loque's story.

I decided I wasn't going to give up that plan. I was still going to do all I could to help Ibara. To help Veelox. To do that, I had to go to Rubic City, find the "mine," and destroy it. With the flume open, Saint Dane could bring more dados from Quillan. He could bring more skimmers and weapons and anything else he wanted. I couldn't let that happen. My duty now was to this territory. In that sense, I was keeping with my decision. I was going to do all I could to help Ibara thrive and bring Veelox back. If that meant going up against Saint Dane again, I was ready to do it.

What I wouldn't do is jump back into the flume. I am no longer a Traveler. Do I feel guilty about that? A little. But by destroying the gate in Rubic City, I'll be making sure that Saint Dane is trapped here for good. That's a good thing for all Halla. How will I do that? No idea. I'll have to figure that one out.

I also have to hope that the Flighters haven't already uncovered the flume. I'm sure that as soon as Nevva left Tribunal Mountain she flew right to her boss to tell him that the masquerade party was over and I knew all about Project Flume. Saint Dane would be ready for me. That made me a little anxious. I'd been out of the game for a while. I was feeling kind of rusty.

All those thoughts fought for brain time while I was supposed to be resting. I may have dozed off a little, but not for long. I wrote some in my journal, then finally decided that lying there was a waste of time.

I first went to Loque's room and woke him up. I needed to tell him all that had happened since he was nearly killed. He deserved to know. But I had trouble finding the right words. How could I tell him the truth, when the truth was so freaking complicated? I decided that the best thing to do was to say that Twig would tell him everything. Once I said the words, I realized it was the perfect solution. Everyone on Ibara had their own way of dealing with the events of the war, and the revelation of their past. It would be better for Loque to hear it from the perspective of someone who was like him—a Jakill who'd lived on the island his entire life. Twig didn't know of Travelers and flumes and Halla. All she knew was that some mysterious evil guy organized the Flighters and launched an attack against their home. The people of Ibara banded together to stop them. That's all Loque needed to know.

"Ask her everything," I said to Loque. "Everybody knows the truth about Ibara now. It's what the Jakills wanted all along."

Loque asked, "What about Siry?"

I decided to go with the story that was commonly accepted. "He's missing," I answered somberly. "Nobody knows for sure what happened to him. I'm sorry."

"He was my best friend," Loque said sadly.

"He's a hero and so are you. Don't forget him."

I then told Loque that I was going to Rubic City to

destroy the mine. He got all worked up and said it was suicide. Not exactly what I wanted to hear, but I didn't back down. I asked him to tell me how I could get into it. At first he wouldn't tell me. He said he wanted to show me. He wanted to go with me! I convinced him that as much as I'd want him to come, between his injuries and his eyes, he'd make the trip that much harder. He started to argue, but gave up quickly. He knew I was right.

"It's hard for me to say exactly where it was," he finally answered. "They brought me back and forth in the dark, and my vision wasn't very good to begin with. It seemed close to the big black triangle building where the Flighters lived. Maybe a short walk. We entered something that looked like a red arch, then immediately went down a ladder. At the bottom of the ladder was the mine tunnel."

Loque sat up and added, "You can't hide. They'll know you don't belong."

That gave me an idea. I grabbed the clothes Loque had worn when he was in Rubic City. They were perfectly disgusting. The idea was to make myself look like a Flighter. I could always make myself dirty; the trick would be to get that rancid Flighter smell going on. I figured a day out on the ocean under the sun would take care of that.

I was about to head out when Loque grabbed my arm and said two simple, sincere words. "Come back."

"That's the idea," I said with more confidence than I actually had.

I started for the door when he asked, "Is everything all right with Telleo?"

How was I going to answer that? The truth was, Telleo was dead. The real Telleo. I didn't think Nevva would be coming back.

"I don't know," I answered.

I couldn't think of anything else to say. I guess I kind of weaseled out. I left Loque with more questions than answers, but I believed the full answers would have been harder to take than the mystery of not knowing the truth. It made me realize something else I didn't want to deal with. Genj. What would I tell him about his daughter? His *real* daughter. He had to know the truth, but I couldn't think of anything to tell him that he'd understand. What could I say? He wouldn't believe me, especially since I started acting all crazy the night before. He might even try to come up with his own logical explanation for why his daughter disappeared and prevent me from leaving.

I couldn't let that happen, so I made a tough decision. I decided to not tell Genj that his daughter was dead. I felt horrible about it. All he'd know was that his daughter had disappeared. He'd have no idea why. My silence would condemn him to the agony of uncertainty and wonder. I promised myself that when I returned I'd tell him everything, even if it meant revealing the existence of the Travelers and Saint Dane. At least I'd be able to give him closure on Remudi, too. Yes, that would be the right thing to do. But not just then. Daybreak was too close.

I gathered a few supplies for the trip. My plan was to make the voyage back on the skimmer that Loque brought from Rubic City. It wasn't a very big craft, so I couldn't exactly load up on gear. I took four canteens of fresh water and some dried fruit, along with a bow and a quiver full of arrows. I didn't know what I'd do with the weapon, but at least it gave me a small feeling of security, as false as it might have been. The final task was to get rid of my lightweight green shorts and shirt and put on Loque's dirty, torn rags.

After putting the shirt over my head, I realized that I didn't have to worry about faking the bad smell thing. The clothes were plenty foul enough.

I walked through the quiet, sandy streets of Rayne, headed for the shore. I didn't hurry. It wasn't that I was having second thoughts; it was more because I wanted to take a good look at what I helped create. I passed newly built huts and many more that were in various stages of construction. The roads were clear. Water lines were being buried. Some homes already had flowers growing around them. It was a beautiful thing. I was proud of this village and its people. I was one of them. I wanted to do right by them. That last walk to the shore gave me the final gut check I needed. One way or another I had to protect this village from Saint Dane and the Flighters.

The skimmer was still onshore where I had beached it. I loaded up my small provisions under the deck and pulled it out onto the water. I had the brief fear that it wouldn't have power. That went away as soon as I started toggling switches and the engines hummed. Skimmers ran on water power. There was plenty of that around.

The sky was already turning from black to blue, extinguishing the stars. A thin line of light appeared on the horizon that said the sun wouldn't be far behind. I needed the sun to get my bearings. Between that and the small compass, they would be my only guides to Rubic City. It was a good thing it wasn't a cloudy day.

I lowered the pontoons into the water. As soon as they submerged, I could feel the power of the skimmer growing. I hesitated. This was really happening. I was going back to Rubic City. I was going to meet Saint Dane. It was something I thought would never happen again, but there I was, poised to go. I took a look back at Rayne and Tribunal Mountain. It was a tropical paradise. I vowed to keep it that way. I looked ahead and throttled the engine. With a quick lurch I was off.

The warm, tropical waters of Veelox were glassy calm, allowing me to fly over the surface. I had made this trip before on a skimmer, in the opposite direction. I knew I was in for a long day, so I settled in and tried not to get bored. A few times I actually broke out in song. Why not? Nobody could hear me. I sang a little Green Day, and in honor of my dad, some Beatles. I'm not a good singer. It didn't matter, unless you were a fish.

I can't tell you how many hours the trip took, because I didn't have a watch. It was many. It took most of the day. That's the best I can say. I kept my eye on the compass and on the movement of the sun, to make sure I was headed in the right direction. When I wasn't rechecking my heading, I stared at the horizon, hoping to see the beginnings of the skyline of Rubic City. It was torture. It didn't help that I was alone. Finally, after what felt like a lifetime, the razor-sharp edge of ocean slowly grew jagged. I knew what that meant. I was seeing the tops of skyscrapers. My first reaction was relief.

My second reaction was fear. I was really going to do this. Was I ready? The answer was no. I had no idea how to prepare myself. To say I was going to wing it would be an understatement. Ready or not, it would soon be showtime. It took another hour or so before I was close enough to make out details of the decaying city. The sun had already traveled across the sky and was heading down. The late afternoon light warmed the cityscape. Things looked pretty much the same as when I'd been there months before. At one time this had been a busy, thriving city. Now it was a hollow, rotting place of the dead. Beneath the water, I could make out the shadowy hulks of ships that had been sunk and left to rust over many generations. You've heard of ghost towns? This was a full-on ghost city. Actually, the only thing I *didn't* have to be afraid of was ghosts. At least I didn't think so.

I saw the pier where we had tied up the pilgrim ship when the Jakills and I first discovered the city. I couldn't bring myself to put in there. It was a place of death. The hull of the burned ship was still beneath the surface. If there were any ghosts in Rubic City, that's where they'd be. Instead, I maneuvered the skimmer toward the large pier under which the fleet of skimmers was kept. My thinking was that the perfect placc to hide the craft was among others just like it. I didn't want somebody stumbling on it and raise some kind of alarm to announce an intruder had arrived and was poking around.

I was about a couple hundred yards out from the pier when I heard an odd sound. I had been listening to the steady drone of the skimmer's engines for the last million hours. This was different. It was steady, but definitely a different frequency. I cut the engines. Water lapped up onto the deck as I came to a stop. Once the sloshing sounds stopped, I listened intently. The sound was faint, but distinct. It wasn't like anything I remembered hearing in Rubic City. The steady sound grew louder. Was it coming closer? The skimmer bobbed gently on the small swells. I scanned the city. There was nothing in sight that could be making that kind of sound, but it was definitely there and getting louder. It sounded like the buzz of a machine. That was impossible. There was nothing mechanized in Rubic City. At least nothing that had worked for centuries.

I was about to hit the throttle and travel the rest of the way to the pier when my eye caught movement. Dead ahead. It looked like a dark cloud moving along a street, between the rows of tall buildings. I strained to get a better look. The cloud grew bigger. It was definitely moving. Was it a dust storm? A minitornado? Whatever it was, it had cleared the last row of buildings and was headed my way. For a second I thought that maybe there really *were* ghosts in Rubic City, because a big, black-looking specter was coming toward me.

That's when I saw the lights. It was almost pretty. Almost. As the cloud grew closer, it seemed decorated with thousands of tiny, twinkling lights. Yellow lights. Like Christmas. The sound grew even louder. The buzzing sound. The lights were the tip-off. It wasn't a cloud. It wasn't a tornado. It wasn't a ghost. It wasn't Christmas.

It was a swarm of bees. Quig-bees. The weird thing was, I wasn't afraid. Not just then anyway. My first thought wasn't that I had to do something or I was going to get swarmed and stung by those monsters. No, my first thought was that there were quigs in Rubic City guarding the flume. That meant that this territory was once again hot. Saint Dane had sent his little demons out to welcome me. There was no chance of surprise here. He knew I was coming.

That's when I got scared.

IBARA

I was alone in the middle of the harbor on a tiny boat with a swarm of quig-bees closing fast. I looked around for some kind of protection. There was nothing. Absolutely nothing. I feared I was done before I even set foot back on dry land.

Dry land. I wasn't on dry land. I did have protection. The water. Could quig-bees swim? I hoped not. I figured I could dive underwater and hide under the skimmer. How long could I last doing that? Were those bees smart enough to hover around, waiting for me to run out of air? If they were smart enough to leave the city to find me, they might be smart enough to bide their time until I poked my head above the surface.

The swarm was out over the water, halfway to me. They weren't fast. I wasn't sure if that was good or just meant it prolonged the torture of my knowing I was about to get stung a million times. My only choice was to go into the water. I was about to jump overboard when I realized if the skimmer stayed dead in the water, I'd be dead in the water too. I had to keep moving toward shore. The throttle for the pontoon engines was on the right handle. It worked like bike brakes. I quickly tore off a length of rotted material from Loque's pants and looped it around the handle and the throttle. I tied it tight, pulling the throttle so it engaged the engine. I didn't want it to go too fast or I wouldn't be able to control it. All I wanted was for the skimmer to move forward. The powerful engine hummed. The skimmer headed toward shore, closer to the swarm of quigs. I tied off the loop and jumped to the back. There were two handles on the stern at water level that the aquaneers of Cloral used to tie up and tow other boats. I was going to use them to try to steer the skimmer from behind. I had no idea if it would work, but it was the only thing I could think of. The dark, sparkling cloud of quigs was almost on me. I put my legs over the stern, grabbed one of the handles, and twisted around while lowering myself into the water. I floated out flat, letting my legs trail behind. I twisted them to the right and felt the skimmer move left. I moved them left and felt the skimmer move right. My legs acted as a rudder. It was working.

Only trouble was, I had no idea where I was going. I was down behind the stern with no view ahead. Okay, maybe that wasn't exactly the only trouble. A few seconds later it grew dark. It felt as though the sun had gone behind a cloud. It had. Sort of. The swarm of quigs had arrived. I held my breath and ducked my head underwater. The handles were above water level, which meant my hands would be too. Would the quigs realize that?

Yes. I felt a sharp sting on my right hand. Without thinking I let go and pulled it underwater. That meant I was hanging on by only one hand. In seconds the quigs would go after that one and I'd have to let go. The skimmer would power off and I'd be dead. I forced myself to grab the handle with my right hand again and pulled my left hand underwater. It was better to have one hand exposed at a time. It gave the quigs less to go after. Though I was underwater I could still hear their demonic buzzing over the sound of the skimmer engines. I can't say how many times I was stung. I switched hands a few times, which seemed to be working. The bees weren't as smart as I gave them credit for. Lucky me. It was a good plan, except for the fact that I didn't know which way I was going.

And I was running out of air. Oh. That. My lungs started screaming. I waited until the absolute last possible second, then pushed my head up, gulped air, and ducked back under again. I didn't get stung. Not once. I didn't know how long I could keep it up. My arms were starting to feel like they were being pulled out of their sockets, and my hands were cramping. Suddenly the few stings I'd gotten didn't bother me so much. I wasn't going to be able to hold on much longer.

I had no idea which direction I was going. For all I knew I had leg-ruddered the skimmer around and was headed back out to sea. Or traveling in circles. The next time I came up for air, I took a quick look behind me, hoping not to see Rubic City growing smaller in the distance. I saw nothing but ocean. Phew. I went back under and tried to duck below the skimmer to look ahead. It was too dark to make out anything, and my vision was blurred. I didn't think I was in the middle of the harbor anymore, but that's about all I could tell. I figured that I had been traveling long enough that I might soon hit land. But where? More important, what would I do when I got there?

The quigs were still after me. I knew that because I kept getting stung. Just when I thought I couldn't hang on any longer, it suddenly got dark. I mean really dark. Night dark. I knew that couldn't be the case. Not that fast. Night didn't really "fall." I took another gulp of air, tried to take a quick look around, and saw nothing but nothing. The world had gone black. Well, not entirely. The quigs were still buzzing above me. Their glowing yellow eyes made them look like fireflies in the dark. What had happened? I ducked back underwater and pushed my head down to look under the skimmer. It was good I did, because a second later the small boat hit something and stopped short. We hit land. Or something else solid. Good thing I was below the surface or my head would have slammed into the stern. The skimmer stopped abruptly, but I kept going. My hand was ripped off the handle. I was now under the skimmer, someplace dark, and running out of air. The skimmer's engines whined. It was bobbing against a hard surface, and with nowhere to go, it started to turn. It wanted to keep going and was looking for a way out. The engines screamed louder. I turned in time to see that one of the pontoons was headed right for me. If that thing slammed my head, it would hurt. I shifted quickly as the pontoon slid by, grazing my nose. I got hit with the stream of water that ejected from the rear. If the skimmer had been at full power, it might have ripped my head off. As it was, it only gave me a mild shove. A moment later the skimmer took off. It must have turned away from whatever had stopped it and found an escape route.

Good for the skimmer. Bad for me. I was stranded underwater. I looked up to see the blurry images of the flickering yellow quig lights hovering above me. I couldn't surface. They'd be on me. I chose a direction and started to swim. Desperately. I didn't know why or where I was going, but I didn't want to be where I was. I half expected to hit the same wall the skimmer had, but I saw what looked like a long beam in front of me that was just below the water. I swam under it. Now I had to get air. I pulled for the surface and hit my hands on something. I was below a dock. If I hadn't been in a panic before, I sure was then, because I was trapped. If the water level went all the way up to this hard surface, I'd drown. I didn't have the energy to swim back out. Not that I even knew which way was out. With my hand touching the hard ceiling, I cautiously surfaced and hit the top of my head. No! There was no breathing room! I kept my wits though. I only needed a few inches of air. The distance from the top of my head to my mouth was what? Six inches? I didn't need that much. I kicked my legs so I was floating on my back. I pushed my face up, lips first, and broke the surface. Yes! I think I gulped more water than air and had to gag and cough. I didn't care. I had air. I pressed my lips against the rough surface to stay as far out of the water as possible. I'm guessing there was about a three-inch gap between the surface of the water and the underside of whatever was above me. It was enough. Once I calmed myself, I actually found it easier to breathe through my nose, because when I opened my mouth, water sloshed inside. It was a nightmare situation, but I was alive.

The surface was rough, like wood. Faint lines of light glowed between the planks. I positioned my eye below one seam to try to see what was above. When I focused, I immediately gasped and dropped below the surface, inhaling a bunch of water. I instantly pushed back up and coughed it out. I had to keep my head together or I'd drown for sure. What I had seen was a bunch of quig-bees trying to push themselves through the cracks between the boards to get to me. They sounded angry, too. If they got through, they'd be on me. The quigs were no more than two inches from my eyes, desperately trying to get at me. All I could do was hope that the space between the boards was too narrow for them to squeeze through.

A few agonizing seconds later, none of them had made it. They were too big. I was safe. Uncomfortable as hell, but safe. The only way they would get me was if they waited me out. No way I'd let that happen. As torturous as it was, I was prepared to float like that for days to avoid those bees.

I'm glad to say it didn't take days. I had been under there for a few minutes at best when the quig swarm suddenly took off. I could see the flashes of light through the thin cracks as they streaked through the darkness, headed someplace else. I waited. The buzzing sound was soon gone. I didn't hear the whine of the skimmer engine either. The only sound was the sloshing of the water against the underside of the structure above my head. I waited a few more minutes, to make sure they were really gone, then made a move to get out. I took a deep breath and pushed underwater. Looking around, I saw that one direction looked brighter than the other. I swam that way. It only took a few strokes before the ceiling I was under, ended. I was back out in open water. Or at least I was back out to where the skimmer had abandoned me. I kicked and broke the surface to take the first comfortable breath of air I'd had since I entered the water.

A quick look around told me several things. Most

important, the quig-bees were gone. Hopefully for good. Second, the skimmer was gone too. I guessed it had spun around and made its way back out to sea. I hoped the quigs were chasing it. The third thing I realized was that I was in a familiar place. I had maneuvered the skimmer beneath the tall pier where the thousands of skimmers from Cloral had been kept. This is where Siry and I stole the skimmer to escape from Rubic City. Most of the skimmers were gone. I saw a few vehicles bobbing against the docks, but that was it. It was like being inside a big, wet, empty airplane hangar.

I had been hiding beneath one of the narrow docks that ringed the place. I took a few strokes back to the dock and hoisted myself up on top. Man, it felt good to have something solid under my butt. It felt even better to breathe. I made two fists. My hands had been stung pretty bad and were swollen. I didn't care. It was a small price to pay. I wished I could have sat around and enjoyed the simple pleasure of filling my lungs with something other than water, but I had business to do. My relief over having survived the quig attack didn't last long. It was time to find the mine that the Flighters had been digging.

It was time to find Saint Dane.

My single goal was to figure out a way to destroy that mine and bury the flume forever. How? I had no idea. If I wanted to save Ibara and return to my life on the island, I would have to find a way. I hoped I wasn't too late. Could the flume already have been found? How long had the Flighters been digging? How deep was the flume buried beneath the rubble of Rubic City? It seemed like an impossible task to unearth something so huge, without tools or digging equipment . . . other than the bleeding hands and tired backs of the poor Flighters. Logic told me that digging out the flume was impossible. Yet Loque said he had been inside the mine. They had made progress. I had to hope that the attack of the quig-bees didn't mean that the flume was already open.

The one weapon I'd brought with me, the bow and arrows, was gone. I had it beneath the deck of the skimmer, which was now headed off to parts unknown. I needed something to protect myself, so I scanned around for a length of pipe or wood. I saw what I needed a few feet from where I came out of the water. It was a wooden rod with a hook on the end that was probably used to control the skimmers from the docks. I picked it up, felt that it was solid, and spun it once. Bad move. I was out of practice. My swollen sore hands didn't help either. I lost control of the rod and beaned myself in the head. Dope. Not only did I nearly knock myself out, I proved to myself that I was rusty. I hadn't fought in months, and it wasn't as if I were an expert in fighting—like Loor—in the first place. I had to have faith that if I needed them, my skills would return. Was fighting like riding a bike? I was afraid I would have to find that out at some point. I hoped I wouldn't knock myself out before then.

I climbed a metal ladder up and out of the pier and got my first close view of the decaying metropolis of Rubic City. Nothing had changed since I was last there. There were a few hundred yards of bare ground that were covered with mounds of debris—I was guessing this was at one time a park. Beyond that, the tall buildings began. The afternoon was so clear I could make out the giant outline of the Lifelight pyramid that was nestled deep within the canyons of skyscrapers. That was where I had to begin my search for the tunnel that would lead to the mine.

I didn't want to run into any Flighters along the way. Or more quig-bees, for that matter. I figured the best thing I could do was keep moving, so I sprinted off the huge dock and headed for the city. Being in the open like that made me feel pretty vulnerable. There could have been eyes on me that were peering out from any number of the thousands of windows that overlooked the harbor area. I darted from mound to mound, trying to shield myself from curious eyes. It was probably a waste of energy.

I hit the first street and decided to hug the buildings. There was always the danger of a Flighter lying in wait and jumping out at me through a nearby window before I had time to react, but it was better than running down the street for all to see. The afternoon shadows were long. I felt fairly safe creeping through the darkened corners. I'd been through this city before, but it still gave me the creeps. The idea that a bustling, modern metropolis could crumble like this was pretty sobering. Nothing had been taken care of in more than three hundred years. I wondered if someday it would all be buried, waiting for archaeological expeditions of future generations to uncover the stores and streets of this dead civilization.

It was also living proof that Saint Dane's quest was nothing short of monstrous. He helped destroy the civilization on Veelox. Why did he think he could convince me that something like this happened for the ultimate good? He was either crazy or delusional. Maybe both.

My plan was to start at the Lifelight pyramid and make my way toward the area of the city where I knew the flume was. When Gunny and I first arrived here so long ago, the gate to the flume was hidden next to a derelict subway track, like on Second Earth. When Siry and I tried to find the flume on my last visit, we discovered that an entire building had crumbled over it and buried everything. Question was, where would it be smart to start an excavation project? Loque said he passed through a red arch when he was taken to dig. It wasn't a lot to go on. Somewhere between the Lifelight pyramid and the flume was a red arch. Piece of cake. Yeah, right.

It was getting late. It would be dark soon. There were no lights in Rubic City. When it got dark, it was deadly dark. If I didn't find that red arch quickly, I'd have to wait until morning. The idea of spending a night alone in one of those buildings wasn't a happy one. Luckily, I didn't see a single soul on my way to the pyramid, which I guess was no big surprise. The Flighters hid within those old buildings like rats. They could have been all around me, and I wouldn't have known. I hated this place.

I finally made it to the last building before the clearing that led up to the pyramid. I figured that was close enough to start the search. I was already on the side of the pyramid that was closest to the flume. Which street should I take to begin my search? I would have to go out in the open, closer to the pyramid, to get a perspective on my choices. That didn't thrill me. I was the only thing moving. An easy target. But what else could I do?

I jogged toward the pyramid for about twenty yards and turned back. I saw that most of the streets that ended at the pyramid were cluttered with debris. Most looked impassable. All but one. It was the obvious choice to start my search. I ran toward that street and moved quickly along the cluttered sidewalk. It didn't look different from any of the other desolate streets of Rubic City. The pavement was cracked, and littered with bits of cement and glass. Skeletons of derelict cars lined the way. Any signage from the stores was worn off long ago. I crossed one block, then another, and a third. I would guess that the distance between the pyramid and the flume was about a half mile. I must have covered at least half of that without seeing anything that looked like a red arch.

I kept glancing back, to make sure I wasn't being followed, which kept me from being totally focused on the search. After traveling several blocks, I feared I may have missed it. Or that I was on the wrong street. The idea of spending a night alone in Rubic City suddenly seemed like the least of my problems. Finding this elusive red arch could take forever. I was about to turn around and retrace my steps to the pyramid so I could start over again, when I saw it. It was built into one of the buildings, looking like an oversized door. It was a big, red frame. The idea of a red frame built into a building made no sense to me until I got closer. There was a single word on top of the arch. It was a mosaic created out of colored glass, which is why it survived so many years without wearing away. The word was "Subway." This was the Veelox version of a subway entrance. Like on the Earth territories, the flume in Rubic City was next to subway tracks. I had found it!

I stepped through the arch into complete darkness. My heart sank. They had no lights. How was I supposed to find my way? I thought back to Loque's description of digging with his hands. He didn't mention that it was done in the pitch dark. I wondered if it hadn't mattered to him because he was nearly blind. It only added to the horror of what Saint Dane put those Flighters through. Did he actually make them dig through the rubble of the city in the dark? How horrific would that be?

My eyes adjusted enough to see gray shadows. That was good. It meant there was at least a little ambient light. I walked farther and sensed that I was in a wide corridor. I was about to take another step when something made me stop. Call it instinct, but before putting my foot down, I looked at the floor to see . . . nothing. The floor ended. I was about to step off a jagged edge into a dark abyss. Talk about a shot of adrenaline! I took a step back and dropped to one knee. That was way too close to disaster.

Once I calmed down, I peered over the edge to find there was a twisted ladder leaning against the edge. This had to be the entrance to the "mine" that Loque described. I gingerly climbed down the rickety ladder, descending even farther into darkness. It wasn't easy since I also had to juggle the wooden pole I'd found. I wasn't about to give that thing up. No way. I climbed down forty, fifty feet. It was hard to tell. Oddly, the farther down I got, the brighter it became. I wondered if there might actually be another tunnel opening down there that was letting in the last bit of daylight. Whatever it was, it was okay by me.

I finally hit bottom to see there was no other tunnel opening, but there was light. Artificial light. Kind of like the lights from Ibara. I saw a crudely strung set of what looked like white Christmas lights stretched along a narrow, low tunnel. They had lights down here after all! I thought back to when Siry and I stepped into the core of the Lifelight pyramid and it powered back to life. Somehow there was still power in Rubic City. It looked as if the Flighters had figured out a way to use that power to light their way into the tunnel. It wasn't bright by any means. I'd say one small light hung every ten feet or so. That was okay. It was enough to keep me from walking into walls.

Before taking another step, I stood there and listened. I wanted to know whether I was alone, or if the Flighters were up ahead, digging. I didn't hear anything, other than the occasional crack or groan of the tunnel. I hoped that was because the Flighters had finished for the day, and it was "Heigh-ho" home from work. The alternative wasn't a good one. If nobody was digging, it might mean that they had already found the flume. I didn't even want to consider that possibility.

The tunnel was treacherous at best. Every few feet I saw something that was used to hastily shore it up. There were flimsy wooden beams and thick cement tubes. It was all pretty haphazard. I even saw a twisted chair straining to hold up an overhang of rock. It wasn't exactly a professional job, but why should it be? Flighters didn't know how to dig tunnels. Even if they did, they didn't have adequate material to help them make it safe. The creaking and groaning made me think that this whole thing could collapse if I so much as farted.

It was eerie, because the walls weren't all rock and dirt. All around me were layers of compressed, man-made objects that had been crushed by other structures that fell on top. I saw street signs, furniture, window frames, and street lights. There were plates and pots and utensils. I passed by tools and doorknobs and even the front bumper of a car. It was like a Rubic City sandwich. Everything was fused into the rock and sand, making it an archaeological trip through the city's history. No need for those future archaeologists to do much digging. It was all right there and exposed.

I walked slowly, with the wooden pole out in front of me in case I didn't see something in my way. The tunnel was low and narrow. It seemed like they didn't want to dig out any more than they had to. Can't say I blame them, since they only had their hands to dig with. For that reason I was surprised to see that, after walking a few hundred yards, the tunnel grew wide and high. Above me, running along the ceiling, were the jagged remains of two steel beams that ran parallel to each other. I didn't understand what they could be, until I walked a few more feet and had to stop short. What I saw above me was impossible, yet it was there. It was the undercarriage of a subway car that was dangling down from the rock ceiling above. I counted twelve steel wheels in all. The parallel steel beams were train tracks. It looked as if they had tunneled beneath this train without realizing it was there. It must have been a mistake, because there were several rickety-looking vertical beams holding the car up. They looked like the wooden cross-ties from the tracks. I could hear the massive train squeak and groan, as if it wanted to break loose from the ceiling and come crashing down. I'm guessing that once they discovered the train, it would have been too much work to stop and dig around it, so they just kept on going. It was a dangerous decision. I hoped it was a bad one.

Beyond that point, the tunnel narrowed again. There were no lights in this section, so it was slow going. I got the feeling that I was nearing the end of the digging, because there was less shoring-up going on. I walked slowly, so as not to slam my face into anything.

That's when I heard the sound. I can best describe it as "hollow." It was a sound that felt familiar, though I couldn't place it. Up until that point it had been deathly quiet, other than the creaks and cracks of settling rock. This sound was different. Was it the quig-bees massing for another attack? No. This was different. It was more like white noise. It was an odd sound to hear down there in that narrow labyrinth. I took a few more steps and saw a sharp turn to the right about thirty yards ahead. Light glowed from around the corner. Something was up there. I stopped and listened. Could the Flighters be around that corner, digging? No. There were no human sounds. No movement. Only that haunting, hollow sound . . .

That I now recognized. My gut twisted. I started to run. It didn't matter that I could barely see where I was going. I had to know that I was wrong. I told myself it could be anything. It could have been another wide cavern. Or a subway station. Or anything other than the one thing I absolutely knew it would be. I reached the turn and stopped. If I was right, I had lost. I knew I was right. Turning the corner was only a formality. I stepped forward, turned, and saw exactly what I feared. The reason there were no Flighters digging was because their work was done. I was too late. Rising up before me was the tunnel to infinity.

They'd found the flume.

Veelox was back in play.

I took a few numb steps toward the tunnel. I wanted it to be a mistake. I wanted it to be some random, natural tunnel that just happened to exist beneath Rubic City. Yeah, right.

"You made it sooner than I expected, Pendragon," came a voice from behind me.

I turned quickly to see someone step up behind me. It was Telleo. No, it was Nevva Winter in Telleo's form. I guess it was a strange thing to think at that moment, but as we stood there facing each other, I found myself wishing I had met the real Telleo. I bet we would have been friends. But that would never be. Telleo was dead. Nevva Winter wasn't. She had followed me down into that tunnel to say the two words I least wanted to hear. Two simple words that made me want to scream.

"He's gone."

JOURNAL #34

(CONTINUED)

IBARA

I clutched the wooden pole and ran at Nevva. I was ready to kill her. I swear I was. Call it frustration. Call it rage. Call it the horror that comes from realizing I was less than worthless. Call it whatever you want, but in that moment I wanted to kill her. Nevva didn't move. She stood there calmly, just as she did when dealing with the leaders of Blok on Quillan. Nothing bothered her, not even an enraged Traveler who had just been told that he was an imbecile. I wound up, ready to crush her.

I don't know why I stopped. It was like an unseen hand was holding back the pole, preventing me from lashing out. There wasn't any unseen hand, of course. I may have been out of control, but I'm not a killer. Still, I needed to vent my fury. I turned and flung the pole into the flume. It disappeared into the dark tunnel. I heard it clatter harmlessly on the rock floor.

"I'm sorry, Pendragon," Nevva said. "You deserve better than this."

"What the heck does that mean?" I snarled.

"You mean well. You're just . . . naive. I'm sorry for using your innocence against you."

"Gee, thanks."

"You wanted what's best for Ibara, and for all the territories. I know that. Saint Dane knows that. You just have no idea how wrong your way of thinking is."

"Let me understand," I said through gritted teeth. "You and your monster boss think I'm wrong for wanting the people of the territories to decide how they live their lives, and you prove it by twisting their worlds into nightmares and then saying it was their own fault for being weak? Is that how it works?"

"I prefer to say that we have proven beyond any doubt that when given the choice, the people of the territories will always take the easy, selfish road. They can be so much more, Pendragon. The heights they can reach are limitless, so long as they aren't held back by the weak and foolish."

"So what's Saint Dane doing? Weeding out the weak, so the worthy can shine?"

Nevva smiled. "Something like that. Which are you, Pendragon? Weak or worthy?"

I was tired of the riddles. "You make this sound like it's all been a contest between Saint Dane and me to prove who's right."

"That's exactly what it was."

I shot Nevva a look. What did that mean?

"And now it's over," she continued. "You ended it."

"Did I? Looks to me like the flume is back open for business."

Nevva strolled past me toward the flume. "That's not

what I meant. You didn't end this by burying the flume. You ended it when you quit."

"What?"

Nevva spun to me with fire in her eyes. "It was the last test, Pendragon. You failed. You gave up the fight. I know what's in your heart. You buried the flume because you were done. You wanted to live a peaceful life on an island paradise, building huts and staring at the stars with Telleo. You . . . gave . . . up."

My anger was building. Not because she was wrong. Because she was right.

"It was only a convenience that Saint Dane was here," she continued. "It pushed away the guilt. You could justify your actions by telling yourself that Saint Dane was trapped along with you. Did you really believe that? Did you honestly think Saint Dane would roll over and die?"

I couldn't answer. I didn't want to admit the truth.

"Of course not, but you pretended, didn't you? This was the ultimate test for you. The lead Traveler. All you did was prove how weak you are. I'll answer my own question. You *aren't* worthy, Pendragon. When the Convergence is complete, you will get what you deserve. Nothing."

I was trembling with anger. With guilt. "What is the Convergence?" I asked lamely.

Nevva's answer was to toss something at me. I caught it without thinking. I didn't have to look to know what it was.

It was my Traveler ring.

"Yes, I took it," she admitted. "Back when I thought you were still a threat."

I clutched the ring, wishing that getting it back might actually mean something. Nevva dashed that hope.

"It doesn't matter now," she said with arrogance. "Go on. Talk to your friends. They'll tell you the truth. The Convergence began the instant you gave up. The first domino has fallen, Pendragon. Exactly the way Saint Dane said it would. You're right about one thing though. The battle is over. You're just a bit confused as to who the victor is. Keep the ring as a memento of your failed mission."

Behind Nevva the flume came to life. As I watched the light grow from the depths of the tunnel, I was grabbed from behind by several strong hands. Flighters. We weren't alone. They must have been creeping up the tunnel from behind me. I struggled to pull free, but there were too many of them. My Traveler ring fell to the ground and rolled away. Gone again. The Flighters wrestled me to the dirt and held me tight. I had to strain and twist my neck to see what was happening.

The rock walls of the flume dissolved into crystal. The bright light turned Nevva into a silhouette. The Flighters didn't let me go, but they hid their eyes. They must have been petrified by what they were seeing, not that I cared. I expected to see Saint Dane step out of the light. I *wanted* Saint Dane to step out of the light. This wasn't about Nevva. She was only the messenger. She stayed on Ibara to keep me occupied, while he was free to roam Halla. That was now painfully clear. How long had the flume been open? How long had he been gone? It probably didn't matter. It could have been open for months or minutes. Saint Dane could go wherever and whenever he wanted to. For the first time in my life, I desperately wanted him to appear.

He didn't. The shadow that was deposited at the mouth

of the flume looked nothing like him. The image was slighter, and much shorter. Whoever it was stood ramrod straight as they walked out of the tunnel. When the light receded, I saw something that made my head nearly spin. It made no sense, but there was no mistake.

It was Veego, the game master from Quillan. The woman looked exactly as I remembered her. She had short dark hair that was slicked straight back from her sharp features. She wore a single-piece dark pants suit that was immaculate. In her hands was the pole I had thrown into the flume.

"Hello, Nevva," she said formally. "Did you misplace this?"

Nevva took the pole and threw it aside.

"Welcome back," Nevva said. "I think you'll be pleased."

This was Veego's original home. Or should I say it was her home three hundred years in the future of her own time. She and her nutbag brother, LaBerge, were brought to Quillan by Saint Dane to run the sadistic Quillan games. What the heck would she be doing back, three hundred years later than when she had lived on Veelox?

Nevva pointed to me and said, "Of course you remember Pendragon."

Veego looked down her nose at me. With a disapproving sneer she said, "I see you're still playing games, Challenger Red."

"She's not a Traveler," I hissed at Nevva. "How can she travel?"

"I told you, the Convergence has begun," Nevva said matter-of-factly, as if she were telling me the time. "Halla is changing. When it is complete, the territories will become one."

Veego ignored me and looked straight at Nevva, saying, "Is everything ready?"

"For quite some time."

"Ready for what?" I screamed, struggling against the Flighters' grasps.

Veego looked at me with a cold stare. "Blok has finally seen its way clear to reward me appropriately for my successful game services. I have to say, it's long overdue."

Nevva added, "Veego and LaBerge have done such a phenomenal job with the Quillan games that the Blok corporation has decided to present them with their very own island." She looked to Veego and added, "It's a beautiful location. I trust it will be up to your standards."

My heart sank. "What island?" I screamed. I didn't want to know the answer.

Nevva gave me a fake smile and answered, "Why, Ibara of course."

I was so angry I nearly broke loose from the Flighters. They forced me back down, pushing my face into the dirt, and sat on me.

"It's not just an island," I shouted. "It's a civilization. You know as well as I do, Nevva, the tribunal won't allow this."

Nevva and Veego exchanged knowing looks. I didn't like that. Knowing looks were never good.

"They won't have a choice," Nevva said.

The flume came back to life. Veego and Nevva stepped out and faced it. I felt as if I were inside of a dream. Who could be coming in now? LaBerge? How could he affect anything? He was an idiot. Saint Dane? I hoped so. Beyond that, I had no other guesses. I figured I would be wrong anyway.

I was. When light from the flume filled the cavern, I saw two men walking out of the flume, shoulder to shoulder. Followed by two more men, followed by two more. And on and on. I stopped fighting. There was no use. I was watching the future of Ibara, and nothing I could do would change it. The men wore the crisp, green uniforms and gold helmets of the Blok security force from Quillan. They were dados. Veego spun on her heel and led the line of robots past me.

"Good-bye, Challenger Red," she spat at me with false warmth. "Pay a visit sometime. You're always welcome."

She strolled out of the cavern, her posture perfect, as if she were leading a military parade. She turned the corner that led to the tunnel out, and was gone. The dados kept marching out of the flume. Twenty, thirty, forty, I gave up counting. They marched in a straight line, two by two, like, well, like robots. They were identical. No expressions. No emotions. No morals other than to carry out their orders. I couldn't stop them. No way. What I needed to do was warn Genj. There was another war coming. Ibara would soon be under attack. In those few frantic seconds I made my plans. These Flighters couldn't hold me forever. Once I got loose I'd make my way out of there and back to the harbor. There were a few skimmers left under the dock. I'd take one to Ibara. It was night. I'd follow the stars. I had no idea how the dados would get there, and I didn't care. I couldn't let them reach Ibara before me. I had to warn the people of my new home that they were in danger. On the voyage I'd have time to figure out a way to defend the island again. Yes, that was my plan.

As the last dados rounded the corner into the tunnel, Nevva walked over and looked down at me.

"This is only one small example, Pendragon. Throughout Halla the strong will thrive and be rewarded. The weak will perish. That's the way it was meant to be."

That was it. I couldn't take it anymore. I kicked out, sending one Flighter reeling back across the cavern. With my legs free, I jackknifed up and grabbed another Flighter around the neck and twisted. He squealed in pain and let go. The third Flighter didn't want any part of that action and let me go too. All three of them took off running after the dados.

"It's not over," I called to Nevva, breathless. "I'm not done."

"But you are, Pendragon" was all she said.

I didn't care about her anymore. My place was on Ibara. I had to get out of there. I had to get back. I ran for the tunnel that led out. I turned the corner and sprinted along the narrow shaft. In the distance I heard something that sounded like pounding. Like metal on metal. Something was being hammered. I was only a few yards from the larger section of tunnel where the subway car dangled overhead. I was about to enter that wider area when I pulled to a stop. I saw what was making the hammering sound. Several dados were using their powerful arms to hammer at the supporting beams that held up the subway car. Were they crazy? Could robots be crazy?

"Stop!" I shouted.

They didn't. Several supports were knocked out quickly. I saw the hanging train shift and groan. Dirt rained down. It was going to fall. Two dados scrambled for the far side, leaving two more to continue smashing out supports. I made a quick calculation and decided to risk it. The train was going to come down. I sprinted for the far side. It was a gamble I had to take. A huge *creeek* sound told me I had made the wrong decision. I was directly under the big chassis. Dirt and rocks fell down on me. The subway train was ready to follow. I was about to be crushed. I had no choice. I put on the brakes and scrambled back the way I had come, just as the train, and all hell, broke loose. With the screeching sound of wrenching metal, the giant car fell through the air. I got thumped by a couple of larger rocks, but it didn't stop me. I dove back into the narrow tunnel, my body parallel to the ground as the whole world collapsed behind me.

The train car plummeted down, crashing onto the cavern floor and bringing tons of rock and dirt and pieces of Rubic City along with it. I scrambled on my hands and knees to escape from the avalanche. The tunnel had become unstable. I was afraid the whole thing would come crashing down on top of me. I rolled to the side and wrapped my arms around my head, in case any more rocks were on their way. I was pelted by a bunch of gravel, but nothing worse than that. After a minute, the sound stopped. All was still. I looked up to see the air was filled with dirt and dust. It took a while for it to settle enough for me to survey the damage.

Behind me, the cavern that had held the train was no more. The train car had fallen straight down, sealing the way out. I was trapped on the wrong side. The dados weren't. Next stop for them, Ibara. I sat there in the dusty darkness, staring at the wrecked train, trying to understand all that had happened. There was too much to get my head around.

There would be more.

A moment later the tunnel filled with light. I didn't register what was happening until I heard the music. The jumble of notes.

The flume had been activated.

"Nevva," I gasped.

I scrambled to my feet and ran for the flume. When I rounded the corner into the cavern, I saw the light receding into the tunnel. The music ended. The cavern was empty.

Nevva was gone.

My heart was beating faster than humanly possible. What was I supposed to do?

Everything was wrong.

Saint Dane had escaped.

Ibara was in danger. Again.

The Convergence had begun.

I still didn't know what that meant.

I was trapped.

Yet in front of me stood the doorway to everywhere.

I couldn't catch my breath. What was I supposed to do?

Nothing. I was through. I wasn't a Traveler anymore.

Did it matter? All that was happening was brought about because I had failed. I had given up. I had chosen not to fulfill my destiny.

Saint Dane's prophecy was coming true.

What was I supposed to do?

I was weak. I was naive.

But I used to be the lead Traveler.

What was the Convergence?

Were the other territories in the same danger as Ibara?

I didn't care. I only cared about Ibara. About Genj and Rayne and the Jakills. About fulfilling Aja Killian's dream. I only wanted to save one territory. Wasn't that enough?

But I used to be the lead Traveler.

It had been my battle to fight. I faced Saint Dane and I lost.

I wanted to see my family again.

I stood in that cavern alone. There was nobody to help me make a decision. Nobody to counsel me. Nobody to watch my back. My mind was in a thousand places and going nowhere.

Something on the dirt floor caught my eye. It was near where the Flighters had held me down. It was a flash of light. A sparkle. I walked the few steps toward it and bent down on one knee for a closer look. Lying in the dirt was my Traveler ring. As always, its stone sparkled because it was so near the flume. I gazed into the glittering gem, as if it might offer an answer. Any answer.

Close by I saw the wooden rod I had taken from the dock, lying where Nevva had tossed it. I reached out and grabbed it. It was a simple nautical tool. Six feet long. Solid. I stood up, holding it firmly with both hands. I held it out, testing its weight. I ran my hands across its smooth surface. It felt familiar. It felt good. I quickly flipped it into my right hand and spun it twice. This time I didn't miss. I snapped it out in front of me sharply. Point forward.

It was a weapon.

I knew how to use it.

I bent down and picked up my Traveler ring. The stone was alive.

So was I.

I put the ring back on my finger.

Things were happening exactly as Saint Dane had predicted. That's what Nevva said. The first domino had fallen. It was something I had heard about years before.

I turned to look into the flume.

The dark tunnel looked back. Waiting. I walked toward

it and stood in the wide mouth, staring into the darkness. Staring into the future. Staring into my destiny.

I clutched the weapon tighter. It felt right.

The first domino had fallen. I knew what that meant. I knew where I needed to be. I knew what I had to do.

I was the lead Traveler.

It was my job.

"Denduron," I growled.

And so we go.

END OF JOURNAL #34

SECOND EARTH

Mark woke up first. It was dark. His head hurt. The faint smell of lemons still tickled his nose. He was sitting in a padded chair that was shaking. How could a chair shake? He thought of those rides he used to go on outside the grocery store when he was a toddler. There were always fire engines or spaceships that you dropped a quarter into, and it shook for a minute. Back then it was thrilling. Now it was making him nauseous. Why was he on a kiddie ride?

As his head cleared, he realized it was a much simpler explanation. He was sitting in a moving car. A real one. Courtney sat next to him, still unconscious. He took a deep breath and tried to focus. It wasn't just a car. It was a limousine. A big one. He had plenty of room to stretch his legs, and he still couldn't touch the seat in front. How did they get there?

Oh. Right. The guys at Courtney's house. The lemons.

Mark leaned over to Courtney and brushed her long brown hair away from her face.

"Hey," he said softly. "You with me?"

Courtney stirred and grumbled.

"I don't want to go to school today, Mom. I'm sick," she whispered.

"You're dreaming," Mark said kindly.

"It was a joke, dork," Courtney quipped. She cracked open her eyes and took in the surroundings. "Nice ride" was her groggy comment.

"Any guesses as to what's going on?" Mark asked.

Courtney sat up and rubbed her face. She looked outside to see they were speeding along the highway. She leaned over and tried the door. It was locked.

"Well," she began. "The guys who grabbed us weren't the police, so that means we've been kidnapped. We're not tied up, so that means we don't scare them. And whoever they are, they're not lowlifes, because we're riding in a limousine. On top of all that, my head hurts and I'm still wearing your mother's goofy freakin' clothes."

Mark stared at her. "Yeah, I guess that about sums it up."

Courtney leaned forward and banged on the smoked glass that separated the rear seat from the front. "Hey!" she called out. "Where are we going?"

No answer. Courtney banged again. "Open up! At least talk to us."

Nobody did. Courtney sat back in her seat and huffed. "That's all I had. Your turn."

"The guys who grabbed us had that star tattoo," Mark said thoughtfully.

"So we've been kidnapped by people from the star cult," Courtney concluded. "Why should they care about us?"

"I don't know," Mark answered. "It's obvious that Saint Dane has to be involved. Maybe he's afraid we'll mess something up for him. It's happened."

Courtney chuckled. "Yeah, it's happened."

The two gazed out at the buildings flashing by.

"My parents are part of this," Courtney said softly. "They had the star over the fireplace. They can't be bad guys. My parents can't be bad guys."

"I don't think they are. Or maybe they don't realize they are."

"What does that mean?" Courtney demanded.

"Saint Dane influences people. They think they're making smart choices when he's actually pushing them toward disaster. What if the star cult or Ravinia or whatever it's called is something Saint Dane has been pushing people toward?"

"So then what's the turning point of Second Earth? The Convergence?"

"No," Mark said quickly. "The Convergence is bigger than that. At least I think it is. There has to be something happening on Second Earth that would naturally happen, and Saint Dane is trying to influence it. Maybe he's doing it through this cult."

Courtney thought about that. "This cult didn't exist on the old Second Earth. Something changed in the past that allowed it to be created."

"That's the mystery," Mark said.

"That and about a million other things," Courtney added. She glanced out the window again and announced, "We're in the city."

The car sped off the highway onto a wide street in New York City. It moved quickly through traffic, headed across town. They soon reached an intersection that was loaded with people. More than normal.

"What's all that about?" Courtney asked.

Mark joined her at the window to look out onto a crowd that was gathered along the sidewalk. Traffic was so heavy, the limo had to slow to a crawl. It gave them a chance to get a closer look at what was happening.

"Looks like a protest," Mark guessed.

"Looks more like an angry mob," Courtney corrected.

It was a raucous crowd, carrying signs that read, WE'RE ALL CREATED EQUAL, TRUTH WILL PREVAIL, and WE THE PEOPLE. They were waving their fists in the air and chanting a phrase over and over again.

Mark said, "Sounds like they're saying 'Stop them here.'"

Courtney listened and replied, "I hope they're not talking about us. Those people look pissed."

"I wouldn't worry about it," Mark said, pointing.

He was looking at several people who were carrying signs with the green star symbol. Each star was surrounded by a red circle with a line slashed diagonally through the center. It was the classic symbol that meant *no.*

"I guess not everybody is part of the star cult," Mark observed. "Look at that guy."

He pointed to a man who stood on a ladder so he could be seen by the crowd. He was a dark-skinned guy, possibly of Asian Indian background. He wore a dark suit with a blue bow tie, looking very official next to the people who swirled around him. He held up a bullhorn through which he chanted, "Stop them here! Stop them here!" while punching his fist angrily toward the sky. The crowd responded, waving their signs and punching right along with him.

"He looks more pissed than anybody," Courtney commented. "He's got them pretty worked up."

The limo slowed and was instantly rushed by a group of people that started to rock it.

"Whoa!" Courtney yelled. "You sure they're not after us?"

"Maybe they think we're part of it."

"Great," Courtney said sarcastically. "We're being attacked for something we don't know anything about."

The limo lurched forward. There were a few thumps, making the car jolt.

"Did we just hit somebody?" Mark asked, aghast.

They looked out the back window to see three people lying on the road, hurt.

"Are you crazy!" Courtney yelled at the driver while slamming on the glass.

"No wonder they don't like us," Mark said soberly.

The car took an abrupt right turn, throwing Mark and Courtney into each other. It quickly descended into an underground garage. The two looked out the back window again to see a group of security people quickly closing a metal fence behind them. Protesters rushed the fence and pounded on it, still chanting, "Stop them here! Stop them here!"

"What the hell?" was all Courtney could say.

The limo sped through the underground parking structure, taking a few quick turns with its wheels squealing on the cement. It suddenly screeched to a stop next to a group of people who seemed to be waiting for them.

"Uh-oh," Mark uttered.

There were five people. Four of them wore the same dark red clothes and short-brimmed caps that were worn by the men who attacked them at Courtney's house. They stood there expressionless. The fifth person looked nothing like the others. He was a man who looked to be in his thirties. He was exceptionally clean cut, with short blond hair and a big, inviting smile. He wore a short-sleeved dark red polo shirt and black pants. In one hand was a clipboard, which made him look official. With his other hand, he waved warmly to Mark and Courtney, who peered out from the backseat.

"Who's the dork?" Courtney asked. "Looks like he's getting ready to play golf."

"At least he's smiling."

The car doors automatically unlocked with a loud click. The smiley guy leaned down and opened the rear door, making a big, sweeping gesture of welcome.

"Hello! You are right on time!" the man said with enthusiasm. "Mark and Courtney, right?"

Mark and Courtney looked at each other in surprise. They didn't move. Or speak.

"Welcome!" the man added.

"Welcome?" Mark echoed. "You kidnapped us."

"Oh, that," the man said, scoffing. "We were afraid you wouldn't make it in time. That's all. But you have! Sorry for the inconvenience."

Courtney erupted. "You broke into my family's house and gassed us. You call that an inconvenience?"

The young man looked at Courtney, still holding the smile. "Yes."

"Oh. Just checking." Courtney banged on the glass separator again and shouted to the driver, "Keep moving!"

The young man reached out his hand in a welcoming gesture.

"Please," he said warmly. "Join me."

The two didn't have a choice. In spite of the friendly welcome, the sober-looking guys who stared them down made that pretty clear. Mark got out. Courtney followed.

"That's better!" the man with the big smile exclaimed. He held out his hand to shake. "My name is Eugene. I'll be your escort."

Mark didn't take it. Neither did Courtney. Eugene took his hand back, but didn't drop his smile. He didn't seem bothered by the snub. "All right then. Let's not dawdle. Wouldn't want to miss anything."

He hurried off past the other four men. Mark and Courtney didn't move. Eugene turned back and gave them a big, overstated frown. "Are we still upset?"

Courtney answered sarcastically. "You're kidding, right?"

Eugene opened his arms in a welcoming gesture. "Let me make it up to you. Come! I promise you're going to see something spectacular."

“What if we don’t want to go with you?” Courtney asked.

“Then you’ll be missing out on what could be the most important moment of your lives” was Eugene’s answer. “And these gentlemen would *really* like you to join me.”

The four goons stared at Mark and Courtney, still with no expression.

Courtney looked at Mark and shrugged. Mark nodded. Courtney turned to Eugene and said, “Does this have anything to do with golf?”

Eugene gave her a puzzled look.

Courtney started walking. “Never mind. Let’s go.”

Mark followed Courtney and the whole group was on their way. They followed Eugene across the underground garage and through a steel door that led into a long, narrow corridor of painted cinderblock walls.

“I hope those rude people outside didn’t bother you,” Eugene said. “They just don’t understand.”

“Understand what?” Mark asked.

“They don’t understand that it’s not their fault. People must accept the fate they’ve been given. Jealousy won’t change that; it only makes them more upset.”

Mark and Courtney exchanged looks.

Eugene stopped short and turned to them. “You understand that, I’m sure.”

Courtney answered, “I don’t understand a word of it.”

Eugene gave her a simple, happy smile. “You will.”

He led them into an elevator. When Mark and Courtney entered and turned around, they saw the door close before the other four boarded.

“There will be other security men when we reach our floor,” Eugene cautioned, as if reading their minds.

The elevator rose a few floors, then opened onto a corridor that was much more plush than the first. It had thick carpeting and large black-and-white photos spaced along both walls. Every twenty feet or so was a closed door with a number next to it.

"This way," Eugene said, and hurried out.

The two followed, looking at the photos. They were enlargements from all different eras. Mark recognized some of them. There was a shot of Muhammad Ali in the ring against Joe Frazier; circus elephants performing in the center ring; and concert shots from such stars as the Rolling Stones, Madonna, and even Justin Timberlake. Courtney focused more on the sports action shots from many eras that featured the New York Knicks and Rangers.

"I know where we are," Courtney said softly to Mark.

"Me too," Mark answered. "I guess we shouldn't be surprised."

"Of course not!" Eugene said happily. "You are exactly where you should be!" He stopped at one door and knocked. A moment later the door was opened from inside by another of the security people.

"You've got the best seat in the house," Eugene said warmly.

Mark and Courtney stepped into what looked like a small living room. To the right was a sitting area with comfortable couches and chairs. To the left was a small kitchen that had a full spread of sandwiches and drinks as if set for a party. They both knew this wasn't the main event. They walked through, headed for the far side, which ended at a glass wall. A glass door opened out to a sitting area where there were a dozen stadium-type seats. Mark and Courtney had only heard about places like this. Neither expected to actually enter one. They both walked past the stadium seats to a safety railing. Spread before them was the vast indoor arena that was Madison Square Garden. Courtney had been there before, for Knicks games. Mark had been there for the circus. Neither had ever been inside one of the luxury suites. The view was perfect, but dizzying. They were up very high.

The Garden was packed. A full house. An elevated stage was

erected in the dead center of the arena, where the tip-off of a basketball game would take place. It was surrounded by a solid pack of eager people. There wasn't a square inch of space available.

Mark nudged Courtney and pointed to a series of large red flags that hung from every level. They ringed the huge arena, creating a circle of bright, fluttering red.

"I think I'm going to faint," Mark whispered.

Each of the red flags had a single, large symbol. The star symbol. A single, huge white star was painted on the floor of the black stage.

"It's okay," Courtney whispered back, her voice quivering. "This is what we wanted, right? We need to know what this is about."

Four huge photos covered each side of the square scoreboard that hung over the center of the arena. They were different close-ups of the man from the television commercial. He looked like a kindly old grandfather, with perfect hair and a warm smile. To Mark and Courtney, it seemed he was staring right at them.

"He personally wanted you to be here," Eugene said, motioning to the photos. He had suddenly appeared behind Mark and Courtney.

"Who did?" Mark asked.

Eugene looked surprised. "Why, Naymeer of course."

"Nay-who?" Courtney asked.

Eugene chuckled as if Courtney had made a joke. She hadn't.

"Why would he want *us* to be here?" Mark asked.

"I believe he's been wanting to meet you since you paid a visit to his home last night. You left in such a hurry, he never got the chance to chat. Enjoy!"

Eugene backed away, leaving Mark and Courtney alone. Mark sat down in a front-row seat. Hard. His legs wouldn't hold him anymore. Courtney held on to the railing, because she feared she might go over the edge.

"No" was all Mark could get out.

"Yes," Courtney countered. "It's the guy from the window of the Sherwood house. With the dog."

"Then the guys who grabbed us from your parents' house—," Mark continued.

"Yeah," Courtney interrupted again. "They were the ones shooting at us."

"That means the man who's running this whole show—"

"Lives on top of the flume."

The lights in the arena went dark. The crowd didn't cheer the way they would at a concert. Instead they grew quiet. Eerily quiet. Grand music swelled. A single spotlight hit the stage, illuminating the star.

The show was about to begin.

SECOND EARTH

(CONTINUED)

The star on the floor began to sparkle, sending out pinpoints of light that danced over the thousands of mesmerized faces. People raised their hands with their palms open, swaying to the music.

Mark and Courtney sat close to each other. Watching. Wide eyed.

The music continued, building in energy. The people moved rhythmically, their eyes closed to allow themselves to be swept away by the sound.

A booming voice echoed throughout the arena. It was a man's voice with a hint of a British accent. The voice was calm, but spoke with the authority that came from total confidence.

"Convergence," the voice began. "All that ever was. All that will be."

Mark held Courtney tighter. "Is this it?" he whispered. "Is this the Convergence?

Courtney stared straight ahead.

"Embrace it," the voice continued. "It is for you. The chosen. The visionaries. The elite."

The crowd let out a gasp of excitement, as if loving the words.

The voice boomed, "When the Convergence arrives, do not have doubts. Do not listen to the skeptics, for they are the lost. The future is yours. Let us enter into it with joy . . . together!"

The sparkling lights stopped abruptly. Several spotlights hit the center of the stage to reveal a man standing in the center of the star. The crowd erupted with rapturous gasps of joy. He was the same elderly man with the perfect gray hair that Mark and Courtney saw on the television commercial. His pictures hung from the scoreboard. He wore a long, deep red robe. On the back of the robe was a golden star. He stood with his hands out and a warm, fatherly smile on his face. Though he was older, he stood straight and tall—his age was not about to slow him down.

"Naymeer?" Courtney whispered.

Mark shrugged. "I guess."

The man stepped off the star and circled the stage so everybody could get a good look at him. People from below reached up, trying to touch his gown. He never got close enough to the edge for that to happen. Mark noticed that there were several security types on the floor, holding the crowd back from touching the man. They all wore the same red shirts as the guys who had kidnapped them. And shot at them. On either end of the arena near the ceiling, two huge video screens flashed to life, each showing a live close-up of the man named Naymeer.

The crowd gasped, as if seeing him this way was more than they could handle. Mark looked around to see that each and every person was transfixed. Some were actually in tears. There were people of all ages and races. Some wore western-style business suits, others wore traditional wardrobe from other cultures. They saw colorful wraps that could have come from African nations. Some women wore saris and several men wore turbans. They also saw what looked like military uniforms from different countries.

As unique as the people seemed, they all had one thing in common—they were transfixed by the man who stalked the stage. Many reached toward him, even from the highest level, as if getting just a few inches closer was a good thing.

"He's loving this," Courtney whispered.

The man circled the stage twice while the music pulsed. Naymeer raised his hand and the music stopped on cue. The people instantly became silent.

"Whoa," Courtney remarked. "They're like trained dogs."

"My friends," Naymeer began. His voice was the same amplified voice they had heard before. "The journey that began for me so long ago is about to end, and a new journey will begin . . . for all of us. I am so very pleased that you have chosen to join me."

As he spoke, he circled the stage. He seemed to be making direct eye contact with each and every person there.

"I was given a gift," he continued. "A gift that means nothing if I cannot share it with you. I have seen the future. I have seen the past. I have seen in each and every one of you the spark of inspiration that will guide our way. You have answered the call. You are the elite. You are the strong. You are the enlightened. You . . . are . . . Ravinia!"

The crowd erupted into a thunderous cheer that lasted for five minutes. The whole while, Naymeer stalked the stage, looking into the people's eyes, soaking up their adoration.

"This could go on for days," Courtney quipped.

Mark said, "This is some kind of cult of the elite. He's telling them that they are the chosen."

"I guess that means those people outside are the not-chosen," Courtney added. "Sucks for them. I guess."

"Yeah, but chosen for what?"

Naymeer held his hand up and the people quickly quieted down. Every last one, instantly.

"That's just odd," Courtney whispered.

Naymeer continued, "You have read the writings. You know my story. I was near death. A poor, weak foundling. Nothing more than an inconsequential spec of sand being blown through a harsh, flawed world. Until I had the vision. The truth. It gave me the strength to live. My friends, I cannot tell you why I was chosen. I like to think that I was an example of what can be. From humble beginnings can grow a mighty force. I believe I was chosen because I had in me the same potential and power that I see in each of you. The power to thrive. The power to create. The power to choose light over dark. Strength over weakness. Right over wrong. From that moment on, I dedicated my life to finding and gathering those who share my vision. Together we will forge a new world. A superior existence. A shining tower. We will cast aside the weak and the needy in order to revel in the glory of a new Halla!"

Mark's stomach turned.

Courtney gasped.

The crowd went nuts.

"H-Halla?" Mark said to Courtney over the screaming crowd. "Do they know?"

For once in her life, Courtney was speechless. All she could do was shake her head in stunned silence. The cheering went on for another ten minutes. Mark and Courtney looked around to see people out of their minds with emotion. People fainted. People cried. People laughed. People hugged.

"This is mental," Courtney gasped.

After several minutes of this rapture, the lights went dark. The crowd became still. The two large video screens flickered to life with a movie. With the same compelling music as background, the crowd was shown a montage of images, all featuring Naymeer. He was seen:

Walking along the Great Wall of China.

Having an audience with the Pope.

Leading a group past the pyramids in Egypt.

Shaking hands with a huge crowd of people outside Red Square in Moscow.

Sitting for a photo opportunity with the president of the United States.

Speaking to an audience in a packed football stadium.

"This guy's for real," Courtney whispered.

"Yeah, but who is he?" Mark shot back.

As the images continued on the screens, Naymeer's voice was heard saying, "We have traveled a far distance together. Our numbers are growing because our cause is just. Now the next step of our journey is at hand."

Images of the United Nations building in New York flashed on the screens.

"A great day is upon us. The next step in our evolution. We are soon to be recognized as the spiritual voice of the entire world by the United Nations."

The crowed roared its approval.

"What!" Courtney gasped.

"There are powers in Halla that are greater than any single one of us," Naymeer's voice continued. "This we have learned. We are humbled in the face of those powers, and steadfast in the belief that we have been chosen to help cast off the shackles of fear. The truth is at hand—the truth of our very existence. Together we will create a glorious future that is greater than anything that has come before."

The movie ended and was replaced by the face of Naymeer. Live. He stood at the center of the stage. The entire arena was dark except for the two video screens, and Naymeer. He appeared to be floating in a black sea.

"I have seen the future," Naymeer said again. "I have seen the past. Separately we are small. Together we have the power to control our destiny. What a glorious destiny it will be."

With that, Naymeer made a fist and held it up above his head. The music stopped. The image of Naymeer's clenched fist was seen in close-up on both video screens.

"Oh my god," Courtney whispered.

"It can't be," Mark gasped. "Can it?"

On Naymeer's index finger was a ring.

A Traveler ring.

Neither had a chance to say anything more, for an instant later, multiple beams of light shot from the ring, as if it were activating and a message were coming in.

"Mark? What's happening?" Courtney asked, trembling.

The fingers of light spread across the arena, lighting up the eyes of everyone there. It played across their faces in a hypnotic dance. What happened next might have been described as a trick. Special-effects wizardry. Computer magic. None of the people in that arena thought it was a trick.

Neither did Mark and Courtney. They knew it was real. The people in the arena had to take it on faith that what they were seeing wasn't a clever illusion. Mark and Courtney didn't have to be convinced, because they had seen it all before. As if being projected from an impossible machine, giant three-dimensional images floated through the darkened space of Madison Square Garden.

The images of Halla.

Floating before them was the same jumble of images that had become so familiar to those who used the flumes. The people in the arena witnessed the floating barges of Magorran and Grallion. Zenzen horses sprinted in space, flying past an army of green-uniformed marching dados. The beautiful city built in the trees, known as "Leeandra," was seen, complete with klee cats scooting across sky bridges. They saw the elaborate stone pyramids of the city of Xhaxhu on Zadaa, around which flew several green and yellow flying machines known as "gigs" from the territory of Eelong. A quig-bear from Denduron reared up against an army of Bedoowan knights, beyond which lay the shining city of Faar, newly risen from the ocean floor of Cloral. The *Hindenburg* sailed past, blotting out in turn each of the three suns of Denduron.

"Ravinia is the power of Halla," Naymeer's voice bellowed. "We are the power of Ravinia. We are the strong. We are the perfect. Those who are not equal to the task will be cast aside. The Convergence will soon be upon us. We must be ready."

Everyone in the arena watched in awe, including Mark and Courtney. As the images danced in the darkness, the crowd was hushed. Slowly, they began to clap and cheer. It started softly, then grew until each and every person was cheering for the swirling images of Halla.

"Th-There's only one explanation," Mark stuttered. "He must be Saint Dane. Naymeer must be Saint Dane."

"Really? Is that the only explanation?" came a voice from behind them.

Mark and Courtney spun around to see a man standing in the glass doorway that led back into the luxury suite. He stood well over six feet tall and wore a dark suit. His blue-white eyes blazed at them.

"There may be another," Saint Dane said with a smile.

Mark and Courtney could only stare.

Saint Dane pointed back to the arena. "You're missing quite a show," he cautioned with a slight snicker.

Naymeer's voice continued, "The Convergence will join together all that is good and perfect in Halla. You will be the leaders. You will control the next step of evolution. You will crush the weak and allow the glory to encompass us all. We will be one with the brothers of all worlds. Those who do not believe will be left behind. Embrace Ravinia, and Halla will be ours."

"Who is that?" Courtney demanded.

"You heard him," Saint Dane answered. "He's the future. He's the past. Very dramatic, don't you think?"

"But who is he?" Mark shouted.

"Isn't that obvious?" Saint Dane answered. "He's the Traveler from Second Earth."

SECOND EARTH

(CONTINUED)

"Bobby Pendragon is the Traveler from Second Earth," Mark said with no emotion.

"He was." Saint Dane sighed. "I'm afraid he decided the task was no longer to his taste. But I'm sure you knew that."

Saint Dane turned and walked into the luxury suite. Mark ran after him. Courtney was right behind.

"How did you get off Ibara?" Mark called after him.

"I'm sure you'll find that out soon enough," Saint Dane answered without turning back.

Courtney asked, "Does that mean Bobby can leave too?"

"Pendragon quit," Saint Dane spat at them. "Why do you think the Convergence has begun? He lost because he didn't have enough faith in himself, or his convictions, to continue. He was flawed, which came as no surprise to me."

"'Flawed,'" Courtney echoed. "You make it sound like a crime."

"Indeed," Saint Dane agreed. "Pendragon was flawed. That is why he quit."

"He didn't quit!" Courtney shot back. "He blew up the flume to trap you on Ibara."

Saint Dane held out his arms and smiled. "And you see how successful he was. Pendragon destroyed the flume on Ibara because he no longer had the will to continue the struggle. Paint that any way you like, but it is the truth. His weakness didn't close a door, it opened one. For me. It's a door that cannot be closed."

"Unless Bobby wants it closed," Courtney threw back at him.

"Why are you so concerned with Pendragon when such momentous events are happening right before you?" Saint Dane chastised. "Pendragon is history. This is what it's all been leading to. The Convergence has begun. Accept it."

"What does that mean?" Courtney yelled desperately. "What is the Convergence?"

"Weren't you listening? It's the creation of a new order, just as Naymeer said. My vision for a unified Halla is one breath away. It's happening on all the territories. Each one is falling into line, just as I said it would." Saint Dane walked to the kitchen area and looked over the tray of sandwiches on the counter. "This is quite nice," he commented. "I may have to attend a sporting event here. What exactly is a Knick?"

"Why are we here?" Courtney demanded to know.

Saint Dane turned to them, but as he moved, he transformed into the character of Eugene, the clean-cut guy who escorted them to the suite. Mark and Courtney both jolted with surprise.

"I told you," Eugene answered brightly. "You're the special guest of Naymeer. He wanted you here."

Mark fought to keep his composure and asked, "Why? He doesn't even know who we are."

"Naymeer is the Traveler from Second Earth now," Eugene said with pride. "He needs acolytes. What better choice than you two? After all, you have loads of experience!"

"You can't be serious," Courtney spat out. "You expect us to give up on Bobby?"

With a quick move to his right, Eugene transformed into the character of Whitney Wilcox—the soccer-playing preppy from Stansfield Academy. He even had a soccer ball that he bounced off his knee.

"You're a winner, Courtney," Whitney said cockily. "The way I see it, you've only got one choice. Take it. Be a winner. You too, Mark. You can come along for the ride." Whitney laughed, bounced the ball off his knee again and kicked it at them. Courtney caught it without flinching.

"Nice!" called Whitney.

"Not gonna happen," Courtney said flatly.

"N-No, it's not," Mark echoed.

Whitney transformed. This time Saint Dane became Andy Mitchell. Mark's nemesis. Mark's partner in Forge. Mark's nightmare. He looked as he did on Second Earth, complete with long, greasy blond hair and a dirty T-shirt. He hawked up a lougie and spit into the sink. Mark and Courtney didn't blink.

"Guess what, Dimond? This one's on you too!" Mitchell cackled.

"What does that mean?" Mark asked.

Andy Mitchell strolled over to the glass partition that overlooked the arena. The lights were back on. The Halla portion of the show was over. Naymeer was once again addressing the audience.

"Naymeer's ring," Mitchell said. "Look familiar?"

"All the Traveler rings look the same," Mark answered through clenched teeth.

"I guess," Mitchell agreed. "But that one. That one's special."

"Why?" Mark asked.

Mitchell smiled, showing a mouthful of yellow, nicotine-stained teeth. "Because it's yours."

Mark and Courtney stared back at Mitchell for a long, confused moment. It was Mark who first put it together.

"Nevva," he whispered, dazed.

Mitchell continued, "First you created the dados, then you offered up the one thing that kicked off the whole show. I pretty much owe you everything, Dimond. The least I can do is offer you a seat at the table. Chetwynde, too, so long as she keeps her mouth shut. She can be really annoying."

Mark stood frozen. Courtney grabbed his arm and pulled him toward the door. Mark didn't move at first, but was too stunned to resist for long, and the two moved toward the exit.

"Hey, where you going?" Mitchell called. "There ain't no place to go. No place to hide. It's all over but the shouting." He let out a scream. "Ahhh!" Then shrugged and smiled. "Oops. Guess now it's over."

Courtney kept pulling Mark toward the door. She backed into it, reached behind herself for the knob, and opened it up.

"Think about it!" Mitchell called. "You're either with me or against me. I don't think you want to be against me. Not anymore."

Courtney pulled Mark through the door and let it slam shut.

"We're outta here," she said to him and pulled him toward the elevator.

Mark didn't move.

"It's my ring," he said, as if in a trance. "That's why Nevva wanted it. It wasn't to isolate Bobby. It was to start the Convergence."

Courtney jumped back and got in Mark's face. "Saint Dane started the Convergence," she snarled. "Not you. Not that slick old dude. Saint Dane."

"If Bobby quit," Mark said flatly, "I think I will too."

Courtney shook him. Hard. "You are *not* quitting! We've been waiting for this moment for years. It's the turning point of Second Earth, Mark. It's not what we expected. Fine. So what? This is our time. It's on us now, just like we always thought."

"But it's all my fault," Mark said weakly.

Courtney wound up and slapped Mark across the face. She didn't hold back, either. She really whacked him. Hard. Mark stared at her, stunned.

"Wake up!" she yelled. "As long as we're still alive, it's not over. But if you give up now, then it really *will* be your fault."

Mark looked surprised, and hurt.

Courtney added, "I don't know what this whole Ravinia thing is leading to, but after what happened to Third Earth, you know it can't be good."

"I wish Bobby was here," Mark said meekly.

"He's not. We are. What's it gonna be?"

Mark's pained look slowly turned to one of resolve. His eyes focused. He stood up straight and said, "What do we do?"

"We get Patrick," she answered quickly.

"And then what?"

"If Saint Dane is here, it must mean the flume to Ibara is open."

"So?"

"So you're right. We need Bobby. Somebody's got to get to him and make him un-quit."

Mark gave this a moment's thought, then shook his head quickly. "Courtney, we can't."

"Yeah we can. We're going to get out of here, get Patrick, and travel."

"Hey!" came a shout from down the hall.

Mark and Courtney looked quickly to see two red-shirt guards running toward them. Both turned and ran in the other direction. They sprinted along the corridor past the photos of famous events. Mark wondered if one day there would be a picture of Naymeer hanging there. The thought made him angry. The anger made him dig in. They ran faster.

"The elevator," Mark shouted.

"No."

They kept running. Halfway down the corridor they hit a fire exit, blasted through the door, and ran down the stairs.

Courtney said breathlessly, "We'll get to Grand Central and take the train home to get Patrick."

"No," Mark argued. "They might expect that. We've got plenty of cash. We'll take a taxi."

"All the way to Stony Brook?"

"Why not? It's KEM's money."

They landed on the next floor and ran through double doors that opened onto a wide, bright walkway that ringed the arena. There were hotdog stands, souvenir counters . . . and two red-shirt guards. The Ravinians were walking toward Mark and Courtney, about twenty yards away.

"They don't know who we are," Mark whispered.

One guard saw them, pointed, and both started running after them.

"Or maybe they do," Courtney countered.

The two turned and ran in the opposite direction, only to see two more red shirts coming toward them. They were trapped. Looking around desperately, they found themselves standing directly in front of one of the tunnels that led back into the arena. Both knew it was the only way to go and ran inside. They had only taken a few steps when a sea of excited people came pouring out. The show was over. The charged-up minions of Naymeer were headed home. Mark grabbed Courtney's hand and pulled her headlong into the crowd. They were like two salmon swimming upstream, fighting their way through. Once inside the arena, Mark took a sharp right and pushed his way farther into the mass of people.

"We'll get lost in the crowd," he called back to Courtney. "Stay low. Go slow."

They had to fight the urge to push faster. Both knew it would only make them stand out. They had to be patient and have the nerve to blend in with the moving mass of humanity. They climbed down a set of stairs and entered another tunnel that led to the outside. The crowd slowly made its way toward escalators going down. Mark and Courtney crouched low, trying to use the people to shield them from their pursuers. They passed a group of red shirts who were scanning the crowd. Courtney saw them first and pulled Mark lower. It took all their willpower not to break into a run. They finally reached the escalator and stepped on.

"Stop!" came a voice from above.

They looked up to see red shirts glaring down on them from two levels up. Courtney looked at Mark and said, "Does he really think we'd do that?"

The escalator dumped them out near a ramp that led farther down. The crowd had thinned and no longer offered cover. Without discussing it, they both ran. They only had to move one more level down before they hit a set of glass doors that led to the street. They pushed through the doors and leaped outside.

"We gotta find a cab," Mark announced.

"Not around here," Courtney offered. "Too much competition."

They were no longer worried about getting caught. There were too many people outside. They walked as quickly as they could toward the sidewalk, but stopped when they saw that blue police barriers were strung along the curb, holding back hundreds of protesters. They held their signs and chanted at the exiting minions.

The same dark-skinned man in the suit and bow tie had moved his ladder into position so he could be seen clearly by the throng exiting the Garden. He stood above the others, pounding the air with his fist and bellowing into his bullhorn. The other protesters gathered at his feet, shouting along with him.

Mark listened and said, "They're not chanting 'Stop them here.' It's 'Stop Naymeer.'"

Most of the people who came out of the show simply smiled at the protesters. Some even waved.

"Look at them," Courtney whispered. "They don't care. They're the chosen ones. The protesters mean nothing to them."

"Look out!" Mark yelled, and pulled Courtney back just as a protester hurled himself over the police barrier and attacked one of the minions. A brawl broke out. The barrier came crashing down as more protesters joined in. The Naymeer people defended themselves, but they were more about getting away than retaliating. Soon the New York City police showed up, complete with riot gear. They fought to pull people apart.

"This is ugly," Courtney gasped.

Mark pulled her away, and the two ran a few blocks until they found a yellow taxi to pick them up.

"Stony Brook," Mark said.

The cabbie's eyes went wide. "Connecticut? That'll cost you."

"Just drive," Courtney commanded.

"Yes, ma'am," the cabbie replied. He hit the meter and they were off.

Mark and Courtney rode in silence. Both were trying to digest what they'd seen. It was the cabbie who spoke first.

"What side you two on?" the gruff little man asked.

"What do you mean?" Mark asked.

"You came from that meeting. You two Ravini-ites?"

Mark and Courtney exchanged looks and shrugs.

"We're still deciding," Mark answered. "What about you?"

"Nah! I think it's all a lot of hocus-pocus," the cabbie scoffed. "All that talk about other worlds and the origins of the universe. It makes my head hurt."

Courtney snickered. "Yeah, tell me about it."

"I'll say this though," the cabbie continued, "I think them guys are dangerous."

"How so?" Mark asked.

"They're trying to run the whole show. Now they got that thing going at the UN 'cause they want to be some kind of international spiritual advisors. That's just wrong. It's what we got governments for. You may not always agree with politicians, but at least they pretend to be fair."

"You don't think the Ravinians are fair?" Mark probed.

"How can it be fair when they only care about the high falutin'?"

"What do you mean?" Courtney asked.

"Hey, I ain't no dummy, but I couldn't join them even if I wanted to. They only take you if you're some kind of egghead. Or you got money. Or a business. I think you gotta have a big fat IQ just to qualify. They don't want regular workin' stiffs like me. I don't know nuthin' about their plans for the future, but it seems to me, they're trying to separate the haves from the have-nots. If you're one of the have-nots, you're gonna have a lot less, if they have a say. It just ain't right."

Mark uttered aloud, "The elite. The strong. The enlightened."

Courtney added, "It's like they're trying to weed out anybody who's less than perfect."

"Exactly!" the cabbie agreed. "I can't get behind that, but a lot of people do. To be honest, it scares me. I'm just a regular guy. It ain't right I tell ya."

Neither Mark nor Courtney said another word until they were dropped off in front of Mark's house in Stony Brook.

"Wait for us," Courtney said. "Keep the meter running."

"You bet I will. Hey, you're not gonna stiff me, are you?"

"Not a chance," Mark said. He dug into his wallet and took out two fifty-dollar bills for the cabbie. "That's a down payment. Wait up the block, okay?"

The cabbie tipped his hat happily. "Whatever you say. It's your dime."

The cabbie put the car in gear, then gave a final warning. "Remember what I told you. Them people ain't right." With that last bit of wisdom, he took off.

"Them people ain't right," Courtney repeated. "Kind of sums it all up, doesn't it."

"Why did you want him to wait?" Mark asked.

"We won't be here long. And I didn't want somebody to wonder why there's a cab outside your house."

"Oh. Smart."

The two circled around toward the back of the house, making sure that nobody saw them. Once inside, they found Patrick right where they had left him, sitting in front of Mark's computer. The only difference was that he was surrounded by bags of Doritos and cans of Mountain Dew. He looked up at them with wild eyes.

"You okay?" Courtney asked.

"I'm fantastic!" Patrick exclaimed. "This sugary drink is incredible!"

"Swell," Courtney remarked sarcastically. "He's wired on Dew."

"But we have problems," Patrick continued, ramping down. He took another hit of soda. "There's a fellow named Naymeer who is the leader of Ravinia."

He stopped talking long enough to gulp down more Dew. Courtney pulled it away from him.

"Easy," she scolded. "You don't want to be up all day."

"Excuse me?" Patrick asked, perplexed.

"We know all about Naymeer," Mark interjected.

He went on to explain all that had happened, from being abducted at Courtney's house to the rally at Madison Square Garden to the meeting with Saint Dane. Patrick listened, wide eyed, while stuffing Doritos into his mouth. When Mark finished, Patrick didn't say a word. He stared straight ahead, digging back into the Doritos bag. Courtney couldn't take it anymore and grabbed it away from him.

"You're making me sick!" she exclaimed.

Patrick barely reacted. He was too busy processing the information. "Traveler from Second Earth," he muttered. "That's not good."

"No," Courtney said with mock patience. "I'd say that's really bad. What did you find out about Naymeer?"

Patrick snapped back into focus and grabbed a stack of papers he had printed out.

"It wasn't difficult," he explained. "This thing you call the Internet is crude, but there's plenty of information about Naymeer."

He handed some printouts to Mark and Courtney.

"His full name is Alexander Naymeer. He's originally from England. An orphan. Apparently, when he was young, he was knocking on death's door, and then he suddenly had a miraculous recovery. The doctors couldn't explain it. The nurses called it a miracle. Whatever it was, from that moment on, the guy started telling stories about other worlds and forces larger than anyone could envision. At first people chalked it up to youthful imagination . . . until he started sharing his visions. Literally. He showed people images of unique people and strange animals and places that didn't exist anywhere on Earth. They would have locked him up except for the fact that nobody could explain how he did it."

"We know how," Mark interrupted.

"He started acting like some kind of prophet, telling of the potential for future glory, and how this world and all others could reach a kind of nirvana, as long as the right path was followed." Patrick dug through the pages, looking for a particular sheet. He found it and said, "Here, this is a quote: *'We must reward excellence and condemn those whose only contribution to society is to burden.'* He said that when he was nine years old."

Courtney held up one of the pages and made a sour face. "Disgusting. You've got Dorito fingerprints all over these."

"Stop!" Mark snapped at Courtney. "This is serious."

"Like I don't know that?"

"Patrick, what year was he born?"

Patrick dug through some papers. "They don't know for sure, because he was abandoned at a foundling home, but the best guess is 1930."

"And what year did he nearly die?"

Patrick scanned the pages. "That one's definite: 1937."

"First Earth," Courtney said softly.

"In England," Mark added. "It happened when we were there. That's when Nevva gave him my ring. It saved his life, and started a revolution."

Patrick said, "'Revolution' is the right word. He's created a cult of excellence. Its members are all special people in one way or another. They're leaders, scientists, athletes, successful business people, brilliant students, military leaders, mathematicians. All races. All nationalities. The one thing they have in common is that in some way, they are exceptional."

"They're flawless," Courtney said, echoing Saint Dane's words.

Mark stood and paced. "It's like he's trying to create a superclass of people to be the new leaders of Earth, and Halla."

"What about everybody else?" Courtney asked. "You know, the regular people?"

Patrick answered, "He never comes out and says it, but from all that I've read, he thinks that the people he considers to be inferior have been the cause of all the world's ills. According to his vision, they'll be marginalized."

"What the heck does *that* mean?" Courtney asked.

"I think it means that according to Ravinia, they're irrelevant and shouldn't be given the same rights as others," Patrick answered.

"Yikes" was Courtney's response.

Mark asked, "So Naymeer's vision for the future says the poor, the sick, the handicapped, the people who need the help of society will be considered irrelevant and treated differently?"

"Not just the poor and sick," Patrick corrected. "It includes anyone whom Naymeer doesn't consider to be exceptional. That means your average person will be treated as a liability to society."

"What about old people?" Courtney asked.

Patrick shrugged. "If they don't contribute to society in some significant way, they're not part of Ravinia and will be treated as second-class citizens."

Courtney added, "Wasn't that kind of what the Nazis were all about? Creating a Super Race?"

"Yes," Patrick answered. "At the expense of several million people who didn't fit the profile."

"How can people buy into this?" Courtney complained. "It's just . . . wrong."

"Not everybody does" was Patrick's response. "There's a whole countermovement to Ravinia. They call themselves the 'Foundation.' They're fighting the cause of the common man, saying how everybody has value, and to follow Naymeer would lead to destruction. Look at this."

Patrick looked to Mark's computer and announced, "Play Gastigian."

On the monitor screen, a video triggered. They saw the image of a dark-skinned man speaking directly to the camera for a TV interview.

"That's the guy from the protest!" Courtney exclaimed. "The guy with the bullhorn."

"Shhh, listen," Patrick admonished.

The man on the screen spoke with passion. *"Naymeer and the Ravinians are putting us on a dangerous course. To disrespect the common man, upon whose backs this world was built, is not only a grave act of injustice, it will certainly bring about the downfall of modern society. If the United Nations votes to accept and perpetuate the teachings of Alexander Naymeer, it will mark the beginning of the fall of modern man."*

The video ended on the frozen face of the passionate man.

"Strong words," Courtney said. "He's predicting doomsday."

"Who is he?" Mark asked.

"His name is Haig Gastigian. A philosophy professor from New York University. He's the leading voice against the Ravinians. From what I've seen, he's a hero to many, and an outlaw to the Ravinians."

Mark shook his head in wonder. "What he's saying is just common sense. You'd think everybody would see that."

Patrick answered, "Many do. But Naymeer's philosophy is pretty appealing to a lot of people. People with power. I guess people like easy answers, and he's promising them a better world. It's great, as long as you're on the right side."

Mark asked, "What's this thing with the United Nations? Ravinia is going to be recognized as the spiritual voice of the world? How scary is that?"

"The UN General Assembly is voting on it soon," Patrick offered. "It could very well be the beginning of the end."

Mark asked, "What do you mean?"

Patrick sighed. "It means Naymeer's vision is wrong and dangerous. The proof of that is on Third Earth. It's created nothing short of chaos and despair. I'm sure he hasn't shown that particular vision to anybody."

"Could that be it?" Courtney asked. "Could that be the turning point for Second Earth? The acceptance of Naymeer's vision by the UN?"

"This isn't Naymeer's vision," Mark corrected. "This is pure Saint Dane. What happened on Third Earth could be the fate of every other territory. Saint Dane is revealing the existence of Halla through this Naymeer guy. This is the ultimate mixing of the territories. How can any society follow its own destiny when they're aware that so much more is out there? Saint Dane is probably going to follow the same model on every other territory."

"Then this is it," Courtney said with finality. "This is the Convergence. Saint Dane is spreading this vision throughout Halla. He's rewarding the strong and punishing the weak. If he succeeds, then what?"

The three fell silent, the weight of those words sinking in. Nobody wanted to ask the next obvious question.

Mark took the plunge. "What do we do about it?"

"I told you," Courtney announced, jumping to her feet. "We travel. This is where it's all coming down. Second Earth. We can't handle this on our own."

"Then why should we leave?" Patrick asked.

"To get Bobby. And anybody else who can help. Alder, Loor, Siry, Aja—"

"Aja's dead," Mark corrected.

"She's dead on Ibara. Not on Veelox. If we went to Veelox, we'd find her."

"And do what?" Mark asked.

"Bring them here! Saint Dane says it's over. I don't think it is. We still haven't hit Second Earth's turning point. Maybe this UN thing is it. I don't know. But things are still happening. The Convergence might have started, but it isn't finished. Naymeer is still gathering his power. We have to try to stop him. No way we can do it alone. The Travelers should be here. All of them."

"What about Bobby?" Mark asked soberly. "What if he really meant it when he said he quit?"

Mark and Patrick looked to Courtney. She didn't answer at first. She knew the importance of her next words.

"I can't pretend to know what's going through Bobby's head after all he's had to deal with, but you know him as well as I do, Mark. No, you know him way better than I do. He may have been frustrated. He may have been tired. He may have felt totally overwhelmed and needed a long rest. But in your heart, do you really believe that he quit?"

Mark and Courtney gazed into each other's eyes for several seconds.

"No," Mark finally said. "No I don't."

"Neither do I," Courtney announced with confidence. "Let's go get him."

Mark looked up to Patrick and said, "Are you up for this?"

Patrick looked pale. "I've never been anywhere but the Earth territories. I—I'm not sure how I'll do."

"You'll do fine," Courtney said dismissively. "Besides, you're a Traveler. We can't use the flume without . . . " Courtney stopped in midsentence.

"What's the matter?" Mark asked.

"I smell something."

"Stop bagging on my room," Mark whined. "I haven't been here in months."

Courtney frowned and walked quickly to the bedroom door. She felt the handle with suspicion, then threw the door open. Black smoke billowed into the room.

"Fire!" Courtney shouted.

"They found us," Mark gasped.

Courtney tried to step through the door, but the smoke drove her back. She closed it quickly. "Can't go that way," she shouted.

Mark went for the door. "I've got to get my parents' papers. And pictures."

Courtney held her arm against the door, not allowing Mark to open it. "Are you crazy?"

"Courtney! My family's life is in that room."

"Your family's life is on First Earth. They can't come back, Mark. This place doesn't mean anything to them anymore."

Mark reached for the door again. "But I have to save—"

Courtney grabbed his arm. She looked him right in the eye and said with dead seriousness, "You have to save *us*."

Mark thought and nodded. "You're right." He glanced around and ran for the window. "We can crawl across the roof and climb down the maple tree. I've done it a million times."

"Wait!" Courtney shouted. "Whoever did this is probably out there."

Mark weighed the problem, then yanked the window up. "I'll see." Quickly he ducked out onto the roof. Patrick didn't move.

"Go!" Courtney ordered.

The Traveler followed Mark. Courtney was right behind him. The shingled roof was sloped, but it wasn't hard to maneuver. Rather than go for the maple tree, Mark scrambled up toward the peak of the roof.

"What are you doing?" Courtney yelled with a strained whisper.

Mark reached the peak and peered over the top in time to see a long black limo driving away. The loud blare of a fire-truck siren was heard in the distance. Help was coming. Mark quickly slid down the roof section on his butt, joining the others.

"It was the limo," he said. "They took off, probably because the fire department's on the way."

"We've gotta be gone too," Courtney said. "We can't let them find us."

Mark nimbly scrambled across the roof until he reached the edge, where the branch of a large maple tree jutted a few feet below. Using skills he hadn't needed since he was a little kid, he grabbed on to the branch, swung his legs off the roof and over the top of the branch. He then shinned toward the trunk of the tree.

"Piece of cake," he called back.

Patrick couldn't move. "I've never done anything like that," he complained nervously.

"You're gonna do a lot of things you've never done before. Move!"

Courtney didn't shove him, but didn't back away from him

either. Patrick gingerly followed Mark's lead and made it out onto the tree. Courtney waited until he got to the center of the tree, then followed. Moments later all three were on the ground.

Flames leaped from the downstairs windows.

"I guess that's the last of it," Mark said sadly.

"Last of what?" Courtney asked.

"My life. Once the house is gone, there'll be nothing left to tie me to Second Earth."

Courtney started to say something, but stopped herself. Instead she put her arm around Mark with sympathy. "Gotta go," she implored.

A loud horn told them the fire engines were almost there. The three rounded the house into the next yard and came out onto the street in time to see several red trucks flash by, headed for Mark's house. They took a quick look back to see the place was an inferno.

"Why would they do that?" Patrick asked. "If they wanted to hurt us, they could have chosen a much more efficient way."

"They didn't want to hurt us," Courtney said. "They wanted to scare us. It didn't work."

The cab was waiting for them, as requested, a block away. They got inside and told the cabbie they were headed back into the city. To the Bronx. To a subway station.

The cabbie shrugged and said, "Whatever you say. I was getting worried about you."

"That makes four of us," Courtney said.

Nobody spoke for the entire journey. Patrick stared out the window, wide eyed, at his home territory in—to him—the distant past. Mark and Courtney tried to nap. They knew they had to sleep when they could. Unlike Patrick, they *had* been to other territories beyond Earth. They knew the drill. It took nearly an hour to get to their destination. Mark nudged Courtney when they were a few blocks away.

"You've been to this flume, right?" Courtney asked Patrick.

"On all three territories."

"Then you know it's dangerous. We've got to time the trains and get down onto the subway tracks without being seen . . . or run down."

"What about quigs?" Mark asked.

"Oh, right," Courtney said, deflated. "There's that."

"Stop the car!" Mark shouted.

The cabbie jammed on the brakes, making everybody nearly fly out of their seats.

"Jeez!" he shouted. "What's the matter?"

"Yeah," Courtney said with equal surprise. "What was that for?"

Mark reached for his wallet, pulled out a wad of bills and tossed them to the cabbie.

"Whoa, chief. That's too much. You got change comin'."

Mark didn't wait. He jumped out of the car.

"Keep it," Courtney said.

"Thanks! I knew you guys weren't Ravinian creeps."

Courtney crawled out of the cab, followed right behind by Patrick. As the car pulled away from the curb, they found themselves at the familiar intersection in a rundown section of the Bronx that Mark and Courtney had been to several times before. Mark stood staring. Courtney joined him and asked, "What is your problem?"

Mark didn't answer. Courtney looked to where he was staring, and her jaw dropped.

"What?" Patrick asked, confused.

"It's the wrong corner," Courtney said.

"No, it isn't," Mark corrected.

"What's the matter?" Patrick asked impatiently.

Courtney slowly looked to him and said, as if in a daze, "The subway station is gone."

Patrick looked to where they were staring. "You're right. That wasn't there when I came through here with Press."

Courtney asked, "So then, what is it?"

"I don't know," Mark answered. "Let's find out."

He stepped off the curb, headed toward the corner where the green subway kiosk used to be. Everything about the neighborhood was the exact same, except for that block. In place of the kiosk was a tall stone building that looked like a medieval castle. Hanging from the second story was a line of flags.

Red flags.

Flags with stars.

SECOND EARTH

(CONTINUED)

The three stood on the opposite corner, staring at the mysterious structure. It looked to Mark like a library. There were high arches and heavy marble columns. Wide marble stairs led up from the sidewalk to the many entrances.

"I've seen this before," Patrick announced.

Mark and Courtney shot him a surprised glance. "Where?" they said in unison.

"Third Earth. Everything changed, remember? When I went to the gate, instead of the underground complex I found this. The flume was inside."

"So this thing is going to last for three thousand years?" Courtney said in awe.

"It wasn't the exact same," Patrick pointed out. "I guess changes were made over the years, and it was crumbling, but it was essentially the same structure."

"What is it?" Mark asked.

"I don't know," Patrick answered. "All I cared about was getting to the flume."

"Look at the flags," Mark announced. "Obviously this is all about the Ravinian cult. Maybe it's headquarters."

"We gotta check this out," Courtney said, and walked toward the strange new building.

All three walked closer with trepidation, while scanning around for any Ravinian red shirts. The street was busy with people, but not crowded. If somebody was looking for them, they'd be seen. They walked up the marble stairs to a long row of glass doors that was the entrance. Courtney tried a door to find . . . it was open.

"This doesn't change anything," she said. "We still have to flume out of here. Whatever this is, we'll have a better shot of getting to the flume here than sneaking into Naymeer's house back in Stony Brook."

Patrick and Mark nodded in agreement. Courtney pulled the door open and stepped inside. Just inside the entrance was a large open area with a marble floor.

"Slick," Courtney said, impressed.

Fresh flowers in vases were placed along the walls. The star symbol was prominent on the wall to the right, a portrait of Naymeer faced it on the wall to the left. Directly ahead was an archway that led farther into the building.

"Doesn't seem like anybody's here," Mark commented.

Courtney walked to the archway to find a wide set of stairs leading straight down. She stood on top and stared toward the bottom. There was no clue as to what they might find below.

"What are the chances of this being some fancy new subway station?" she asked over her shoulder to the others.

"No chance," Mark answered.

"I didn't think so."

The three started down slowly, shoulder to shoulder. With each step they saw more of the floor below. It seemed to be one big room. A few more steps down revealed a long row of green theater-style seats that stretched out to either side, facing away from them. It was followed by another row and another and another. A wide center aisle separated the seats into two halves. Left and right.

"This is no subway station," Courtney muttered.

"It looks like a big theater," Mark replied.

The room was huge. There looked to be enough seating for several hundred people. The rows of seats all faced the same direction. When they reached the bottom, Courtney saw why.

"This is no theater," she gasped.

There was no stage. No movie screen. No performance area. Mark, Courtney, and Patrick stepped down onto the floor and saw the truth. On the far side of the vast space, facing the seats, for all to see, was the flume. To the right of its mouth was a red star flag on a pole in a stand. On the opposite side of the mouth was a U.S. flag.

"I can't swallow," Mark croaked.

"It's like some kind of shrine," Courtney murmured.

Mark walked to the first row of seats and picked up a thick book that was all too familiar. "Or a church," he said, holding the book up for the others to see.

The cover was deep read. The word "Ravinia" ran vertically down one side in gold letters. Next to it was the star symbol. It was the exact same cover that Patrick had brought from Third Earth. The cover that Richard, the librarian, was willing to die to hold on to. Every other seat had the exact same book.

"I guess the mystery is solved," Patrick commented. "It's the Ravinian Bible."

"Yeah," Courtney quipped. "The Bible according to Naymeer."

"According to Saint Dane," Mark corrected.

Mark tossed the book back onto the seat. The three slowly drifted down the wide center aisle. Far ahead of them, the flume loomed large.

"It wasn't out in the open like this on Third Earth," Patrick commented. “A similar structure was aboveground, but the flume was behind a series of doors.”

“Like they decided to hide it again,” Mark commented.

“Exactly,” Patrick agreed.

Courtney asked, “What’s the point? Do they all sit here staring at a tunnel, reading about Naymeer’s twisted philosophies?”

“Maybe it’s like what we saw at the rally,” Mark offered. “Maybe Naymeer somehow produces images of Halla.”

“Yeah, like a movie,” Courtney agreed. “Unbelievable.”

“It’s gone further than we thought,” Mark concluded. “If the Ravinians know about the flume, they know everything.”

They heard a voice from the top of the stairs call to them. “Indeed. There are no secrets.”

All three spun and looked back up to see a man standing on top. He no longer wore his deep red robe. Instead he had on a gray business suit with a red tie. Embroidered into the tie was the star symbol.

“Welcome, my friends,” he said warmly. “My name is Alexander Naymeer. This is my conclave.”

To either side of him was a red-shirt guard. Unlike the guards at the Garden, these men were armed with pistols in hip holsters.

“I’m so glad you’ve come to visit,” he said kindly as he strolled casually down the stairs. “We have so much to talk about, and plan.”

“I don’t think so,” Courtney shouted. She looked to Mark and said, “We are so gone.” With that, she turned and ran for the flume.

“Stop!” a guard yelled. Both red shirts pulled their pistols and started to run down the stairs.

Mark ran after Courtney.

“Let’s go!” Mark shouted back to Patrick.

Patrick hesitated a moment more, then ran to catch up.

“Where to?” he asked breathlessly.

"Doesn't matter," Courtney shouted back. "Zadaa, Denduron, Quillan. Anywhere but here."

Bang! A shot was fired.

"Down!" Mark yelled, and pushed Courtney to the side, between two rows of seats. They were still over thirty yards from the mouth of the flume. Thirty long yards.

Patrick jumped the other way. They were on opposite sides of the aisle, both far from the flume.

"We can't let them trap us here!" Courtney hissed.

"We can't let them kill us!" Mark countered.

"They won't! He wants us to be acolytes." Courtney jumped up and started for the flume. Another shot was fired, kicking up a splinter from the chair in front of her. Courtney screamed and dropped back to the ground.

"You can't travel without me," Patrick called to them. "Follow me!"

"Patrick don't!" Mark yelled.

Patrick didn't listen. He jumped up, ran into the center aisle, and sprinted for the flume.

"C'mon!" he yelled back to the others.

He got only a few steps when another shot was fired.

Courtney screamed in horror.

Patrick stiffened instantly and spun back around in surprise. The look on his face said it all. He couldn't believe what had just happened.

Patrick had been shot.

"Get down! Lie down!" Courtney yelled on the edge of hysteria.

Patrick staggered backward, stumbling toward the flume. He twisted his arm up to try and touch his back, as if to swat away an annoying bee. Mark and Courtney peeked over the tops of the chairs to see the Traveler from Third Earth twist and stumble as though he were drunk. A red patch of blood spread on the back of his shirt. His eyes rolled in his head.

"It hurts," he cried, more in surprise than pain.

Courtney jumped up to go to him. Another shot was fired, hitting the seat in front of her. Mark grabbed Courtney and pulled her back down for protection.

"Stay down. They'll shoot us all!" Mark cried.

Courtney was in tears. "Patrick! Sit down! Don't move."

Behind them, the red shirts hit the bottom of the stairs. Both had their guns drawn.

Patrick's heels caught on the edge of the flume. He stumbled and fell down flat on his back, hard. Mark and Courtney clutched each other. Mark was ready to scream with anger and frustration . . .

When the flume came to life.

"What?" Mark gasped with dismay.

"He activated it," Courtney whispered.

"Where is he going?" Mark asked.

"Who cares?"

"Get him out of there!" one of the guards yelled. The two took off running, sprinting up the aisle toward the flume.

Light began to shoot from the tunnel and fill the immense room. Patrick's crumpled body became a silhouette on the floor of the flume.

"He won't make it," Courtney sobbed.

"Yeah, he will," Mark said, and leaped from behind the seats, into the aisle, throwing himself at the first guard as he was about to pass them. Mark's feet were off the ground as he nailed the guy in the ribs, knocking him into the opposite row. The musical notes grew louder. The second guard stopped. He knew he wouldn't make it in time. Instead he raised his gun and took aim at Patrick. The wounded Traveler was in his sights for one second. The second after that, Courtney was in his sights. She stepped right in front of him, the barrel of the pistol pointed at her nose.

"Too late," she said with a smug smile.

Brilliant light and music filled the massive room. The guard blinked. He didn't know what to do.

"Put it down," Naymeer's calm voice said from the bottom of the stairs.

Reluctantly the guard lowered his pistol.

Courtney kept her eyes locked on the guard's. Her back was to the flume. A moment later the light disappeared. The music ended. Patrick was gone.

"I do so abhor violence," Naymeer said wistfully. "It is a tool of the ignorant."

The guard stepped away from Courtney, revealing the elderly man as he strolled up the aisle. The first guard got to his feet, grabbed Mark, picked him up by the collar, and shoved him toward Courtney. The two stood together, facing Naymeer.

"We should be introduced formally," the man said. "I am the Traveler from Second Earth."

"No, you're not," Mark said quickly.

Naymeer raised a surprised eyebrow.

"Of course," he said with a knowing smile. "I respect your loyalty. Won't you please accept my humble offer and join me for dinner?"

"No, thank you," Courtney answered.

Naymeer took a tired breath. "Really? I would think you two would be interested to hear about all the wonderful work I've been doing here."

"She said 'No, thank you,'" Mark said adamantly.

Naymeer shrugged. "It would be so much easier if we did this on my terms."

Mark and Courtney didn't budge.

"Easier for who?" Courtney asked in defiance.

"Please!" Naymeer said jovially. "Let's not be contentious. I'm sure you'd enjoy seeing what I've done to my house in Stony Brook." He leaned into them with a sly wink and added, "After all,

I didn't get the chance to give you a tour the other night."

He smiled, turned on his heel, and strode back down the aisle toward the stairs.

"The car is waiting outside," he called back.

Mark and Courtney didn't move. The two guards had to grab them by the arms and shove them toward the stairs.

"Where do you think Patrick tried to go?" Courtney whispered to Mark as they were pushed along.

Mark shrugged. "It doesn't really matter . . . if he's dead."

JOURNAL #35

DENDURON

They say the truth hurts.

They're right. I've been getting hit with a lot of truths lately, and it hurts. I didn't realize just how badly I had messed things up until the moment I hit Denduron. Yeah, things got worse. What can I say? I was an idiot. I was kidding myself. I gave up. I was tired. Guilty guilty guilty. On all counts. I'm not trying to defend myself or justify what I did, but for the record, I truly thought I was doing the right thing by burying the flume on Ibara and trying to trap Saint Dane. It wasn't about being selfish. Okay, maybe it was a little bit, but I really thought it was the right thing to do.

I was wrong.

As I write this journal, I can only say that I now know *how* wrong I was. Saint Dane will not be defeated by a single clever move. It's gone way beyond that. The only way I will be able to stop him now is to destroy him. Mark, Courtney, I don't know if you'll ever get the chance to read this, but I want you to know that I've finally come to the realization that he's been manipulating me from the very beginning. I don't know if things have gone exactly as he planned, but that doesn't really matter. What counts now is that the battle is nearing its completion, and unless I can do something more than I've done, he will win. The Convergence has begun. The territories are tumbling toward chaos. The one glimmer of hope I have is that as far as I know, things haven't hit bottom. Yet. That's a scary thought, because things have gotten pretty bad. We're on a path that's leading toward the complete breakdown of Halla, so that Saint Dane can remold it the way he chooses. As grim as that sounds, at least we haven't reached the end of that path yet. I've got to try and stop him before we do.

For that, I will have to crush him.

When the flume dropped me at the gate on Denduron, it first looked as if I wouldn't be doing much of anything anymore. Normally the end of a flume ride is marked by a gentle deposit. I didn't expect this arrival to be any different.

Wrong. Again. My feet touched the ground, gravity took over, and all hell broke loose. I was ramrodded square in the chest and knocked back into the flume. It happened so quickly I didn't know what hit me. That's not just a figure of speech. I really didn't know what hit me. I was slammed down onto the hard rock floor of the flume, wishing that the receding light would have been thoughtful enough to take me back along with it. It didn't. I was stuck with whatever it was that wasn't happy about my arrival. Before I had the chance to see what had slammed me, I heard it. It was a growl. A familiar growl. It took all of two seconds for me to put it together.

The quigs were back on Denduron.

I didn't try to figure out what that might mean. There would be time for that later, assuming I could get out of there and create a "later" for myself. I didn't jump to my feet. I didn't want to be a threat. At least not yet. I lay on my back and twisted my head to try and see my nemesis. My eyes hadn't adjusted yet to the dark, so all I saw at the mouth of the flume were two eyes. Yellow eyes. They seemed to be floating in the air. I knew they weren't. They were inside the head of a quig-bear. Locked on me. I heard its heavy breathing. This thing was going to attack again, and there was no place for me to go. I couldn't even activate the flume and travel somewhere else. By the time the light came for me, I would be hamburger. I couldn't just lie there either. It would be the easiest meal that quig ever had. There weren't a lot of options. Actually, there was only one option. Attack.

I rolled forward and leaped for the mouth of the flume. It was a totally insane move, but the only thing I had going for me was surprise. I hoped that jumping at the monster would be the last thing it expected.

"Ahhhh!" I screamed, trying to sound more threatening than I was. Between my sudden move and the lame scream, I bought myself a second to act. That's about how long the quig hesitated. I lunged at the eyes, but I wasn't about to grab it. That would have been suicide. I remembered the multiple rows of sharp teeth set into the strong jaw of those prehistoric bears. It would have bitten my head off before my hands could reach its throat. The quig didn't know that. For that one second it must have felt threatened, because it didn't move. Or maybe it just couldn't believe I was being such an idiot. Didn't matter to me. I had bought another second to do something. That was the good news. I cut hard to my left, trying to get past the beast. I almost made it too. Almost. That was the bad news.

Two seconds isn't a very long time. I had drawn parallel with the quig, thinking I might get past it. That hope didn't last long. The beast realized I wasn't a threat and made its own move. It lashed out with one oversized paw and slashed my left shoulder. It clubbed me so hard that the impact spun me around. I found myself reeling backward again. I desperately tried to keep my balance, but couldn't stop from slamming the back of my head on the rock wall on the far side of the gate cavern. I forced myself to stay focused, because I knew if I didn't, the next thing I'd hear was the sound of the quig chewing on me. Followed by my own screams. I looked up to see the beast on all fours near the mouth of the flume. It was exactly as I remembered the quigs from Denduron. It was a brute of a mutant bear with long bonelike spikes rising from its back. Though it was one of the smaller quigs, it had to be six hundred pounds. Its jaws were impossibly huge for its head. So were its teeth. So were its eyes, and they were looking right at me. I don't know why it didn't pounce right away. Maybe it was still surprised that I had the guts to try to escape. Or maybe it knew there was no rush. I was helpless. And hurt.

I forgot to mention that. It hadn't just clubbed me with its paw. My adrenaline was pumping so hard I didn't realize it at first, but it had sliced right through the thin material of my shirt from Ibara with its sharp claws. It had also sliced right through my shoulder. When I tried to push up on my left arm, I felt the pain. A quick look down showed me the grim reality. I was bleeding. Badly. The tattered shirt was already soaked with my brown blood and the wet patch was growing fast. I remembered back to when Uncle Press had speared the quig that had been chasing us down the snowy mountain as we escaped on a sled. The other quigs smelled the blood and attacked. They went after the wounded quig with a horrifying, cannibalistic bloodlust. I'll never forget the pained screams of the injured quig as it was eaten alive by its buddies.

The quig in front of me had the same idea. I saw its big nose working, sucking in the blood smell that was filling the cavern. In a few seconds its own blood would start to boil. A few seconds after that the rest of my blood would start to spill. I only had a few seconds to save myself. Looking around quickly, I saw something that made absolutely no sense, but I didn't stop to try to figure out the explanation. Lying in the dirt, not five feet from me, were four dado-killing rods from Quillan. Instinct took over. I rolled for the long, metal spears.

The quig let out a screeching bellow that made me shudder. I didn't let it stop me though. It was coming for me. I would have only one shot. I grabbed for one of the rods. I needed two hands to control it, but didn't have two hands. My shoulder burned with pain. It was useless. Too bad for me. The quig charged. It was making the first move. If there was anything I learned from Loor and Alder at the warrior training camp of Mooraj, it was to never make the first move. Lucky for me the quig hadn't trained there as well. Since my back was to the beast, I had to sense its movement. My hope was, in its mindless bloodlust, it would attack without thinking. I swept up the long rod, clutched it with one fist, and spun around.

It all happened so fast it's hard to describe exactly *what* happened. I remember seeing its eyes flash yellow. I also remember seeing its jaws opened wide, ready to chomp. In that brief flash of a moment, I remember thinking that it must have had a few hundred teeth in its mouth. Every last one looked sharp. For me, it was a target. I whipped the rod around and jammed it into the beast's throat. I could feel the solid rod pierce flesh. The beast howled and gasped but didn't stop its charge. It was the worst thing it could have done. The back end of the rod was planted against the rock wall of the cave, so the only place the other end could go was through the beast's neck. I jumped out of the way and quickly grabbed another rod off the ground. The quig whipped its head back and forth, as if trying to shake the dado rod loose.

I quickly realized that the quig was just as dangerous that way as when it thought it was in control. The monster was in pain. It was angry. At me. The fight wasn't over. I grabbed the second rod and did something that, as I write this now, seems too hideous to even consider, let alone pull off. But you do strange things when you're fighting for survival. I lifted the weapon high like a javelin, but didn't throw it. The chance of missing was too great. I had to make sure this weapon found its mark. I ran forward, timing my move so that I attacked at the exact moment the quig shook its head away from me. When it whipped its head back my way, I jammed the dado rod straight into its eye. The beast screamed. I didn't back off. I forced the weapon farther in, no doubt piercing its brain. Gross? Well, yeah, but so what? It was him or me. Thinking back now, it kind of makes my stomach turn, but at the time all I could think of was killing that bad boy. It's hard to describe the feeling. My heart was racing, obviously. I was desperate, but if I were to be honest, I'd have to say that I was also a little out of my mind.

It was a quig. A freakin' quig! We had won Denduron. Its turning point had passed. Why was a quig guarding the flume? The monster stumbled. It may have been done, but I wasn't. I had to make sure. I let go of the dado rod I had drilled through its brain and grabbed another. The beast fell onto its side. I didn't hesitate. With my one good arm, I raised the third rod high and stabbed it down through its chest, where I imagined its black heart was beating. Now that I look back, I'm sort of ashamed to admit this, but writing these journals is about telling the truth for the ages, right? I stabbed the beast once, pulled out the rod, and stabbed it again, and again. I don't know how many times I pierced the monster. More than I had to. At that point it was more about anger than self-preservation.

With each thrust I gritted my teeth and snarled, "I . . . am . . . not . . . done . . . yet!"

I stood over the dying beast, covered with blood, not sure how much was mine and how much was the monster's. I had beaten it. I had survived. I wanted to stumble back into the flume and get out of there, but that wasn't an option. Saint Dane had said that the first domino of Halla to fall would be Denduron. I thought we had prevented that many years before. As I stood looking down at the dying quig, I knew I was wrong. Denduron was back in play. I was in the right place. I also realized that Alder was on Denduron. The dado weapons were proof of that. They were the weapons he was supposed to return to Quillan. Why he hadn't done that, I had no idea, but I was glad he hadn't. They saved my life.

Once I calmed down, I realized I wasn't out of danger. Far from it. If there was one quig, there would be more. If they smelled blood, they'd come running, looking for a frenzy feed. Since I was bleeding, I'd be on the menu. I had to be gone. I started to go for the leather and fur Denduron clothes that were lying around the flume cave, but soon realized I had a bigger problem. I was seriously hurting. If I wanted to make it out of that cave and down to the Milago village, I had to stop the blood flow. I pulled off my Ibara shirt, which wasn't easy, because my left arm was useless. The pain from the slash felt like fire. Loque's shirt was a rotted mess. That helped. I was able to half-pull and half-tear it off. Once I wrestled off the shirt, I saw two deep gouges that ran across my shoulder and my left pec. They were deep, too. Muscle was cut. I was in a bad way. How the heck was I supposed to bandage that up? Since my arm was useless anyway, I used the old shirt like a bandage and wrapped it around the top of my arm. That only covered half the wound. I looked around the cavern and saw some wide leather straps that could have been belts. I tied those under my armpits and around my chest. Would that stop the blood flow? I didn't know. It was better than nothing.

The next trick was to get dressed. I knew it would be freezing outside, and I had to protect myself, so I worked my way into some of the leather clothes I found lying around. The toughest part was lacing up the leather shoes. At least my left hand still worked. Between that, my good right hand, and my teeth, I was able to strap myself up. The final touch was a furry cloak that I threw over my shoulders. I hoped it would be enough. There were no sleds in the cave. I was going to have to walk down that mountain, through the snow. It was going to be cold. Really cold. I picked up the final dado weapon, thinking I could use it as a walking stick. I leaned on the long rod, testing to see if I could hold my own weight. It wasn't perfect, but it would have to do. It was time to get going. As I stepped out of the dark cavern, into the bright light of the three suns of Denduron, I had real doubts about whether or not I would be able to make it down that mountain.

My confidence bottomed out when I saw the bony spikes of quig spines sticking up in various places around the snowfield in front of me. At least they hadn't yet smelled the blood that was pooling inside the cavern. I knew that would only be a matter of time, and wind direction. I had to move. Walking across the snow was hard. There was a thin crust of ice on top that wasn't strong enough to hold my weight. I'd take a step and plant my foot, but as soon as I put weight on it, I'd break through the top layer and sink down to midcalf. Every time. Over and over. It was like walking in cold mud. I was glad I had grabbed the dado rod. It was the only thing that kept me from toppling. If I had gone over, I didn't think I'd be able to pull myself back up.

I chose a route that kept me going downhill and as far away from the dormant quigs as possible. All I needed was for them to catch a whiff of my blood, and it would be like: "Come and get it!" Each time my foot broke through the snow with a loud crunch, I winced. Did they hear that? Would they hear the next one? I trudged a few hundred yards before clearing the final, buried quig. Huge relief. From then on, each agonizing step took me farther from danger . . .

And closer to exhaustion. I was freezing. Literally. My feet were so cold I couldn't feel them. The bleeding had almost stopped, but I don't think it was because of my makeshift bandages. I think it was freezing up. It would have been a tough trip even if I'd been healthy, but after losing all that blood I was getting weaker by the second. After a torturous hour I still couldn't see to the end of the snowfield. I had made this journey a few times on a sled, traveling ten times as fast, and it still took a long while. When I came back up the mountain, it had been on horseback or in a mechanized dygo. I had never done this on foot. I was in trouble.

After another hour, things started to spin. I think I was being pulled forward more by gravity than by my own horsepower. I stopped thinking about what I might find on Denduron. I pretty much stopped thinking about everything. My brain was too blood starved for that. Colors swirled. I knew that I would soon pass out. Far ahead I saw the snow was thinning, giving way to brown dirt. I would soon reach the end of the snowfield. I was also reaching the end of the line. I wasn't going to make it to the Milago village.

Far up ahead I sensed movement. In my dazed state it looked as if the distant trees were moving toward me. That didn't make sense. Or did it? I couldn't think clearly about anything. The trees seemed to be moving in a line toward me. I still had enough sense to realize that was impossible. Still, there was no other explanation, other than the fact that maybe I had lost my mind. Or maybe it was a mirage? Do mirages only appear in the desert? I didn't know. I was too dazed to think straight. Instead of looking at the moving trees, I should have been looking where I was stepping, because my foot hit a small boulder. It couldn't have been more than six inches high, but it was enough to trip me. I fell forward, face-first, and slammed onto the gravel-covered ground. It didn't even hurt. I was too far gone for that. I couldn't move. My energy was gone. My feet were frozen. I had lost the will to move. I kept looking down the mountain at the moving trees, which of course weren't moving trees at all. They were Bedoowan knights on horseback. An entire line of them. There had to have been thirty across, followed by another line and another. They walked in tight formation like an army.

An advancing army. My throat clutched. Why were the Bedoowan knights marching up the mountain?

"There!" I heard a voice shout.

A lone knight charged forward, headed for me. He galloped up the steep slope, his horse's hooves kicking up small pebbles in his wake. For a second I thought he would trample me. To be honest, I didn't care. The knight pulled up a few yards short and leaned forward on the horse to get a better look at the strange, frozen, bleeding guy who was nearly passed out miles from nowhere.

A second knight galloped up and stopped next to the first.

"Is it a Lowsee scout?" the second knight asked.

"No," the first knight answered. He dismounted and walked cautiously toward me. "He is too light-skinned to be a Lowsee."

What the heck was a Lowsee?

"Dead?" the second knight asked. He didn't even bother getting down from his horse.

The first knight knelt down to find out. When our eyes met, his opened even wider in surprise.

"You!" he exclaimed, as if he recognized me.

"Who is it?" the second knight asked, finally getting off his horse.

"You are hurt," the first knight said, actually sounding worried about me. "We will get help." He stood up straight and called back to his advancing army. "A stretcher!" he called. "Hurry!"

By this time the second knight was staring at me too.

"Who is it?" he asked.

"It is Pendragon," the first knight answered. "We owe this man our future. Without him, we would not have the weapons to attack the Lowsee."

The second knight shot me a quick, surprised look. "This is the man who unearthed the tak?"

"It is," the first knight answered. "He has changed the future of all Denduron."

It was the absolute last thing I wanted to hear. *I* had become the merchant of death.

I closed my eyes and let darkness fall.

JOURNAL #35

(CONTINUED)

DENDURON

It felt like my shoulder was on fire. It really did. I actually thought it was burning. I forced myself to wake up, thinking I had to find some water and put out the flames. I wasn't on fire of course. I was feeling the effects of a foot-long double slash that ran across my shoulder onto my chest. I cracked open an eye to try and get my bearings. Disoriented? Yeah, you could say that. I stole a quick glance at my arm to see there were no flames, only a clean white bandage that wrapped my left arm to my side like I was a half mummy. Oh, right. The quig. Ouch. I twisted my head one way to see that I was in a hut. A big one. I was on my back on a cot. A long string of cots were lined up next to mine. All were empty. I twisted my head back to the left to see even more cots lined up. Looking past my feet toward the opposite wall, I saw still another row of cots. Also empty. It seemed I was the only guest in this very big hospital.

"Would you like some water?"

I shifted my gaze to the voice and saw a young girl headed my way with a pitcher and a cup. She may have been pretty, with long dark hair tied up into a practical knot, but this was no candy striper. She wore the lightweight, black leather armor of a Bedoowan knight. I nodded. The girl knelt by the cot, lifted my head with one hand, and brought the cup to my lips. I took a small sip. I didn't want to choke. It felt great. It was like washing away a coating of sand inside my throat.

"That's enough," she said as she gently lowered my head.

"Thank you," I croaked. "Uh, where am I?"

"The hospital," she answered. "You were lucky the advance force found you."

I reached up with my right hand and felt my burning shoulder.

"One hundred and twenty stitches," she said, as if reading my mind. "You lost a lot of blood. How did it happen?"

How the heck was I supposed to answer that? I decided to tell the truth. Sort of. I was tired of playing games.

"Wild animal," I answered. "He lost more blood than I did."

"Why were you up on the mountain?" she asked.

"Sightseeing."

She gave me a strange look. I shrugged.

"No matter," she said dismissively. "You are here now and you will survive. Your wound is already showing signs of healing. It is quite remarkable actually."

I shrugged again. It hurt to shrug. I stopped shrugging.

"Why is the hospital so empty?" I asked. "Hard to believe that I'm the only sick guy around here."

"It will not be empty for long," she answered solemnly. "This ward was built to treat the wounded."

"Lotta cots. Expecting more patients than normal?" I asked, confused.

She frowned. "It is what happens in war."

"War?" I shouted, and sat up quickly. Just as quickly, I wished I hadn't. My head spun. I wasn't healing so fast after all. I dropped back down and closed my eyes, trying to hold on to consciousness.

"Rest," she said professionally. "We will move you once the wounded begin to arrive."

I think I slipped in and out of reality awhile. For how long I didn't know. Images of the advancing Bedoowan army kept dancing through my head like a feverish nightmare. There was going to be a war. The Bedoowan knights who found me on the mountain were an advance team. Who were they going to fight? The knights talked about using tak, which meant the worst had happened. By digging out the tak to defend Ibara, I had given Saint Dane a second shot at Denduron. The turning point of the territory was the discovery of tak. By destroying the tak mine, I had only shifted the turning point. Worse, I feared that I had begun a chain of events that would be felt throughout Halla. Denduron was on the verge of a war. Dados had returned to Ibara. What else was happening? What would it all lead to? The answer was obvious.

Convergence.

History-changing events were being influenced by events on different territories. It was the ultimate mixing of worlds. The destiny of each territory was no longer its own. This was Saint Dane's Convergence. I was the one who was given the task of stopping it. Instead, I was the one who started it. It made me wish that the slash from the quig had been a bit higher and hit my throat.

I was vaguely aware of people hurrying in and out of the

large ward, preparing the cots for the wounded. Every so often somebody would check on me. I didn't care. I wanted to die. I think a night went by. Maybe two. I lost track of time, which is kind of an understatement, since I had actually lost track of time the very first moment I stepped into the flume when I was fourteen. What made me finally rejoin reality was the feeling that somebody was standing over me, watching. Unlike the many caregivers who came and went, this person didn't move. He kind of hovered there, as if waiting for me to say something. It gave me enough of an uneasy feeling that I willed myself to crawl from the darkness where I had been living. When I focused, I was surprised to see Rellin, the chief miner of the Milago. But something wasn't right. He was wearing the armor of a Bedoowan knight. Stranger still, this armor had bright yellow stripes on both arms. It looked like a fancy-dress version of the familiar black armor.

"Welcome back, Pendragon!" Rellin exclaimed warmly. "I was afraid we had lost you."

Rellin sat down on the cot next to me. I did my best to focus on him.

"I want to hear about your adventure," he exclaimed. "Did the tak serve you well?"

It took me a few seconds to understand what he was asking. When I came to Denduron with Siry, I told Rellin that we needed to unearth more tak to help a tribe on the other side of the mountain. I didn't mention that the people happened to be on the other side of the mountain . . . on a territory called Ibara.

"Yes" was the only answer I gave him. I didn't want to tell him just how effective the tak had been.

"I am glad," he said with a smile. "And I am glad that you have returned to us."

"There's going to be a war?" I asked.

Rellin smiled. He actually smiled. You'd think that somebody on the verge of war would be kind of, oh I don't know, nervous? Sober? Tense? Not Rellin. The idea of going into battle made his eyes sparkle.

"The Lowsee are threatening our very existence by hoarding triptyte," he explained. "Without it, our village would go dark. And all because they are greedy for glaze. What is more important? Light or wealth? They have chosen wealth. They will suffer for it."

"You're going to use tak on them," I said softly.

"We are going to destroy them!" Rellin exclaimed, jumping to his feet. "We have given them every chance to make a fair arrangement for their triptyte. They have proven to be greedy and shortsighted. We have broken off discussions and will now speak with our swords . . . and with tak."

Most of what he was saying didn't matter to me. It was all just a lot of blah blah blah. The bottom line was what mattered. The Bedoowan had tak and they were using it to attack another tribe. After that . . . what? Would the Bedoowan and the Milago become the aggressive force that Uncle Press feared? What would that mean to the rest of Denduron? Was the territory going to be ruled by fear and aggression? Was this what Saint Dane wanted? Was the territory going to be laid waste like Veelox? Was this going to be the future of every territory? My head hurt worse now than when I had first been brought to the hospital.

"I'd like to see Alder," I said.

Rellin scowled. "Alder has been imprisoned."

I wanted to jump up and scream, "Why?" but forced myself to keep calm. I had already learned that lesson.

"You are not a Bedoowan," Rellin explained. "The fact that you left to help another tribe was your choice. Alder did not have that choice, yet he deserted us. Still, that would not have been enough to imprison him."

"Then why?"

"He tried to destroy our tak mine," Rellin answered. "I do not know why. He would not answer me. I am sorry to say that Alder has been branded a traitor. For his actions he has been sentenced to death."

My head swam. Things were happening fast, but they were all too clear. Alder must have returned to find exactly what I found, and tried to destroy the tak. He failed, and now he was going to be executed for doing his job as a Traveler. My job. I should have been here. This was my fault too. Halla was crashing down around me in every possible way.

"I am sorry, Pendragon," Rellin said. "I know that Alder was your friend. I believed he was my friend as well. I suppose we do not always know everything about our friends."

"When?" I gasped.

"Tomorrow morning. It is the last official duty I will attend to before leaving to lead the attack on the Lowsee. I would not expect you to be there. I understand how difficult this must be for you." Rellin knelt down by me and took my arm. "Do not dwell on the negative. Did you know that I am now king?"

"Uhhh, no."

"Kagan and I were married. Our union has brought the Milago and the Bedoowan together. We are now a single, mighty tribe that will soon rule all of Denduron. You are here at the start of a glorious new era. Revel in it. When the history of our world is written, you will hold a place of honor. When the battle is complete, we will talk again about what role you wish to play in our new tribe. You have earned that right, Pendragon."

He smiled and left. I didn't feel much like reveling. I didn't feel very honorable. I didn't want any part of his new tribe. I felt I had done everything wrong since the moment I left home as a Traveler. As I lay there on that cot, alone, in pain, I felt as if everything were lost. Denduron would only be the beginning. Stories like the one I'd just heard from Rellin would play out across Halla. I don't believe it's possible to feel any lower than I felt at that moment. All the sacrifices the Travelers had made were for nothing. Saint Dane had won. It would have been so easy for me to roll over and close my eyes. All I wanted was to go back to sleep and hopefully never wake up. There was only one thing that stopped me from doing it.

Alder.

He was still alive. I may have lost Denduron. I may have lost Halla. There was no way I would let my friend die. It had nothing to do with Saint Dane. It was about saving Alder. It was all I had left. Of course, that meant I actually had to stand up and move. Not an easy thing. I threw my legs over, sat up, and immediately puked. All over the floor. Nobody saw. Nobody cared. Least of all, me. I wasn't going to let a little thing like uncontrollable nausea stop me. I wiped my mouth on my sleeve, stood up, and puked again. I was a mess. I didn't know if it was from my injuries or the blood loss or from whatever medicine they were giving me. I was a step above worthless. I struggled to put on the leather clothes I'd found at the flume. It took forever, since I was doing it with only one arm. My pounding head and weak stomach didn't help. The pain that tore through my shoulder and chest made it nearly impossible to dress. But I didn't give up. After a grueling twenty minutes, I was ready to stagger out of the hospital.

Next to the cot was the dado-killing weapon I'd used as a crutch on my way down the mountain. I still needed it. With every muscle in my body screaming in pain, I bent over to pick it up. It was worth the effort. I needed the heavy stick for balance. I held it close to my side and started limping for the door . . .

Just as the Bedoowan knight-nurse walked in.

"What are you doing?" she demanded, surprised.

She tried to force me to sit back down. I don't know how, but I didn't let her.

"Listen," I said. "My friend is going to be executed tomorrow. I have to see him."

"You are not well enough to move."

"You're a knight," I shot back. "What would you do if your friend were going to die in the morning? Would you lie down and nurse your wounds?"

I saw her eyes soften. "No," she said softly. "I know Alder. I do not understand his actions."

"Doesn't matter," I said quickly. "He's my friend and I'm going to see him before he dies."

The girl nodded. She understood.

"Where is he?" I demanded.

"There is a stockade near the ruins of the Bedoowan castle," she explained. "That is where he is being kept and where the execution will take place."

"Thank you," I said. I meant it too. I pulled away from her and staggered toward the door.

"Pendragon?" she called. "Alder was a good knight. Why would he betray his own tribe?"

"That's exactly why," I answered. "Because he is a good knight."

I left her with that totally confusing explanation. Alder did what he had to do. He knew the tak had sent the tribes down a destructive path, and he risked his own life to stop it. It may have been too late to save Denduron, but there was no way in hell I was going to let Alder die. I limped out of the hut to see that the hospital was on the edge of the Milago village. The town had been rebuilt since the tak-mine explosion. It was the beginning of a new society. Thanks to me, it was a society that had chosen the path of war and aggression instead of peace and growth. I looked out toward the ocean, where I knew the Bedoowan castle had once been cut into the bluffs. Several stone huts had been erected along the old path. Alder was in one of them.

The suns were setting. It was cold. The village was surprisingly quiet. Most of the people I saw walking between the huts were women. My guess was that most of the men had been pressed into war duty and were now marching up and over the mountain, toward their date with the Lowsee. Lights glowed in several of the huts. Nobody paid any attention to a raggy, staggering stranger who could barely put one foot in front of the other. I followed the winding dirt path toward the bluffs, passing several of the stone huts. My feet hurt. It was probably frostbite from my trek down the snowy mountain. I thought back to how my feet had gone so numb I couldn't feel them. I kind of wished they'd go numb again. Each step was torture. If not for the dado weapon to lean on, I wouldn't have made it very far.

Finally, after walking a few hundred yards that felt like a few hundred miles, I saw a larger stone hut that sat several yards away from the closest structure. A Bedoowan knight stood guard at the door. It had to be the stockade. I limped slowly up to the knight, trying to look every bit as weak as I felt, so that he wouldn't think I was a threat. The guard had a cross-stave that he held out when I got within five yards of him. I stopped and held my hands out.

"I want to see the prisoner named Alder," I announced.

"No one is allowed to enter," the knight replied coldly.

"I'm his friend," I said. "If he's going to die tomorrow, he should be allowed to say good-bye."

The knight blinked. He wasn't a jerk. "I am sorry that it has come to this."

"Tell me about it," I replied.

"I cannot let you in, but you may speak with him through his window."

The guard retracted his stave and motioned for me to go around to the far side of the hut. Swell. More walking. I wasn't complaining though. I rounded the hut to see a row of six windows that ran the length of the building. Each had strong vertical bars. I guessed that meant there were six cells. I walked along the row of windows, peering in each to look for Alder. The cells were empty, except for the last. I looked inside to see a man sitting on the floor with his head on his knees. He wore the same kind of leather I wore, which was strange because, when we were on Denduron, Alder always dressed as a knight. Not anymore. Seeing my large friend sitting there, looking so small, made my heart ache. Of all the Travelers, Alder was the most open, honest, and positive. He had saved my life more than once, never with any fear for himself. He was truly a noble warrior. It hurt to see him look so beaten.

"Hello, Alder," I whispered.

The knight looked up, confused. His hair was ratty. His

eyes unfocused. He was thinner than when I had seen him last.

"Who's there?" he asked, dazed.

"I'm sorry, Alder. This is my fault," I said softly.

"Pendragon!"

Alder shot up as if the ground were hot. He ran to the window and reached through the bars, grabbing the back of my neck in a warm hug with one of his big paws. The transformation had been instant and complete. Gone was the beaten boy. Alder was every bit the outgoing, positive knight he'd always been. When he grabbed me, it felt as if an electric charge flashed through my body. I don't know how else to put it. It was more than just a surge of relief. It was an actual, physical sensation. My head suddenly felt a bit more clear. My nausea was forgotten.

Alder beamed. "I knew I would see you again."

"But not like this," I replied.

A dark look came over him. "I have failed you."

I grabbed Alder's hand and squeezed it. "Don't go there. If anybody failed, it was me. Now you're the one who's going to pay the price."

"So much has happened," he said, shaking his head. "So much has changed."

"You don't know the half of it," I replied. "I have a lot to tell you."

"Speak quickly," he said with a sorry chuckle. "I will not be around much longer to hear it."

Alder kept his hand on my good shoulder while we spoke. I felt his strength flowing into me. I don't mean it was an emotional thing. I swear, I felt I was gaining strength from his touch. My head was clearing. My mind started clicking again. After crawling through the depths for so long, I actually felt as if possibilities might exist. I can't say for sure what guided me to do what I did next. Maybe it was instinct. Maybe it was desperation. All I can say is that it felt right. I grasped Alder's hand, pulled it off my shoulder and placed it square on my chest, over the wound that had been torn open by the quig. Alder gave me a quizzical look.

"We're Travelers," I said, staring him in the eye. "I don't know where we came from or why we're here, but we are like no others."

Alder nodded. He knew.

"We are bound by our destiny. We must not accept defeat."

"We will not accept defeat," he said, his conviction growing.

"As long as we're breathing, there's hope."

"There is always hope," he added with growing confidence.

In that moment I actually believed it. We stood there, two Travelers. The future was in our hands. The past was in our hands. My life was in Alder's, his in mine.

"I'm hurt," I said, not shifting my gaze from his. "Heal me."

Alder didn't question. He didn't flinch. He didn't look away. I felt his hand press against my chest. It was warm. No, hot. I thought back to the moment at the gate on Zadaa when Loor was in my arms, dead. Saint Dane had driven a sword through her heart. She was gone . . . but I saved her. I healed her. We were Travelers. We were illusions. We had the power. We would not be denied.

My body started to tingle, as if blood were being pumped through my veins by a force beyond my own. Alder's eyes grew sharp. He felt it too. The spark was back. I felt my strength return. Not only physically, but mentally. I felt like myself. I was Bobby Pendragon. I was the lead Traveler.

I stood up straight on feet that no longer ached. I released Alder's hand. He pulled it back through the bars. We stood staring at each other, both breathing hard. I didn't have to tear off my bandages to know what had happened. I knew the wounds would be gone. Saint Dane was right. We weren't normal. We were illusions. What that meant, I still didn't know. All I could say for sure was that we weren't like other humans, and right then, it was a good thing.

Alder smiled. "We are not done yet, are we?"

"Not even close," I replied.

JOURNAL #35

(CONTINUED)

DENDURON

The Milago village had changed since my first visit to Denduron. What had once been a small village of farmers had been destroyed by an underground explosion (thanks to me), rebuilt using Bedoowan technology, and was now being developed as a jumping-off point for a conquering army—complete with training grounds, hospitals, armories, and barracks for newly inducted knights. Even with all the advances, it was still primitive by Second Earth standards. The huts were made of stone or wood. The streets were dirt. Horses pulled wooden wagons. The only signs of modern technology were the street lights, which were powered by something called "triptyte," a mineral that glowed in the dark. Triptyte wasn't electricity, but it was valuable enough to start a war over. A war that would put Denduron on Saint Dane's path to destruction. Could Alder and I stop it? I had no idea, but we had to try. Together. That's why the first thing I needed to do was get my friend out of prison.

The Bedoowan armory was exactly where Alder said it would be. I recognized the area as the old Milago training ground. This is where I first saw the Milago miners having target practice with tak. It was a skill that was quickly developed into a method for waging war. Finding the armory wasn't exactly tricky. It was the largest building in the village. Alder told me that there were two armed guards. I saw only one. I was in luck. Still, it was broad daylight. If I made trouble, there was a good chance I'd be seen. Whatever I did had to be fast.

I looped around to the side of the barnlike building, clutching the dado weapon. I wanted to get as close as possible before announcing my presence to the guard. Surprise was a good thing. Loor and Alder taught me never to make the first move. That didn't apply when it came to surprise. The trick with surprise was to make sure the fight was over before it began. The first strike had to be the last.

The Bedoowan guard didn't know what hit him. For the record, it was me. I crept to the corner of the building, waited until his attention was away from me, leaped at the unsuspecting guy, and knocked him cold with two swipes of the dado weapon. Before he had the chance to hit the ground, I grabbed him and dragged him inside the building, closing the door behind us. It was fast. It was efficient. It was violent. It was the new me. So far so good. Really good. I felt great. Physically, I mean. Alder had healed me. The mystery of what it meant to be a Traveler would continue, but that didn't mean we couldn't take advantage of the powers we possessed. I felt strong and hopeful. I might even say invincible. Why not? It was proved that we could cheat injury and even death. I wish I could say that we were able to cheat pain, but that wasn't part of the program. Oh well. It's hard to put this into words, but the feeling of knowing we had that kind of power shot me full of such confidence,

I actually thought we might have a chance of stopping the war on Denduron. Why not?

That feeling of confidence lasted for about as long as it took me to look into the armory building. Alder had described it as the storehouse for the Bedoowan arsenal. He told me about the rows of cannons and the stacks of bows and arrows that sat waiting for war. He said there was enough firepower contained in that building to overrun the simple Lowsee, destroy their tribe, and move on to any other enemy the army decided to victimize next. I didn't doubt him. Trouble was, what I saw inside the armory was in some ways more frightening than knowing such an elaborate arsenal existed.

What I saw was nothing. The armory was empty. Cleared out. Not a single arrow or cannonball was left. Alder had described a huge stockpile of weapons. There was nothing like that in sight. It suddenly made sense why there was only one guard stationed out front. There was nothing left to guard. The weapons were gone and I knew where they went. They were headed over the mountain with the Bedoowan knights, who were on their way to destroy the Lowsee. My heart sank. Our plan was to destroy the arsenal, but there was no arsenal left to destroy. We were too late.

We would have to find another way to stop the war. But first, Alder had to be rescued. I moved quickly, following his description of the armory. Finding the tak mine wasn't hard. Near the mouth of the tunnel was a small pile of tak bricks.

I took two, along with a length of fuse and one of the friction starters Alder described to me. I had a fleeting thought that I should run down into the mine and just ignite the tak again. But that was too risky. Alder had failed at that once. There were probably miners and guards down there. I didn't need to be caught and dumped into the jail cell next to my Bedoowan friend. No, I had to stick to the plan and spring Alder.

I took one of the bricks and gingerly broke off a piece of the soft mineral. If you remember, it was gritty and pliable, like clay. It was also volatile. I had to be fast, but careful. I ran to one of the inside walls of the armory and gently pressed a line of tak along the base of the wooden wall. The process scared the heck out of me. If I handled the tak too roughly, it would hit back with a big boom. I kept breaking off pieces and smearing the soft mineral along the base of the wall, making a long, rust-colored line.

I heard a sound from down in the mine. *Clang!* Somebody had dropped a tool. It was innocent enough, but I feared that somebody might be coming up. I had to work faster. After smearing most of the tak brick on the wall, I was ready. I took a small piece of fuse no more than two inches long and jammed it into the space between the wooden boards, making sure the end touched the smear of tak. I sparked the starter and lit the fuse. Backing away, I hoped I had smeared the right amount on the wall. I didn't want an explosion, I wanted a fire. A diversion. I had made a thin line of tak about twenty feet long on the wooden wall. If it didn't blow up, it would burn. At least, I hoped it would.

I backed away to the door of the armory and waited. It wouldn't be long. The fuse would only take a few seconds to reach the tak. I actually put my fingers in my ears, in case I hadn't spread it thin enough. Two seconds later I heard a sharp fizzle. The fuse hit the tak and instantly shot along the line, faster than I had imagined. The flare was brighter than I had imagined too. I had to squint or I would have been blinded. I waited for an explosion. It didn't come. Perfect. The wall of the armory was burning. The tak was so powerful it had already eaten through the wood. Flames began to lick up the side of the huge wooden structure. We were in business. The armory would soon be blazing.

I couldn't leave the unconscious guard in there to die, so I quickly dragged him outside and dumped him a safe distance from what was about to be a burning building. If all went well, help would soon arrive to put the flames out and he'd be in no danger. If things went badly, well, I didn't want to think about that. So I didn't. I ran back inside, grabbed the dado weapon and the second tak brick, then ran out for good.

I sprinted across the training ground, jumped over the berm of dirt, and turned back to watch. Smoke was already filling the air. The tak was doing its job. If this fire wasn't put out quickly, the whole place would go up. It was exactly what I wanted. I got up and moved quickly back toward the village. I had gotten about halfway back to the stockade when I heard the urgent clanging of a bell. It had to be a fire alarm. Whoever was ringing it wasn't announcing lunch. The ringing was furious. Instantly people emerged from their houses and looked around nervously. A patrol of Bedoowan knights ran past me, headed for the armory. They knew where the problem was. What they didn't know was that I was about to cause another problem somewhere else.

I made it back to the stockade easily. The whole way, I passed Bedoowan knights sprinting the other way, toward the burning armory. My hope was that Alder would be left unguarded.

He wasn't. One guard remained at his post. That was

okay. I could handle one guard. The poor guy was about to get a very big surprise. I ran quickly to the back of the stockade, where I gently broke a Silly Putty egg-size chunk off the tak brick and molded it along the upper edge of Alder's barred window opening.

"Do not use too much," Alder cautioned as he peered at me from inside. "I have no protection in here."

I didn't know how strong the bars were. If I didn't use enough tak, all we'd do was alert the guard. If I used too much, there wouldn't be enough left of Alder to break out of anywhere. It wasn't an exact science. I decided to use only one piece of tak. I pressed the explosive along the entire top edge of the window and jammed a fuse into the soft material.

"Under the bed," I commanded.

Alder didn't need to be convinced. Before I could ignite the fuse, he was hidden safely under his cot. At least, I hoped it was safely. I sparked the starter. Ten seconds to detonation. This time it wasn't about the fire. It was about the boom. When that tak went off, there was no telling which way the bars would fly, so I ducked around the corner. I put my back to the wall and waited. And waited. It felt like forever. I was second-guessing myself, thinking I should have used less tak when *boom!* The tak erupted, much more strongly than I expected. I quickly glanced back around the corner to see the square frame of bars flying away from the building, with smoke trailing behind as if it were jet propelled. I sprinted to the window, choking on the smoke.

"Hey!" I called. "You okay?"

Alder's head popped up from below the charred, gaping hole that was once a window frame. He was smiling. "I guess there is no longer need for secrecy," he announced with a grin.

Before he could climb out, I was tackled from the side. I never saw it coming. It was a total blindside hit. It took me a second to realize that the guard had heard the explosion too, no big surprise. It wasn't subtle. He had run around to investigate and jumped me without so much as a "Halt!" or a "What's going on here?" The guard hit me. I hit the ground. He sat on top of me, pinning my arms with his knees, and wound up to punch me in the head. There was nothing I could do but wince. The punch never came. I looked up cautiously to see Alder looming over the guard. He had caught the guy's hand at the top of its arc.

"Please do not hit my friend," he said calmly.

The Bedoowan guard didn't have time to react. Alder clocked him with his other hand. Simple as that. The guard tumbled off me. He wasn't knocked unconscious, but he was reeling.

"Now what?" Alder asked as calmly as if we were planning a picnic. The answer came in the form of a shout from the direction of the sea. We turned to see a dozen Bedoowan knights with cross-staves, sprinting directly toward us from the ruins of the castle.

"We get gone," I said, and ran toward the village.

We both knew the best place to escape to would be the village. With any luck we could get lost within the labyrinth of huts. We needed time to think and to plan.

"The armory is on fire," I said as we ran.

"Perhaps it will destroy the weapons as well."

"The building was empty, Alder. The weapons are in play. The war is about to begin."

Alder's only response was a quick, dark look.

We hit the village and sprinted along the narrow streets, winding our way on a route we thought would be impossible to follow. There weren't many people around. They were either out in the fields to work the farms or marching over the mountain to work the war. Alder pointed for me to run down a narrow alleyway of huts. We moved quickly until we came to a central, open courtyard.

"Stop here," he ordered.

We both leaned against one of the wooden buildings to catch our breath.

"The tak mine," I said, gulping air. "Maybe we can still take it out."

Alder shook his head. "It would not matter," he said gravely. "The Bedoowan already have all they need. Once they see the power it gives them, they will never be denied again. If we buried the mine, they would only dig it out again. We cannot turn the clock back."

I hated to admit it, but he was right. The damage was done.

"It is too late for Denduron," Alder added. "We cannot stop an army."

Alder dropped his head in defeat. This was the new turning point for Denduron. The first domino was about to fall, and there was nothing we could do about it.

"I'm sorry" was all I could say. It was a painfully inadequate apology. After having saved it once, Alder's home territory was now lost.

He frowned. "We cannot let the events that happened here stop us."

"Agreed," I said quickly. "I'm not giving up. Not again."

"Perhaps the Convergence has not yet touched other territories," Alder offered. "There may still be hope."

I nodded. "We've got to get to the flume."

Zing! An arrow nearly hit me in the face. It stuck in the wall of the hut where we had been resting, not a foot from my head. Alder shoved me out of the way. I hit the ground, rolled, and came up running. We sprinted for a large wooden structure on the far side of the clearing.

Zing! Zing! Arrows flew around us. I swear I could feel the ripple of air as they sped past. None found their mark, but I didn't think we could dodge them for long. Alder leaped through a large wooden door, into a dark room that my nose told me was a stable. He knew exactly what he was doing. Horses were lined up along the far wall, all with simple saddles and halters.

"Can you ride?" Alder asked.

"Can you keep up with me?" I answered.

I grabbed what looked like a leather saddlebag. I still had the rest of the tak brick I'd used to blast open Alder's cell. No way I could hold it while I rode, but I didn't want to give it up. It was the only weapon we had. I quickly but gingerly slipped the chunk of explosive into the bag and tied it to the saddle of a deep brown horse. Alder was already up on his own horse, ready to go.

"Hurry, Pendragon," he said calmly. Alder didn't know how to panic.

"Right behind you."

Alder kicked his ride. The animal responded and bolted for the door. I did the same, clutching my legs so hard I was sure I'd crack ribs. Alder blasted out the door just as the Bedoowan knights arrived. I don't think they were expecting to face two charging horses, because they scattered in surprise, jumping out of the way to avoid being trampled. I didn't know where to go. Alder did. I stayed focused on the butt of his horse, urging my own to stay close. Clods of dirt and gravel were kicked up by Alder's animal. I didn't care. I didn't care if my horse cared. We weren't about to stop. I cringed, expecting to get hit with an arrow from behind. Alder smartly rounded a hut to put a barrier between us and the knights, then galloped on a course directly away from them.

Turned out it wasn't the knights from the stable that we had to worry about.

Alder's horse was faster than mine. Or maybe it was because Alder was a better rider than I was. As we broke into the open, he quickly pulled way ahead. In no time there was a gap of about twenty yards between us. Another patrol of knights appeared far off to our left. They were too far away to do anything but shoot arrows, but that was enough. A wave of missiles flew in front of me like the swarm of quig-bees from Ibara. Most missed. One didn't. Alder's horse took an arrow square in its left flank. The animal whinnied and reared up. Alder wasn't ready for that. He rolled backward, falling off the horse and landing square on his back. Alder's horse wasn't hurt badly, because it continued to run. The animal would be fine. I wasn't so sure about Alder.

I shot a look to see the group of knights about fifty yards away and closing. They weren't moving all that fast—they were busy fumbling to reload their bows. It wouldn't be long before another round of arrows would be incoming. I hadn't slowed down. In seconds I would be next to Alder. What would I do? I was an okay rider, but I wasn't a circus guy. It wasn't like I could lean down and swoop him up off the ground at a full gallop. I only had a few seconds to make a decision. I had no idea what to do.

Alder solved the problem. When he hit the ground he never stopped moving. He did a complete backward somersault and landed on his feet. It wasn't like he jumped up with a "Ta da!" or anything. He was shaken and looked pretty wobbly. His balance was obviously off as he struggled to stand straight. But he was aware of everything that was swirling around him. I knew it the instant he glanced over his shoulder, looking for me. He knew where he was. He knew where I was. He needed a ride.

I slowed my horse, not sure how to get Alder on board. Again Alder took care of it. He was a knight. A soldier. He knew horses. He grabbed the back of my saddle and vaulted onto the rear of my horse.

"Go" was all he said.

I kicked my horse and launched back into a gallop . . . as another wave of arrows arrived. The knights' timing was off. They were aiming at where we were, not thinking we'd be moving so fast, so quickly. The missiles flew behind us. None came close. We were gone.

"Head for those trees," Alder said, pointing to a stand of pine trees far ahead. We weren't moving as fast as before. Two riders on one horse tends to slow things down. Didn't matter. We weren't being chased. I maneuvered the strong horse into the trees, but kept moving forward, trying to get as much distance between us and the Milago village as possible.

"You okay?" I asked Alder.

"I have been thrown worse than that" was his understated answer.

The guy was amazing. Nothing got to him. He could be hit by a bus and he'd shrug it off as if it were a tricycle. That is, if there were buses on Denduron. Or tricycles. Whatever. I was glad we were together. I knew that no matter how the final moves of the battle with Saint Dane would play out,

Alder would be by my side. And why not? He didn't need to be on Denduron anymore.

Neither did I. Denduron was lost. A victory had turned into defeat. What we needed to know was, what other territories were in danger of turning. Zadaa? Eelong? Everything we had done was thrown into doubt because of Saint Dane's Convergence.

As we climbed the mountain together on the back of that horse, I realized there was yet another concern. I don't know why it took me so long to get it.

"There are ten territories," I said to Alder. "Until today we stopped Saint Dane on six of them. Veelox was a loss, but by winning Ibara, I thought it had become a victory. The only solid loss was Quillan . . . until now."

"Now they are all in danger of turning," Alder replied with no emotion.

"That's not all. There are still two territories that haven't been targeted. Second and Third Earth. If territories are defined by their turning point, what's the deal with those two? If Saint Dane's big plan was to create a convergence of territories, why did he skip those two?"

"Perhaps he did not need them," Alder offered.

"Or maybe he's been waiting until now."

The thought made my stomach twist. That always seemed to happen when reality paid a visit. Especially if it was bad, which was often. All I knew about events on Second Earth had to do with the change in technology that happened because of Forge. Same with Third Earth. As far as I knew, neither had reached a definite turning point. As we spoke, the truth became obvious. Unfortunately.

"It's about Earth," I announced soberly. "It's always been about Earth."

"Why do you say that?"

"Because everything leads there," I answered, my mind racing. "Second Earth is where Saint Dane got Mark to invent Forge. First Earth is where the evolution of the dados began. The dados attacked Ibara. We took tak from Denduron to battle the dados, which is why things have gone sour here. Dados are everywhere on Quillan, and they were trying to get to First Earth. They're already on Third Earth, and they're headed back to Ibara. I'm the lead Traveler. I'm from Second Earth. It's like Earth is the hub of a wheel. Everything spreads out from there. All the events that have led to the Convergence began on Earth."

Alder let that sink in, then asked, "What do you believe that means?"

"I think the turning point of either Second or Third Earth might be the turning point for Halla."

Alder shook his head. "I do not know, Pendragon. For all that I have seen, the concepts of which you speak are still beyond my grasp."

"Yeah, I'm not far ahead. I'm reaching here, but I think I know what we should do. We'd be wasting our time by going to any other territories. We've got to go to the source. We've got to see what Saint Dane is doing on Earth."

"So do we go to Second Earth?"

"No, Third Earth. From there we can use the computers to look back on everything that has happened on Earth. That's where we'll find answers."

Alder didn't say anything. I wasn't surprised. He was a simple guy from a primitive society. The ideas I was throwing out were completely alien to him. They weren't exactly comfortable to me either, but I had been through a lot more than he had. I hoped he would continue to trust me.

We climbed silently for several minutes. The horse was strong. Once we entered the snowfield, the animal barely slowed as it trudged across the icy expanse. Finally, after rolling our dilemma over in his head for the better part of our trek, Alder spoke.

"I do not know if your theory is correct, Pendragon, but I do agree with one thing."

"What's that?"

"We should not look back. The Convergence has begun. I fear that if we revisit any of the other territories, we may not have the power to change events. Even if we did, what would prevent Saint Dane from manipulating events yet again to create other turning points?"

He was exactly right. It was the reality that had been eating at my stomach since I discovered that Ibara was the future of Veelox. Saint Dane was in control. More than I had ever imagined. He seemed to have the ability to travel between times at will. We only had the power to chase after him and trust that the flumes would put us in the right time. I didn't know why that was. I didn't know who made up the rules, but it was the truth. We could be chasing Saint Dane between territories from now until forever, and he would always have the ability to change the rules.

"If we are to stop him," Alder continued, "we have to understand exactly what his goals are. It is the very essence of warfare. The only way to defeat an enemy is to understand what he wants. Until we do that, we have no hope of victory. We need to learn why we have been fighting this battle."

Alder may have been a simple guy. He may have not understood modern concepts or technology, but with those few words he had defined our mission perfectly. We had to stop thinking small. This wasn't about a single territory, or even about ten individual territories. This was about Halla. This was about flumes. About Travelers. About Saint Dane's ability to change shape. It was about the Travelers being able to heal one another. It was about our being illusions. About traveling through time. It was about Saint Dane saying that he wanted to prove his superiority. We needed to know who he was proving it to. We had to learn it all.

"You're right," I declared. "I think we have the best chance of doing that on Third Earth."

"Then Third Earth is where we will go."

We heard a distant rumble. The horse stopped, spooked.

"Thunder?" I asked.

More rumbles followed. I looked back at Alder. His eyes were sharp. His hearing focused.

"No," he answered somberly. "The battle has begun. The Bedoowan have used tak against their brothers. Denduron is lost."

What we were listening to was the sounds of war. There was no way we could change things for the better on Denduron. Those distant explosions proved it.

"Are we that close to the Lowsee village?" I asked.

"No. It is well beyond the far side of this mountain. That will tell you how devastating the tak is. Right now, people are dying."

"So is Denduron."

We listened to the explosions. The power was incredible. The snow beneath us shook. More explosions echoed over the mountains. The snow shook again. And again. Something was wrong. The sound of the explosions and the shaking beneath us weren't coinciding. There was something else happening.

"Earthquake?" I asked, jittery.

Alder didn't know. We heard more explosions.

We weren't the only ones who heard them.

The snow continued to rumble and shift. I realized the real reason for all the shaking a split second before it all came apart. Thirty yards in front of us, the snow started to boil. I saw the surface crack and crumble. A few yards beyond that, more snow shifted. Another area began to roil. It wasn't the whole surface of the snowfield; it was only in specific areas. Areas where things were buried. Things that were awakened by the sound of exploding tak. An area of snow erupted like an ice-filled volcano, sending sparkling shards into the air. Through the cloud of snow that blew into the sky, I saw the cause.

The quigs were awake.

JOURNAL #35

(CONTINUED)

DENDURON

All around us the vicious bears that had been hibernating under the snow were coming to life. We were nowhere near the gate to the flume. There was nothing around us for protection. We were in the middle of a pack of quigs, who weren't happy about having been rudely awakened from their slumber.

As the first quig rose up out of the snow, our horse panicked and reared.

"Whoa, whoa!" I shouted, as if that would do any good. The poor horse was terrified. I didn't blame him. All around us, quigs erupted from below. It was all I could do to stay on the horse and control it. Control? Not exactly. It was more like desperately holding on to the reins to keep from falling off. Alder had nothing to hold on to but me. The horse brought its front legs back down and turned to run, only to be faced by another quig that had appeared behind us. I pulled with every bit of strength I had, just to keep the horse from bolting.

"Take the reins!" I shouted to Alder.

He reached around me and grabbed on to the leather straps.

"I have it," he shouted.

I ducked under Alder's outstretched arms and dove off the animal.

"Pendragon?" Alder yelled with surprise.

"Keep it still," I ordered.

I knew we had only one chance. If the horse took off, we'd have no chance. Alder wrestled with the animal, who was spinning and bucking like a wild mustang. Its eyes flared. It must have seen what I saw: The closest quig had zeroed in on us. If it's possible for an animal to look angry, this beastie was there.

"Get up here!" Alder commanded.

I ignored him. There was no way we could outrun a charging quig on that horse. We had to make a stand.

"Keep it still!" I shouted again.

Alder struggled to keep the horse in place. The horse was winning. That didn't stop Alder from trying. He tugged on the reins, forcing the horse's head down. He would only be able to keep it still for a little while longer. I hoped it would be enough.

The quig huffed and stalked toward us. Stalking was good. Better than charging. If the quig ran to attack, we'd have been done, because I wasn't ready yet. The other quigs circled behind it. I guess there's some kind of honor among quigs. Closest to the prize gets the first nibble. Unlike the quig I had fought in the flume cave, this guy was big. Bigger than any quig I'd ever seen. It was like the T. rex of quigs. Maybe that was why the others let it have first dibs on the prey.

"Pendragon?" Alder called again, his voice cracking, which

for him was the same as a totally panicked breakdown.

"It's okay. Let him come," I said.

"I do not believe I have a choice."

"We need him closer."

"Any closer and I will feel its breath."

The horse bucked, hit my shoulder, and knocked me back. I stumbled, but didn't fall. There was no time for that. I quickly leaped back at the horse, grabbing for the leather bag that was attached to the saddle. The bag with the tak brick. The horse was between me and the advancing quig.

"I'm only going to get one shot, maybe two," I said. "When I say so, rear up."

"If I can."

"You have to," I said firmly.

I pulled out the small brick of tak and tore it in two. Putting one half under my arm, I formed the other half like a snowball. I quickly shifted hands and formed the other tak ball.

The quig roared and stood up on its hind legs. It was getting ready for the kill.

"Pendragon?" Alder called again nervously.

"Not yet," I cautioned.

The quig's eyes flashed yellow. Hunger was all that mattered to him. As soon as its front paws landed back on the snow, it charged. It had decided that we posed no threat. He was wrong.

"Now!" I shouted.

Alder pulled back on the reins with a grunt. The horse whinnied and reared up, lifting its front hooves into the sky, giving me a clear shot. The quig was maybe fifteen yards away and closing fast. I heaved the tak ball sidearm, for fear I might hit the horse. The ball flew square at the quig's head . . . and exploded on contact.

I was blown off my feet. It was like being hit with a wall of hot bricks. I landed hard on the snow. The horse landed right next to me. The only thought I had was to protect the second tak ball. If that was slammed too hard, there would be a second explosion. Closer than the first. Too close. I cradled it next to my stomach as if it were a precious egg. Or a high explosive. I didn't know where Alder was. I couldn't hear anything except the ringing in my ears from the explosion. It started to rain, only the rain was traveling sideways. And it was too cold to rain. I soon realized the truth. I was being pelted by wet bits of quig. Chunks of flesh and fur and blood flew everywhere. A hunk of bone flew past. A tooth skidded across the snow. If I hadn't been so dazed, I probably would have retched. Through the smoke and snow and flying gore, I saw Alder lying a few yards from me. I scrambled over quickly and rolled him onto his back.

His eyes were open, but unfocused.

"Hey!" I shouted, shaking his head.

Alder blinked, coughed, and met my gaze.

"I believe the correct word is . . . 'wow,'" he said with wide eyes.

I had to laugh. Nothing bothered this guy.

We weren't out of danger. There were other quigs lurking around. I looked back to where I had hit the lead quig and saw exactly what I'd hoped to see. There was nothing left of the quig but a huge chunk of blood and bone. I made out a couple of furry masses that were probably paws. The rest was scattered across the snow. The red snow. More important, the other quigs took the bait. Or the lunch. They didn't care about us anymore. There were good eats to be had. They climbed over one another to get a piece of their exploded pal. One would grab on to a piece of flesh and pull away, only to have another quig bite the same piece and wrestle for the prize. Yeah, disgusting.

I hate quigs.

The horse was long gone. The trail of hoof prints in the snow showed that he had decided not to make the rest of the trip with us and had run for home. I guess he'd had his fill of being a Traveler.

"We have to go the rest of the way on foot," I said. "Can you walk?"

Alder's answer was to stagger to his feet. The guy stood up tall over me. He had to be at least six-four. He was a heck of a sight, standing there in his blood-spattered leathers.

"I am looking forward to being somewhere else."

The two of us staggered away from the carnage, headed for the top of the mountain and the flume. It took another half hour of trudging through the snow until we saw the rocky cave. I'm happy to say that there were no quig spines poking out from the snow. They were off having a bite to eat. We were nearly at the cave when Alder put his hand out to stop me.

"Look," he said.

Bright light flared from inside the cave. We both knew that meant only one thing. We sprinted the last few yards and ran inside in time to see the light disappearing into the depths of the flume, along with the musical notes. Between us and the tunnel was the white skeleton of a quig. Two of the dado weapons I had used to kill it were still jutting out from the bones, right where I'd left them. The quig looked as if he had been picked clean by his pals. Gross. But the quig skeleton isn't what held our attention. Alder and I stood staring at something beyond. Something in the flume.

On the rocky bottom, just inside the mouth, was a body. We stood stock still, waiting for the guy to move. He didn't.

"He may be dead," Alder said.

The body groaned. He wasn't dead. But he looked hurt. We ran for him. I got there first and rolled the guy over.

"Patrick!" I shouted.

"Who?"

"The Traveler from Third Earth."

My hand was under his back. I felt something I didn't like and quickly pulled my hand back to see it was covered with blood. Fresh blood. Patrick's blood. Alder and I exchanged looks. We knew what to do. We both put our hands on the Traveler. I slid my bloody hand under his back, to where I thought the wound was, and held my other hand over his heart. Alder rested both his hands on Patrick's chest. I didn't know the exact procedure, other than to concentrate on willing Patrick to heal. Alder's eyes were closed. I closed mine as well. I thought of Patrick the way he was on Third Earth. Smart, quick, and maybe a little neurotic. I pictured his face and the way he moved. I tried to imagine his voice.

My hands felt warm. Both of them. It wasn't painful or anything. It was a strange feeling, but also kind of comforting. We were Travelers. All three of us. We were brothers. We were part of something bigger that we had yet to uncover. Of all the things that were still unknown, still a mystery, still maddeningly elusive, there was one thing that I had total confidence in.

We could save one another.

The warm feeling became a tingle that spread up my arms and through my body. I opened my eyes and stole a look at Alder to see a small smile on his face. He was feeling the same thing. The event lasted only a few seconds. I looked down at our Traveler friend.

"Patrick?" I said softly. "You there?"

Patrick's eyelids fluttered. He gasped, as if refilling his lungs with air. Slowly his eyes opened. He glanced around in confusion until he focused on me.

"Pendragon?" he croaked.

"Do you know where you are?" I asked.

"Denduron?"

I nodded. "Why did you come here, Patrick? What happened?"

"I . . . I was shot," he gasped. He hadn't fully focused. He was still trying to get his bearings.

"By who? Who shot you?"

"People who worked for the Traveler," was his strange answer.

I looked to Alder. Alder scowled.

"What Traveler?" I asked quickly.

Patrick grasped my hand and whispered, "The new Traveler from Second Earth."

I was rocked back on my heels. Nothing could have prepared me for that. In three seconds my mind raced to a million possibilities and a million dead ends.

"Pendragon?" Alder said calmly.

I looked to him, hoping he had an answer. He did. He may not have known what was happening, or what the news from Patrick meant, but he knew exactly what had to be done.

"I believe we are no longer going to Third Earth," he declared.

"No, we're not," I said, getting my wits back. "I'm going home."

END OF JOURNAL #35

SECOND EARTH

Mark and Courtney sat stone faced in the back of the same limousine that originally took them into New York City. They didn't bother to try and get out. It was parked and surrounded by Naymeer's red-shirt guards. Not that it mattered. The events of the past few minutes had shocked them into submission.

There was a flurry of activity outside the car. One of the guards opened the door next to Mark. Mark didn't react. It was like he didn't care anymore. They were soon joined by another passenger. The door was slammed shut, and an instant later they were rolling.

Sitting across from them was Alexander Naymeer. He looked every bit as calm and together as Mark and Courtney looked worn. Not a single one of his silver-gray hairs was out of place. In spite of all that had just happened, he was as relaxed as if going on a drive through the park.

"Finally," he said with his arms spread out in a warm welcome. "We meet."

Mark and Courtney stared at him blankly.

"Mark Dimond and Courtney Chetwynde," Naymeer continued.

"I've heard so much about you, I feel as if I know you. Would you like something to drink?"

He reached for an expensive-looking crystal decanter full of water. Mark and Courtney didn't respond. Naymeer replaced it and chuckled like an amused grandparent.

"If we don't converse, this will be a very long ride," he said playfully.

"You killed him," Courtney said flatly. "Patrick is dead."

Naymeer frowned. "A horrible mistake. It should never have happened. Heat of the moment and all. My guardians used poor judgment. I am absolutely sick over it."

Mark added, "You destroyed my house. Was that in the heat of the moment too?"

Naymeer raised his hands in a gesture of surrender. "Please, don't judge too quickly. There are larger issues involved."

"Larger than murder?" Courtney snapped.

Naymeer cocked an eyebrow and answered, "Yes, actually."

Courtney sat forward in the seat. "Who the hell are you!" she shouted.

Mark put out a hand to stop her from moving any closer to Naymeer.

"You already know that answer," Naymeer said without flinching. "I am the Traveler from Second Earth."

If Mark hadn't held Courtney tighter, she would have leaped at Naymeer's throat.

"Bobby Pendragon is the Traveler from Second Earth," she hissed.

"He was," Naymeer said with sympathy. "But he has abdicated the position, so the honor is now mine."

"How can you say that?" Mark asked, trying to control his emotions. "Who told you?"

Naymeer looked between the two and shook his head. "After all that has happened, you truly do not understand, do you?"

"A-Are you Saint Dane?" Mark asked tentatively.

Naymeer laughed. "Hardly. I am but a mere Traveler. Though I am at his disposal."

Mark and Courtney sat stunned. Naymeer was slick. His British accent made him seem all the more superior. He was worshipped by millions. He consulted with world leaders. He was a force to be reckoned with.

All Mark and Courtney saw was a murderer who had aligned himself with Saint Dane.

"How do you know so much about Halla?" Courtney asked. "I've never heard of you, and I know all about the Travelers."

"You may know of the Travelers, but I'm beginning to realize you don't know much about Halla. You are aware of Ravinia, aren't you?"

"It's your creepy cult," Courtney said. "So what?"

Naymeer held up his hand and looked at his ring, admiring it. "What do you know of this?" he asked.

"I know it's mine," Mark grumbled.

Naymeer ignored the comment and continued. "Do you question how it works? How the flume performs as it does? What powers it all?"

"You're kidding, right?" Courtney said sarcastically. "Try, like, every minute of every day."

Naymeer removed the ring and held it up to the light coming in through the car's window. "It's not a very attractive stone. Until it comes to life, that is. Of course you understand that the stone in this ring is the same material that makes up the flume."

Courtney and Mark exchanged looks. They didn't.

"Scientists have debated its existence for some time now. It's quite extraordinary actually. From this simple material, a universe was born."

Mark's eyes widened. "No way," he gasped.

"No way what?" Courtney asked, shooting a surprised look to Mark. "You know what this guy's talking about?"

Mark stared right at Naymeer and asked, "You're saying the rings and the flume are made up of the dark matter?"

"The who?" Courtney asked, totally confused.

"It's been called many things," Naymeer explained. "But you are correct. It is most commonly referred to as dark matter. Whatever the name, its nature is undeniable. This amazing material provided the foundation of Halla. Planets, stars, moons, civilizations, cultures, everything we know of grew from this most basic substance. It is the oldest material in existence. It is also the most powerful."

"How do you know that?" Mark asked. "No one's proved its existence."

"No one on Second Earth," he answered slyly. "Surely you realize there is more to existence than this one territory."

Mark and Courtney didn't reply. They knew about the other territories. The other worlds. They knew there had to be greater powers at work on their lives. The flumes were proof of that. Now, for the first time, it seemed they were with someone who had the answers.

"So, who told *you* about it?" Courtney muttered.

Naymeer smiled. "A raven."

Mark and Courtney stared at him blankly.

Naymeer returned the ring to his finger. "Many years ago I was given a gift. This ring. It was brought to me by a raven."

"I know how you got it," Mark spat. "From me. I was blackmailed into giving it up."

"Were you?" Naymeer responded. "If it was in your possession, why did you not explore its wonders?"

Mark didn't have an answer.

"Perhaps it was in the wrong hands," Naymeer concluded.

"What kind of wonders?" Courtney asked.

Naymeer closed his eyes, as if remembering a time long past. "I quickly realized that the gift was more than a simple trinket. The power contained in this stone saved my life and opened the door to Halla. Whenever I held the ring, I saw visions of the fantastic. The impossible. I saw other worlds full of unique animals and alien civilizations. There were ancient tribes and modern spectacles. Initially I was frightened, but I soon learned they weren't fantasies, or spirits sent to haunt me. I was getting a glimpse into the vast reality of Halla."

"You traveled to other territories?" Mark asked.

"No!" was the quick answer. "I have never left Second Earth. There is no need. The ring provided me with all the answers. I grew up alone, you know. In a foundling hospital. The ring and its truths became my whole life."

"I don't buy this," Courtney said. "No way a kid could figure all this out on his own."

"You are correct. I was adopted by a young woman, who raised me. Together we explored the wonders of Halla. She showed me all that was good, and so much that was wrong. Together we formed the plan to ensure that the good would triumph."

"Nevva Winter," Mark gasped.

"Yes, sweet Nevva. I cannot say she became a mother to me. She was more of a mentor. But she is as much responsible for all that has happened as I."

"So what happened?" Courtney asked impatiently. "What is the point of Ravinia? What are you promising these people?"

Naymeer leaned forward. His eyes sparkled with an intensity that made Mark and Courtney press back into their seats.

"I'm giving them hope for the future," he answered. "I started slowly, appealing to children and their parents. The war drove them to me. London was in turmoil for many years. People knew there had to be a better way. They needed to know there was something bigger, something more important, in order to make sense of their misery. To organize the chaos. I showed it to them. With this ring I treated them to glimpses of other worlds. Other civilizations. I introduced grand possibilities that reached past their limited lives. I convinced them to look beyond their borders and strive to become citizens, not of their towns or their countries, but of Halla!"

"That's it?" Courtney scoffed. "You showed them some floating pictures and they lined up to follow you? You can get that in the movies."

"Except motion pictures aren't real," Naymeer countered.

Courtney backed down.

Naymeer continued, "I showed them how their lives would have no limits, no restrictions, as long as they believed in me and my vision of a greater future. Not everyone has the prescience. I had to appeal to the proper type of person."

Mark said, "The elite. The strong. The enlightened."

Naymeer's eyes widened with pride. "I'm flattered. You listened to my speech."

"We didn't have a choice," Courtney growled.

"I had a difficult upbringing," Naymeer continued. "It became clear early on, that the only way to survive was to excel. To be better. To rise above the rabble. Every world of Halla is faced with the same challenge: From individuals to cities, tribes to armies, governments to families—societies throughout time have crumbled due to their tolerance for weakness. Instead of encouraging the strong, they waste resources on those who don't contribute. Halla can be so much better than that. Imagine if our prime goal were to transcend mediocrity? Think of the possibilities! Instead of being held back by the weight of failure, we should reward those who strive for excellence. The doctors. The scientists. Teachers. Generals. Mathematicians. Athletes. Those who excel in finance.

The visionaries. The leaders. Excellence will be rewarded. Failure and apathy will not be tolerated. Once that philosophy is universally accepted, Halla will soar to greater heights than could ever be imagined. Let me quote one of your most popular presidents: *'Ask not what your country can do for you, ask what you can do for your country.'* That is the philosophy of Ravinia. That is what we will achieve throughout Halla."

"But you twisted it," Mark argued. "That wasn't what Kennedy meant. He was making a plea for people to think beyond themselves and consider the needs of others."

"Exactly," Naymeer said with satisfaction.

"You're only considering one side," Mark complained. "I can quote you, too: *'We must reward excellence and condemn those whose only contribution to society is to burden.'* You said that, didn't you?"

Naymeer smiled. "You know more about me than you've let on."

Courtney sat forward and said, "What about the people who don't live up to your high standards? The burdens to society? They're going to be 'marginalized,' right? What does that mean?"

"It means they are inconsequential," Naymeer said. "What is the saying you Americans are so fond of? *If you're not part of the solution, you're part of the problem."*

"Problem?" Mark shouted. "Just because somebody might not have some special talent, doesn't make them a problem. Every life has value."

"Indeed," Naymeer agreed. "It is up to every individual to find their talent and use it for the common good."

"And who decides if they're contributing enough?" Courtney bellowed, getting red faced. "You? Not everybody is a leader. Or a genius. What about all the people who are just . . . normal?"

"They will be encouraged to be productive," Naymeer said easily. "If they choose otherwise, there will be repercussions." Naymeer touched a button on the console on the side of his seat and spoke to the driver. "Take us to Horizon One."

"This is unbelievable," Courtney cried. "What about the elderly? The sick? You're saying that millions of people will be tossed aside?"

"Believe me," Naymeer countered. "There are millions who agree with my way of thinking."

"Brought to us courtesy of a bird," Courtney scoffed. "A raven. Ravinia. Cute."

Naymeer laughed. "All I've done is appeal to the common sense of those who want a better way of life. This isn't about race or religion or nationality. All we are doing is concentrating on the positive and eliminating the negatives."

"You're eliminating humanity," Mark said softly. "You sound exactly like Saint Dane."

"That is the greatest compliment you could have paid me," Naymeer said with smug satisfaction.

All three fell silent. Courtney and Mark held hands for support. The words of the man sitting across from them played over and over in their minds. In a few minutes the car turned off the highway and came to a stop. Immediately one of Naymeer's guardians opened the door. Mark and Courtney looked at the old man.

"You inquired, you should see," he said as he got out of the car.

"Is this possible?" Courtney whispered to Mark. "Can this one guy change the thinking of an entire world?"

"It's not just this one guy," Mark answered soberly. "This is all about Saint Dane. And it's not just about this one world."

They both got out to see several of the red-shirt guardians surrounding them. Two motorcycles had been leading the limo. Two more black cars had been trailing. Alexander Naymeer was well protected.

"This way," Naymeer said, and walked off.

Mark and Courtney followed. They were on the edge of a vast

construction site. Mounds of dirt were everywhere, being pushed around by heavy machinery. The first sections of a tall, cement wall could be seen, on top of which was a line of red flags with gate stars, flapping in the breeze. Naymeer climbed up on a scaffold to get a better view. Mark and Courtney joined him. Red-shirt guards were never far away, keeping a watchful eye.

Naymeer surveyed the site proudly. "Not long ago this area was littered with derelict warehouses and ramshackle homes. Now it is owned and controlled by Ravinia. I'm going to call it 'Horizon One.'"

"What are you making?" Courtney asked. "A mall?"

Naymeer chuckled. "This is the first of several compounds that are being constructed to house the people we refer to as Horizon Class. We will provide simple single-family homes, recreation, shopping, hospitals—everything they will need to live comfortable lives."

"And all be surrounded by a big fat wall to keep them inside," Mark said somberly.

"You make it sound like a prison," Naymeer countered. "It isn't. The Horizon Class will live normal lives. Most will work outside the compound. It will be their choice to live here or not, though they would be wise to come here, for there will bo nowhere else for them to go. Slums will be razed to make way for progress. There will be no more poverty, for there will be no place to harbor the poor. Eventually there will be immense compounds like this built all over this country, and then the world. It is a model that will be copied throughout Halla."

Mark and Courtney shot him a look.

"You're serious," Courtney said in awe. "This isn't just about here, it's about Halla."

"That is what I have been telling you!" Naymeer said with excitement. "Once societies are free to flourish without restriction, we will truly achieve paradise."

Mark frowned. "So everybody who isn't pulling enough weight

will be thrown into these compounds so they won't interfere with progress."

"That's one way of putting it," Naymeer agreed.

"They'll be treated like cattle," Mark groused.

Naymeer shrugged. "The choice is theirs."

"No, it isn't!" Courtney shouted. "The choice is yours! This isn't a housing compound, it's a concentration camp! What happens when overcrowding becomes a problem? Or disease? Or crime?"

Naymeer gave them a dark look. "Those who cause problems will be marginalized."

Courtney winced. Mark balled his fists.

"Earth is actually behind the curve," Naymeer said lightly. "Things have progressed further on Denduron, but life is far less complicated there. Change will be brought about with much less fuss."

"Denduron?" Courtney exclaimed. "What's happening there?"

"Every territory will have its own spiritual leader," Naymeer explained. "As each Traveler is cast aside, they will be replaced by a Ravinian, who will guide the world toward its new and greater destiny. I believe the name of the fellow on Denduron is Rellin."

Courtney felt dizzy. Things were coming at her too fast.

"And everyone will answer to Saint Dane," Mark declared, stunned.

"Of course," Naymeer said with a shrug, as if that went without saying. "After all, this is his vision. He is the architect. We are merely devout followers who believe in his plan."

"Why are you telling us all this?" Mark asked. He had to work to control his voice from turning into a cry. "You know we've been helping Bobby to stop Saint Dane."

"I was hoping to appeal to your common sense," Naymeer answered. "You have played as large a part in this revolution as anyone. You are acolytes. You could be instrumental in shaping the future of Earth."

"You can't be serious," Courtney said, incredulous.

"Let me show you one more thing," Naymeer said, heading down the scaffold stairs.

Courtney and Mark stayed on the scaffold, staring at the expanse that would become Horizon One.

"This is it," Courtney said softly to Mark. "This is Saint Dane's vision for Halla. He wants to create an elite society at the expense of the common man."

"It's more than that," Mark said. "Saint Dane is taking away people's ability to control their own lives."

"Coming?" Naymeer called as he strode toward his limo.

Mark and Courtney had no choice but to follow. They climbed down, got in the car, and rode the rest of the way in silence. Their destination wasn't a surprise. When the car finally stopped, they found themselves in front of the Sherwood house in Stony Brook. Naymeer's home. The location of the second flume.

Naymeer's black Lab ran up to meet his master. The dog was all wags and smiles as Naymeer petted him lovingly.

"I thought people who liked dogs were the good guys," Courtney said caustically.

"Having the strength and vision to make difficult decisions doesn't make me a bad person, Courtney."

"Depends on the decisions you make," Mark countered.

Naymeer shrugged and looked to one of his red-shirt guardians. "Bring them to my study."

Naymeer hurried off toward the front door, his dog running alongside obediently.

Courtney looked at Mark and frowned. "Where's a quig when you need one?"

They were escorted into the house and brought to a warm, wood-paneled room near the front door. Mark and Courtney had been there before. When it was empty. Before things changed. Naymeer sat down behind a large mahogany desk. Wooden bookcases were lined with leather-bound books. A welcoming fire crackled in the fireplace. Naymeer's dog was already curled up in front of it.

"In spite of what you might think, I am not a monster," Naymeer said, taking on the friendly grandfather role once again. "I truly believe in the vision of Ravinia. Every world of Halla is flawed. You cannot deny that. Our vision is to mold Halla into a utopia where there will be no wars. No strife. No prejudice. It is not a bad thing to encourage greatness."

Mark said, "Sure, so long as it's not at the expense of everyone else."

Naymeer stood and rounded his desk toward them. "You of all people should understand, Mark. You are brilliant. You are the father of the dados."

Mark winced as if Naymeer had hit him.

"We are on the verge of something wonderful here," Naymeer continued. "When the United Nations General Assembly convenes, they will vote to make Ravinia the world's spiritual leader. Many, many people agree with our way of thinking. Once we are validated by the UN, there will be no stopping the change. We offer something that everyone so desperately wants. Clarity."

Naymeer held up the ring in front of Mark.

"This is what allowed it to happen," he explained. "This is proof that life is greater than our own singular world. This is what people believe in. They will not be disappointed."

"I'll ask again," Mark said, seething. "Why are you telling us this?"

Naymeer walked to the far corner of his study. "I am a wealthy man," he continued. "Donations to Ravinia are staggering, as you might imagine. It isn't enough. Not if we are to expand throughout the globe."

"What do you want?" Courtney chided. "A donation?"

"Something like that" was Naymeer's strange answer. He

stopped at a closed door that might have been a closet. "I want you to join me. Given time, I believe you will understand that my way of thinking, our way of thinking, is the only way to ensure a peaceful Halla for all eternity. To expedite matters, I suppose you could say I do indeed need a donation."

Mark looked to Courtney. The two burst out laughing.

"Sure!" Mark laughed. "I've got a couple of bucks."

Naymeer smiled. "You have much more than that."

He opened the closet door. Mark gasped. Courtney held on to him for strength. What they saw inside the closet . . . was Mark.

"I had some very good financial advice many years ago," Naymeer continued, enjoying the reaction his revelation caused. "I invested in a company that showed great promise. You may have heard of it. Keaton Electrical Marvels."

"KEM," Mark croaked. "You own part of KEM?"

"Half of it, to be exact," Naymeer corrected. "It was my idea to make the first prototype of a human dado in your image, Mark. I thought it was a fitting tribute since you were the inventor of Forge . . . and your parents owned a quarter of the company."

"What?" Mark shouted.

"Oh, yes. They did quite well after you left them on First Earth. KEM flourished due to your technology. Their stake in the company grew. Actually it was *your* stake, but since you gave them control of the company they did what they saw fit. Your father was a shrewd man. I'm sorry to say that they both passed away tragically in the early 1970s. I believe it was an automobile accident."

Mark staggered to sit in a chair. "My parents are dead?"

"My condolences, though it shouldn't come as a surprise. If they had lived, they'd be over a hundred years old today."

Mark was reeling. "I—I hadn't thought of it that way."

Courtney touched Mark's shoulder to console him.

"Life goes on," Naymeer added casually. He touched the cheek of the Mark dado that stood in the closet. "This is only a prototype. It doesn't function. It will be used as a design guide for the dados of the future."

"It's all coming together," Mark whispered to Courtney.

Naymeer closed the closet door and continued, "It wouldn't be right of me to use funds from Ravinia to help KEM. No, it would be illegal, and that kind of activity will not be tolerated. What I need, Mark, is your piece of KEM."

"My piece?" Mark shouted. "I don't have a piece of KEM."

"But you do," Naymeer countered. "When your parents died, they didn't make provisions to dispose of your shares. They have been lying dormant, gathering value since their death. Most of the technology you see around you today sprang from that initial, small invention you brought to England in 1937. KEM's reach is global. I'd estimate that your piece of the company is worth somewhere in the range of a few billion dollars. Give or take."

It was Courtney's turn to sit down. "Give or take . . . " She couldn't continue. The words caught in her throat.

Naymeer stalked toward the two.

"I need control of those shares, Mark," he said. "Your place in history is secure. Your place in the future can be just as dramatic. If you do not agree with all my teachings, fine. We can debate. I can bend. But do not throw away this chance. Sign your shares over to me, and you will stand beside me at the United Nations. Together we can create a new world. A new Halla. It can be paradise, Mark. You can end war. You can end hunger. All you need do is have the strength to make the difficult choices, as I have."

Mark put his head in his hands. Courtney kept her arm around his shoulders. Naymeer stood over them, waiting.

Mark didn't lift his head to look at the man. "What if I say no?"

"I will take control of the shares anyway."

"How can you do that?" Courtney asked.

Naymeer scoffed and said, "No one will ever know you were here. The mystery of what happened to Mark Dimond will continue and the remaining shares will become mine."

"Not while I'm alive," Mark said.

Naymeer's eyes sparkled. He smiled and said, "Exactly. You too can be marginalized."

The room shook. Naymeer's dog barked. It was like an earthquake was rocking the mansion. The crystal chandelier swayed and clinked. A lamp fell onto the floor. The event lasted only ten seconds before all became still once again.

"What was that?" Courtney asked, stunned.

Naymeer shrugged. "I believe we have visitors."

JOURNAL #36

SECOND EARTH

Reality.

I have no idea what that word means anymore. Everything I believed in since I was a kid has been thrown to the wind. Scattered. Shattered. Lost. The irony is that, with so many truths being revealed, I think I finally have a handle on the conflict I've been in the middle of for so long. Out of confusion comes clarity. Sort of. I don't have all the answers yet. I may never. But I now believe that with what I've learned, I can end it all.

I know, I've said that before, only to discover that Saint Dane had yet another curve to throw at me. That could happen again. Easily. As I make my final play, I would not be surprised if it turns out to be a false end. A shadow. A dream. It's happened before, right? As frustrating as that is, I can't let it dictate my actions.

I know how to end this war. I have to make my move.

It isn't without risks. That speaks to the larger reality that I'm still pretty much in the dark about. Alder told me that the only way to defeat your enemy is to understand what he wants. I now believe I know what Saint Dane wants. Just as important, I know how he plans to get it. That's huge. It gives me hope that we can actually defeat him. I get it. I understand.

I think.

What still remains a mystery is the engine. How can this all be happening? I may understand the rules enough to play this game now, but the grander reality of how it all came to be is still floating out there somewhere. I wish I knew how to reel it in. I have to believe that it all comes down to the truth about who I am. The truth about all the Travelers. A big part of me still feels like the kid who lived for fourteen years in Stony Brook, blissfully unaware of the worlds that swirled around him. I miss that life. I miss my family more with each day. Not that I didn't miss them before, but now that I'm questioning the truth of my own existence, it's as if I've lost not only my family, but my core. If, as Saint Dane said, the Travelers are illusions, does that mean my family was an illusion too? As impossible as that sounds, the fact that they disappeared along with any sign that they ever existed doesn't seem so far fetched. What about the time my dad finally got me to balance on my two-wheeler? Or the time my mother jumped off the dock into Chautauqua Lake to save me from drowning? Or all the times I read books to Shannon? Or picked up Marley's poop? Or Thanksgiving dinners or school plays or trips to Disney World or getting my freakin' boo-boos kissed! Did any of that actually happen?

That's one truth I'd just as soon not know, because I'm afraid of the answer. One of the driving forces behind every action I've taken is the hope that I would one day see my family again. What if there is no family to see? It would mean that all my memories, my emotions, my security, everything that makes me *me*, isn't real. It's not a good feeling. The only way I can deal with it, is to not deal with it. I have to stay focused on the here and now. The challenge at hand.

Saint Dane.

The rest will come when it comes, though I'm not sure I want it to.

As I write this journal, I am preparing to make our final play. Or what I hope will be our final play. I ended my previous journal where Alder, Patrick, and I were at the flume on Denduron, preparing to return to Second Earth. I wanted to end the journal there because I felt I was closing a chapter. Everything that had happened up to that point was prelude. I wanted it to remain separate, so I finished that journal and kept it safe.

This next journal marks my return to Second Earth for what I believe will be the final time. The story has come full circle.

The battle for Earth is the battle for Halla.

It is about to begin.

"His name is Alexander Naymeer," Patrick began. "He lives on top of the flume."

I was all set to jump right into the flume and head home. Patrick convinced me to wait. Why not? Time never seemed to be an issue. The flumes would put us where we needed to be, when we needed to be there. We could afford to take a little time and get up to speed. It wasn't easy. With every word he spoke, with each new revelation, each new twist, it made me want to leap into the flume all the more. I didn't. I was patient. We stayed in that chilly cave and listened to it all.

Patrick told Alder and me about Alexander Naymeer and his Ravinian cult. He explained how Second Earth had changed, and how Naymeer used your ring, Mark, to introduce the reality of Halla to the people of Second Earth. Talk about mixing territories! I wanted to scream.

He told us how Naymeer created a cult that is all about molding a superior society while eliminating those who don't contribute. He explained how the United Nations was about to vote on whether his Ravinian cult should be considered the spiritual leader of the world. Maybe most shocking of all, he told us of the changes that happened on Third Earth. That was the ultimate proof that Naymeer's cult would drive Earth toward disaster.

The only good news he had was that you two were back home together, Mark and Courtney. And Mark, you're okay. I wished that were the only news he had to give me.

"So it's true," I said once Patrick finished.

"What is?" Alder asked.

"It's about Earth. Saint Dane has influenced this Naymeer guy and his followers into putting Earth on a path that will divide everyone into two groups. The haves and the have-nots. It'll be great if you're a 'have.' If not . . . yikes."

Alder asked, "What of the other territories?"

"The same thing," I exclaimed. "Why not? Look at Quillan. There's Blok and then there's everybody else. Right here, the Milago and the Bedoowan have formed a supertribe that's going to march on Denduron. The same could happen on Zadaa. The Rokador are a more advanced tribe than the Batu. Now that they're aboveground, who knows how their influence will spread? And on Eelong—the gar may have won a victory, but the klee are still way ahead of them intellectually. With the right influence, the klee could turn on the gar in a heartbeat. It's a reverse revolution. Instead of the oppressed people rising up to tear down the elite, the elite of each territory are gathering their resources to wipe out the lower classes. Earth will be the model for others to follow."

Patrick added, "And with each territory, Saint Dane is influencing the elite. They will have total power over their world, and Saint Dane will have total power over them. He will rule Halla."

"Can a society exist like that?" Alder asked. "Not everyone can be a leader."

"Of course it can't," I shouted. "You heard what Patrick said about Third Earth. Earth evolved into a world that was in perfect harmony with the people and the environment. Now it's a mess. That's what Saint Dane's influence led to. That's what'll happen on every territory."

I paced the cave nervously. "Saint Dane always said that in order to build Halla up, he would first have to tear it down. I always thought he planned some kind of superbattle with armies and bombs and whatever. It's much more devious than that. He's been inciting social revolution all over Halla. It never mattered that we won a battle or saved a culture, it was all about creating the environment where these revolutions could begin."

Patrick said, "That's exactly it. This Naymeer fellow is a revolutionary in the guise of a prophet."

Alder asked, "He said he was the Traveler from Second Earth?"

"That's what Saint Dane said," Patrick answered.

"So then, what am I?"

Patrick looked to the ground nervously. "You quit."

I wanted to shout in anger. I might have, but I thought it would attract a few nosy quigs. "Now Saint Dane's using

Travelers to influence the people of the territories," I said angrily. "First Nevva, now this Naymeer character."

Patrick added, "I believe the turning point of Second Earth is the vote at the United Nations. Perhaps if that vote goes against Naymeer, his cult will not be handed enough influence to do any more damage."

I looked between Alder and Patrick. My blood was boiling. "Okay, so I'm not the Traveler from Second Earth anymore? Too bad. I'm still the lead Traveler." I walked to the quig carcass, grabbed a dado-killing rod and yanked it out of the ick. It made a sucking sound. Patrick cringed. I was beyond that.

"Here," I said, tossing it to Alder. I grabbed the second rod, that had gone through the quig's eye. No, that I had jammed through the quig's eye. It came out easily, though I think that turned Patrick's stomach again. Like I said, I was beyond that.

"Patrick, go home," I commanded.

"What? No! I want to be where—"

"You should be on your own territory. Third Earth hasn't hit its turning point yet. That's where Alder and I were headed before we found you. Learn what you can about the history of Ravinia and Naymeer. A perspective from the future might help."

"But the computers no longer exist!"

"Then research the old-fashioned way, with books and newspapers."

"I do not believe they exist either."

"Find them," I snapped. "There have to be more people around like that Richard guy. You might come up with the one piece of information we'll need to derail this whole thing."

Patrick frowned.

"What's the matter?" I asked, maybe a little too impatiently.

"It's unnerving on Third Earth" was his answer. "It's like, every time I close my eyes, the entire world changes."

"I know. Chances are it'll happen again. No, it *better* happen again."

"Excuse me?" Patrick exclaimed, horrified.

"It's the whole point. Once we start causing trouble on Second Earth, it *should* change things on Third Earth. For the better."

Patrick wasn't happy.

"I'm sorry, man," I added with sympathy. "It's where you can be the most help."

Patrick nodded. He knew. He didn't like it, but he knew. He looked me right in the eye and said, "Promise me one thing. When it's getting near the end, call for me. I don't want to be watching from the sidelines anymore."

I had to smile. Patrick may have been a neurotic intellectual, but he was a Traveler. The good kind. He wanted to stop Saint Dane as badly as any of us. Alder and I each hugged him good-bye and watched as he stepped into the flume for his journey home.

"Third Earth," he called out, and waited for the flume to take him. Before the light enveloped him, he looked back and said, "Remember. I want to be there at the end."

I nodded. Though the truth was, I had no idea if I'd be able to call for him. I had no idea what to expect at home. I had no idea about anything. But I made him a promise. If I could, I would get him into the game. A moment later he was gone.

"We should get out of these bloody clothes," Alder suggested.

I looked down at my filthy leather and fur clothes that were spattered with quig blood. Actually, it was more like they were drenched in quig blood.

"Nah, I think we should show up like this."

"They will think we are savages."

"Maybe they're right," I said slyly. "Let's go make a house call."

I clutched my blood-encrusted dado weapon, stepped into the flume, and called out *"Second Earth."*

Alder stepped next to me as the flume went hot. "I have never been to your territory," he said. "What can I expect?"

"I wish to heck I knew," I said, and we were off.

The trip through the flume was jarring. The ride itself was the same as always, but the images of Halla floating in space were so dense, it was hard to make out any one vision. The truth was obvious. Halla was in chaos. Faces jumbled on top of animals on top of buildings on top of armies. It was frightening. The destinies of the territories had been mixed, that much was clear. The question was, would we be able to do damage control? As I looked out onto that horrifying show, to say that I had doubts would be a huge understatement. I didn't think we stood any chance at all.

Thankfully, the trip was over quickly. I didn't know how much more of that insanity I could stand. Before we landed, I realized that I didn't know which gate we would show up at. Would it be in the basement of the Sherwood house? Or the temple that had been built around the flume in New York City? Either way, we had to be ready to deal with the security team of the guy called "Alexander Naymeer." The guy who thought he was the Traveler from Second Earth. I wanted to meet that guy.

I *really* wanted to meet that guy.

The instant my feet touched ground, I knew where we were. It was dark. From what Patrick told me of the cathedral that had been built around the flume in New York, it was wide open and full of light. We were at a gate that was anything but wide open. We were in the root cellar of the Sherwood house. Naymeer's home.

Before I had a chance to focus, I felt a jolt of something blow through my body like an electric shock. My body went rigid. My head spun. My hands went limp and I dropped the dado weapon. I was aware of activity swirling around me, but I was too stunned to react. I sensed a jumble of arms and legs and men barking orders. I tried to stand and got hit with another jolt that made me see stars. It was so violent that I was thrown off my feet. I was vaguely aware that I was being dragged along, but I couldn't tell where, that's how out of it I was. Most of what I'm describing now I have to think back and try to piece together. At the time I was too stunned to think. My arms were held tight. I felt myself being carried up stairs. I knew they were stairs because my feet trailed behind and banged into each step as we climbed higher. At the top a door was pushed open, and I was dragged farther along. I tried to look around, but couldn't focus. The place looked familiar, but I was too loopy to put it together. It wasn't until I was thrown down on the floor that I saw something that made sense.

"Bobby!" Courtney yelled, and ran over to me.

It was like a dream. I'm not sure whether it was a good dream or a nightmare. Seeing Courtney was good. She sat down next to me and threw her arms around me. Looking around at the red-shirt guards who were standing over us was bad. They each carried short metal prods. I knew then what had hit me. They were carrying Tasers.

"Are you okay? We haven't heard from you in forever! We never thought you'd leave Ibara. And . . . and . . . " Courtney pulled back in disgust. "And you're covered with blood. Yuck."

I tried to force the room to stop from turning sideways. It wasn't easy. My arms weren't being cooperative either. I tried to lift up, but it was next to impossible. It was the effects of the Taser. I realized that Alder was lying next to me in the same incoherent state. He had a dazed, faraway look in his eyes. So far I didn't think he was a big fan of Second Earth.

"Mark?" I mumbled to Courtney through lips that would barely move.

"I'm here, Bobby."

I heard his voice from across the room. It was a voice I feared I would never hear again. It was lower than I remembered. We had grown up. The last time I saw him, he was diving into the crumbling flume on Eelong. How long ago was that? Years? So much had happened since then. I moved my wobbly head around to see Mark sitting in a chair on the far side of the room. I wondered why he didn't come over to talk to me, but there were more things to worry about than etiquette. If he wanted to sit in that chair, that was okay. I didn't particularly want to be sitting on the floor, but I didn't have a choice.

"You must be Bobby Pendragon," a man said as he walked toward us.

I slowly raised my head to see a slick-looking old guy. He was exactly as Patrick described him. The first thing I noticed was his perfect silver hair. It was like a helmet. Or robot hair. Why the heck did I notice something as dumb as that? He wore a suit like a business guy, but I knew we weren't in an office. We were in the Sherwood house in Stony Brook. Patrick wasn't kidding. This guy had set up housekeeping on top of the flume.

He also claimed to be the Traveler from Second Earth.

I felt some control returning. It's amazing what'll happen when your blood starts to boil.

"Alexander Naymeer," I gurgled.

The guy looked shocked. I swear, it was like I had slapped him.

"And how would you know that?" he asked, as if it were the best-kept secret of all time.

I looked to Courtney. She was staring at me with a mix of curiosity and pride. It took every bit of concentration I had, but I winked at her. It was worth it. Courtney beamed. My strength was coming back. The effects of the Taser were wearing off. I didn't want to let anybody know. I looked to Alder. He gave me a small wink. He was nearing okay too. I wasn't sure if he was "fighting okay," but I wasn't planning on starting anything. Not yet, anyway. I looked at Naymeer and gave him the most confident smile I could manage with my numb lips and said, "I've been doing this a lot longer than you, Al."

I saw blood rush to his face. Naymeer was flustered. I'd only known the guy for a grand total of eight seconds, and I could already tell that he was used to being in charge and didn't like being treated as an equal. The fact that I had just dropped in from another territory and knew who he was, threw him. Thank you, Patrick.

"You have come at a perfect time," Naymeer bellowed, pretending that I hadn't thrown him. "Your friend Mark Dimond and I were discussing the glorious future we are going to share."

"You were?" Courtney said sarcastically.

I knew exactly what the score was from Courtney's reaction. Naymeer wanted something from Mark. Mark didn't want to give it. I knew my friends.

"Yes," Naymeer said as he strode toward a big-old fancy desk. "Certainly you weren't planning on choosing the other option, were you, Mark? Especially not now, when we have both your friends here. Along with this other . . . person. Who exactly are you?"

"My name is Alder," the knight answered. "I am the Traveler from the territory of Denduron."

"Denduron!" Naymeer bellowed. "I understand that events are moving along quite briskly there. How exciting it must be."

Even though I was a few feet away from him, I could feel Alder tense up. Naymeer had no idea how close he was to being clocked.

"Now. Mark," Naymeer continued. "We were discussing the future of KEM."

KEM. The company that made the dados. Things were starting to fold in on themselves again. Of course, I didn't know the details, but I could tell that Naymeer had threatened Mark. It seemed as if Alder and I had dropped in at a critical moment. Yes, the flume had once again put us where we needed to be, when we needed to be there.

Mark stayed seated. When he spoke, it was with a calm, assured voice. "We're leaving, Naymeer. All of us."

Naymeer seemed taken aback, as if Mark had spoken in Swahili.

"Apparently you do not appreciate the gravity of your situation," Naymeer said with a puzzled look. "I am not giving you a choice. If you do not sign over your piece of KEM, I will have you killed. I will kill the girl. Now it appears as if I will also have to end the lives of two more Travelers. Is that the choice you are making?"

I was feeling stronger by the second. A quick scan of the room told me there were two guards with Tasers. Two on two. That wouldn't be fair. At least, not once Alder and I got back up to speed. The ball was definitely in Mark's court. I hoped he knew what to do with it.

He stood up and said, "We're leaving, and you're going to give us one of your cars."

Naymeer sat back in his chair, stunned. He couldn't believe what he was hearing. I wasn't so sure I believed it either. I didn't know much of anything at that point.

Naymeer looked at his two guards as if they might have an answer. They didn't. Guards never did. He finally asked with dismay, "What makes you think I would allow that?"

I wanted to hear this. I think we all did, no matter what side we were on.

Mark didn't hesitate. He didn't stutter. "You are an important person, Naymeer. Heads of governments look to you. Heads of religions look to you. You are about to go before the United Nations General Assembly to try to convince the entire planet that they should follow you."

"And?" Naymeer said, intrigued.

"How would it look if someone in authority were to walk in here right now and find us? Two young people you kidnapped and a couple of bloodied knights from another territory? How do you think that would go over at the UN?"

A quick look of doubt crossed Naymeer's face as he surveyed the room and the odd group of people assembled.

"Why on Earth do you think I would let anyone come in here?" Naymeer asked.

Mark smiled. He really smiled. I'd never seen him so confident. My buddy Mark Dimond had changed.

"You're a smart guy, Naymeer. Just not smart enough to keep an eye on us while your guardians wrestled with my friends here."

"What are you saying?" Naymeer asked with growing impatience.

Mark stepped aside to reveal a table next to the chair where he was sitting. I realized why he hadn't gotten up when Alder and I were thrown into the room. Sitting on the table . . . was a telephone.

Naymeer saw the phone and let out a small gasp.

"You didn't have the chance to call anyone," he said with confidence, though the hitch in his voice proved that he wasn't entirely sure.

"Three words," Mark said. "Numbers actually. Nine-one-one. I'm guessing in about five minutes the Stony Brook police are going to be knocking on your door, wondering why you called."

"Oh *yeah*!" Courtney shouted, then looked to Naymeer. "In your *face*!"

"Take them to the basement!" Naymeer commanded to his guards.

One guard made a move toward me, raising his Taser. Bad move. He thought I was still stunned. I wasn't. I deflected his move and jammed the heel of my palm into his chest. I actually felt the air leaving his lungs as he collapsed. A quick look over my shoulder showed me that Alder had the other guard under his foot. Two guards down. Two Travelers up. It was good to be back home.

"Whoa," said Courtney. "That was . . . interesting."

"Get us the car," Mark said calmly.

I thought Naymeer's head was going to explode from all the blood that had rushed to it. His eyes flashed with anger. He started to say something, but Mark cut him off.

"We'll probably hear the sirens any second."

Naymeer grabbed his own phone and barked, "Bring a car round front. Open the gates. Now."

The guy was barely holding it together. Like I said before, he was somebody who was used to being in control. And just then, he wasn't.

"Take the weapon," I said to Alder.

We each grabbed the Tasers from the red shirts. I really wanted to zap the guy who had zapped me. Instead, I stepped over him and walked up to Naymeer. I looked the guy up and down. "You have to know," I said cockily, "this isn't over."

Naymeer took a breath. He was already getting himself back under control. The guy was good. I could see why so many followed him.

"Perhaps not," he admitted. "But soon."

Something was off. Maybe it was the confident way he spoke, or the evil he represented. I couldn't put my finger on it, but a red flag was raised. I turned to Courtney with a questioning look. She knew exactly what I was thinking.

"No," she answered. "He's not Saint Dane."

I looked back to Naymeer. He was smiling. "I'm flattered."

"Don't be," I shot back.

"We'd better go," Mark cautioned. "It wouldn't be good for us to be found here."

I turned and strode for the door. Alder, Courtney, and Mark followed. Before leaving, I turned back to Naymeer and said, "By the way, Al, I unquit."

"It's too late for that," Naymeer sneered.

"Keep telling yourself that" was my answer.

I strode out the door, followed by the others. In the foyer of the mansion, Naymeer's red shirts surrounded us. One made a move, but Alder held the Taser out and the guy backed off.

"Let them go," Naymeer commanded. He was standing in the doorway to his office.

The guards backed off and we went out the door. I didn't even stop to think about how odd it was that the deserted, empty Sherwood house was no longer deserted. There would be time to catch up later. We had to be gone. The large, wrought-iron gates in front of the mansion swung open to reveal a dark car waiting in front, its engine running.

"Pendragon!" Naymeer called.

I looked back.

"Welcome home."

I really didn't like him. Just as well. It would make taking him that much easier.

"I'll drive," Courtney announced and got in the driver's seat.

I opened the rear passenger door and motioned for Alder to get inside. He had never been in a car before. He had no idea what was going on. I climbed in back with him; Mark jumped in the shotgun seat. Courtney sat with her hands on the wheel.

"The police will be here any second," I said.

"They would be," Mark answered, "if I had actually made the call."

He looked at me and smiled. "We've got a lot to catch up on."

It had been a bluff. This definitely wasn't the same old Mark. I liked this guy even more.

Mark asked Courtney, "When did you learn how to drive?"

"Long time ago," she answered casually, putting the car in gear.

"How long?"

"About three seconds."

She hit the gas and the car lurched forward. With a squeal of tires on asphalt, we were off. Before we cleared the opening of the stone wall in front of the place, I took a quick look back to see two of Naymeer's guards running toward a pair of motorcycles.

I hoped that Courtney had learned a lot about driving in those three seconds.

JOURNAL #36

(CONTINUED)

SECOND EARTH

Look out!" Mark yelled.

"You think?" Courtney said calmly as she spun the wheel, barely missing a dog that had foolishly gone for a stroll around the time that a crazy girl with three seconds of driving experience was gunning the gas behind the wheel of a huge car while making a desperate escape. The dog yelped and jumped off the road. Safe but scared.

Alder pushed himself back into his seat. He had never been in a car before, let alone one driven by someone whose only experience was in driver's ed class. At least, I hoped Courtney had taken driver's ed. The way we were lurching from side to side, I wasn't so sure. Poor Alder. He was thrown into a terrifying situation in an alien world. Poor all of us.

"That would be a stop sign," Mark said, trying to be calm as we flew past one without stopping.

"I saw it," Courtney snapped.

None of us asked the obvious question as to why she didn't actually do what the sign said.

"I can drive," Mark said calmly.

Screeech! Courtney slammed on the brakes, making Alder and me hit our heads on the backs of the front seats.

"Whoa!" I shouted. "Easy. We've got enough problems."

"Fine," Courtney huffed. "You drive."

She got out, turned to run around the car, and stopped. "Uh-oh."

"What?" Mark asked as he climbed over to the driver's side.

"They're coming."

Courtney sprinted around and jumped inside. I looked back to see the two motorcycles with the red shirts on board, pulling out of the Sherwood house.

"You up for this, Mark?" I asked.

"Let's find out" was his answer.

I was happy he didn't stutter. Confidence was good at this point. Before Courtney had time to slam the door, Mark jammed his foot down on the gas pedal, and we were off.

"You don't know how to drive any better than I do!" Courtney complained.

As if to answer, Mark spun the wheel hard, made a ninety-degree turn, and gunned the engine. It almost seemed as if he knew what he was doing. Almost.

Mark explained, "I was all set to get my license, but some things came up."

That was a pretty big understatement.

"We've got to find a place to hide," I said.

Courtney corrected, "We've got to shake those guys first."

Good point.

Mark said, "We've got an advantage."

"What's that?" Courtney asked.

Mark made another quick turn, throwing Alder into me.

"I've been riding my bike around here for years. I know every street. They don't. We might not be able to outrace them, but we can make it tough to follow us."

The car was some big-old American sedan. It didn't exactly handle like a hot street racer, which was probably just as well. If we crashed in this land yacht we were in, none of us would even be scratched. That was negative thinking. We weren't going to crash. I hoped.

Mark took a quick left on two wheels. We probably weren't actually up on two wheels, but it sure felt like it. Alder looked white but didn't make a sound. I think maybe he went into some Zen-like state to avoid an all-out terror puke.

"There!" Mark shouted, pointing.

"Where?" Courtney asked.

"There's a dirt road that leads through the old cemetery on King Street."

I looked ahead to see two old, crumbling stone pillars on either side of a dirt road to our left.

Courtney shot him a look. "You're not thinking about—"

Mark didn't give her time to answer. He spun the wheel and accelerated into the turn. The car skidded, then sped between the two pillars with inches to spare on either side. We were on a rutted dirt road that probably hadn't been driven on in months, if not years. It was overgrown with bushes that slapped at the car as we sped by.

"So much for the paint job," Courtney commented.

The road continued on through an old cemetery that Mark and I used to ride our bikes to all the time. It was the kind of place that had more graves from the 1800s than from the present. Mark knew exactly where to go. He maneuvered the big car past an ancient, stone mausoleum and quickly braked. We all looked at one another, wide eyed.

"Okay, maybe you *can* drive," Courtney gasped in awe.

Mark turned around and said, "If they didn't see us come in here, we're good. If they did, it's the perfect place for you two to take them out with no witnesses."

I had to smile. Mark was still a thinker. "I missed you, man."

Mark gave me a big, proud smile. For a moment I saw the kid I had known for so long. It was great to be back with my friends.

We all jumped out and took up positions behind tombstones close to the road. If the motorcycles showed up and went for the car, we'd wait for them to pass and then attack from behind. We waited a solid five minutes—plenty of time to be sure that Mark had pulled off the impossible.

He had. We were free. The four of us stood up, surrounded by ancient graves. I looked at Alder in his bloody leathers and laughed.

Courtney did too. "I hope nobody sees you guys looking like that in a creepy cemetery. They'll think the place is haunted by Viking ghosts."

Mark and I laughed. Alder didn't get it.

"Mark, Courtney, this is Alder. The Traveler from Denduron."

Mark gave Alder a firm handshake. Alder wasn't quite sure of what that meant, but he went along. "We've read all about you, Alder. I'm glad you're here."

Courtney actually gave Alder a hug. Alder wasn't sure what to do about that. He didn't seem to mind though.

"What was that for?" he asked.

Courtney answered, "For bringing Bobby home."

"We have to find a safe place to regroup," I said. "What about your house, Courtney?"

"No way. They already found us there once. And Mark's house was torched."

"What!" I shouted.

"We have so much to tell you, Bobby," Mark said. "It could take months."

"We don't have months," Courtney added. "It's all happening here, Bobby. On Second Earth."

"I know," I said. "We saw Patrick."

Mark and Courtney stared at me with wide, expectant eyes.

"He's okay," I assured them. "We sent him back to Third Earth."

"But he was shot," Courtney yelped.

"We got him help. He's fine now, I promise you" was all I said. It wasn't time to get into the whole "Travelers are illusions that can heal one another and I have no idea why" conversation.

"Man, that's good news," Mark said. "We needed some."

"I know where we can go," Courtney blurted out. "My parents' boat is in a slip on the Signet River. They always put it in by the first of March. By the way, happy birthday, Bobby. You're eighteen."

It took me a second to get my head around that. "That feels . . . odd," I said.

"What kind of boat?" Mark asked.

"Big sailboat. Sleeps six. They always have it geared up for overnight trips, so there'll be dry clothes on board. We can't have these guys running around like cavemen, and I am seriously tired of wearing your mother's goofy clothes. No offense."

I knew the Signet River. It flowed from upstate all the way into the Long Island Sound. Before it hit open water, the river turned from fresh water to salt and widened enough to hold a big marina with tons of docks and slips for small boats. Courtney's idea was great, though I was pretty nervous about getting there. My biggest worry was that a cop would pull us over for something random. We'd have a heck of a time explaining who we were, why Mark didn't have a license, and why we were covered with blood.

I'm happy to say that I was worried for nothing. We made it to the marina with no problem. Mark drove the car as if he'd been driving for years.

A lot of people in Stony Brook loved sailing. Though it was only March, the floating docks were all in the water, and most of the slips were already filled. Once the chance of a freeze was over, people were quick to get their boats into the water to take advantage of the short sailing season. The marina was so vast, I was sure we could easily lose ourselves in the labyrinth of docks and boats and not be seen from the shore. Better still, the sun had gone down and being March, it was cold. People may have loved sailing, but hanging out on a boat when it was nasty-raw cold wasn't fun. We didn't see a single person there. Which was perfect for what I had planned.

"Wait here," I instructed everyone, and got behind the wheel of the car.

"Where are you going?" Courtney asked.

"Just taking a short trip," I answered.

"Uh . . . what?"

I gave her a wink of assurance. While the others watched, I put the car in gear, hit the gas, and drove down the cement ramp that led down into the water. It was the ramp people used to launch their boats. They would back their trailers onto the ramp until the boat was floating in the water, then push the boat off and drive the trailer out. I had planned something similar, though there would be no driving out. It was the first time I'd driven a car since I got behind the wheel of Max Rose's big old black sedan on the way to my date with the *Hindenburg* on First Earth. I didn't know any more about driving than Courtney did. No, I knew less. Luckily, figuring out how to get this car moving was a lot easier than it was with Max Rose's car. And I didn't have far to go. I drove slowly down the steep, concrete grade and straight into the water until the car wouldn't go anymore. I made sure all the windows were open so it would fill quickly. I climbed out of the driver's window and into the cold water of Long Island Sound. The car was actually floating. I pushed it out even farther until water started flooding into the windows, and it got too heavy to maneuver. It was over in less than thirty seconds. The car was underwater. Invisible.

I sloshed back up onshore to meet the others, who stood watching.

"The next person who launches a boat is going to get a big surprise," I said.

"Was that necessary?" Courtney asked. "I mean, now we don't have any way of getting around."

"It was," Mark declared. "That car would have marked us."

Alder added, "I am not sorry to see it go."

I didn't blame him.

The three of us followed Courtney onto the dock.

"Things have changed," Mark said as we walked along the maze of floating docks. "Let's hope your parents still have a boat on this new Second Earth."

"Most everything is the same," Courtney said. "It would be really bad luck if this wasn't."

Courtney knew exactly where to go. We walked past many types of boats of all sizes. Speedboats, cabin cruisers, and sailboats. Toward the end of one dock we came upon a medium-size sailboat with a red flag flying from the mast. Seeing that flag was probably the most jarring thing I had experienced in a long time. And that's saying something. On the flag was the star symbol that marked the gates to the flumes.

Courtney saw that I was staring at the flag. "Long story," she said. "Let's get changed first."

The Chetwyndes had already outfitted their boat for the season. We found plenty of clean, dry clothes, though they weren't exactly the kinds of things I was used to wearing. The Chetwyndes were suburban sailors. They mostly had khaki pants and worn deck sneakers. They also had some T-shirts and a few thin sweaters. I chose a white T-shirt and a dark brown sweater. Alder took a deep green sweatshirt; Courtney, a dark blue hoodie. Before getting changed, we needed to wash. The Chetwyndes had a bottle of biodegradable soap that was okay to dump in open water.

"It's cold," I said to Alder.

"No colder than the rivers on Denduron" was his answer. Oh. Right. They didn't have hot water on that territory.

While Courtney stayed below to change, Alder and I peeled off our crusty leathers and sank them underwater. We slipped quietly into the river and washed as best we could. It wasn't ideal to be bathing in salt water, but it was better than nothing. We needed to get rid of not only the grime, but the dried blood. As cold as it was, it actually felt good. Call it symbolic, but I felt I was reacquainting myself with the sensations of home. Of course I didn't usually go swimming in March, but it was still a great feeling. In some small way it made me feel centered. I was in familiar surroundings. I was home.

It was time to learn about how unfamiliar my surroundings had actually become.

Courtney found some canned tuna fish, and crackers that were kept in a plastic container to keep them fresh. It wasn't exactly a feast, but it was better than nothing. I was starved. After we got dressed, the four of us sat down to eat.

"Look at us," Courtney said, chuckling. "We look like a bunch of preppies in our khakis and sweaters."

"What are preppies?" Alder asked.

How did you explain that to a knight? I took a shot. "Preppies are wealthy, conservative people who all dress alike."

"Like the Bedoowan?" Alder asked.

That made me laugh, but he wasn't far off. "Yeah. Preppies are like the Bedoowan. In Top-Siders."

Mark and Courtney laughed at that one. Seeing Alder in clothes that were two sizes too small didn't help. He looked like a monster preppy kid who had outgrown all his clothes. His pants were above his ankles, and his sleeves didn't come close to reaching his wrists. Seeing that made us laugh even harder. Alder didn't exactly get it, but he laughed too. It felt great. These were my best friends in the world. No, in Halla. Mark and Courtney had been with me since the beginning of this adventure, either in spirit or in person. It was as much their adventure as it was mine. It now looked as if we would be together at the end. That felt right, like it was the way things were meant to be. Though it feels odd writing this journal now, since Mark and Courtney are part of it. But I have to continue. Who knows where it will eventually end up and who will be reading it?

"I knew you didn't quit," Mark said.

The laughter stopped. That kind of killed the fun part of the reunion. The mood turned dark.

"But I did," I admitted. "I wanted this to be over. I thought it was."

"We don't blame you, Bobby," Courtney said. "We just weren't sure about what happened or why we couldn't reach you."

"I lost my Traveler ring," I said. "But it's back."

"I wish I could say the same," Mark said glumly. He held up his hand to show that his ring was gone. "Everything that's happening here is my fault."

"That's not true," Courtney corrected quickly.

We spent the next few hours catching up. There was a lot to hear. Courtney and Mark gave Alder and me the story of what had happened since I left Courtney on First Earth to search for Mark. We learned all about KEM and how Mark was tricked into delivering his Forge invention to the company that would create the first dados. We learned how Nevva had actually saved Mark's parents and then threatened to execute them if he didn't give up his ring—the ring that was made from the same material as the flumes. The dark matter. The foundation of Halla. I didn't know what to think about that one.

They told us of Naymeer's history and the Ravinian cult and the Horizon compound and, most important, the upcoming vote at the United Nations. Between their story and what we learned from Patrick, I was pretty confident that we were up to speed on all that had been happening on Earth.

It was the only thing I was confident about.

"Patrick went back to Third Earth," I said. "He's going

to look for any information about how Naymeer and the Ravinian cult influenced events. From everything I've heard, the turning point on Second Earth is the vote at the United Nations."

"That's what we thought too," Mark added.

Courtney shook her head in dismay. "How can so many people be influenced by such a nutjob? A slick nutjob, but still."

"People believe what they want to believe," I said. "I've seen it all over Halla. Guys like Naymeer tell people what they want to hear. Everybody thinks their lives can be better, and guys like Naymeer say they can make it happen."

"The grass is always greener," Mark said.

"Exactly. It's powerful stuff. Naymeer has taken it a step further. He's giving them proof that there's something greater out there. Something bigger than their own ordinary existence. Imagine the leader of a religion telling people he can get them to heaven, and then actually showing them heaven! That's what Naymeer is doing. All they have to do is follow him, no matter how wrong his ideas are."

"But Halla isn't heaven," Courtney corrected.

"No, but it proves there's life beyond our own," I pointed out. "That's pretty dramatic stuff. From there, Naymeer can spin it any way he wants. I'm not surprised he has so many followers. Saint Dane must be loving this."

"Do you know where the demon is?" Alder asked.

"No," Mark said quickly. "He took the form of one of Naymeer's people, so he's definitely in the inner circle of Ravinia. Beyond that, he hasn't shown himself."

"What's the big deal?" Courtney chimed in. "All we have to do is get to the United Nations and convince them to vote no on Ravinia."

The three of us looked at Courtney with blank expressions.

"I'm being facetious, dorks," she said, rolling her eyes. "Sheesh. Don't you think I know that's impossible!"

"So what *can* we do?" Mark asked.

Nobody had an answer. It seemed hopeless. It was a strange feeling. With every territory I'd chased Saint Dane to, I always found a way to get involved in the conflict. On my home territory, I was stumped.

"Naymeer is the key," Courtney offered. "He's Ravinia. Without him, it all means nothing. If we can somehow stop him, we'll stop Ravinia."

Courtney's words put a thought into my head. It was a fleeting idea. One that I could hardly believe even occurred to me. It might have been a solution, but it wasn't something I was willing to think about seriously. At least not yet. Things would have to get desperate before I went there. I hoped we hadn't already reached that point. Still, I had to put it out there as a possibility.

"There is one way," I said. "It's a last resort but—"

"Courtney?" came a voice from outside. A woman's voice.

We all froze. I motioned toward the battery-powered lantern we had been using to light the cabin. Mark killed it.

"Courtney honey, are you in there?" the voice called.

Courtney's eyes went wide. She whispered, "It's my mom."

Another voice was heard. A man's voice. "It's all right, sweetheart. Come on out."

I looked at Courtney. She nodded. "My dad," she whispered.

Nobody knew what to do. How idiotic was that? Here we were discussing the future of all existence, yet we were terrified about getting busted by Courtney's parents, as if we'd been caught skipping school or something. I guess old habits die hard. Courtney made the first move. She motioned for us to stay still and went for the hatch. I was able to peer through the curtains that covered the porthole, to watch as Courtney climbed onto the deck of the boat.

On the dock her mother and father stood waiting for her.

"Hi, guys," she said, sounding like a meek little girl. "Going for a sail?"

"Honey!" her mom shouted with genuine relief. She ran for the boat and hugged her daughter tight. "You're all right," she cried, in tears. "We thought . . . we thought . . . "

"It's okay, Mom, I'm okay. I'm sorry I had you so worried."

Courtney's dad joined in the group hug.

"It's over," he said, also in tears. "You're back with us now. Everything's going to be all right."

"Yeah, it is," Courtney said. "Let's go home."

She tried to maneuver her parents back along the dock, away from the boat. Away from us. Her parents didn't move.

Her mom said, "I'm sorry, sweetheart. We did what we thought was best."

"What do you mean?" Courtney asked suspiciously.

Mr. Chetwynde looked to the boat and called out, "Mark? Come on out, son."

Mark stiffened. He shot me a look, as if to say, "Now what?"

"You too . . . Bobby."

My head swam. This couldn't be happening. I had disappeared from town years before. Nobody on Second Earth had seen or heard from Bobby Pendragon in all that time. How could they know I was there?

I whispered, "It must be Saint Dane."

"Maybe Nevva, too," Mark added.

Alder didn't know how to react. "We should find out," he declared.

"No. Stay here. I'll figure this out." Then to Mark, "We better go."

Mark nodded. The two of us crawled up and out of the hatch.

Courtney stood on the dock being hugged by both her parents. When they saw Mark, Mrs. Chetwynde began to sob.

"You're all right." She wept and turned to her husband. "He's all right."

When I appeared on deck, I thought they were going to faint. Can't say I blamed them. Bobby Pendragon had returned from the dead. Or at least the missing. Mrs. Chetwynde leaned against her husband for support. They truly looked stunned. If this was Saint Dane and Nevva Winter, they were putting on a great show. But for who?

Courtney pulled away from her parents and wiped a tear from her own eye. "Mom, Dad, you should go home and leave us alone."

"I wish we could, sweetheart," Mr. Chetwynde said. "This is too important."

"What is?" Courtney demanded.

Mr. Chetwynde looked nervous. He ran his hand through his hair. When he did that, we all saw the same thing: On his arm was a green tattoo. A star. The mark of the Ravinians. The Chetwyndes were definitely followers of Naymeer.

"We can help you, Courtney," Mrs. Chetwynde sobbed. "You're confused. We can make this all better. For all of us."

Courtney backed away from them, toward Mark and me. "Mom, what did you do?"

Mr. Chetwynde answered, "What we had to."

Floodlights flashed to life onshore, lighting up the dock as if it were day. Our backs were to the water. We had nowhere to go. Below the white lights, several flashing red lights appeared. Police lights. The Chetwyndes had called the cops.

Behind the Chetwyndes a lone silhouette of a man came walking along the dock. He wasn't in any hurry. He knew we weren't going anywhere.

"Almost four years," the man said. "I've been on this case for almost four years. Thought for sure it would never be solved . . . until right now."

The man stepped out of the shadows and stood next to the Chetwyndes. He wore a plain suit that looked as if he had slept in it. There was nothing familiar about the guy. To me, that is. Mark and Courtney knew him very well.

"Captain Hirsch?" Mark called out.

"Hi, guys," the man said. "Looks like we're finally going to find out what happened to Bobby Pendragon and his family. Believe me, the town, the state, and I'd pretty much guess the whole country wants to know. I, for one, cannot wait to hear."

JOURNAL #36

(CONTINUED)

SECOND EARTH

Hi, Bobby," the policeman said warmly. "I'm Jim Hirsch. Lot of people have been worried about you. And your family. We've got a lot to talk about."

I was in a brain freeze. This couldn't be happening. Of all the odd twists that had been thrown at me, this was the most surreal. I looked to Courtney for help.

"Captain Hirsch is the guy who's been investigating your disappearance from the beginning," she explained. She looked at the cop and boldly asked, "It is you, isn't it?"

Hirsch gave her a confused look. "Who else would I be? Except it's Chief Hirsch now."

Courtney gave me a concerned look. She thought the same thing I did. Saint Dane. There was no way to know for sure. At least the guy seemed genuinely confused by the question.

Mr. Chetwynde explained, "We got a call from the Ravinians. They said you had broken into their compound along with Mark and Bobby and another young man. They didn't want the police involved, but we said there was no choice in the matter. That's when we called Chief Hirsch."

Courtney said, "And you figured we might come here."

The Chetwyndes nodded.

"So where is Naymeer and his red-shirt clowns?" Courtney asked.

"They are good people, Courtney," Mrs. Chetwynde said quickly. "They don't want to cause any trouble. They left it up to us to decide what to do."

"Yeah, I'll bet," Courtney said sarcastically. "They're swell."

"Don't be disrespectful," Mr. Chetwynde admonished.

"Courtney, where have you been?" Mrs. Chetwynde asked with concern. "Why did you break into the home of such an important man? Did you steal a car from them?"

Mr. Chetwynde added, "And where's the other fella who was with you?"

Hirsch said, "I think it's best we all get out of the cold and go somewhere to talk about it."

Mark interjected, "You mean somewhere like the police station?"

Hirsch answered with a shrug.

Time slowed down for me. It was a standoff. We were on the end of the dock, at least thirty yards from shore. I had to assume there were more policemen waiting onshore near the floodlights. Fighting our way off the dock wasn't an option. Not when policemen had guns. As of that moment, I didn't think we were considered dangerous. Fighting through the police would change that. But we had to make a move. Who knew what the police would do with us? Did they think I had done something evil to my family? Would they actually arrest us? The only thing we were caught dead to rights on was car theft. Maybe breaking and entering. Even if no trouble came from that, we'd be tied up with the police for a long time. The glare of public scrutiny would shine brightly. On me. And what about Alder? How would we explain him? If we went with the police, any chance of derailing Naymeer and his cult would be gone. Second Earth would be lost. Halla would be lost. It couldn't end this way. There was only one thing to do.

"Alder?" I called. "Come on out."

Alder had been waiting below the hatch. As soon as I called him, his head popped out. Mr. and Mrs. Chetwynde took a surprised step back and watched him move, as if he were an alien from another planet . . . which is exactly what he was. Alder was a big guy. A warrior. With clothes that were too small, he looked even bigger and more formidable. Hirsch tensed up. I don't think he expected to see a guy looking like a defensive lineman rise out of that boat. He shot a quick glance back toward shore, as if he wanted to call for backup. He didn't though. The situation was too fragile. Alder stepped off the boat and onto the dock, beside me.

"Listen," I said to him. I didn't care that everybody else could hear. It would make absolutely no difference if they knew what I was thinking or not. It was more important that my friends and I were all on the same page. "The police want to take us into custody to talk about the disappearance of my family. They're the good guys. They don't want to hurt us. But if we go with them, they'll take us out of play."

"Understood," Alder said calmly.

I turned to Mark and Courtney. "Guys, I'm sorry but you're going to have to handle this situation on your own."

"Got it," Mark said with confidence.

"Not a problem," Courtney added.

Hirsch took a step forward. His eyes darted between us nervously. "Let's . . . let's all be cool and head for shore, all right?"

I put my hand up. It stopped him.

"Jim, I know you might not believe this, but we are not criminals."

"I'm not saying you are—"

"I know. I get it. You don't know what's going on, and you're going to want to talk all about it and solve all the mysteries. I'm sorry, but we don't have time for that."

Hirsch shook his head quickly, as if not believing what he was hearing. "Wha—you don't have time? I'm sorry, son, but four people have been missing for a long time and—"

We didn't give him time to finish the sentence. Alder and I dove off the dock into the cold waters of the river. I could only imagine the stunned looks on everyone's faces. I hoped that would translate into a few frozen moments of inactivity before Hirsch triggered his cops into action. Alder and I both swam for the next dock over. When we hit it, we hung there to take a few seconds to form our plan.

"We'll split up," I gasped. "Swim underwater as much as you can. Hide under the docks. Take your time. Don't splash. Make your way as far away from the lights as you can before hitting shore." I pointed upriver and added, "On the far bank of the river, beyond the highway, is a rope swing. It's not far beyond the road, on a steep hill. I'll meet you there."

Alder didn't waste time with a response. He took a gulp of air and dove underwater with nothing more than a wink of reassurance. The guy was a pro. I had no doubt he'd make it. I wasn't so certain about my own chances.

"Bobby!" Hirsch called out. "Don't do this! You're not in any trouble."

"Yeah," I thought to myself. "Not yet."

I dove below the surface and dropped under the dock. It was dark. And cold. It was going to be harder than I thought. Visibility was next to zero. I'd been around docks like this all my life. They were each roughly six feet wide, with boats tied to cleats on either side. I knew there was airspace below. I surfaced to find myself looking up at the rows of wooden planks that ran the width of the structure. My hope was to zigzag from dock to dock, swimming underwater and resting underneath, slowly making my way toward shore. The docks were built like fingers, stretching out in all directions like a floating maze. I fought the urge to stay under the dock where I was and make my way toward shore beneath it—I was afraid that would be the first place they'd look. I needed to get to another dock to make the chase impossible. Alder had gone downriver, so I chose to go upriver. I took a few deep breaths, filled my lungs, and pushed myself down, headed for the next dock over. It was hard to see how far it was. I didn't want to surface short. I'd be seen for sure. I kept one eye looking above, trying to see the shadow of the float. The floodlights helped. They cast the wooden docks into sharp relief. I made it to the next dock and surfaced beneath it with no problem.

"Spread out!" I heard Hirsch yell to his men. "Two on each dock."

He knew exactly what we were doing. It didn't take Sherlock Holmes to figure it out. But knowing what we were doing and actually finding us were two different things. As I wrote before, there were a lot of docks and many, many boats. I gulped air and dove below again. It was risky, because I had to maneuver between the keels of a few big sailboats. There were many places to hide, and just as many places to bash my head. I had to be fast, silent, and cautious. The shadow of a shallow-draft cabin cruiser loomed ahead of me. I swam beneath it and surfaced below the dock. . . .

To hear footsteps directly above. The sound echoed through the airspace over my head. Did they know I was there? I looked toward shore to see the beams from flashlights shining down through the spaces between boards.

"Slow, slow!" a voice said. "Don't miss him."

"I can't see anything," another shouted back.

Yelling was good. So long as they were yelling at one another and clomping around on the wooden boards, they wouldn't hear anything below, and I'd know where they were. I waited until they were nearly on top of me, then took a breath and dove straight down. I figured depth was good. No light could penetrate more than a few feet into that murky water. I forced myself to hover below without moving. Light would catch movement. I waited until my lungs felt as if they would burst, then drifted slowly back up. When my face broke the surface, I fought to keep myself from taking a huge gulp of air, for fear they would hear. Keeping my teeth from chattering was almost as hard. I was freezing. I sensed a flash of light behind me, and turned to see they had passed over me and were now farther out on the dock. I didn't want to risk having them walk over me again, so I gulped air, dove down, and pushed off, to head for the next dock over.

It was getting harder to see, because I was getting beyond the throw of the floodlights. There was less chance of them spotting me out there, but there was also more chance of me finding the hull of a boat with my head. I lost all sense of direction. I didn't know which way was up or down, let alone where the next dock was. The only thing I could do was surface. I stopped swimming, and let the air in my lungs float me to the surface. When my head broke out of the water, I found myself between the hulls of two big sailboats, a few yards short of the dock.

"There he is!" came a shout.

The voice seemed far away. I wasn't sure if I should dive under the dock and swim for it, or climb out of the water and fight for it. I figured that if they had spread out over all the docks, odds were good that I'd only have to deal with one or two cops. My chattering teeth told me to go for the fight. At least that would keep me warm.

Before I officially made the choice, I heard the unmistakable sounds of a fight. It wasn't me they saw. It was Alder. I pushed off of one boat and swam out into the open to see that Alder was onshore about fifty yards from me. He wasn't alone. The police were closing on him. I could see that cops were spread out all over the docks to search for us, which meant only a few were left onshore, which meant they didn't stand a chance against Alder. It would take more than two policemen to take him down, unless they started shooting, which I didn't think would happen.

Alder made short work of both the cops who got to him. They had no idea what they were up against, but found out fast. The fight was short and violent. Within seconds both cops were on the ground, either unconscious or wishing they were. Alder didn't wait for the others. He disappeared into the shadows. I would have shouted "Yeah!" in victory, if I hadn't been still floating in the middle of the marina. I had to find my own way out of there.

I dove underwater and kicked the rest of the way toward the dock. I surfaced below its planks and waited. It didn't sound as if any cops were overhead, so I cautiously swam beneath the dock, toward shore. I heard the sounds of far-off yelling. Orders were being thrown out. The police were getting desperate. I was sure that some had taken off after Alder, which meant there were fewer looking for me. My hopes rose. I had a chance.

After a few minutes of winding my way beneath the wooden floats, my feet touched bottom. I was almost onshore. It was time to come out of the safety of the shadows. I dove down, pushed off the bottom, and surfaced to find that I was faced with a rock wall. The dock I was under was built parallel to a sheer wall that rose up out of the water and ran along the shore for about thirty yards on either side of me. I knew where I was. It was a retaining wall, on top of which was built the dockmaster's hut. The tide was low, so the dock level was several feet below the top. If I wanted to get out this way, I had to climb up the slick wall of rocks. It was a stroke of luck, and a total pain. Climbing those wet, barnacle-covered rocks wasn't easy. Still, it shielded me from shore and hunting eyes. It was all I could do to keep from slipping off and falling back into the water. I wouldn't have gotten hurt, but the splash would have given me away for sure.

The climb was torture. Between the slick seaweed that clung to the rocks and the slime from the salty water, it was like climbing up a vertical Slip 'N Slide. A couple of times I slipped back down into the water and held my breath, waiting to hear if anybody noticed the splash. It was totally frustrating. The cold made it even worse. I was having trouble convincing my hands to grip. I actually started to think that maybe turning myself into the Stony Brook police wouldn't be such a bad idea. They were the good guys, right? Maybe I could somehow convince them of what Naymeer was up to. The idea of us stopping him on our own seemed impossible. Maybe I could appeal to the police. Maybe I could tell them everything. As I stood in that freezing water, feeling very alone, the idea of looking for help started to appeal to me.

I tried one last time to make the climb and struggled to the top. It wasn't graceful, but I had made it. When I finally gripped the top and peered over, I saw something that knocked any thoughts of turning to the police out of my head.

The cop named Hirsch stood maybe thirty yards from me, under a streetlight in the parking lot of the marina. This was the guy who had been searching for me on Second Earth since the day I had disappeared. He was the local police chief. He was one of the good guys. Yet he stood next to a long, black limousine, talking to somebody who sat in the back. Police didn't drive limousines. Attached to the hood of the car, above each headlight, was a small red flag with the star symbol. I didn't want my paranoia to spin too far out of control, but if whoever was in that limousine was part of Naymeer's cult, why was Hirsch talking to them? Could it mean that Hirsch was part of it? Worse, could the entire police force be part of it? I wanted to scream. It was looking like even the good guys weren't the good guys anymore.

I waited until Hirsch's back was turned and quickly threw my legs up over the side and ran stiffly for the dockmaster's hut. My legs were so cold I could barely bend them. I crouched behind the small building and scanned the area for an escape route. Several policemen were still out on the docks, searching. A few others were helping their fallen friends who'd introduced themselves to Alder. I had to assume that others had taken off into the woods that surrounded the marina, searching for him. That wouldn't be a smart way for me to go. I didn't want to end up running into the policemen who were running after Alder. My best choice was to keep to the bank of the river, using as cover the sea of boats that were still in dry dock.

I crouched and ran. In seconds I was among hundreds of boats. I knew it would be like trying to find me in a hedge maze. They would need incredible luck. Each time I rounded a boat, my confidence grew. I was going to get away. The next challenge would be to reconnect with Alder. The river flowed under a high bridge that was the New England Thruway. The marina continued beneath it. That's how high the bridge was. It was perfect cover. I was about to run under the bridge when I heard sirens. Looking back, I saw several police cars with lights flashing and sirens blaring turn on the road that led into the marina. One of the cars was an ambulance. I hoped it was for the downed policemen and not for Alder. Either way, they were going in the opposite direction from me. I was free.

The next trick was to get to the far side of the river. For that I had to climb out onto the road. No way I was going back into the water. The road ran along a dam that was the changeover point of the river between fresh and salt water. The road was wide and well lit. Too well lit. It was a major thoroughfare. I stood on the edge, ready to come out of the bushes, wondering how best to make the crossing. Should I run and risk standing out to cars driving by? Or walk casually? It would take longer, but there would be less chance of being spotted. I decided to jog. Simple as that. People in Stony Brook ran all the time. It wasn't odd to see somebody running along any road, anytime of the day or night. So I put myself in the mindset of one of those guys who lives to train for the local 10K races, and jogged along the road to the far side.

Nobody stopped me. I got to the far side and ducked back into the bushes. I was now on the same side of the river as the rope swing where I was to meet Alder. I don't like to be negative, but I was worried that he had been captured. After he took out those two policemen, I had to believe that the effort to bring him in would intensify. He may have taken the heat away from me and allowed me to escape, but what if they got to him? What would he tell the police? Would they turn him over to the Ravinians? There were too many horrors to consider, so I decided to put them out of my head and hope he showed up.

I don't know who first put up the rope swing on the bank of the Signet River, but it was there for as long as I can remember. It was on a steep bank that allowed you to get decent height when you swung out, and a rush of a plummet when you let go. It was a great way to spend a hot summer afternoon. It wasn't a great way to spend a cold March night, but I had no intention of using it. I pushed my way through the bushes, wondering how long I should wait there before giving up on Alder.

I shouldn't have worried.

"I thought you would never get here," Alder said as I broke into the clearing near the swing. He sat beneath the tree as casually as if he were kicking back and thinking of taking the plunge. I actually felt dumb for worrying about him.

"We need to find a warm place to spend the night," I said. "I'm totally beat."

It had been an impossibly long day that started on Denduron. We needed some downtime to recharge our batteries.

"Your territory is very busy," Alder commented. "How are you able to live in such confusion?"

I'd never thought of it that way. He was right. Compared to the simple world of Denduron, Second Earth was like living inside a frantic video game. For all its busyness, it was going to be tough to find a safe place to hide out. There would certainly be a manhunt on for us. Where could we go for the night? We could break into a store, but there might be alarms. We could find a dark house and hope nobody was home, but what if they came back? I thought of stories I'd heard about escaped convicts. Where were they always found? Churches? Their girlfriends' houses? Hiding in a ditch somewhere? We couldn't go anywhere that was remotely associated with me or my friends, because they would be searched for sure. I knew this town inside out and couldn't think of a single place we could go that would be safe.

Except for one.

"Where should we go?" Alder asked.

"To the absolute last place they'll think of looking for us."

We stayed on the far side of the river for nearly two hours, wet and shivering. From that perch we could see through the trees over to the marina. At first there was a flurry of activity as the ambulance took away the policemen that Alder had clocked. Shortly after, we saw the long limousine pull out.

Alder asked, "I thought the local soldiers were the good guys?"

"So did I. Things have changed."

Finally a long line of police cars drove off. They knew we were gone. The manhunt was on. Alder and I waited another half hour to be sure that they were definitely gone, and quickly made our way back to the marina. Yes, back to the marina. A few minutes later we were resting comfortably, and warm, back in the Chetwyndes' boat. We even finished our tuna and crackers. Why the heck not? I figured they'd never expect us to go back there. We took off our wet clothes and hung them in the bow to dry. After eating our fill and wrapping ourselves in blankets, Alder and I settled down to get some sleep. We decided on taking two-hour shifts. Somebody had to stay awake in case my idea proved to be idiotic. Alder slept first. He was out and snoring before I had the chance to say good night.

It was a strange feeling. I was a fugitive on my own territory. In my hometown. Our task of trying to stop Naymeer was already tough enough. Now it seemed we had to watch out not only for Naymeer's people, but the police as well. As I lay on that bunk, rocking on the waves, I had no idea what we were going to do.

I spent my two-hour watch writing my journal. I found a pad of paper in a waterproof pouch that I figured Mr. Chetwynde used for, well, for a journal. That's where I finished my Journal #35. I took the pages and stowed them in a compartment beneath some navigation gear. I figured it was safer there than on me. One more dunk in the water and the journal would be gone. I figured that at some point the Chetwyndes would find it and give it to you, Courtney. Okay, maybe that's a long shot, but I couldn't think of anything else. I then began my Journal #36. Why not? There was nothing else to do but worry.

By the time I was tired of writing, my shift was almost up. I was looking forward to putting my head down and getting some long-overdue rest . . .

When my ring came to life.

My first thought was to wake up Alder. No, I take that back. My first thought was: *I can't believe this is happening now!* My *second* thought was to wake up Alder. I didn't. Whatever was coming in, there would be time to share it with him later. At least one of us would be well rested. I took off the ring and placed it on the bunk beside me. I wanted to shield the light, so as not to disturb my friend. The ring grew; light flashed from the depths while the sweet musical notes drifted out from the pathway between territories. A moment later the event was over. The ring was back to normal. Lying next to it was a torn piece of paper with writing on it. It looked as if it were smudged with something, but it was too dark to tell. I held the note up to the porthole to allow moonlight to shine on it. As soon as the light hit it, I saw the smudge for what it was.

Blood. Wet blood.

THIRD EARTH

Patrick Mac, the Traveler from Third Earth, returned to his home territory. There was no place like home. Literally. It felt nothing like home. At least not the one he was used to.

He landed back at the flume that was hidden beneath the ruins of the stone cathedral they had entered on Second Earth. The Ravinian cult may still have been active on Third Earth, but they weren't using the flume for gatherings anymore. Patrick didn't want to be there any longer than necessary. Being there reminded him of being shot.

He climbed up the stairs to the ruined street that was in the Bronx, New York. Having been to Second Earth, the surroundings seemed a bit less alien than when he had left. Looking around at the crumbling buildings, he could imagine what they had looked like centuries before. Not a soul was on the street. It was as good as a ghost town. Patrick stood stunned, taking in the evidence before his eyes. This was what Naymeer's teachings led to. This is what Saint Dane wanted. The territory was in ruins.

As much as Patrick dreaded returning, seeing the nightmare that Third Earth had become lit him up . . . with anger. His world had been as close to perfect as could be. The people of Earth had gotten it right. Naymeer's cult changed all that. The so-called elite had driven Earth to ruin. The proof was all around him. Patrick had a mission. He had to stop it from happening. He had to help Pendragon change the past. Again.

The lead Traveler had asked him to dig through history to find whatever he could about the Ravinian cult. Anything that might help stop them from accomplishing their mad plan. If anybody could do that, Patrick could. He decided to go to the source. To the one person who seemed to have a decent grasp on the past. He needed to see Richard, the elderly librarian. Richard had told him that all the records from that time were destroyed, yet he still seemed to know a lot about what had happened. *Yes,* thought Patrick. Richard would be his first resource. But where would he find the man? Richard had been beaten by the Ravinians. Had he survived? People said they would take him to the hospital. What hospital? Patrick knew nothing about this transformed Third Earth. How long ago had it all happened? *When* had the flume returned him to Third Earth? Was Richard beaten earlier that day? Or years before?

Patrick decided to tackle the challenges one at a time. It was the only way to fight off the panic. He had to calm down and act logically. The place to start was obvious. He had to go back to the library.

It was a long walk downtown. The subways no longer ran and no taxicabs cruised the streets. The farther south he went, the busier the streets became. New York was still alive, though barely. Most people got around on bicycles, but after he crossed a bridge to Manhattan, he saw ancient buses cruising the avenues. He would have loved to catch one, but he didn't have a penny to his name. He resigned himself to walking the full distance, just as he had made the walk from the library up to the flume before.

It took several hours, but Patrick finally arrived at the library. When he looked up at the stone facade, his heart sank. The front of the once proud building was marked with ugly black streaks. They were scars from the fire the Ravinians had set. It gave him even less hope that he'd find Richard there. But he didn't know where else to look, so he willed his aching legs to climb the steps.

The foyer was badly damaged but not destroyed. Patrick took a few steps toward the corridor that led to the room where Richard had hidden the Ravinia book cover, but he stopped before getting very far. The corridor was impassable. It looked as if this was where the fire was centered. Charred wooden beams had crashed down, closing off the hallway. There was no use trying to go that way. Patrick returned to the foyer and decided to try the other direction. When he turned to head back, Patrick froze. Standing in the center of the burned foyer was Richard. For a moment Patrick actually thought he was looking at a ghost—that's how thin and pale the man looked.

"You came back," Richard said in a thin whisper.

Patrick went to him quickly. "Are you all right?"

Richard scoffed. "Depends on your definition of 'all right.' I'm alive. Does that count?"

Patrick was flustered. He hadn't expected to find Richard so quickly. He had a million questions and couldn't think of a single one.

"How long?" he asked. "I mean, how long ago did they, you know, burn the library?"

Richard gave Patrick a curious look. Patrick realized he had asked a ridiculous question. Richard didn't know about traveling between time and territories.

"Why do you ask?" Richard replied. "Did you go somewhere else in Halla?"

Or maybe he did. Patrick had forgotten that Naymeer pulled the curtain back on Halla many centuries before.

"What do you know about Halla?" Patrick asked.

"Enough to know that the promise of living in a world better than our own was never fulfilled" was Richard's angry answer. "Is there anything else to know?"

"No," Patrick said, glum. "I guess not."

"Yesterday," Richard said.

"Yesterday what?"

"Yesterday they burned the library and sent me to the hospital."

"Oh. Right."

"Why did you come back?" Richard asked. "Still looking for answers, Teacher?"

Patrick perked up. "Now more than ever."

Richard gave a tired nod. He reached for his sleeve and pulled it up to reveal an ugly red blotch on his right forearm.

Patrick gasped.

It was a scar where there once had been the tattoo of a star. "How's this for a start?" Richard asked.

"You're one of them?" Patrick asked, stunned.

"I was. Until I learned the truth."

"Tell me," Patrick begged. "I need to know. Everything."

"Why?" Richard asked.

"To try to stop it," Patrick answered bluntly.

Richard sniffed skeptically. He looked Patrick right in the eye and asked, "Are you strong enough?"

"To stop it? I don't know."

"No. I'm asking if you're strong enough to learn the truth."

The ominous question made Patrick flinch. "I have to be."

Richard nodded and shuffled off, headed deeper into the library. Patrick followed him down a long corridor with a cracked marble floor. They soon reached a small room with an unmade bed along the far wall. Clothes were strewn everywhere. The place smelled of smoke and dirty laundry. A small hot plate for cooking was on a scarred old desk.

"You live here?" Patrick asked, incredulous.

"This is my world now," Richard said as he dug through mounds of clothing and paper containers. "Homey, don't you think?"

"This isn't your world," Patrick corrected. "Your world is those books out there."

That made Richard stop. He seemed to soften. "Thank you," he said sincerely. "It's a dying world. I'm tired of living in it."

He found what he was looking for—a set of car keys.

A few minutes later Richard and Patrick were driving up Broadway in an ancient, gas-powered automobile. Richard was behind the wheel. Patrick was white-knuckling it in the passenger seat. The old car was falling apart. Every time it hit the slightest crack in the road, it bounced and groaned as if about to crumble. Patrick glanced nervously at the old man. He was actually relieved to see that Richard looked better. He had a happy spark in his eye. He obviously enjoyed driving.

"Haven't taken this old wreck for a spin in a decade," Richard explained. "Impossible to get gas. All I do is start it up every so often to keep things working."

"Where are we going?" Patrick asked.

"To get the answers you've been looking for."

"I thought all the records from the early twenty-first century were destroyed."

"They were. Most of 'em, anyway. Things get passed around. And hidden. I've read enough to piece some things together. But I'm not taking you to see some old papers. You're going to see reality." He reached into the glove compartment and pulled out a pad of paper with a pen attached. He tossed it to Patrick, saying, "Take notes. Let's start our own documentation of history."

Patrick took the pad but didn't write anything. He was too terrified of Richard's driving to look at anything other than the road.

"He was some kind of prophet," Richard began. "Or so the stories go. He promised a better life. He promised paradise. All his people had to do was buy into his way of thinking."

"You're talking about Naymeer?" Patrick asked.

"Who else? He gave people a glimpse into other worlds. 'Halla,' he called it. People ate it up. Everybody wants to live in a better place. It's only natural. Halla wasn't some mystical afterlife you had to die to get to. No, it swirled all around, all the time. All you had to do to get there was prove your worth."

"By being perfect," Patrick added.

Richard gave him a look. "You know more than you let on, teacher."

"I'm learning," Patrick answered. "How did Naymeer show them these worlds?"

"He had a ring," Richard continued. "He said it was made from the stuff that created all existence. Not many doubted him. There was a tunnel in the Bronx. They had big gatherings where he'd use the ring to make that tunnel come alive with visions of Halla."

"The flume," Patrick muttered.

"Yeah, the flume. I understand it was quite the show."

"That was a long time ago," Patrick said. "How did it all go wrong?"

"It didn't at first. Naymeer was all about reward and punishment. Those he considered worthy were given wealth and comfort. Those he thought were a drain on society were given, well, nothing. No, worse than that. They were stripped of everything, including their pride."

"What about the sick and the elderly?"

"No exceptions. Once you were judged to be a burden, your rights were taken away, and you were forced to live in these camps they called Horizon Compounds. There were thousands of 'em, all over the world. That's where they kept the people who didn't contribute. They were as good as slaves. Occasionally somebody would prove to be worthy and got sprung to join the elite, but mostly they spent their lives between the compounds and whatever job they were assigned to keep the wheels of the world moving."

"And they weren't allowed to see the rest of Halla?"

"They weren't allowed anything," Richard snapped. "They were treated like a subspecies. The Horizon Compounds were filthy places full of crime and disease."

Patrick sat back in his seat, stunned. "That's incredible."

"What's incredible is how so many people allowed it to happen. That's what Ravinia is all about. It's the essence of their philosophy. They believe that prosperity comes only from rewarding excellence and crushing weakness."

Patrick shook his head sadly. "Yet society crumbled."

"Not according to the Ravinians. They're still around, you know. Who do you think gave me that beating? They haven't given up. They consider all this just a transitional phase before the true glory will rise from the ashes, or some such nonsense."

Patrick looked to Richard. "You were one of them."

"I took on the symbol," Richard answered. "I was never one of them. I joined to keep the library open and the memories alive. The truth alive. But I was *not* one of them."

"Why do they care so much about burying the truth?" Patrick asked.

Richard gave him a sideways glance. "Look around. Reality hasn't exactly lived up to the promise. They fear that if enough people learned the truth, it could lead to a revolution."

"Why did you get rid of the star symbol?"

Richard didn't answer at first. Patrick saw his eyes fill with tears. Patrick didn't push him. He would answer when he was ready.

"I'm an old man," Richard finally said. "I won't be around much longer, and I'm okay with that. I've seen too much as it is. I played the game, to do what I thought was right, but every man has his limits. I'd dance through hell, but I'd never make a pact with the devil. When I learned the truth, I reached my limit. So I burned off the star."

Patrick stared at Richard, wide eyed. The old man looked back at him through tears. "Now I'm going to show you the truth. Who knows? Maybe you're the one to start that revolution."

Richard turned back to his driving. Patrick didn't ask him anything else. He felt as if he had already pushed the old man too far. Was he stable? Patrick didn't know. He was upset for sure. Wherever it was they were going, Patrick felt sure he would find answers. Answers he hoped would help Pendragon and Alder stop the growing insanity on Second Earth.

Richard drove them north. They left the island of Manhattan and traveled through what used to be the suburbs. On Patrick's Third Earth it was beautiful, green countryside. It was now filled with blighted trees, abandoned tracts of homes, and trash. Lots of trash. From derelict cars down to paper wrappers. The thruway hadn't been repaved in ages. It looked more like a spider web than a solid roadbed.

"People still live out here," Richard said. "They're like wild tribes, sticking together for security. This isn't the kind of place to be spending time if you're an outsider."

"Really? What about us?"

"Let's just say it will be better if this old jalopy doesn't break down," Richard answered ominously.

When they had driven for nearly an hour, Patrick noticed changes. They first drove past a series of small, crumbling cement structures that spread out to either side of the thruway.

"Security outposts," Richard answered, as if he knew what Patrick was wondering. "Back in the day they were filled with armed soldiers."

"What for?"

"To keep the curious away. If you didn't have business out here, you'd never get past this perimeter. It circles around for miles."

"What were they protecting?"

Richard didn't answer and Patrick didn't press.

Once past the abandoned military-style bunkers, the signs of civilization became fewer and farther between. The trees grew more dense. Green foliage became thicker. It was the first pleasant sight Patrick had viewed on the new Third Earth.

"Pretty," he commented without thinking.

"That was the idea," Richard said with a snarl. "If you were brought out here, you first had to travel through this pleasant, green forest. I guess it calmed people down and made them feel like they were going someplace swell."

"People were brought here? Why? What is this place?"

Richard answered, "They called it Stony Brook."

Patrick shot Richard a stunned look. "Stony Brook?"

"You heard of it?" Richard asked, surprised.

Patrick wasn't sure how to answer. "I knew people who came from there."

Richard gave a skeptical laugh. "Not this place. Nobody comes from Stony Brook."

Patrick didn't press Richard any further. He knew he'd get answers soon enough. The forest they passed through bore no resemblance to the hometown of Bobby Pendragon. Patrick couldn't imagine why people would have been brought to the home of the Traveler from Second Earth. They drove several miles through dense forest, until the trees opened up to reveal a long, stone wall that at one time was probably white, but was now dirty gray. It stretched out before them for several hundred yards before turning at right angles away and continuing on for a distance that Patrick couldn't see. On either front corner were large round turrets with peaked roofs. At dead center were huge, wrought-iron gates that hung open on rusted hinges.

"It's like a castle fortress," Patrick gasped.

"I think that was the idea. Coming up here, you had the feeling you were entering someplace special. To the best of my knowledge, it's been empty for over a hundred years."

"How did you find out about it?"

"I told you, there are still records," Richard answered. "Hidden around. Here and there. People trade bits of information like contraband. I came across an ancient transfer order that sent a huge shipment of 'relos' to Stony Brook. I'd never heard of Stony Brook before that. Or relos for that matter. The more I dug, the more I learned." Richard looked at Patrick with a mischievous gleam in his eye. "Once I started putting things together, I couldn't resist taking a look for myself." The gleam turned into a tear. "I wish to all that's good and decent that I hadn't."

Richard hit the gas and drove them past the rusted, hanging gates.

The front half of the compound was nothing more than a large, empty courtyard that was half the size of a football field. It was full of dust and weeds that poked up through the cracked asphalt. Rising up on the far side, opposite the gates, was an elaborate structure, with stone pillars that reminded Patrick of the cathedral-like Ravinian building built over the flume entrance in the Bronx. The structure had seen better days. Large chunks of marble had fallen from the ornate molding that skirted the roof above the columns. Though far past its prime, it was still a majestic site.

"What is it?" Patrick croaked.

"It's the gate into hell," Richard answered as he got out of the car.

Patrick followed quickly as the old man shuffled across the cracked courtyard, toward the imposing columns.

"Quite the sight, isn't it?" Richard asked as they walked. "Who knows what people thought when they came here? Apparently they were told they were going to be shown the wonders of Halla."

"Isn't that what the flume in the Bronx was for?" Patrick asked.

Richard stopped and looked at Patrick. "That place in the Bronx was for Ravinians. This place was for everyone else. People would be driven here in buses. I believe they disembarked right here, where we're standing. They'd be led through these pillars. From what I've read, they all went willingly, though they must have wondered why there were armed guards up in those turrets."

Patrick looked up to the round turrets that were on each corner of the tall wall that surrounded them. It suddenly felt less like a magical castle and more like a prison.

Patrick asked, "Who was brought here?"

Richard began to tremble. "At first they brought the weak. The handicapped. The elderly. Those with debilitating diseases. As time went on, they weren't as discerning. If you lived in one of the Horizon Compounds, there was always a chance you might end up here."

Patrick croaked, "I don't like where this story is going."

"No?" Richard blurted out. "You said you wanted the truth."

"I do," Patrick confirmed adamantly.

"I believe the term they used was . . . 'marginalized,'" Richard said. "That's what they did with relos. They were marginalized."

He left Patrick and walked toward the columns. Patrick glanced around the empty compound, a knot of dread twisting his stomach. He wanted to get the heck out of there, but he had to know the whole truth. It's what his mission was all about. He followed Richard up to a set of massive, steel doors. One was open slightly. Barely enough for a person to squeeze through.

"Had to pry this open," Richard explained. "I never would have gotten in if the locks hadn't rusted. Even after they shut it down, they didn't want people wandering in."

Richard squeezed through the opening, followed right behind by Patrick. Inside was a grand marble foyer. No electric lights burned. The only illumination came from sunlight that was sneaking in through high windows. Patrick saw that the space was ringed by austere marble columns.

"Feels like a tomb," he commented softly.

Richard gave Patrick a quick look, an ironic chuckle, then walked to the far side of the room, where a flight of stairs led down into the dark. The librarian continued down without stopping. Patrick didn't follow right away. As soon as he saw the stairs, it clicked. He felt certain he knew what he would find down below. What he didn't know was what it meant. To find that answer, he had to follow Richard.

Patrick went for the stairs and had to descend only a few steps to see it, just as he suspected. Sitting on the far side of a plain, cement-walled basement room, recessed in the wall, was the flume.

"It's the Sherwood house," he gasped.

"I don't know anything about a Sherwood house," Richard said. "Seems to me it was more like a house of horrors." Richard stepped into the mouth of the flume and continued. "From the accounts I've pieced together, Naymeer himself would preside. The poor people they called 'relos' were led down here and told to walk inside the tunnel. Naymeer would stand here with his ring and activate this infernal device. The people would walk in and that would be the last anyone ever saw of them. This was how the Ravinians got rid of those they didn't feel worthy."

"No!" Patrick blurted out. "That doesn't make sense." His mind was working too fast to worry about being discreet. "The flume only works for Travelers. It's dangerous for anybody else to use it."

"Dangerous?" Richard scoffed. "Those poor people were executed! Can't get any more dangerous than that!"

"No," Patrick blathered. "That's not how it works. The flume doesn't kill people."

"Then what happened to them?" Richard shot back. "They went in and didn't come back out. By the thousands. If somebody didn't fit the Ravinian profile, the person was either used as a slave, or categorized as a relo and sent here. That's what they're trying to hide, Teacher. Genocide. It lasted for decades. Once Naymeer got too old to continue, he passed the ring on to his acolytes. That's what he called them. Acolytes. The Ravinians purged the world of anyone they thought was inferior or didn't agree with their philosophy. It wasn't about race or religion or even politics. It was all about the individual's ability to contribute. If you fell on one side of the line and were a productive, intelligent person, you lived comfortably. If you fell on the other side of the line, you could end up a relo and sent here. It was all about reducing the excess population, taking stress off of an overburdened system, and allowing the elite to thrive. That's how they were able to take control. If you caused trouble, you were gone."

Patrick paced, shaking his head. "It can't be."

"Why not?" Richard asked. "Because you don't believe people are capable of such evil? That they can flat out exterminate their enemies? History proves you wrong, Teacher. The Ravinians prove you wrong. Heck, what happened up here was nothing compared to the Bronx Massacre."

Patrick whipped a look at Richard. "Bronx Massacre?"

"You never heard of that either?" Richard snarled. "What kind of a teacher are you?"

Patrick stalked toward Richard. "A confused one. What was the Bronx Massacre?"

Richard sniffed. "Only the event that started it all. It put the Ravinians in power. They showed what they were capable of and took the world hostage."

Patrick was doing his best to control his voice and his emotions. "Richard, what exactly was the Bronx Massacre?"

Patrick heard a pop. It sounded like a firecracker. The sound reverberated off the stone walls of the flume.

"What was that?" Patrick asked.

He looked to Richard. The old man gazed back with glassy eyes. He opened his mouth to speak, but instead collapsed. Patrick caught him.

"Richard!" he called out.

Patrick pulled his hand away, to find it covered with blood. Richard's blood. He'd been shot. Patrick looked up quickly. The only place the shots could have come from was deep within the flume. Patrick was in the dead center of its mouth.

"I'm sorry, Richard," he whispered, and rested the old man down on the rock floor . . . and ran. He dodged to his right as two more pops were heard. They missed him, slamming into the stairs. Patrick pumped his knees, taking three steps at a time. It wasn't just about survival. Patrick knew he had to get this information back to Pendragon. He had to let Pendragon know that Naymeer and the Ravinians were using the flume to exile their enemies to other parts of Halla. The flume was being used as the ultimate weapon in Saint Dane's quest to control Halla. He no longer had to destroy those who didn't fit in with his plans—all he needed to do was send them elsewhere. But where? There was no way to know.

Then there was the Bronx Massacre. What was it?

Patrick reached the top of the stairs, squeezed through the opening in the steel doors, and sprinted for the car. He stayed low, hoping to make a smaller target. He got to the car without having another shot fired at him, and dove inside. Patrick had never driven an old car. He was used to the quiet, electric vehicles of his Third Earth. He had watched Richard. He twisted the ignition key. The engine turned over.

"Yes!"

He hit the gas and spun the wheel. The car skid across the asphalt, kicking up dirt and gravel. Patrick aimed for the front gates and jammed his foot to the floor. The old vehicle squeaked and complained, but it moved. Fast. With each second he felt more comfortable behind the wheel. He felt sure he was going to make it. All he would have to do was figure out how to drive the car back to the Bronx and the other flume. He didn't want to leave Richard, but there was no choice. He had to get to the other flume. He had to get to Bobby.

He was ten yards from the front gate when a large truck shot in front of the opening, directly in front of the speeding car. The truck skidded to a stop, blocking the way. Patrick wasn't an experienced driver. Even if he had reacted quickly, he was still driving too fast. He slammed on the brakes. It was too late. He hit the side of the truck at full speed. The crash was violent. Patrick flew into the windshield, vaguely aware of glass shattering. He bounced back into the front seat, stunned. The world swam around him. He was hurt. Badly. He knew it. He knew he'd never make it to the flume. He forced himself to focus. He had to warn Pendragon.

Gasping for breath, he found the pad of paper Richard had given him. He couldn't move his right arm. It was broken. The pain told him so. He used his left. Patrick fumbled for the paper and wrote. He coughed, sending a spray of blood splattering across the page. Patrick knew he didn't have much time left. The pooling blood on the floor was proof of that. He would have to convey all that he knew in a few words. As he wrote, more of his blood dripped onto the page. He fought the dizziness that was quickly overtaking him. He forced himself to think. What words to use? What words?

He finished writing and took off his Traveler ring.

"Second Earth," he croaked weakly.

The ring came to life. Relief. He fought to stay alert for a few seconds more. The world swirled. He wished the ring would work faster. Light blasted from the circle. The portal was open. Patrick's last act was to clutch the bloody piece of paper and drop it inside.

He had done it. His mission was complete. The ring returned to normal.

Patrick was alone. There were no Travelers there to help him. No one to heal him. No one to save his life. He had dodged death once. This time he wouldn't be so lucky.

"Good luck, Pendragon" were the last words spoken by Patrick Mac, the Traveler from Third Earth.

JOURNAL #36

(CONTINUED)

SECOND EARTH

What does it say?" Alder asked, groggy, as he rolled over in his bunk.

I clutched the bloody note. The message was cryptic and hurried. It was barely legible. I hoped it was because Patrick only used computers and had lousy penmanship. I was kidding myself. Patrick was in trouble. Or worse. Blood is never an indication of something good.

"It's from Patrick," I answered.

Alder sat up, suddenly wide awake. "Did he learn something of Naymeer?"

I nodded and handed him the note. He looked at it carefully, feeling the moisture. He gave me a concerned look and read Patrick's words: *"N. exiles enemies through flume. Begins w/Bronx Massacre. Patrick."*

Alder read the words aloud once, then twice. "'N.' is Naymeer?" he asked.

"That's my guess," I replied.

"What is a Bronx?"

"It's where the other flume is."

"How can Naymeer send people into exile? The flume can only be used with a Traveler."

"Unless the Convergence has changed things," I said soberly.

Alder added, "Then where would Naymeer send them?"

I sat up and rubbed my eyes. I was tired and wired at the same time. "I don't know. What if he doesn't send them anywhere? Massacre and exile aren't the same things."

"The flume is not an execution device, Pendragon," Alder corrected.

Reading Patrick's note may have raised more questions than it answered, but it cemented something in my head.

"Patrick wrote this Bronx Massacre is where it begins," I said thoughtfully. "Sounds like a turning point to me."

Alder nodded. "Perhaps it is the first time that Naymeer will use the flume to exile his enemies."

"Or murder them," I cautioned.

"Whatever it is, we must stop it," Alder declared.

I looked down. I didn't like where my head was going. The last-ditch plan I'd thought of earlier suddenly felt a lot more like a possibility. Unfortunately.

"Tell me your thoughts, Pendragon," Alder said softly.

"This is too big for us," I answered. "You said it yourself. This is a busy territory. You have no idea how right you are. We're not talking about primitive tribes or local conflicts here. The problem is global. I'm telling you, altering world events isn't a simple thing. Naymeer has a huge following. His cult is about to get recognized by the United Nations. That's a worldwide organization! It'll be impossible for us to convince enough people that he's leading them down a dangerous path. I wouldn't know where to begin."

"But we must try," Alder muttered.

"Trust me, we can't handle something that big. Our only hope is to think small."

Alder nodded thoughtfully. "Have you an idea?"

I took a deep, uneasy breath and continued, "This is all about Naymeer. He's the center of it all. Saint Dane may be pulling his strings, but Naymeer is the voice of Ravinia."

Alder gave me a sober look. I think he knew where I was headed. I didn't like it any more than he did.

I continued, "If we take Naymeer out of the picture, Ravinia might crumble."

"Are you suggesting what I think you are?"

I nodded. "We should try and get him off Second Earth. If we remove the head, the body might die."

"We would have to get him to a flume," Alder said thoughtfully. "That will be difficult. He is protected."

"It'll be next to impossible," I shot back. "Short of that, there's only one other thing we can do."

Alder said it first. "Are you suggesting we kill him? Kill a Traveler?"

Hearing the words made it sound even worse, but it was exactly what I was thinking. I nodded. I couldn't believe it. I was actually thinking that we would have to kill Naymeer. "Unless you have a better idea," I added hopefully.

Alder leaned back against the hull. I didn't think I'd ever seen him look so centered. So serious. I waited for him to respond, but he stayed silent, lost in his thoughts.

"Talk to me, Alder!" I finally shouted. "Am I crazy?"

Alder was calm. He spoke softly, but with authority. "We have done many things that go against our mandate as Travelers. Killing would certainly be one of them."

"We made the choices we had to make," I said defensively. "If we hadn't broken a few rules, the turning points of many territories would have gone the wrong way."

"Would that have been so bad?" Alder asked quickly.

I couldn't believe what I was hearing. "Well, yeah!" I argued. "We stopped Saint Dane most every time."

"To what end?" Alder asked. "He is on the verge of controlling Halla in spite of our efforts. I cannot help but wonder what would have happened if we had not broken the rules. Would we be in any worse of a situation than we are right now?"

I was getting angry. Alder was questioning everything we had done as Travelers.

"I don't buy that," I shot back. "Anything we can do to stop Saint Dane is justified."

"I would agree," Alder stated calmly, "if we had stopped him. We have not."

I wanted to argue, but he was right. All the battles up to that point didn't matter. Everything was happening as Saint Dane predicted. In spite of all we had done, all our victories, he was on the verge of controlling Halla.

"So what do we do? Give up?" I shouted in frustration.

"No," Alder answered quickly. "I am saying we should use every possible method at our disposal, before once again doing something we know is wrong."

"Of course we will!" I shouted. "You think I *want* to kill somebody?"

We sat silently for a few moments. I had to cool down. Alder was on my side. Arguing wouldn't help things.

"Taking a life is a frightening step," Alder continued. "Maybe a step too far. If we murdered someone in cold blood, would we be taking the final step down to Saint Dane's level?"

"Yes" was my honest answer.

Alder thought for a few more seconds, then said, "You have never taken a life, have you, Pendragon?"

I shook my head. I had been surrounded by death and destruction from the moment I became a Traveler, but never at my own hands. Even with the *Hindenburg*, it was Gunny who allowed the rocket to be fired. Not me.

I swallowed hard and admitted, "I'm not even sure I could."

"You must not find out now," Alder concluded.

"What other choice do we have?"

"Only one. If it comes to it, I will kill Naymeer."

I hadn't expected that. "What? Why?"

"It is wrong to take another life," Alder explained. "However, if it would mean stopping the Ravinians and righting Second Earth, I believe it would be justified. If it would prevent a massacre, it would be justified. If it would end the Convergence and protect Halla, it would be justified. I believe that. But I also believe it would be disastrous for you to do it."

"Why? What difference does it make?"

"You are the lead Traveler, Pendragon. You are the way. You have always been the way. You must rise above. If Halla is to be put right, many will look to you for guidance. I believe that is the way it was meant to be. If we are to believe that our way is the right way, you cannot become a killer. If it came to that, I believe Halla would truly be lost, and Saint Dane would have his ultimate victory."

Alder's words rang true. We were the good guys. Or so I always thought. Yes, we made mistakes and didn't always play by the rules, but I always believed our intentions were right and our actions justified. This was different.

Deliberately taking a life, in cold blood, felt like it crossed the line. Even more so than mixing territories. I wasn't sure it would be okay for Alder to do it and not me, but I was willing to accept the possibility. Saint Dane told me so many times that this was a battle not only for Halla, but between the two of us. He wanted to prove himself superior to me. I still didn't know who he wanted to prove it to, but some higher power had to be involved. Maybe I was kidding myself by thinking that condoning a murder, without actually doing it, got me off the hook. That felt like a technicality. But if this were truly a battle between Saint Dane and me, I had to think that taking the high road and not actually having blood on my hands was the right way to go.

"All right," I finally said. "We'll try to get Naymeer off the territory. If we fail and have to do something more drastic, I'll step aside for you, Alder. But not if it means losing him."

"Very well. Please remember, though, that there may be a lot more to lose if you do *not* step aside," Alder said.

With those ominous words in my head, I lay back down on the bunk and closed my eyes.

"I gotta sleep," I said. "Tomorrow is going to be a long day. Wake me up in two hours. We have work to do."

SECOND EARTH

Courtney and Mark sat behind the same long table in the Stony Brook police station where they had been interrogated years before by Captain Hirsch. It was Chief Hirsch now. Both Mark and Courtney remembered him as being a good guy. A friend. He was genuinely concerned back then about what had happened to Bobby and his family. They trusted him.

Not anymore.

Hirsch wasn't an enemy, but he and the Stony Brook police were standing in the way of their mission to derail Naymeer and the Ravinians. Mark and Courtney knew that whatever happened, they had to keep the police away from Bobby and Alder.

Hirsch had left them alone in the simple, bland room for over an hour before rejoining them. The whole time, Mark and Courtney didn't say a word to each other. They knew they were being watched from behind the two-way mirror that took up most of one wall. When Hirsch finally entered, he came in with a uniformed officer who went immediately to the back of the room and stood with his arms folded. Hirsch brought Mark and

Courtney sodas and chips. Neither cared. Neither ate. Hirsch took off his gray suit jacket and sat down in the chair across from the two friends.

"So?" he said casually. "Where have you guys been?"

It was such a simple question that had an impossibly complicated answer.

Courtney jumped in first. "I just took off," she said bluntly. "I was going through a lot at home, you know, with getting injured and all. When Mark's parents died, it was just too much to handle. So I left. It was wrong, I know. What can I say?"

"Where did you go?" Hirsch asked, sipping on a Coke.

"New York," Courtney answered. She wanted to keep as many elements of the truth as possible in her story, in case she slipped up. "I stayed in different places. Worked some odd jobs. You know, just to get by."

"We can check on that, you know," Hirsch said bluntly.

"Do you really care that much?" Courtney asked.

Mark winced. He was afraid Courtney would get combative and say something foolish. Hirsch didn't answer her. Instead he turned to Mark. "How about you, Mark?" Hirsch asked. "I'm very sorry about your parents by the way."

"Thanks," Mark said softly. He had to play the role of a grieving son who had lost his parents in an air disaster. "We were together. Courtney and I. We were just hanging out, you know?"

"Okay, why?"

"I don't know," Mark said evasively. "It's tough losing your parents and finding out you're alone in the world. I didn't want to live with my aunt in Maryland."

"He's my friend," Courtney added. "I was helping him get his head back on straight."

"Without telling your parents?"

"If you were my father, would you have let me go?"

Hirsch nodded thoughtfully. "Why did you break into Alexander Naymeer's house?"

Mark was about to answer, but Courtney sat forward, cutting him off. "We didn't. Why would he say that? We were hanging around outside, but we didn't break in. Does he have proof? Were things stolen?"

"Uh, yes, a car."

That made Courtney hesitate. Her plan was to deny everything. She didn't think Naymeer wanted any of this to get out either.

"You think we stole it?" Courtney asked. "Prove it!"

"We found the car submerged at the bottom of the boat ramp at the Signet Marina," Hirsch answered with no emotion.

"That doesn't mean we took it," Courtney shot back. "We ran away. So what? We didn't do anything wrong. We don't owe anybody any explanations."

Mark put his hand on Courtney's arm to calm her down.

Hirsch didn't react. He simply looked back and forth between the two.

"You're both seventeen," he finally said. "You're minors. You go missing for four months, then suddenly show up out of nowhere, along with a guy who dropped off the face of the earth almost four years ago. A guy whose entire *family* disappeared almost four years ago. I'd say you owe people a lot of explanations."

Courtney pulled away from Mark and stood up. "This isn't about us," she barked. "It's about Bobby. That's who you really want to know about, isn't it?"

Mark gave Courtney a wide-eyed look that screamed, "Shut up!"

"I'm not your enemy, Courtney," Hirsch said calmly.

"Then stop treating us like you are!"

Hirsch sized the two of them up. It seemed to Mark that he was debating about how to proceed.

"I don't know what happened at the Naymeer compound," Hirsch said. "They aren't filing charges, so it's not a criminal matter."

"Good!" Courtney declared. "Then we can go." She went for the door. It was locked. She rattled the handle and turned back to Hirsch petulantly.

"Don't we get lawyers or something?"

"You're not being charged with anything," Hirsch said patiently. "I just thought you could shed a little light on the mystery. Is that too much to ask?"

"You can ask," Courtney shot back. "But we don't know anything. We're just as surprised as you are. Bobby showed up tonight, looking for a place to stay. I suggested my parents' boat. Before he got the chance to tell us anything, the storm troopers showed up. End of story."

Hirsch stared at Courtney. Courtney stared back. Hirsch looked to Mark.

"What's your version?" he asked Mark.

Mark shrugged. He was just trying to keep up with Courtney's thinking.

"Same as hers," Mark answered. "Courtney and I got back to town tonight and ran into Bobby."

"And what about that big galoot friend of his? What's his story?"

Courtney strode back to the table. "Weren't you listening? We don't know! We have the same questions you do."

Hirsch looked between the two, thinking. He let out a breath, leaned back in his chair, and rolled up his shirtsleeves, as if preparing to get down to some serious work.

"The journal I read back then, when Bobby first disappeared," Hirsch said. "The one that talked about flumes and territories. What was the name of that lowlife who stole it? Right. Andy Mitchell. Maybe I should take another look at that thing."

"I—I told you back then," Mark stammered. "I wrote that journal."

"Maybe," Hirsch said. "I still think I should take another look."

When he finished rolling up his sleeves, Mark and Courtney saw it at the same time. Tattooed on Hirsch's arm was a green star tattoo.

"You're a Ravinian," Mark gasped.

"Is that a problem?" Hirsch asked.

"Is that how you got promoted to chief?" Courtney asked.

Mark winced again. Courtney just couldn't keep herself from stirring up trouble. Hirsch snickered, stood up, and walked to the mirror. He stared at it. Mark and Courtney exchanged looks.

Courtney called out, "What are you doing? Getting instructions from somebody?"

Hirsch quickly turned away from the mirror. Gone was the calm, friendly officer. His frustration over not getting any information from Mark and Courtney was starting to show. He strode back to the table. "This would be so much easier if you told me the truth," he said impatiently.

"Weird," Courtney said.

"What is?" Hirsch asked, his voice cracking.

"We're being interrogated, but you're the one who's all nervous. Why is that? You getting pressure from somebody behind the mirror?"

Hirsch started to answer, but couldn't find the words. He was flustered. Mark gave Courtney a stern look. She shrugged. Hirsch paced. He was definitely nervous. He stared down at the floor, deep in thought. The phone on the table jangled, making him jump.

"Wow," Courtney said. "You really are under pressure."

Hirsch swiped at the phone quickly, snatching it before it could ring again. He didn't speak. He closed his eyes and listened. Whatever he was hearing, he didn't like it. He nodded, as if the person on the phone could see.

"Bad news?" Courtney asked.

Hirsch shot a quick glance to the mirror and gently put the phone back down.

"Hey, you okay?" Mark asked with genuine concern. Both he and Courtney actually liked Hirsch. He once tried to help them.

"Is there anything you can tell me?" Hirsch asked. "Anything?"

To Mark it sounded like a last, desperate stab at solving an impossible problem. Both he and Courtney answered the same way—with a shrug. Hirsch's shoulders fell. He looked beaten. He shook his head, as if resigning himself to something he didn't agree with.

"Take off," he ordered the uniformed cop who had been watching the scene silently.

The cop walked for the door without question. Before leaving, he threw a troubled look to Mark and Courtney, then left without a word.

"What's up with that?" Courtney asked. "I think you'd better get my parents."

Hirsch picked up his suit jacket and walked for the door.

"I hope this works out for you guys," he said. "I think you're good kids. Do the right thing, and everything will be fine. Good luck."

Hirsch opened the door and left quickly, without so much as a look back. Courtney stood there, staring at the door. Mark didn't move.

"Did that creep you out as much as it did me?" Courtney asked.

"I don't like this," Mark announced, standing up. "Something's going on."

"What do we do?"

"We leave." Mark started for the door, but got only a few steps closer before it opened.

"Mom? Dad?" Courtney called out.

It was neither. Entering the room quickly were two of Naymeer's red-shirt guardians. They wore the same masks as when they'd captured Mark and Courtney at her house.

"No, no!" Courtney shouted.

She picked up a chair and flung it at the first guardian. He ducked, and it clattered harmlessly against the wall. There was no way out of the room. Courtney ran to the mirror and hit it with her fists.

"You can't do this!" she screamed at the unknown faces beyond. "You aren't above the law!"

It was the last thing Courtney said before the smell of lemons filled the room.

SECOND EARTH

We were going after Naymeer.

My plan was to move before dawn. Alder and I were wanted by the police. We would stick out on the streets of Stony Brook like, well, like two guys who were wanted by the police. There would be no place to hide in daylight. Not in the busy, crowded suburbs. We had to get to our destination before the sun came up.

The predawn hour was the best time to stage our attack. Our target? The Sherwood house where Naymeer lived. It made all sorts of sense to go after him there. As much as we debated about whether or not it was right to kill him, that wasn't our first plan. We wanted to get him into the flume and off the territory. The flume was in the Sherwood house. Hopefully, Naymeer would be too. It was also a place where we stood the best chance of getting to him. Once he was out in public, surrounded by his guardians and worshipping followers, we wouldn't even get close. If we could get into his house, in the quiet hours before dawn, hopefully his guards would be a little less alert. Hopefully. There were all sorts of things that could go wrong with this plan, but it was the only one I could come up with.

Alder woke me at three thirty a.m. I didn't have near enough sleep. It would have to do. We had roughly three hours until sunrise. I figured it would take around an hour to get to the Sherwood house on foot. We quickly and quietly got dressed, splashed water on our faces, and finished off the last of the packaged food that the Chetwyndes had stowed for their next voyage. With a silent nod to each other, we were off.

It would have been risky to travel on a main road, so I led Alder on a trip through the backyards of Stony Brook. I had no problem finding my way. Up until I was fourteen, I must have explored every inch of my town. Most of them with Mark. Alder and I ran along train tracks, snuck across school parking lots and ball fields, and skirted private swimming pools. Whenever possible, we stayed on paths through woods that had yet to be developed. It was a piece of cake. We jogged the whole way. Both of us were in great shape. I think the anticipation of what was about to happen burned off any residual fatigue. We both knew that each step brought us closer to a showdown.

We made it to the Sherwood property with no problem. We crept behind a hedge that bordered the yard across the street from the imposing mansion. From there we got a decent view of our target.

"I trust you have a plan, Pendragon," Alder whispered.

"Not exactly" was my answer. "All I can think of are negatives. There are the guards. Who knows how many? They're the least of our worries. They're armed, but I don't think they'll shoot us."

"Why not?"

"Because Saint Dane wouldn't allow it. At least, I don't think he would. He wants us around for the end. I can get us over the wall, but I don't know what kind of surveillance they have."

"Surveillance?"

"Cameras, motion detectors, microphones, anything that would alert them to intruders."

"I do not know what any of that means," said the knight from Denduron.

"It means they're going to know we're here pretty quickly. All we can do is take on the guards and force our way in. I'm guessing Naymeer's bedroom is upstairs. The big one is on the second floor, off the center of the hallway. If he's here, that's where he'll be. We've got to grab him and get him down to the basement."

"He will resist," Alder added.

"He's an old guy. If we get that far, it shouldn't be a problem."

"What if we do not get that far? If we are separated? Or if Naymeer is not there?"

"No matter what happens with Naymeer, get to the flume. It'll be our only hope of escape."

"And go where?"

"Third Earth," I answered quickly. "That's the one thing I'm sure about. We need to find out what happened to Patrick. If we're lucky enough to have Naymeer, we'll see if getting him out of here changes Third Earth back to normal. If we don't have him, we'll regroup there."

"There is a third scenario," Alder reminded me. "If we find Naymeer, but are unable to get him to the flume, you must allow me to do what needs to be done."

"Are you sure?" I asked.

Alder looked me square in the eye. "No, but I am capable."

I grabbed Alder's arm and squeezed. "You're my brother. There's nobody I'd rather be here with. Actually, I'd rather not be here at all, but since I am, I'm glad you are too."

Alder laughed. "It is good you have not lost your sense of humor."

I shrugged. "It's pretty much the only thing I have left."

We stayed low and crept out of the neighbor's yard, headed for the Sherwood house. We moved quickly along the base of the high stone wall, like commandos, looking for the tree that Mark and Courtney always used to climb over. I held my breath. Would it still be there? It was a pretty huge security risk. If they were really trying to protect Naymeer, that tree would be the first thing to go. When I rounded the corner, I let myself breathe again. The tree was there. Idiots. We stopped at the base and looked up.

"There might be something on top," I whispered. "Like barbwire that'll make it tough to get over. Be careful."

Alder gave me a leg up and I quickly climbed. When I reached the top of the wall, I scanned both ways, looking for anything that might hurt us, or maybe trigger an alarm. There didn't seem to be anything. That was weird. Naymeer was a controversial guy. I thought for sure he'd need big security. Things didn't look any different from when the house was empty. Dumb for him, good for us. I reached down for Alder and helped him climb up. I didn't want to be on top of that wall for a second longer than necessary. As soon as Alder was up, I dropped my legs over the other side, lowered myself until I was fully stretched out with my hands on top, and let go. After a drop of a few feet, I was on the ground, inside the compound. I crouched down against the wall, wishing I were invisible.

A second later Alder's huge form dropped down next to me. We were in. No alarms were triggered. No floodlights bathed the place. No hounds came running. Until that moment I didn't think we stood a chance of getting close to Naymeer. After getting as far as we did, I was beginning to think we actually had a shot. I tapped Alder's shoulder. The two of us crouched, and sprinted across the grass toward the house. We made it to a large bush of something-or-other that had grown next to the rail of the porch. We stayed close to it and rounded toward the front door. We had yet to see a single guard. The thought hit me that maybe it was because Naymeer wasn't even there. That might explain the lack of security. Alder and I could be going all Navy SEAL while Naymeer was halfway around the world. I pushed the thought out of my head. If Naymeer wasn't there, fine. We'd go to the flume and find Patrick.

I led Alder up onto the porch, trying not to make the wooden stairs squeak. Our next challenge would be to get inside the door. That's when the fireworks would start. I figured the door would be hooked up to an alarm, and once we broke in, there would be people descending from all over.

"Do we break it down?" Alder whispered.

"I think that's the only way," I answered.

We both took a step back, ready to smash it open with a double kick and start the party.

"Wait," I said.

I stepped forward, reached out for the door handle . . . and opened the door. It was unlocked! I looked at Alder and shrugged. This wasn't making sense. I had to figure that if the perimeter security was lacking, at least the security of the house itself would be good. It wasn't. Alder and I were able to walk in as if we owned the place. He followed me in; I gently closed the door behind him; we both turned for the stairs . . .

And came face-to-face with Naymeer's dog.

We froze. At first I thought it was a quig, but this dog was a sweet-looking black Lab. She sat on the bottom step with her ears up and her head cocked, as if thinking: "Who the heck are *you* guys?"

I knelt down and put my hand out in a friendly, nonthreatening gesture. I wanted to give her a good scratch behind the ears and send her on her way.

That's not what happened.

The dog must not have understood the universal "I've put my hand out, so I'm cool" gesture. She started barking. Loud. Really loud. The house was so deathly silent, it sounded like thunder exploding inside. I guess Naymeer didn't need a fancy alarm system when he had Old Yeller standing guard. The clock had started ticking. We had to get to Naymeer before his guards got to us. Alder and I started for the stairs just as one of the red-shirt guards made an appearance. He ran into the foyer from deeper in the house. One guard. A single guard. What were they thinking? They'd have to do better than that if they were going to keep us from Naymeer. Alder and I leaped at the guy. He didn't stand a chance. He went for his Taser. I launched myself at his legs, feetfirst, knocking him forward. Alder hit him as he fell. The guard had been in the room, conscious, for maybe three seconds. He wasn't anymore. Conscious, that is.

I ran for the stairs.

"Pendragon?" Alder called.

It surprised me that he called so loudly, but quiet didn't count anymore. Not with Underdog still bellowing at us. I looked back to see Alder kneeling over the fallen red shirt.

"Leave him," I commanded.

"Look at this," Alder said, ignoring me.

"Alder, c'mon. There's gonna be more."

"That is what I am afraid of."

It was something about the grave way he said that that made me stop and focus. I jumped back down the stairs, past the barking dog, and ran to the kneeling knight. Alder held up his hand. In it, was an ear. The guard's ear. My first thought was to retch. My second thought was to wonder why Alder would pick up the gruesome trophy. My third thought was the only one that counted. I took the ear. It didn't feel right. Not that I'd ever held an ear before, but something was definitely off. It didn't feel human. I looked at the unconscious guard. He was lying injured-ear-side up. Alder had knocked the ear clean off when he pounded the guy. There was no blood and no wound. Where the ear had been was a smashed piece of computer board.

"It's a dado," I gasped.

"Of course it is," came a voice from across the foyer.

Alder and I both jumped to see Alexander Naymeer standing in the doorway that led to his office. He wore a deep red bathrobe over pajamas. Even at that early hour, the guy looked perfectly put together, like some kind of magazine ad for elderly slick guys in Vegas or something.

"All of my guardians are dados," he continued. "They make excellent guards."

The dog continued barking, even though her master was there.

"Nevva!" Naymeer commanded. "Come."

The dog instantly stopped howling and ran to him.

"You named your dog 'Nevva'?" I asked.

"After my former nanny. I believe you know her."

I didn't answer. I hadn't thought about Nevva since I left Ibara. Was she lurking around somewhere? Could she possibly have taken on the form of a dog? It didn't seem likely.

"Please," Naymeer said cordially. "Join me, won't you?"

He turned and went back into his office, leaving Alder and me alone in the foyer.

"This is just odd," I whispered.

Alder followed the old man. I followed Alder. When we entered his office, Naymeer was headed for his desk, to pick up what looked like a TV remote control.

"I'm pleased that you two are here," Naymeer said calmly. "It saves us all the trouble of hunting for you."

It would have seemed so normal and cordial, if he hadn't used the word "hunted." That wasn't a cordial word. Still, the whole British thing with the accent and the civility made it seem as if we were welcome guests.

On one wall was a huge, flat-screen TV that I hadn't noticed the first time we were there. It looked like it was tuned to CNN.

"I am surprised you arrived so early in the day," he continued. "Why is that? Did you expect to catch us all napping?"

Of course he was right, but we didn't give him the satisfaction of answering.

"I don't sleep much," he continued. "There's too much happening. I've already had breakfast. Would you like something to eat?"

Our answer was to stare at him. Naymeer shrugged and pointed the remote at the screen. Instantly the news went away as the on-screen image divided into several smaller pictures. A close look showed the feed from surveillance cameras that covered every possible angle of the compound. I felt Alder tense up. He wasn't used to watching TV. Heck, he wasn't used to any kind of technology. He'd probably freak if he saw an electric toothbrush.

"Are you surprised how easily you made it through to me?" Naymeer asked.

He gestured for us to look at the screen. We watched several different images of ourselves being played back simultaneously. We were recorded running toward the house from next door, creeping along the wall, climbing up the tree, climbing over the wall, and running to the house. Here we thought we were being so stealthy. They were watching us from the second we got within shouting distance.

"What is this magic?" Alder asked in awe.

"It's not magic," I answered. "It's the surveillance I told you about. Oops."

Naymeer added, "Suffice it to say, leaving the compound won't be nearly as easy."

He pointed the remote, and the screens changed to what looked like live pictures from the same surveillance cameras. Several red-shirt guards took positions at the front gate, at the front door, and at the four corners of the outside walls of the compound. In other words, we had walked into a trap.

"No matter," Naymeer said jovially. "I'm sure you don't wish to leave so quickly. Not after going through such trouble to see me." He put the news program back on and sat behind his desk. "You caught me as I was preparing for this evening's conclave. I would love it if you honored me by attending as my guests."

"What's a conclave?" I asked.

"A small gathering of the faithful," Naymeer answered, waving his hand as if it were nothing. "Tonight should be especially eventful though. We're preparing for the big night tomorrow."

"What will happen tomorrow?" Alder asked.

Naymeer's eyes went wide. "You can't be serious! It's the night of the General Assembly vote! It's nothing less than the event that will decide the future of mankind." He got a mischievous gleam in his eye and added, "And the future of Halla."

I wanted to jump over the desk, yank him by his expensive robe, and drag him down to the flume right then and there. I might have tried, too, if the TV news show hadn't caught Naymeer's attention.

"Shhh!" he commanded, looking to the screen.

Alder and I looked to see a dark-skinned man being interviewed. He was introduced as Professor Haig Gastigian of New York University, the leader of a group called the "Foundation." Mark and Courtney had told us all about the guy. He was the one sane voice that anybody seemed to be listening to.

On the screen, Gastigian said, "To say this has gone too far is a gross understatement. For the General Assembly of the United Nations to allow a single entity to dictate matters of morality is nothing short of fascism. There are far too many people who will not sit still and let these Ravinian people impose their value system on the world. We plan on staging a protest outside of the United Nations, beginning today and carrying through the vote tomorrow evening. In addition, as a show of strength and unity, there will be a major rally beginning tomorrow evening—"

Naymeer clicked off the TV and tossed the controller onto his desk in disgust. "Gastigian and his people call themselves the 'Foundation,'" he scoffed. "Foundation of what? Failure? Excuse? Whimpering? Thinking that a group of loudmouthed ne'er-do-wells can stand up to us is exactly why we have become so powerful. Ravinia is about taking positive, decisive action, not whining and fearing change. Do they have any idea that their complaining and negativity is their downfall?"

There was plenty to discuss with Alexander Naymeer. But not then. Not there. I glanced at Alder and nodded. It was time.

"I want to hear all about it," I said as the two of us stalked toward Naymeer's desk. "Let's take a trip first."

"Excuse me?" Naymeer said, genuinely confused.

"And please," I added. "No whimpering."

"Wha—"

Alder grabbed the guy's arm and twisted it behind his back.

"You're hurting me," he complained.

"Nuh-uh," I cautioned. "No whimpering."

"I will not hurt you, so long as you do not resist," Alder said to the man.

Naymeer didn't fight. "You realize this is futile," he said.

"Let's find out," I replied, and walked for the door.

Alder followed with Naymeer. The dog named Nevva sat on the couch and didn't so much as whine in protest. It seemed as if this Nevva was just about as loyal as the original. When we exited the office, four red shirts arrived, each carrying Tasers.

"Stand back," Naymeer ordered them. "I must not be harmed."

The guards looked confused. Or as I've written before, as confused as a dado can look. They kind of bumped into one another as they jockeyed to get out of our way. I ran to the door that led to the cellar and the flume.

"Go," I commanded after opening it.

Alder pushed Naymeer ahead and down the stairs. I looked back at the dado guards and said, "You bozos wait here. We won't be long." I closed the door, leaving them standing there, befuddled.

"What is the point?" Naymeer asked as Alder wrestled him down the stairs and through the basement. "Do you think taking me away from Second Earth will change anything? Ravinia is more powerful than any one man. All will continue as planned whether I'm here or not. This is all so futile."

"Maybe," I said. "Maybe not. We'll know for sure in a couple of minutes."

"What? How?" Naymeer asked.

"We're going to see the future."

We stopped at the wooden door with the star. The gate to the flume. I took a second, and touched the star symbol that had been burned into the door.

"This star used to represent something special," I said to Naymeer. "Something bigger than all of us. This star said Halla. But you took it and made it into something small and hateful. You feel good about that?"

Naymeer lifted an eyebrow and said, "What makes you think that star ever represented anything other than the pursuit of perfection that is Ravinia?"

I wanted to hit the guy. Especially if he was right. I didn't want to believe that the star was put at all the gates solely to mark the way for Saint Dane's crusade. That would have been too horrifying to even think of. So I didn't. I pulled open the door and motioned for Alder to take him into the root cellar.

"We'll all travel together," I said as I stepped into the

mouth of the flume. "I don't want to risk this guy getting away and—"

The flume came to life.

It began to crack and writhe as light appeared in the deep distance. I shot a look to Alder. I wasn't sure why. He didn't have any more answers than I did.

"This is my lucky day," Naymeer said with a confident grin. "It looks as if I'm to be receiving additional guests."

I jumped out of the flume and stood with Alder and Naymeer, our backs to the far wall. The gray stones of the flume turned to crystal. A shadow appeared. A tall shadow. A single Traveler had arrived. He walked slowly from the depths of the flume and stood with the light at his back.

The light didn't disappear. That meant only one thing.

"I'm honored that you've all come to greet my return," Saint Dane said. "I trust you're getting acquainted."

"We're taking him out of here," I shouted.

Saint Dane laughed. "Why would you do that? You wouldn't want him to miss all the fun, would you?"

"Let's go," I growled to Alder, taking his arm and pulling him toward the flume. I didn't care if Saint Dane was there. I was ready to bowl him over. We had to get Naymeer away from Second Earth. We had to change the future.

It was going to be harder than I thought. More shadows appeared from deep within the flume, walking toward us in two military-like lines.

Alder and I stopped short. "Dados," he declared.

They all wore the red-shirt uniforms of Naymeer's guardians. Naymeer was right. It was going to be a lot more difficult leaving the house than it had been getting in.

We weren't ready to give up. I spotted the two dado-killing rods that we had brought from Denduron. They were still on the dirt floor where we had dropped them when we were Tasered on our arrival.

"Let him go," I commanded Alder, while diving to the ground and grabbing the rods.

Alder pushed Naymeer away. I tossed him a weapon.

Saint Dane stood in the center of the flume with his legs apart and his arms folded. He wasn't about to move.

"Must you always be so difficult, Pendragon?" he asked, bored.

"Uh, yeah" was my answer, and the fight was on.

The dados jogged past Saint Dane on either side of the demon, headed for us. I dropped my rod down to my waist, ready to use it like a prod. I nailed the first dado in line, instantly feeling his power going out. I pulled the weapon back and jabbed again at the second. They didn't know what hit them. Wherever these dados came from, it wasn't Quillan. They knew nothing about the power of these weapons. We had a chance.

Naymeer ran from the root cellar. I didn't care. We had to get out of there and go to Third Earth, where we could figure out another plan of attack. Alder took out the dados one by one. The bodies were piling up, but more red shirts marched from the depths of the flume. Many more.

I heard Alder gasp. He'd been hit. I wasn't sure by what. A Taser? The butt of a gun? He staggered. I went to him to try and keep the dados off him. It was the last move I made. There were too many of them. As soon as I jumped to Alder's defense, I felt a sharp shot to the back of my head. I fell forward, dropping the weapon. Alder was already flat out. I was on my knees, about to join him. I took another shot to the side of my head and went down, hard. The last thing I remember seeing was Saint Dane's smiling face looking down at me.

"Always the hard way," he said, shaking his head.

JOURNAL #36

(CONTINUED)

SECOND EARTH

"How are you feeling?"

It was a deep voice that sounded vaguely familiar. How was I feeling? I wasn't sure I wanted to know the answer.

"Like I was hit by a bus," I croaked. Of course, I'd never actually been hit by a bus, but I was pretty sure that this was what it would feel like. I struggled to pull myself out of the dark pit of the unconscious, knowing that when I got out, I wouldn't want to be where I found myself. I opened my eyes. At least I think I did. It was hard to tell, because everything was black.

"Alder?" I asked.

"He is fine," came the deep voice.

Who was that? Why did he sound so familiar? I blinked. It didn't change anything, other than to make my head hurt. I decided not to blink anymore. I was lying out flat on something soft. At least somebody had tried to make me comfortable. Good for them, whoever they were.

"Over here, Pendragon," the voice said.

The third time was the charm. I recognized the voice. I

wanted to be unconscious again. I looked toward my feet to see him standing over me, lit by a small lamp near the end of the couch I was on. The light hit him from below, like when you hold a flashlight under your chin to look all spooky. But Saint Dane didn't really need any lighting effects to help with his creep appeal. He loomed over me like a vulture, his bald head in shadow caused by the light of the single bulb.

"Welcome back," he said warmly, as if he actually meant it. "I was afraid you'd miss the festivities. Close your eyes; I'll put some lights on."

What a courteous guy! He didn't want me to be uncomfortable when he flicked on the lights. How thoughtful. I'd have thanked him, if I hadn't wanted to hurt him.

Saint Dane walked slowly to a wall panel and turned a dimmer switch. The room slowly grew brighter, and I got a view of the space. It looked like the waiting room at a doctor's office. I didn't think for a second that Saint Dane would have taken me to a doctor. There were a couple of couches and chairs with tables. One whole wall was covered by heavy red drapes that were probably blocking a window. I was lying on a couch along one wall. My head hurt. I wasn't sure if I had been knocked out by getting hit or being Tasered. Probably both. Bottom line was, I felt like, well, like I had been hit by a bus.

Saint Dane walked toward me. Except for the fact that he had lost his gray hair when his head caught fire a while back, the guy hadn't changed a bit since the day I'd first seen him. He still stood tall and ramrod straight. He still wore that black suit. He still had those blue-white eyes that burned into my head whenever he looked my way. He still made my skin crawl.

"Can I ask you a question?" I said groggily.

"I'd be disappointed if you didn't."

"How many of those suits do you have? Do you like, send them to the laundry, or just toss 'em out and put on a new one when it gets all gamey?"

Saint Dane chuckled. I amused him.

"Does it matter?" he asked.

"It was a joke, idiot." On top of everything else wrong with him, Saint Dane didn't have much of a sense of humor. Except when I amused him. Which happened a lot, I'm sorry to say.

"I'm glad to see that you're in a good mood. You should be. Our struggle has finally come to an end. Perhaps we should celebrate."

"Perhaps you should bite me."

Saint Dane cocked his head, confused. "I'm afraid I don't understand that remark, but I'll assume it's a provocation. There's no need for hostility between us anymore, Pendragon."

"I'll be the judge of that."

He sat down in a chair across from me. I tried to sit up, but decided my aching head preferred that I stay on my back. What the heck. I didn't need to be polite to this guy.

"You'll soon learn that I speak the truth," Saint Dane said calmly. "The Convergence is well under way. The territories are becoming one. All is as I anticipated it would be. Our duel is complete."

"You keep talking as if this were a contest between us," I said.

"It is. It was."

"Then why didn't somebody tell me that from the beginning? You can't have a competition when only one side knows the rules."

"It was the only way," Saint Dane explained. "This has been a battle to determine the future of Halla. Though not in the conventional sense. If you were to have understood the stakes from the beginning, it would not have been a fair demonstration."

"Demonstration of what?"

"The quest for control of Halla was never about armies or physical strength or even technology. It was about a battle between two basic, philosophical differences. It was about determining which is the more effective way to play out one's destiny. By chance or by design. I, of course, believe in design. You and your sort prefer to let fate lead you where it may. If you knew that issue was at the core of our struggle, you would not have had a fair chance to prove your philosophy."

I finally sat up. I didn't care that my head was being pounded by a sledgehammer. "What philosophy? I don't have any philosophy."

"But you do. At every turn you have made choices based on the belief that the people of Halla know what is best for them. Correct?"

I didn't answer.

"Press told you that the territories should never be mixed. Each culture, each society, each world, each *individual* should be given the chance to live its own destiny without interference. Am I wrong?"

"No."

"Of course not. And I have proved time and again that the people of Halla will consistently make the wrong choices."

"Because you've pushed them into making the wrong choices," I exclaimed.

"Only to prove my point. Do you honestly think the

battles we've been through are the only cases of misery in the history of Halla? Pendragon! I know you are still just a boy, but certainly you know that each world has its own legacy of violence and strife that has nothing whatsoever to do with me. I didn't invent conflict. Quite the opposite. I'm trying to end it."

My head hurt, and not just because I had been beaten up.

"So what?" I exclaimed. "What's the point? Let's pretend you're not lying. Again. Let's say that everything that's happened between us was all some huge philosophical debate that used the people of Halla as pawns. Why? Who are we trying to prove something to? Who's running this, Saint Dane? What's the prize? If this war is truly over, then it won't make any difference if you let me know what's going on."

Saint Dane blinked. I saw it. He didn't answer right away either. It was the best possible response I could have hoped for.

I smiled.

"It's not over, is it?"

"It was over when you quit, Pendragon," he spat at me. "It was the ultimate display of weakness. You are incapable of making difficult decisions. You flinch in the face of adversity. Your so-called morals have been your downfall. When you buried the flume on Ibara, it opened the door for the Convergence."

"But it isn't over, is it?" I said, goading him.

Saint Dane's face grew dark. His eyes flared. He stood quickly and strode to the panel with the dimmer switch. He hit another button. The red drapes that covered the one wall parted automatically. I struggled to stand and look at what was being revealed. There was a long glass window, but it didn't look outside. I had heard all about this place from Mark and Courtney and Patrick, but seeing it was still a shock. Hearing about it and seeing it for myself were two different animals. I couldn't breathe.

The window overlooked a huge room that seemed to me like a cathedral. Or a big theater. There were multiple rows of green seats all facing the same direction, with a center aisle dividing them. It was exactly as my friends had described it. It wasn't a cathedral. It wasn't a theater. Roughly ten yards in front of the seats, was the flume.

"Look familiar?" Saint Dane asked. "This is the flume that was unearthed next to the subway tracks in the Bronx. It's now the Conclave of Ravinia."

The room we were in was some kind of private viewing area that overlooked the seats from a level above. To the rear of the huge space was a wide staircase. I saw people coming down and filling up the rows. They could have been arriving for a church service. Or a movie. Or a school play. There were all kinds of people. All races. All ages. I saw families with little kids and people who arrived alone. They all seemed to be dressed pretty well. Some had what looked like traditional costumes from other countries, and some even wore military uniforms. They filed in quickly and quietly. Several of the red-shirt guards were stationed around, leading people to their seats like ushers. They didn't have guns. I wondered if the people knew they were robots.

There were two flags on stands up front, one on either side of the flume. There was an American flag and a red flag that had the star symbol on it. Saint Dane and I stood there, looking down at the growing crowd. He let me take in the scene for a few minutes before speaking again.

"This conclave is the prototype," he explained. "The first. It will be repeated throughout Halla. I will admit to you, though the end result was never in doubt, events did not play out precisely as I anticipated."

"So what's different?" I asked.

"I fully expected you to become the leader of Ravinia."

I laughed. "Me? You thought I was going to be like that guy Naymeer?"

Saint Dane nodded. "How many times have I asked you to join me? I felt certain that eventually you would see reason and take your place at the forefront of this movement. I was wrong. It was not meant to be. I'm not sure if I should commend you, or pity you."

"There was zero chance of that happening."

"Apparently. And so the honor went to Naymeer. He is now the Traveler from Second Earth and the leader of a revolution. Your loss."

"What's this all about?" I asked, gesturing to the rapidly filling space below. "What are they doing here?"

"Naymeer was given the key to Halla," Saint Dane answered, pointing to the Traveler ring on my finger. "A key you have as well, but Naymeer was not afraid to use it for more meaningful pursuits than sending mail. He opened the door for the chosen. The Ravinians. They will be the leaders of a new Halla. The same will happen on each and every world. The truth of the grander existence of man will be revealed to those who are worthy of leading the way. Those people down there are the first. Many more are joining every day, from all over the world. They are not necessarily people of wealth or power, but they share a common philosophy. They do not tolerate anything less than absolute perfection."

"There's no such thing as perfection," I countered.

His eyes flared. His lips curled into a smirk. "Not yet."

I wanted to hit the guy.

"Weakness will not be tolerated. On any level. The advancement of our societies will be the singular goal. It is all about the greater good. There will be no room for pity or second-guessing."

"And no room for humanity," I added.

"Humanity is nothing more than an acceptance of failure. We do not accept failure. The goal is too great."

"And what exactly is that goal?" I asked.

"Utopia."

I had to let that sink in. Saint Dane really believed he was working to create an ideal Halla. Trouble was, there was no place in that ideal world for most of the people already in it.

"What about Third Earth?" I asked. "You destroyed an ideal society. That's not exactly Utopia."

"It is no longer about territories, Pendragon. There were ten territories but only seven worlds in Halla. Each will have to be torn down and stripped of its prior imperfections before it can be allowed to truly flourish. What happens on Earth is simply part of that process."

"Do those people down there know that they're setting something in motion that will lead to the ruin of their own society?" I asked.

Saint Dane chuckled. I was amusing him again.

"They know sacrifices must be made. They accept that. Part of their strength is the ability to make difficult choices. That's why it was so important to reveal the true nature of Halla. They understand there is life beyond the few meager years they will spend here. They are working to create a perfect, eternal life for themselves as citizens of Halla. The same will happen on each world. It will begin with conclaves such as this. The strong will join together to unify Halla. There will no longer be barriers."

Things were becoming clear to me, and totally overwhelming. The Convergence was going to create a single, unified Halla that was under the control of Saint Dane. For the first time, I was beginning to see how it might be possible.

"You know you're a total hypocrite," I said.

"And how is that?"

"You've based your whole philosophy on the fact that the people of the territories make dumb, selfish choices that hurt them in the long run. Yet that's exactly what you're taking advantage of. You're tempting these people with the promise of some kind of perfect existence. Aren't those people down there being just as selfish as anybody else? I guess that means you think it's okay to be selfish, so long as it helps you get what you want."

"There is a difference," Saint Dane replied. "Yes, I've influenced these people through Naymeer. I've tempted them. I've given them hope for a better world. But in this case, the choice was mine, and I am correct. If Halla is to flourish, my way is the only way. These people simply recognize that fact."

I looked at the demon, who was keeping his eyes on the people as they filed in. The room was nearly full.

"Then what have you proved?" I asked. "Only that people will always try to make a better life for themselves."

"I have proved that left to their own devices, they will never find it. People need guidance from a higher authority. Someone with vision. I have that vision. It will now become a reality."

"This is insane. You can't create two different classes and think that the normal people of the world will let it happen. No way."

"Then how do you explain the stand taken by the United Nations? That august, respected voice of this world will vote tomorrow to adopt our positive way of thinking as an international standard. Is any more validation needed than that? People want simple answers, Pendragon. They want to be shown how things can be made better. They're tired of pulling the deadweight of society. Ravinia gives them the chance to fly, not just survive."

"And what happens to those who don't fit your perfect profile?" I asked.

"They will perform important functions. There will always be a need for pure, simple laborers."

"Slaves," I said with disdain.

"Call it what you like."

"They'll try to stop you," I warned.

"They will regret it," Saint Dane said ominously.

Before I could ask him what he meant by that, a door opened to the rear of the room. Two red shirts entered, followed by two more. It took four of them to keep Alder under control.

"Ahh, our dear friend from Denduron!" Saint Dane exclaimed. "Just in time."

Alder's hands were tied in front of him. I imagined the hard time he had given the dados.

"You all right?" I asked.

He nodded. I saw a huge black-and-blue mark on his cheek. I wondered how many of the dados he took out before they stopped him. Two of the red shirts left. The other two stayed and stood inside the door. I guess they were expecting more trouble.

"Look," Saint Dane exclaimed, gesturing to the viewing window. "It begins."

Alder and I stood together at the window and looked down. The place was packed. Every last seat was taken. The lights went dark. I felt a collective rush of anticipation from the people below. Everyone was at attention, waiting for . . . what? A pin spot of light hit a sole figure that stood near the mouth of the flume. Naymeer. He wore a long, dark robe, making him look like a monk. The crowd gasped, as if they were in the presence of a rock star.

"Behold," Naymeer's amplified voice boomed. "Halla."

Naymeer held up his fist. Beams of laserlike light shot from his ring, spraying the room with color. The light danced over the faces of the assembled, who let out a collective sigh. They all had these serene looks, as if they were being kissed by a thousand tiny angels. I was less impressed. It was the same kind of light that sprang from the flume whenever it was activated. Okay, maybe I never saw it come from a Traveler's ring, but still. It wasn't all that new to me. I found myself rubbing my own ring. I had no idea it contained that kind of power. I looked at Alder. He stared at the spectacle, expressionless.

The light flashed into the flume. Instantly the gray rocks of the tunnel began to glow. Naymeer had activated the tunnel. The rocks turned crystal. Light sprang from the flume itself. Was somebody on the way in? A ball of light erupted from the mouth of the tunnel, creating a brilliant flash. When the flash subsided, it was my turn to gasp. Three-dimensional images floated near the mouth of the flume.

Images of Halla.

"The island city of Faar from Cloral," Naymeer announced.

I saw the mountain city that had risen from beneath the sea. Hauler submarines floated around it, as if suspended in space. It was incredible. The image was clear, yet transparent.

I couldn't take my eyes off it. I didn't think anybody else could either. No wonder they were all so impressed by Naymeer and his promises of other worlds.

"Faar will be the home for Ravinia on Cloral," Naymeer's voice boomed. "As will the village of Leeandra on Eelong, and Xhaxhu on Zadaa. Each world will have its own Conclave of Ravinia, as we have here in New York."

My stomach now hurt as much as my head. It felt like a fantasy come true. A horrible, evil fantasy. As amazing and real as it was, I didn't get how these people could buy into it so easily. I mean, I knew it was real, but to the people of Earth it just as easily could have been a hologram movie as a glimpse into another world. Why did they buy into it without any doubt?

My answer came quickly. Shadows appeared through the image, moving forward. I soon realized they weren't shadows at all, but very real people, who were walking out of the flume. The brilliant images of Cloral were sucked back in by the flume, as if it were a vacuum cleaner that controlled light. In a moment the flume went dark, and a spotlight shone on a group of five people standing beyond the mouth. I didn't recognize any of them. They were five normal-looking people. Two men and three women. They wore clothes from Second Earth. They stood together, holding hands. As soon as the light hit them, they raised their clasped hands in triumph. The crowd jumped to its feet with excitement while applauding and cheering. Another group of people ran from the side to greet the five who had arrived through the flume. They hugged and kissed as if they were greeting loved ones who had returned from a long trip—which is exactly what they were.

Naymeer's voice proclaimed, "Our latest travelers, back

from Cloral, where they enjoyed the wonders of that world of water."

"So it is true," Alder said softly. "Anyone can travel."

"With the help of Naymeer," I corrected.

Naymeer continued, "Ravinians are joining together throughout Halla, sharing our views, planning our future. We are not alone. There are no boundaries. There is so much more to life then we ever imagined. It is there for us all to share. The chosen. The visionaries. The elite."

"As I have been saying," Saint Dane declared, "the Convergence has broken down the barriers between worlds."

I realized how Naymeer was able to convince his followers that Halla was real. He showed them. He let them explore other territories. Other worlds. It truly was a Convergence. Of all the things I had seen in my years as a Traveler, this spectacle seemed the most incredible. Yet it was all too real. Ravinia was going to spread throughout Halla, dividing the classes and mixing the destinies of every world. Saint Dane's vision was becoming a reality.

A group of red shirts hurried in and gently escorted the newly returned travelers and their loved ones away. The spotlight returned to Naymeer, who stood in the center of the flume. He raised his hand and the crowd instantly grew quiet.

"They will soon share with us the wonders of their travels to another world—wonders that, in time, you all will have the opportunity to experience yourselves. But first we must acknowledge the wonder that is about to happen right here on our own world. We are on the verge of seeing our dreams become reality. Tomorrow is a day that will go down in history as the beginning of a new Halla. Tomorrow is the day when, if all goes as we expect, the United Nations will accept us as the voice of our world."

An excited cheer went up. These people were out of their minds with joy. Through Naymeer, Saint Dane had done a real number on them. They fully bought into Ravinia and its philosophy. And why not? They were being tempted with the ability to travel to other worlds. It had to be pretty staggering to learn that there was so much more to the universe than they thought, and that they were the only people who were going to be allowed to take advantage of it. I guess the same kind of thing had happened to me, only I saw the darker side to it all. It didn't seem like these people got any hint of that. No way.

Naymeer raised his hands again.

"As much as this is a time to celebrate, we must remain humble. There are those who still oppose us. Those who do not understand. Those who will never share in the glories of Halla. They are deserving of our sympathy."

The crowd didn't peep. I didn't feel a whole lot of sympathy going on. Man, who did they think they were? How could they be brainwashed into believing they were so superior? I glanced over to Saint Dane. He had a small smile on his face. That was my answer. Saint Dane had convinced them. Through Naymeer, he had seduced them into helping him begin his final assault on Halla. As Alder and I stood in that room, next to the guy who was the architect of this horror, I had no idea what we could do about it. I was beginning to accept the fact that Saint Dane was right. I was beaten.

Naymeer continued, "Right now, outside the sacred walls of this conclave, a group has gathered to protest our very existence. Might I say, once the teachings of Ravinia are instituted, such crass showings will be a thing of the past."

I saw the people nodding to each other knowingly. Creeps.

"There will be no more protests. No more dissension. No more violence. There will be only one voice. The voice of Ravinia. The voice of Halla. Your voice."

"There goes freedom of speech," I said.

Saint Dane didn't react.

"On the eve of such a historic occasion, I would like to invite some of our detractors to join us. To see what we are about. To get a small taste of the wonders of Halla."

A concerned murmur went up. The people didn't expect that. How could Naymeer suggest bringing the unwashed masses into their perfect little temple? Naymeer raised both hands and added, "I assure you, this will be a night that none of us will forget. Nor will our detractors. I beg your patience and understanding."

The room lights went on. Naymeer strode away from the flume, walking directly up the center aisle. He was quickly joined by six guards, who surrounded him in a protective cocoon. They walked past the adoring yet confused eyes of the Ravinians, toward the rear of the room, and climbed the stairs.

"What's going on?" I asked.

Saint Dane left the window and walked to the opposite wall. There was another red drape, much smaller than the one that was pulled back from the window looking down onto the flume. Saint Dane touched the wall panel. The smaller drape slid open the same way, revealing another window. He gestured for us to join him. I didn't want to be anywhere near the guy, but I had to see what was happening.

Alder and I reluctantly joined him and looked out of the window to the street below. It was night. We were in the familiar Bronx neighborhood that used to be home to the subway station that held the gate to the flume. Mark and Courtney had described the huge, marble structure that we were now in. We were looking down from the second or third floor. I could see the marble steps leading down to the street . . . a street that was packed with people. Protestors. They carried signs that read: WE THE PEOPLE . . . and LIBERTY AND JUSTICE FOR ALL. According to Saint Dane, these were the bottom-feeders of society. The losers who were nothing more than a drain on the world's resources. From where I stood, they looked like regular people. *Angry* regular people. I could hear them chanting, "Stop Naymeer. Stop Naymeer."

A long line of red shirts kept the crowd from climbing the stairs. Unlike the dados inside, these guys were armed. They looked pretty imposing with their Tasers. Suddenly the chants turned to a chorus of boos. I looked directly down to see that a podium was set up on the stairs that led from the sidewalk up into the conclave building. Whatever was about to happen, it was planned. This wasn't some impromptu moment. A group of red shirts marched down the steps toward the podium and surrounded it. Naymeer followed soon after and stood at the podium, looking out over a sea of his enemies.

"My friends," his voice boomed over speakers.

This was definitely planned. They even had speakers set up. The booing grew louder. Naymeer was patient. He raised his hands to try to quiet them. These people weren't as obedient as the ones inside. They kept screaming and booing him angrily.

"Stop Naymeer! Stop Naymeer!"

Naymeer stayed cool. "Please," Naymeer continued. "I understand your concerns."

The people were having none of it. Good for them. The boos got louder. This went on for a solid ten minutes. Naymeer didn't give up. He kept trying to get them to listen, but that only made them yell louder. Finally, either they got tired of screaming or they actually decided to listen to what he had to say, but the crowd settled down enough so that Naymeer could be heard.

"Before you judge, I would like to invite some of you to come inside and see for yourselves what Ravinia is truly about."

If it was possible for an entire crowd to be confused, they were. It didn't seem as if they expected that olive branch. Their surprised looks proved that they didn't know what to think about the surprise offer. Naymeer started pointing to people.

"You, and you," he called out. "Bring your daughter. You, young man, join me inside, won't you?"

Slowly, each person he pointed to stepped forward and onto the steps of the conclave building. The red-shirt dados parted, allowing them to pass.

"Yes, come forward," Naymeer encouraged from his podium. "Don't be afraid."

The people were tentative, but they climbed. A few red shirts met them and escorted them up and into the building. Before the last volunteer went inside, he turned and threw his arms up in a sign of victory and defiance. The little girl who was the guy's daughter did too. The crowd cheered, then started to chant again. It now felt like a charge to those who were headed inside.

"Stop Naymeer. Stop Naymeer."

I looked to Saint Dane. "Has this ever happened before?"

"No," he said coldly. "It is unfortunate that it had to come to this."

He left the window, leaving us with that ominous statement. What was going on?

"I don't like this," I whispered to Alder.

We followed Saint Dane back to the inside viewing window. The Ravinians were as well behaved as the crowd outside was unruly. When Naymeer appeared at the bottom of the stairs, they turned to him and watched politely. There was no cheering. No chanting. No urging him on. Following Naymeer were his red shirts, after which came the group of nervous outsiders. A quick count told me there were ten people, including three kids. They didn't seem scared, but they were definitely intimidated. All eyes were on them. They huddled closer to one another for support as they made their way toward the flume. One of them caught sight of the tunnel and nudged another. Soon they all saw the tunnel that led to the territories. Their mouths hung open as they drew closer.

Naymeer was back in his position, next to the opening to the flume. "Come now, right this way," he urged the people warmly. Invitingly.

They were brought to the front of the audience and stood in a group near the mouth of the tunnel.

"There," Naymeer said cordially. "Thank you for joining us. This is a night you will not soon forget, nor will your friends outside. You are about to experience the true power and majesty of Halla."

Alarms were going off in my head. Something was wrong. Why were these people crowded together in front of the flume like this? Like . . . like sheep. The words that Patrick had written suddenly came back to me.

N. exiles enemies through flume.

Was that it? Were these poor people going to be made an

example of? Was that going to be his demonstration of the power of Halla? My mind was racing. I had to do something, but what?

"Ahh," Saint Dane exclaimed. "A few stragglers have arrived."

We looked down to see the red shirts were escorting two more outsiders up the aisle. These two weren't going as easily as the others. The red shirts held each by the arm and pushed them forward. The two didn't fight; they knew it was futile. But they didn't go quietly, either. The people in the seats whispered nervously as they passed. They began to realize something was wrong too.

Alder stiffened. My knees went weak. I pressed my face against the glass. My heart raced. The two new arrivals were Mark and Courtney.

Alder gasped out Patrick's other words: *"Begins with Bronx Massacre."*

"Yes," Saint Dane confirmed. "This is where it truly begins."

JOURNAL #36

(CONTINUED)

SECOND EARTH

I whirled to Saint Dane.

"What's going on?" I demanded.

Saint Dane was smug. I hated smug. I've mentioned that before, right?

"You predicted that the enemies of Ravinia would try to stop the movement," he declared. "Once they understand the consequences of their opposition, their will to rebel will disintegrate."

Mark and Courtney were gently, yet forcefully, pushed into the group. The twelve stood huddled together directly in front of the flume. What they didn't realize was that a group of red shirts was moving in behind them. Circling them. Cutting off any chance for escape.

Naymeer stood in the center of the flume, facing them. "I am sure you've heard rumors about the worlds of Halla," he announced to the newly arrived group. "It's true. The people in this room have witnessed the wonders. Now, tonight, you will be given the same privilege." He raised his hand. Light flashed from his ring. The people huddled closer as the flume activated.

Naymeer continued, but when he spoke, his benign grandfatherly tone took on a firm, dark edge. He stared the group down and declared, "When those who oppose us learn of what transpired this evening, they too will realize that the rise of Ravinia is inevitable. There can be no opposition."

With that, Naymeer stepped aside to reveal the light that had appeared deep in the recesses of the tunnel. The group stood together, transfixed, staring into it like deer caught in the headlights. Mark and Courtney tried to move away, but were forced back into the group by red shirts who were ready for them. Mark looked concerned, but Courtney was clearly scared. The people in the audience whispered to one another. They were just as clueless about what was going to happen as I was.

I take that back. I wasn't totally clueless. I feared that we were about to witness the Bronx Massacre.

"Stop it!" I shouted to Saint Dane.

Saint Dane remained calm, with his arms folded. "Now why would I do that?"

These people were about to become victims. Whether it was to be exiled somewhere in Halla or to be executed, they would never see this life again. They were to become a warning to the world not to challenge the Ravinians. Naymeer promised his own people Utopia. He was about to promise something much worse to those who opposed him. They were about to be sacrificed in the name of Ravinia. This was the beginning of Ravinia's reign on Earth. . . .

And Mark and Courtney were caught in the middle.

I ran for a table that sat against the far wall.

"Guards," Saint Dane called out, barely concerned by my move.

The red shirts ran for me. Too late. Alder launched himself at the dados, laying them out flat with his body parallel to the ground. I picked up the table and hurled it at the glass. Saint Dane dove out of the way. That was okay. He wasn't the target. I wanted to break glass. The table hit the window, creating a spider web of cracks without breaking through.

Alder took on both the red shirts, keeping them away from me. His hands were tied, which made it more of a fair fight. I didn't know how long he could keep them occupied. I didn't need long. Saint Dane stepped directly in front of the cracked glass and faced me. The growing light from the flume filled the huge room below, casting him in shadow.

"Must you always prolong the inevitable?" he asked, sounding bored.

"Uh, yeah," I answered.

He was in the perfect spot. Right in front of the damaged glass. This was going to feel good. I sprinted right at him. His eyes opened in surprise. He didn't have time to react. I nailed the demon dead on, driving my head into his chest, knocking him back into the glass. The already damaged glass shattered, and the two of us launched into space. We fell through a blizzard of glass, plummeting toward the poor people who were directly below. I grabbed on to Saint Dane's jacket, determined to keep him between me and the ground. If anybody was going to get hurt, I wanted it to be him. Not that I had thought it through, but I suppose I had a flash of hope that we'd land on some unsuspecting, soft Ravinians who wouldn't be able to get out of the way in time.

I don't know what or who we landed on, but we did land. Hard. I was aware of a jumble of arms and legs and screams as people dove out of the way. I was shaken, but okay. I landed squarely on Saint Dane and was thrown against the backs of some chairs. When I looked to him, he was gone. No, that's not right. He was still there, but he had changed. Transformed. He had become a clean-cut-looking guy with short hair and a red golf shirt. He sat up, not hurt in the slightest.

"Stop him!" he shouted while pointing at me.

Nobody listened. They didn't want any part of me. They backed away as if I were radioactive. Saint Dane may have considered them perfect. I considered them cowards.

Crash! I looked up to see one of the red shirts had been thrown through the window. Alder was back in charge. The guard plummeted down, along with the shattered glass. He landed against the back of a chair and bounced. Seriously. Dados bounce.

Bedlam was breaking loose. Between the flume activating and bodies crashing down from above, the Ravinians wanted out. They starting pushing their way toward the stairs.

Bright light filled the room. I didn't have much time.

"Courtney!" I shouted. "Mark!"

I climbed up on a chair to see the red shirts pushing the group of frightened people toward the flume. Courtney heard me and turned.

"Bobby!" she screamed.

Her eyes were wild. She was terrified. She tried to fight her way back, but a red shirt grabbed her by the waist and pushed her forward. Closer to the flume. By this time the other people in her group knew something was wrong. They tried to resist, but the ring of dados closed on them, forcing them toward the light. I jumped down from the chair, pushing my way through the fleeing Ravinians, desperate to help these people. To help Mark and Courtney. It was impossible to move. There were too many people pushing against me, moving the other way. I was stuck. The music from the flume grew louder. I climbed back up on a chair just as the group of people were shoved into the tunnel, along with several red-shirt dados.

Mark fought his way out of the crowd. For a second I thought he was going to get away, but he turned back and tried to grab Courtney's hand to help her. He was more worried about her safety than his own. That was Mark. The move cost him. A red shirt ran up from behind and pushed them both back into the pile of victims. The light enveloped them all. The music was deafening. A moment later it ended. The light disappeared. The music died. The last sound I heard was the faint echo of Courtney's voice calling, "Bobby!"

The Bronx Massacre.

They were gone. But to where? Were they dead? Or exiled to some unknown location? Whatever the truth was, Naymeer had sent a message. Don't mess with the Ravinians. Or else. I couldn't let myself believe that Mark and Courtney were dead. I had to tell myself that they were just . . . gone. Thinking any other way would have crushed me. Knowing that they were out there somewhere, needing my help, gave me new strength. That was good, because I was still in the thick of it.

Naymeer was gone. So was Saint Dane. The red shirts weren't. From my perch on the chair I saw several of them pushing their way through the crowd to get to me. I was about to jump down when I felt my legs go out from under me. The dado that Alder had bounced down from above was still in play. He flipped me to the ground, but I went down kicking. I nailed his knee. Hard. It may have been a dado, but feeling his knee give way was gruesome. It didn't stop the dado from coming after me. After all, it was a robot. He reached down, and was about to grab my shirt when he was suddenly picked up and thrown aside like a puppet.

Alder stood over me. His hands were untied.

"We must go," he said.

I bounced to my feet and looked around to find the best way out. I thought of going for the flume, but there were too many Ravinians and red shirts between us and the tunnel. The only logical way to go was with the flow of people who were desperately pushing to get to the stairs that led up out of there.

"Go with the crowd," I instructed Alder.

We pushed our way through the mass. The dados were after us. Our best hope was to keep as many Ravinians as possible between us and them. I didn't think the dados would hurt the Ravinians to get to us. After all, they were the chosen people. They were the future. All I cared about was that they would be our shields. Politeness didn't count. I barged past them, not caring if they were offended or bruised or angry. We fought our way to the stairs and climbed to the top. I kept glancing up and around, to see how close our pursuers were. They were all still at the bottom of the stairs and having just as much trouble getting through the crowd of Ravinians as we were. I actually thought we were going to make it, until we reached the top of the stairs and ran outside.

The line of red-shirt dados that was holding the crowd back was still there.

The Ravinians were quickly funneled off to the side of the building, where two columns of red shirts formed a clear alley for them to hurry past the angry protesters. A line of buses was fired up, and waiting to take them away from the madness. We couldn't go that way. The corridor of dados was too narrow. They'd spot us for sure. Even if we made it to a bus, we'd be stopped before we got on. No, we had to break free from the crowd and take our chances on our own.

The protesters on the stairs crowded against the line of red shirts. There were thousands of them, all wanting to break through and storm the conclave.

"Pendragon, look," Alder shouted.

A group of red shirts had climbed up and out of the flume room, headed for us. We were trapped between them and the line of red shirts below us on the stairs. We were moments away from being swarmed. I could only think of one thing to do.

I started a riot.

"They're not coming out!" I shouted to the angry mob of protesters. "Naymeer killed them all!"

Under normal circumstances, shouting something like that would have been a totally irresponsible thing to do, like shouting "fire" in a crowded movie theater. These weren't normal circumstances. The effect was instant. The crowd turned violent. While some ran off in fear, most of them pushed past the line of red-shirt dados to storm the conclave. The guards Tasered a few, in a futile attempt to keep them back. No go. There were too many. The red-shirt dados were stampeded. Now the crowd was headed toward us. We stood frozen on the stairs as the mob came our way. I glanced back up to see the dados who were chasing us had decided it was more important to protect Naymeer than to recapture Alder and me. They fled back inside the building and were quickly shuttering the large doors. The conclave would survive intact. I wasn't so sure I could say the same for Alder and me.

Alder grabbed my arm and took off to our right. I felt like a tailback running behind a pulling guard. Alder picked a spot that wasn't so dense with people and bulled through. I tripped down the stairs, banging into people as I went. Frankly, there were so many of them, it kept me upright. I kept bouncing off of people like a pinball. Alder didn't do much bouncing. It was more like mowing. I don't know how many people he ran over. Too many. These people were victims. They had only begun to live a life of misery, thanks to the Ravinians. A life they didn't deserve. I hated to have to start it with violence, but we had to get away. It only took a minute for us to land at the bottom of the stairs and the backside of the surge of people. I grabbed Alder's arm as a signal for him to stop. We both looked back up the stairs to see the crowd banging on the doors of the austere building, desperate to get inside and learn the fate of their friends.

"We gotta get away from here," I said to Alder, and took off running.

The farther we got away from the conclave building, the sparser the crowd became. We made it. We got away. But our night was only beginning. I saw a subway entrance and led Alder down. I didn't know where to go other than to get as far away from the Ravinians as possible. We didn't have any money, so we both jumped the turnstile and walked out onto the platform to wait for a train. I had to give Alder credit. He followed me through this strange world without question. I couldn't begin to imagine what must have been going through his head as he experienced the alien world that was Second Earth. Or maybe he wasn't shaken by any of it. After all, there were bigger issues to deal with than learning what a subway train was.

Thankfully, a train pulled into the station quickly. The

doors opened and Alder followed me on. We took seats at the rear of the near-empty car. It was the first chance we had to catch our breath since I saw Mark and Courtney being led to— I won't even finish that sentence.

"What do you believe happened to them?" Alder asked.

"I don't know. I can't believe they were all just . . . executed. What would the purpose be?"

"To eliminate their enemies and intimidate those who remain," Alder answered.

"Yeah, but Patrick wrote that Naymeer exiled his enemies. I said before, exile isn't execution."

"Then why was it called the Bronx Massacre?"

I didn't know. I didn't want to know. What I wanted was to have Mark and Courtney back. I think I was in shock. That's the only way to explain how I could keep going without being crushed by the events we had witnessed. We were traveling downtown into Manhattan. With each stop, the subway car took on more passengers. I didn't know what to do. After having bounced around between territories for so long, it was a strange feeling to be home and not know where to go. I had to think, but the memory of Courtney and Mark being tossed into the flume kept invading my head. If nothing else, I swore to myself that I would find out what happened to them.

The train made a stop at a busy station. I didn't know which one. The platform was crowded and people jockeyed to get off and on before the doors closed. At the far end of the subway car, I saw a cop get on. A regular old New York City cop. Nothing strange about that, except that he seemed to be looking for something. Or someone. Or two someones . . . us. That wasn't the worst part. The cop wasn't alone. With him was a Ravinian red shirt. They were both searching the faces of the people on the subway car. That meant the Ravinians and the New York City police force were working together. The implication was huge. The Ravinians were already working their way into positions of power with the government.

"We gotta go," I whispered, and pulled Alder toward the door. The bell rang. The doors began to close. I threw my arm out and pushed the sliding doors back open. There was no way I'd let us get trapped on a moving train. We weren't going to make it that easy for them. It was my turn to get Alder through the crowd. We couldn't be as bold as we'd been in the Bronx. We didn't want to attract attention. We were being hunted by the Ravinians and now the police. We were fugitives here, just as we were in Stony Brook. It was going to be easier melting into Manhattan than the suburbs, but still, eyes were everywhere. We were going to have to find somewhere safe to hide.

I led Alder up and out of the crowded subway station, to discover we were in the middle of busy Times Square. Alder finally balked. I guess being bombarded by the lights and sounds of one of the busiest intersections in Halla was a little much for a knight from a primitive village. He stood frozen, staring up at the noisy spectacle. I didn't push him. The chances of us being seen by the police were slim. The sidewalks were packed with tourists. No way we'd stand out.

At least that's what I thought, until my eyes settled on the giant video screen that loomed over the crossroads.

"Pendragon, it is you," Alder said with surprise. He saw it too.

It was a still picture of me that must have been taken

from the surveillance cameras at the Sherwood house. It was a grainy blowup of a video freeze-frame, but it was definitely me. As stunning as that was to see, the words superimposed under the picture were even worse. Beneath my admittedly guilty-looking face were the words "ROBERT PENDRAGON—SUSPECTED DOMESTIC TERRORIST."

It was a news report. A warning. There was no sound, but the words that ran along the bottom of the screen said it all. "WANTED IN CONNECTION WITH ATTACK ON RAVINIAN CONCLAVE. EXTREMELY DANGEROUS. IF SIGHTED, DO NOT APPROACH. CONTACT POLICE."

My picture was replaced by another. Alder's. Alder gasped. It was also taken from the surveillance footage. Similar words crawled beneath his picture, warning people to contact the police if these two dangerous terrorists were sighted. The feeling was hard to describe. We were standing in the middle of a thousand people, yet I suddenly felt alone. Naked even. It was like one of those dreams where you find yourself out in public in your underwear. Only we were being accused of a lot more than walking around in boxers. I was a fugitive in my own home.

"They are hunting for us," Alder said in a small voice that was not like him.

"It's worse than that. It means they've gotten to the media. There's no report about a dozen people disappearing in the Bronx, only about us. The Ravinians' influence is everywhere."

"Then we are truly too late," Alder said, defeated.

The image of Alder on the giant screen was replaced by another. It was the man we had seen on TV that morning in Naymeer's office. Again there was no sound to the report, only words that crawled across the lower part of the screen. He was identified as: "HAIG GASTIGIAN—NEW YORK UNIVERSITY." The scrolling words read: "PROFESSOR CONDEMNS IMMINENT UNITED NATIONS DECISION. CALLS FOR WORLDWIDE PROTEST AGAINST ALEXANDER NAYMEER AND THE RAVINIANS."

"Maybe not," I said. "That guy's the leader of the opposition. What's it called? The 'Founding'? No, the 'Foundation.'"

"What about him?"

"He may be the only person with any power who's left on our side."

An hour later Alder and I arrived in Washington Square Park at the bottom of Fifth Avenue. We walked the whole way, for fear of being spotted on the subway. The park was the center of New York University, the college where Gastigian was a professor. It was pretty simple to find him. I looked in the white pages of a phone book. Duh. There weren't a whole lot of Haig Gastigians listed. In fact there was only one, and it was in Greenwich Village, near the university. The address was on Sullivan Street, a quiet, tree-lined street of brownstones. Finding the address was easy. Getting to see Gastigian wasn't. I knew we had come to the right place when we turned onto Sullivan Street and saw a group of scary-looking guys camped out in front of Gastigian's address under a streetlight.

"Guards," Alder said, reading my mind.

"Smart move. It's not healthy to mess with the Ravinians."

We saw more men stationed at every street corner, watching for trouble. They were ordinary-looking guys, but not the kind you'd want to mess with. They were big and they were serious. They must have heard what had happened at the Ravinian compound. These guys looked like the type to want revenge.

"Act unintimidating," I said as we walked toward the building.

"How do I do that?"

"Smile and don't take a defensive stance."

"What if they attack us?"

"Let them."

We had only gone a few steps when I sensed that we were being followed. I didn't have to turn around to know there were a couple of big goons shadowing us. I was pretty sure that Gastigian didn't have high-tech surveillance cameras like Naymeer, but his security was just as effective. Before we could step up to Gastigian's door, a ring of thugs closed around us.

"Remember," I whispered. "Unintimidating."

Alder put on a totally false smile that looked more creepy than friendly.

"Lose the smile," I said quickly. "Just don't hit anybody."

"Can I help you fellas?" said one of the larger characters, who stood between us and the door.

"We'd like to see Professor Gastigian," I said in my most polite voice.

Two other thugs joined the first. They exchanged looks. It was pretty clear that they had no intention of letting us see him.

"Really?" the first guy said sarcastically. "What for?"

"We have information about the Ravinians he'll want to hear" was my honest answer.

The thugs exchanged looks again. They didn't look like rocket scientists. I wasn't sure if that was good or bad.

"Tell you what," the guy said while pressing closer. He had to be six inches taller than I was, which made him even taller than Alder. I stood my ground and hoped that Alder wouldn't pop him. "Make an appointment. The professor's a busy guy."

"I'm Bobby Pendragon," I blurted out.

The guards looked at me blankly.

I took a breath and added, "We're the ones who attacked the Ravinian conclave tonight."

The big guy raised his eyebrows in surprise. He opened his mouth to speak, but nothing came out. Instead we heard a man's voice coming through the security speaker in the door. "Send them up."

Apparently Professor Gastigian had electronic eyes and ears after all.

Professor Haig Gastigian lived in a simple, neat apartment that had a cool view of Washington Square Park. It was exactly the kind of place I expected a professor of philosophy to live. It was small and full of books. Alder and I had to move several volumes off the couch so we could sit.

Gastigian entered the living room carrying a tray with a teapot and three cups. He treated us like welcome guests. The guard who sat at the door, though, let us know we weren't completely accepted. Gastigian looked to be in his sixties, with dark skin and a head full of pure white hair that he combed straight back. He wore big, square glasses right out of the seventies that made his eyes look twice their size. He wore a buttoned-up sweater, a blue bow tie, and walked with a kind of stoop and shuffle. If I were making a movie and had to cast a guy to play a philosophy professor, Gastigian would get the nod.

"Is it true what they say?" he began. "Are you terrorists?"

"Depends on your definition," I answered. "Are we trying to spread terror? No. Are we trying to stop the Ravinians?

Absolutely. So to them we're terrorists. I guess that makes you a terrorist too."

Gastigian gave me a sly smile. "Call me Haig," he said. I think he liked me. That was good. People who liked me were in short supply lately. He poured us tea. I was never much of a tea guy, but I was starving. Alder was too. We didn't waste any time in downing our cups and polishing off the stale cookies he put out.

Haig took his own cup and sat back in his easy chair, totally relaxed. "It never ceases to amaze me how gullible people can be. The promises that Naymeer feeds the world on a daily basis are shameless. He tells people what they want to hear, like a politician running for office. It would all be laughably harmless if people weren't actually listening, and if his ideology didn't involve the persecution of so many. Those are the people I speak for. The people who will be left out of his grand scheme. There are plenty of us, I'll tell you that. We aren't going to sit still and let this fascist consume us." He took a sip of tea and continued, "So tell me, gentlemen, how is it that you found yourselves giving Naymeer a run for his money, hmmm? I must say, I've never had terrorists to tea before."

I hadn't thought about what I would say to Haig. He might have been the last person in the world who had any kind of hope of slowing down the Ravinians, but I was afraid that when he heard what I had to say, he'd throw us out. Still, we had to take the chance. I decided that the only way to go was to tell him the truth.

"You're not going to like what we have to say," I began.

"I don't like much of anything I hear these days. Try me."

"Okay. The trouble is, the things that Naymeer is saying aren't fantasy. You may have trouble believing it, but it's all true. Halla is real. There are other worlds besides our own. You said you speak for the people who will be left out of his grand scheme? You have no idea how many people that really is. What's happening here is going to happen everywhere else. If he isn't stopped now, it will be the end of it all."

Haig held the teacup to his lips but didn't take a sip. He stared at me for a long moment, placed the cup back onto the saucer, put the saucer back on the table, then sat back and folded his arms across his chest.

"You have my attention," he said.

Alder and I spent the next hour telling Haig the highlights of what we thought he needed to know. We skipped over many details of the struggle with Saint Dane. In fact we skipped over Saint Dane altogether. What we concentrated on was Naymeer, and his use of the flume to show his chosen people the other worlds of Halla, and how he planned on creating a superrace of achievers to control all that exists, at the expense of those who might have less to offer. Haig listened intently. More so than the guard at the door, who I think fell asleep. Haig never took his eyes off us. Besides trying to digest what we were saying, I figured he was also trying to judge if we were crazy or not. I wouldn't have blamed him if he decided we were.

I ended by saying, "What happened tonight at the conclave was the beginning of something evil."

"The Bronx Massacre," Alder added.

"There's no other way to say it," I continued. "If given the power, Naymeer will do the same to anyone who threatens him. The fear of being shipped up there and tossed into the flume will get his enemies to back down. I think that if the United Nations accepts Ravinia, there won't be anything stopping Naymeer. That's why we came to you. You have the ear of the opposition. You are the voice of the Foundation. The voice of reason. Something must be done to stop Naymeer. Now. Today."

I grabbed my cup of tea and remembered it was empty. I didn't care. I had to do something other than look into Haig's questioning glare. The man sighed and stood up. He ran his hands through his white hair. He was sweating. He was shaken.

"I know," I added. "It's impossible to believe."

"Not so impossible," Haig said. He stood before us and pushed up his sleeve. On his arm was the Ravinian star tattoo. Alder sat up straight, as if he had been hit with another Taser. I probably did the same thing.

"I—I don't get it," I gasped.

"I have seen many of the things you speak of," Haig said. "I have sat in that conclave and witnessed sights from throughout Halla. I am a believer."

"But . . . " was all I managed to croak.

Haig pushed his sleeve back down and returned to his chair. He sat forward, leaning his hands on his knees, speaking with passion. "Knowing that we aren't alone in this life is both frightening and thrilling. But instead of treating this reality as an opportunity to enrich everyone's lives, Naymeer and his people have used it as a weapon to further their own elitist goals. Yes, I was a Ravinian. *Was.* I'm a professor of some note. I was selected. Once I realized where it was all leading, I left. I couldn't be part of it. Instead I used my knowledge and influence to build the Foundation. I was the first to raise a negative voice against the Ravinians. I'm sure they want me dead, or to throw me into the flume as they did those poor people this evening. Why do you think I need the protection of these guards? If not for them, I'm sure I would be gone by now. So yes, Pendragon. Alder. I believe you."

I wanted to jump across the table and hug the guy. We had an ally. A true ally. With power.

"So maybe there's still hope," I exclaimed.

Haig shook his head gravely. "Hope? That's a fragile concept. For all that I've done, I'm afraid we're tilting at windmills. Ravinia has become very powerful. Naymeer is spoken of in the same breath as respected world leaders. People believe in him. They don't want to hear the downside of his vision."

"So that's it? We're going to roll over and give up?"

"No," he said adamantly. "There is one last opportunity. Call it my last hurrah. The United Nations is voting tomorrow evening. Of course we have organized a protest to take place outside their headquarters in midtown. But the truly impressive display will happen at the same time in another venue. The Foundation has reached out to people from all over the world who fear the Ravinians. I'd venture a guess that there are more people out there who are against Naymeer than with him. Call them 'the silent majority.' I'm anticipating a showing that is seventy thousand strong. The eyes of the world will not only be on the United Nations, they will be on us. The common people. We will not be ignored. We will not be silent anymore. Our numbers are strong and we will prove it, in force."

"That's incredible," I said. "Do you think it might sway the UN vote?"

Haig shrugged. "Who's to say? At the very least, it will be seen by people all over the world. Perhaps it will convince them to think twice about Naymeer and all that he stands for. Your coming to see me could help with that."

I looked to Alder. He shrugged. "How?" he asked.

"Your name is known, Bobby Pendragon. A few years ago you made national news when you disappeared along with your family. It's a fascinating mystery that has never been solved, until now. Your return, and the story you can tell of Halla, might open the doors of possibility for all people, not just the Ravinians. Naymeer has guarded the truth about Halla, keeping it for himself and his minions, excluding those who were deemed unworthy. You can change that. You can offer up the truth to the world. The whole world. Present Halla as a wonder for all to share. You'd be empowering the common man. Who knows? Armed with the truth, it might give them the will to reject Naymeer and his cult of the elite."

My head was swimming. Haig wanted me to go before seventy thousand people, no, the entire world, and reveal the truth about Halla. How could I do that? It was a huge request. A huge responsibility. On the one hand, given what was happening with the Ravinians, Haig could be right. It might actually help. Still, my first thought was to say no. In my gut it felt like the exact opposite of what Uncle Press said was one of the most important responsibilities of a Traveler. We were not supposed to mix territories and their natural destinies. Explaining the nature of Halla to the people of Earth felt like I would be doing exactly that.

But things had changed. With the Convergence, was that no longer an issue? There were plenty of people who knew about Halla already. Heck, the Ravinians were traveling to other territories, thanks to Naymeer. The flumes had become busy highways. Maybe keeping silent about Halla was actually giving the green light to Naymeer. If his people knew the truth, why shouldn't everyone?

It was a bold step, but I decided that Haig was handing us the one tool we didn't think we had. He was offering us a platform to speak to the world. I had told Alder that world opinion was much too vast and complicated for us to influence. I told him we had to think small. I was wrong. With Haig, we were able to think as big as Earth. That was worth the risk. We had to take the chance. Besides, we had nothing to lose.

"All right," I said. "I don't know what I'll say, but I'll try."

Haig reached out and gave me a friendly slap on the knee. "Good man," he exclaimed. "Who knows? Perhaps your mission as a Traveler was always about this one moment. Seize it, Pendragon. Your words to the world might be the deciding factor in saving Halla."

I looked to Alder. He smiled, but uncertainly.

"If we're not arrested first," I said, half joking.

"You won't be," Haig answered. "You'll be my guests tonight. Sleep here. Order pizza . . . or whatever it is you eat on—what's the name of your home, Alder? Denderoon?"

"Close enough," Alder answered, actually having fun with it.

Haig jumped up. He was excited. "Boys," he said, "for the first time in a very long while, I'm thinking we might actually stand a chance."

Alder and I did exactly as instructed. We ordered pizza. Pepperoni. It was delicious. Alder drank Coke for the first time and didn't like it. I didn't know why. Maybe he's a Pepsi guy. Haig set us up in his guest room, where there were twin beds. It was a luxury compared to the places we'd been crashing lately. I spent a few hours writing this journal, to try and get my thoughts down. Writing this one has been tougher than most, because I don't know if Mark and Courtney will ever get the chance to read it.

You know what? Lose that. I have to be positive. Mark, Courtney, you *will* read this someday. Since day number one, writing these journals as if I'm talking to you has helped keep me sane. I'm not going to stop now. When you read this, know that I'm worried as all hell about you right now, but I have faith that you're all right, and someday we'll see one another again. Count on it.

Alder and I went to sleep that night with the faint hope that in spite of all that had happened and all that had gone wrong, there was still a slim chance that the people of this territory, of Second Earth, would see reason. We had to find hope somewhere. As someone once said, without hope, you have nothing.

It took a while for me to get to sleep. As exhausted as I was, I couldn't get the image out of my head of those poor people being thrown into the flume. Of Courtney. Of Mark. I tried to think ahead to what we would do if Haig's rally failed and the UN passed its resolution, but I couldn't. It was too much. One major hurdle at a time.

Once I finally conked out, I slept like the dead. I think we both did. We didn't wake up until almost noon. Haig had breakfast waiting for us. Or maybe it was lunch. Whatever. It was a delicious feast of bacon and eggs and pancakes and so many other delights I hadn't had since I lived at the Manhattan Tower Hotel. Haig was off making preparations, so Alder and I watched TV. We saw news reports of the members of the General Assembly arriving in New York for the vote. Those images were countered by footage of people arriving from all over the world for the Foundation's rally. It was like Super Bowl Sunday, with planeloads of people flooding out of the airport. It was a welcome change to see the other side of this drama. There were people out there who cared. Who didn't buy into Naymeer's elitist cult. They were regular people who feared what their lives would become under this new and frightening way of thinking.

We also saw news bulletins about the hunt for the terrorists. Us. There were stories about the strange disappearance of Bobby Pendragon and his family. The newscasters actually speculated that since my disappearance, I had been training in terrorist camps in Asia. Unbelievable. Naymeer's propaganda machine was in high gear. I took it as a good sign. People were being reminded about Bobby Pendragon. That could only help when I went before the world that night to tell my true story.

Yikes.

Finally, at around three o'clock, Haig returned to his apartment.

"Ahh!" he exclaimed with a smile. "I see that you were not arrested."

"So far so good," I replied.

"It's time to go. I have two cars waiting outside. You will follow me."

Alder and I got up and grabbed our sweatshirts.

"Hey, you never told us where this rally is going to be," I said.

Haig smiled proudly. "I managed to secure one of the most hallowed venues in all of New York. Arguably in the entire world."

"Really? Where?" I asked.

"Yankee Stadium," he announced with a sly wink.

"We're going to the Bronx! Tell me that won't get noticed!"

With a spring in his step, Haig left the apartment.

Alder and I didn't move. Haig's words were like a shot to the gut.

"What is a Yankee Stadium?" Alder asked uneasily.

"A sports arena," I answered, numb. "Home of the most famous team in baseball."

"It is a large venue?" Alder asked.

"Huge. Think of the battle arena that was part of the Bedoowan castle. You could fit ten of them inside Yankee Stadium."

"And it is in the Bronx?"

I nodded. "Seventy thousand people. All together in the same place. All enemies of Ravinia."

The two of us stood there; we were both thinking the worst.

"Pendragon," Alder finally said with caution, "is it possible that the horror we witnessed last night at the Ravinian conclave . . . was *not* the Bronx Massacre?"

JOURNAL #36

(CONTINUED)

SECOND EARTH

Alder's fear was the same as mine. Twelve people had been thrown into the flume the night before. The jury was still out as to their actual fate, but even if they had been executed, did that constitute a legendary massacre that would be spoken about in dreaded whispers for centuries? Would the disappearance of twelve people create such fear of the Ravinians that the entire world would tremble and fall to its knees?

It suddenly seemed unlikely. The loss of twelve people, though tragic, wouldn't have that kind of impact. The loss of seventy *thousand* people would.

"We must stop it," Alder declared.

"How?" I shot back. "Thousands of people are showing up from all over the world. You think they're going to cancel the whole show just because we said so?"

"Think of the alternative," Alder said with a lot more calm than I was feeling. "Seventy thousand people may be in danger. That truly is a massacre."

"*May* be!" I repeated. "We don't know for sure. What if

we're wrong? Haig said it himself. This is the last best hope to try to stop Naymeer. To stop Saint Dane. If we somehow pull off a miracle and abort this rally, we'd be killing our last chance of saving Halla."

"If we do *not* stop it, it may be the turning point of Second Earth and the beginning of Naymeer's dominance. Stopping it would save thousands of lives and alter the course of Earth's history. This might truly be our chance to stop Naymeer."

"Unless we're wrong," I argued again.

Alder and I stared at each other. Neither of us knew what to do. I grabbed my sweatshirt and headed for the door. "We won't solve anything by hanging around here."

We blasted out the door and ran down the stairs to the front entrance of the brownstone. Two black SUVs were waiting outside, along with several of Haig's bodyguards.

"We've got to ride with Haig," I said to the first guy I came to as we ran down the outside steps.

Before he could answer, the first SUV took off. Haig was on his way north. The guard shrugged an apology. I didn't waste time and went for the second SUV. Alder and I jumped in the backseat and slammed the doors. Behind the wheel was a big guy with a neck as thick as his head. He turned to us and said, "Hey, how come you two bozos get special treatment?"

I wasn't in the mood to explain anything to anybody. Especially somebody who called me a "bozo."

"Drive," I snapped.

The big guy shrugged and revved the engine. "Whatever you say. The professor says I gotta get you there, I'll get you there. That's my job. But I was wonderin' why do you two get the VIP treatment when—"

"Drive!" I shouted again.

He did. With a quick lurch, we were off.

Traffic was light, so we were able to move quickly uptown, toward the Bronx. Toward a potential massacre.

"You got a phone?" I called to the driver.

"Sure? Want it?"

"Yeah."

He grabbed his cell phone off the seat next to him and tossed it to me. "Don't go making any long-distance calls."

"I have to talk to Professor Gastigian. What's his number?"

"He doesn't have a cell," the big guy answered.

"You're kidding! Somebody in that car must have one!"

"Nope. The professor hates 'em. He doesn't let anybody carry one around him. He says we all got by just fine for a long time without cell phones."

"Until today," I grumbled, and tossed the useless phone back into the front seat.

"I do not know what to do, Pendragon," Alder said, sounding less than his usual confident self. "I am at a loss to understand your territory."

"We might be wrong. Wiping out a stadium full of people isn't exactly a small thing. Naymeer has a lot of power and influence, but unless he's got some kind of massive weapon, things might be okay."

The driver turned around and gave me a strange look. "Do I want to know what you're talking about?"

"No," we both said together.

"I hope you are right," Alder said. "My instincts tell me otherwise."

Mine did too. We had gone from thinking this rally might be the salvation of Halla, to fearing it would be the most horrific disaster in history. The Bronx Massacre. That's what Patrick wrote. We thought for sure it was the incident at the flume. But that would seem like a footnote if something horrific were to happen to a stadium full of people. Was Naymeer capable of doing something so diabolical? To what end? Fear? Intimidation? Or was having so many of those opposed to him, all in one place, too tempting to pass up? With one deadly swipe he could wipe out the most vocal of the people who resisted him. Would the rest of the world stand for that? Or would they be too frightened of Naymeer to bring him to justice?

How could he wipe out an entire stadium of people anyway? It was all seeming kind of far fetched. I hoped I wasn't talking myself into believing that everything was going to be fine, but the hard truth was that even if we knew for certain the people in the stadium were in danger, we had no way of helping them.

I had been to Yankee Stadium many times before. I'm a Yankees fan. Or I *was* a Yankees fan. I had no idea who was on the team anymore. Or who the manager was. Or who had won the last four World Series. It seems strange to think how important baseball used to be for me. My dad took me to a lot of games. He even took me and Uncle Press to a World Series game. Yankee Stadium was a special place for me.

When we crossed the bridge to leave Manhattan, we saw it. I caught sight of the familiar blue letters that ringed the upper rim of the stadium and made a brief wish that someday I'd get the chance to see a ball game again. Any ball game. Anywhere. I might as well have wished to sprout wings and fly.

The parking lots surrounding the stadium were already packed. The rally was under way.

"Where do we go?" I asked the driver.

"We're gonna drive right inside near left field," he answered. "I never been down on the field. Maybe I'll get a Yankee autograph."

The guy was an idiot.

Alder stared up at the stadium, wide eyed.

"You were not exaggerating," he said. "It is colossal."

There was a big police presence. I guess that's what happens when a protest is going on. Especially one with multiple thousands of angry people. Alder and I ducked down, in case some overeager cop recognized us and decided to be a hero by bringing down the terrorists. We drove along the outer wall of the stadium that ran parallel to the third-base line. The police waved us through with no problem. As we swung around toward the gate in left field, my eye caught something. Parked across the street from the stadium was a line of buses. They looked like the same buses that had picked up the Ravinians after the abrupt end of the conclave. I wouldn't have thought twice about it, except that standing at the doorway to each of the buses was a red-shirt dado. Why were they there? This wasn't a Ravinian show.

I nudged Alder and pointed. He saw the dados and frowned.

"That is not a good sign," he said gravely.

We didn't have time to wonder what it could mean. Our car was being waved inside an open gate. We had arrived. Though I had been to Yankee Stadium many times, the first moment that I got a peek inside the park itself was always a breathtaking one, if only for the sheer size of the place. A day at the ballpark was as much about the sensory experience as it was the game. I loved seeing the perfectly manicured, brilliant green grass and razor-sharp diamond.

We drove through the gates, past the bull pen, and right onto the warning track in left field. It was like a dream come true for a baseball fan. Too bad I wasn't enjoying it.

Alder was so overwhelmed by the sight that he pushed himself back into his seat. It wasn't exactly like going to a ball game, but the experience wasn't any less impressive. The place was packed. I mean, totally packed. World Series packed. There wasn't an empty seat anywhere. You couldn't even see the aisles, because people crowded the stairs. A big stage was erected over second base, complete with a lighting grid and a huge bank of speakers. If I didn't know better, I'd say it was set up for a rock concert. It even sounded like one. A guy with a guitar was onstage singing. I recognized him but couldn't remember his name. I know my parents listened to him a lot. I guess he was real popular back in the day, but I doubted that he ever played to an audience this big. The giant screen in center field showed his image as he sang some old song that I didn't know the name of.

People were allowed down on the field in front of the stage. They were packed in, shoulder to shoulder. Behind the stage, the grass of the outfield was empty. A couple of cars and limos were parked there, which is probably how the performers got in and out. Even the outfield bleachers were packed. Standing room only. In all, it was an impressive rally. Professor Gastigian had done his job. It was actually good to see how many people were willing to take a stand against Naymeer and the Ravinians. I had to believe that these people represented only a fraction of the people in the world who didn't agree with him, or his vision. It made me feel as if there might be hope yet.

It also scared the hell out of me. If anything bad were to happen here, anything, lots of people would get hurt.

The idea of Naymeer trying something so villainous seemed impossible. But the impossible often happened. Every day.

The driver steered us behind the stage, where a big, eighteen-wheeler truck was parked.

"The professor's in there," he said. "And hey, if you see a Yankee, get me an autograph, all right?"

"What is a Yankee?" Alder asked.

The driver gave him a sideways look. "Where you from? Mars?"

"Denduron, actually."

I had had enough of the witty banter with the driver, so I jumped out of the car. As soon as I opened the door, I was hit with a rush of noise. Besides the old guy onstage singing some ancient song, the people in the stands were chanting and singing. They swayed back and forth, repeating phrases like the protestors used outside the conclave: "We the people," "Liberty and justice," "All men are created equal." It seemed that whichever way I turned, I was hit with a different wave of singing. Unlike the protesters outside of the conclave, these people were calm. Police were patrolling everywhere, but there were no problems. There were homemade signs everywhere, and hands waving in the air. It was a totally peaceful, positive event. Maybe everyone was on good behavior because the world was watching. Or maybe they knew they were fighting a losing battle and this was their last party. There were TV cameras all around us, mostly on the backs of camera guys who ran around catching the flavor of it all. It was an amazing, impressive spectacle. I hoped it would stay that way.

Alder and I ran to the truck and climbed the few metal stairs that led to a door. Inside we saw it was a TV control truck. One whole wall was taken up with small video monitors that showed the feeds from the various cameras roaming the stadium. Some were on the guy with the guitar, but most of the cameras were trained on the faces of the people. As different as they all were, they shared the same sad, frightened look. They all feared that their world was about to change, and not for the better.

A couple of technicians sat in front of the monitors, with a guy I figured was the director because he was calling out camera changes.

"Camera One, pan left. Let's see some faces. Take! Ready four, pull back from the guitar. Take. Dissolve to three. Dissolve to six. Nice!" He went on and on like that. It would have been interesting if I hadn't been thinking about imminent genocide.

"Pendragon! Alder!" Professor Gastigian bellowed.

Haig strode toward us from the far end of the truck. In his hand he grasped a handful of papers. The guy was totally lit up with excitement. His eyes sparkled.

"Isn't this wonderful?" he announced. "Seventy thousand plus. They have to be taking note of this at the UN. They have to be listening." He held up the pages. "Look. E-mails. Hundreds of them. Thousands. From all over the world, offering support for us and condemnation of the Ravinians."

"Professor," I said, "we have to talk about something important."

"What's more important than this? Look!"

He led us back to the TV monitors and pointed at the screens on the far right side.

"Look there," he said. "The UN."

On several video monitors were shots of the protest happening in front of the famous United Nations building.

Hundreds of people marched with signs, chanting. It was as peaceful and impressive as the event at Yankee Stadium.

"Yeah, it's terrific," I said. "But there's a chance that—"

"Look at them. Five thousand strong at the UN alone," Haig declared. "These images are being sent all over the world, live. Every network is carrying it. Live. The news channels too."

"When is the vote?" Alder asked.

"It's happening right now," Haig answered. "They should make an announcement at any time. The eyes of the world are on us. I have to believe that goes for the General Assembly as well. This has to give them pause."

"Professor, listen, these people might be in danger—"

"Of course they are! That's what this is all about!" He leaned down to the TV director and said, "Be sure to get lots of close-ups in the stands. We have to put a face on the Foundation. We want the world to see that we're all just regular people."

Haig was too wired to listen to anything I had to say. He was like a Ping-Pong ball bouncing around the trailer. But I had to try.

"Something might happen here. Right now."

"I certainly hope so," Haig replied. "Are you ready to go out there and talk to them?"

Talk? I'd forgotten all about it. Haig wanted me to speak to this crowd. To the world. He wanted me to tell them about Halla. I wasn't ready for that.

"No, listen, we saw buses with red-shirt guards outside and—"

"Intimidation tactics. Nothing more. Are you sure you won't speak? Now is the time."

"Professor! I'm trying to tell you that Naymeer might be

planning something to hurt these people right here! Right now!"

Haig finally focused on me. I had gotten through.

"You have my attention," he said soberly.

"Alder and I heard about an event called 'the Bronx Massacre.' After what we saw Naymeer do to his enemies last night, who's to say he wouldn't try something just as horrible right here? He has seventy thousand of his enemies together, all in one place. He'll never have another chance like this."

Haig looked shaken. I'm sure he was thinking the same thing we were. If something nasty was going to happen, how could they quickly evacuate so many people? It would be impossible.

I looked to the many TV screens and the thousands of faces. I couldn't imagine the nightmare. The guitar guy had finished singing, and there was now some actor dude and his actress wife onstage, talking about the evils of Ravinia. The people had stopped their chanting and singing. All eyes were focused on the couple. I watched as one camera panned a row of people who were all looking at the stage. As the camera moved past them, I saw so many different people with so many different lives that—according to the Ravinians—were worthless. I imagined the same happening all over Halla. There would be Batu and the gars. Milago and Novans. The worlds would change, but the frightened looks would be the same.

How could Saint Dane consider these people to be worthless? Maybe they weren't geniuses. They might not have had any special talent or calling. They might not be leaders. Or visionaries. But they cared. Their being at that rally proved it. These were people who had families and friends. They cared about their futures as much as any of Naymeer's "chosen." They had come from all over the world to show just how much they cared. Didn't that count for something? As I looked at their faces, I realized that Naymeer had gotten it wrong. Saint Dane had gotten it wrong. *These* people were the chosen. These ordinary people were the life and soul of the world. Every world. There is no such thing as perfection. Anywhere. No world is perfect. It is the spirit and heart of people like these—the ordinary people—that keep it all from falling into chaos. These people are the backbone of Halla.

That's why Saint Dane wants them gone. I had been witness to countless horrors unleashed by Saint Dane. It wasn't until that moment, as I watched the faces of his next victims, that I fully appreciated how truly evil a creature he is.

I watched as one camera continued its slow pan across the many faces. Oddly, it moved past a guy who wasn't looking in the same direction as everyone else. It was so strange that it nearly made me jump. He was actually looking right into the camera, as if he knew it was there. He even had a little smile on his face. The camera continued past him and on to more people, who were focused on the stage.

"Go back. Go back!" I shouted to the people at the control panel.

One guy wearing a headset glanced back at me. "Go away!" he barked, and went back to work. I got right into his face and shouted, "I have to see somebody on that camera!" I pointed to the screen where I had seen the strange guy.

The man with the headset looked to Haig. "Who is this guy?" he asked, meaning me.

I answered, "I'm the terrorist. Do what I say or I'll terrorize *you*."

The guy focused on me. I saw a look of recognition as the color drained from his face. "It *is* you," he gasped. "The one who disappeared."

"Yeah, nice to meet you. Get that camera back where it was."

"Do it, please," Haig chimed in.

The guy was shaken. He ran his fingers over the buttons in front of him as if not sure what to do. "Uh, uh . . . which camera?"

"That one," I screamed, pointing to the monitor.

"I can play back what you saw," he mumbled nervously.

"Do it!" I demanded.

The guy fumbled with a few buttons as we all stared at the screen. He finally got the right one, and the picture did a quick rewind.

"Stop!" I shouted. "Go from there."

He hit play. We all watched the same shot I had been staring at a few seconds before. The camera panned across the sea of faces that were all looking in the same direction. It then moved past the guy who was looking right into the camera.

"Whoa, that's kind of creepy," the technician muttered.

"Freeze it!" I shouted.

The technician froze the frame. I looked right into the eyes of the smiling man onscreen. I knew him. It was the guy with the short hair and golf shirt from the conclave. It was Saint Dane.

"What is it, Pendragon?" Alder asked.

"He was at the conclave," I said. "He's a Ravinian."

"Are you sure?" Haig asked.

I grabbed the guy with the headset and squeezed his shoulder. "Where is he sitting?"

"Uh, uh . . . field level. Behind the third-base dugout."

I ran for the door. Alder caught up and stopped me before I could run out.

"Who is that man?"

"It's Saint Dane. That was the guy he turned into after we crashed through the window at the conclave. He's here, Alder."

"I will go with you."

"No, stay with Haig. Don't let anything happen to him."

"What will you do?"

"I don't know."

I left the trailer and sprinted around the stage, hitting the crowd that was being held back by blue police barricades. There was a sea of people between me and the third-base dugout. I plunged in, trying to move quickly without knocking anybody over. The crowd was pretty calm as they listened to the actors speak. Everyone moved aside to let me by. For all they knew, I was just some guy who was desperate to get to the bathroom. I finally made it to the edge of the dugout and scanned the crowd. The dugout was about twenty yards long, with hundreds of people behind it. I didn't think there was any way I would find him. Turned out I didn't have to.

He found me.

While everyone was focused on the stage, the guy who was Saint Dane was turned toward me. He was standing in the front row eating popcorn. Popcorn! We made eye contact. He waved at me. I moved along the field in front of the dugout, until we faced each other across the roof. He looked like an unassuming, clean-cut guy who was there to enjoy a day at the ballpark.

"Quite the show," he called out. "Are you enjoying it?"

"What's going to happen?"

"That would be telling," he said, teasing. "Look!"

He pointed to the giant video screen above the bleachers in the outfield. On the screen was a live image of the General Assembly room of the United Nations. It was unmistakable. The giant UN logo hanging behind the podium was an image that everybody knew. I'd seen it in a million movies, but this was the real deal. The assembly room was packed. A sober-looking man in a suit stood behind the podium. What was his title? Secretary General? General Secretary? President? Whatever. He was the guy in charge. The guy who held the future of Halla in his hands.

At the stadium, people's attention shifted quickly to the screen. The actor onstage stopped talking. An eerie quiet fell over the stadium. It was hard to believe that so many people could become so still so quickly.

This was it. This was the announcement. I knew that in a few seconds, one way or another, I would be witnessing the turning point of Second Earth. Of Halla. The man cleared his throat, stepped up to the microphone, and spoke in English.

"We live in troubled times," he began. "We speak of world peace, but that is an elusive goal. The United Nations was formed to promote peace, security, and international cooperation. Our mandate is the same today as it was then, but the challenges have evolved. We enjoy a global economy. Technology has made the world a smaller place, yet disputes between nations, peoples, tribes, and ideologies still tear at the very fabric of peace. The road we have been on for so long is deteriorating. If positive, dramatic change is not effected, the future will be a bleak one. The world needs vision. The world needs hope. Not for any individual nation, but for the world as a whole. With that in mind, today, the General Assembly of the United Nations has voted by an overwhelming margin, to designate the Conclave of Ravinia as the spiritual advisor to the member nations of the United Nations—"

I didn't hear another word the guy said. He was drowned out by boos. And shouts. And whistles. And sobs. I turned to Saint Dane. The demon gave me an innocent little shrug and fake frown, as if to say, "Sorry!"

The last bit of hope was gone. As impressive as this rally was, it had failed to make a difference. I stood there among the people of the Foundation, genuinely fearful of what would become of them in the new world order that was being formed by Alexander Naymeer. By Saint Dane.

The boos and whistles were suddenly drowned out by another sound. At first I thought it was rolling thunder, but the sky was clear. All eyes looked up toward the video screen, but it wasn't the screen that was giving off the sound. Moving through the sky, appearing over the scoreboard, were three large military-style helicopters. They swooped over the top of the stadium like three giant birds of prey, scanning for their next meal. They entered the airspace over the stadium, hovering above the empty outfield. Simultaneously, three lines dropped down to the ground, one from each helicopter. The crowd watched in wonder as Ravinian red shirts began to slide down the zip lines, headed for the stadium grass.

At the same time, the outfield fences opened and buses began rolling in—the same buses we had seen outside. I looked around to see how the police were reacting. They were gone. Not a single blue uniform was in sight.

I glanced at Saint Dane. He was gone. That surprised me. I thought he would have wanted to stick around to witness the Bronx Massacre for himself.

JOURNAL #36

(CONTINUED)

SECOND EARTH

One helicopter landed in center field. The other two remained hovering and disgorging dados. The buses charged into left and right field, digging up grass. When they stopped, the doors flew open and red-shirt dados began pouring out.

The crowd wasn't in full-on panic. Yet. As a whole, they began moving backward, as if repelled by the sight of the sudden, dramatic arrival of the red shirts. I think there was as much confusion going on as anything else. Still, the people in that stadium looked as if they all felt it might be a good idea to be somewhere else. Those who were standing in front of the stage climbed back into the stands. The people in the stands moved toward the exits. It wasn't a mad rush, but it was a definite, massive movement...

That was abruptly ended.

Red-shirt dados, spewing from every exit that led under the stands, pushed the people back. To keep them in. There was one big difference between these red shirts and any others I'd seen. They weren't carrying Tasers.

They were holding machine guns.

I looked to the higher levels, where the same thing was happening. Dados appeared at all the exits, blocking the way. Nobody was allowed to leave. The scene on ground level was more intense because of the people trying to push their way off the field.

Confusion was quickly turning to fear.

People scrambled past me, but there was nowhere to go other than to jam the field-level boxes, which were already packed with people. I knew it would only be a matter of time before panic set in. The crowd would try to rush the dados. What would happen then? Would they start shooting? Was this how the Bronx Massacre would play out? Were thousands of people about to be gunned down in cold blood?

"My friends!" came a calming voice over the stadium speaker.

I looked back to the stage to see another performer had arrived. Alexander Naymeer. He stood alone onstage, wearing his dark red robe. His face appeared on the giant video screen above.

The crowd reaction was all over the map. Some booed. Some cried. Some angrily tried to shout him off the stage. Naymeer was unaffected. He stood there with a benign smile, gazing out at the madness as if proud of his handiwork. The guy actually looked happy. And why not? He had just been given the keys to the kingdom.

"The choice has been made," his voice boomed. "Our noble cause has been recognized. A glorious future awaits, but there is much work to be done."

People tried to scream him down. Some tried to jump onto the stage, but they were thrown back by the dados that had arrived on the buses and choppers. The nightmare had been carefully planned.

"Today is the beginning," Naymeer declared. "It is a day that will forever be looked back upon as the turning point of mankind. It is the day when we grab hold of our own destiny and begin to create the life we so richly deserve."

This couldn't go on much longer. The crowd wouldn't stand for it. It was going to get real ugly, real fast. While the madness swirled around me, I was strangely calm. I guess it was because there was nothing I could do. However this was going to play out, I wasn't going to be a factor.

Or maybe I was.

Professor Gastigian was the voice of the people. If there was any hope of standing up to Naymeer, the people were going to need somebody to rally behind. I might not be able to save the thousands of poor people in that stadium from whatever fate awaited them, but I had to try to save at least one: Haig. He had to get out of there.

I took off running for the stage, which wasn't easy, because I had to weave my way through the people who were pushing the other way, desperately trying to get off the field. I knocked over more than one person as I fought my way back toward the TV truck.

"You are here today because you have made a choice," Naymeer continued. "Rather than rising to your fullest potential, you have chosen to let others lead the way for you."

Naymeer's voice had taken on that edge again. He was transforming from kindly father figure to harsh judge.

"You have chosen to tear down rather than build up. You criticize rather than strategize. Instead of working to improve your lot, you are satisfied with being carried on the backs of others."

Naymeer stalked the stage, pointing an accusing finger at the crowd. He was getting worked up. It was all building toward something that I knew couldn't be good.

"For that, I pity you. If we are to see our way through to a greater world, we will no longer make excuses. No longer tolerate lethargy. Idleness. Sloth. You have chosen your own path. You could have reveled in the glory of Halla. Instead you will be swept away by the tide of purification."

With that, he thrust his hand into the air. A single beam of light shot from his ring, headed for the sky. The crowd let out a collective gasp. They no longer pushed their way toward the exits. Every last person froze, transfixed by the dramatic sight.

I didn't stop moving. I couldn't. I was on a mission. The infield was nearly empty. The few stragglers who remained stood staring at the impossible display coming from Naymeer. From his ring. Mark's ring. The beam of light shot skyward with no end. It could have reached into space and beyond. What was it? What did it mean?

A shadow flashed on the stage. Somebody had gotten through security and was headed for Naymeer. I looked away from the beam of light in time to see who the brave intruder was.

It was Alder. He must have gotten onto the stage from behind. I guessed the guards weren't expecting an assault from backstage. It was as if time slowed down. Alder was doing what he always did—he was taking charge. He was a warrior. A knight. While I was in brain lock, already admitting defeat, Alder was taking action. Whatever the light was that sprang from Naymeer's ring, I figured it couldn't be good. Alder must have thought the same thing, because he was making a full-on assault. He sprinted across the stage. His target was Naymeer. I held my breath, waiting for the tackle.

It never came. As Alder coiled to launch himself at Naymeer, two red-shirt guards stepped onto the stage from opposite sides. Their machine guns were leveled at their waists.

"Alder!" I screamed to warn him. There was no chance that he heard me. Even if he had, it wouldn't have made a difference. I changed direction and sprinted for the stage. For my friend.

The dados fired. Both weapons clattered loudly. Alder was hit so hard and so furiously, it knocked him off course and threw him from the stage. The sight was so jarring and violent, it made me stop short. Alder landed on the dirt of the infield. He didn't move. His blood quickly mixed with the light brown dirt. People screamed in horror. The violence had begun. And Alder didn't move. Naymeer never took his eyes off his beam of light. I don't think he even knew what had just happened. He stared up at the shimmering laserlike ray as if he himself were in awe of its majesty. And Alder didn't move. I started running again. I could save him. I could bring him back to life.

I never got the chance.

Before I could reach him, I was tackled by two red shirts. All I wanted to do was get to Alder. To get my hands on him. To will him back to life. I nailed one dado in the head with an elbow, sending him reeling. The other one wrapped his arms around me in a bear hug that I tried to break, but couldn't.

"Alder!" I shouted desperately. "You're all right! You will not die!"

Two more dados joined the guy who held me. They dragged me away. Away from Alder.

"Alder!" I screamed again. "Hang on!"

I didn't have the strength to break free of the dados. I couldn't lay my hands on Alder. I couldn't work whatever impossible magic we Travelers had. There was nothing I could do to help my friend. My fellow Traveler. The guy who followed me unquestioningly. The knight who'd saved my life so many times before. Alder was dead.

He died the way he had lived, fighting for what he knew was right. I didn't even react. Seriously. How could I? Call it shock. Call it denial. Whatever. I couldn't focus on the fact that the knight from Denduron was lying dead in the dirt. Not him. Alder was invincible. It was something I knew I would have to deal with at some point, but not just then, because my nightmare was only beginning.

I desperately struggled to break loose from the dados. It was a waste of energy. They dragged me to the side of the stage, away from Naymeer. The Ravinian leader hadn't moved. The beam of light from his ring shot straight into the sky. I heard a clap of thunder. At least, it sounded like thunder. It could have been the seam between territories cracking open. Then another beam of light shot down from the sky, next to the first. It was as if the first beam hit something in the heavens and bounced back. The light hit the ground in front of the stage with another thundering boom, as if it were a bomb. The ground shook. The force of the impact knocked us off our feet. The dados lost their grip. I nearly got away, but the dados were too fast. They wrapped me up again and dragged me off. I kept my eyes on the infield. The ground was glowing. Whatever the light was, it had heat. Smoke rose from the point of impact.

Both beams of light disappeared. Naymeer took a quick look at his handiwork, nodded in satisfaction, and strode off the stage. What had he done? The light spread across the ground, creating smoke and sizzle. Every eye in the stadium was on it. Except for minc, that is. The dados pulled me behind the stage.

I saw Naymeer coming down the backstage stairs. He was met by two dados, who escorted him toward the helicopter that had landed in the outfield. Whatever was about to happen, Naymeer wasn't going to be around to see it. Or maybe he wanted to watch it from the air.

The door to the TV trailer flew open. Two more red-shirt dados blasted out. They were holding Professor Gastigian. They too must have realized how important Gastigian was to their enemies. Haig struggled against them, but it was no use. The old man couldn't battle two dados. I wasn't doing such a great job either. There was nothing I could to do help the professor. There was nothing I could do to help Alder. It was a complete and total loss. Haig was dragged toward the waiting helicopter. Surprisingly, I was too. Up ahead, the rotors of the big chopper started to whine and turn. Naymeer climbed aboard, followed shortly after by Haig, who was thrown aboard. I was last. The red shirts took me right to the door and pushed me in. I hit the deck and tried to bounce back to my feet, but a dado followed me in and pushed me back down onto the deck. He stood over me with his machine gun ready. I wasn't going anywhere.

The door was slammed shut from the outside. The dado on board reached back with one hand and threw the handle to lock it tight. The rotors whined. The chopper shuddered. Moments later we were airborne.

The helicopter looked like a military troop carrier. It was pretty much a big, flying room with bench seats along either side. Haig was on the floor in a heap. I didn't see Naymeer. I figured he must have gone to the cockpit. I rolled to my right and crawled toward the window. I needed to see what was happening below. The dado didn't stop me. I guess he figured there was nowhere for me to go. The helicopter rose quickly and hovered between the other two choppers, giving me a blimp's-eye view of Yankee Stadium. Looking down, I saw the area in front of the stage was burning. What seemed like a random fire from ground level looked very different from above. It wasn't simply burning grass. There was a pattern to the fire. A very distinct pattern. Burning on the field below was the star symbol. The people in the stadium were actually drawn to it out of curiosity. With Naymeer off the stage and the helicopter gone, they must have thought the show was over. I could see them pushing closer to the field from every level, straining to get a look at the burning symbol, as if it had all been some spectacular stunt.

It was spectacular all right. But it was no stunt.

The fire seemed to have a life of its own. Instead of burning out, it flared brighter. This was no ordinary fire. It burned into the ground, sinking lower, eating into the earth. Smoke swirled, nearly obliterating the flames. As if that weren't impossible enough, the fiery star began to spin. It was as if the symbol were a physical object. Like a demonic dygo, it burrowed into the ground, creating what at first looked like a deep pit. As it dug deeper, I could see there was more to it than that. The spinning star went straight down into the earth, leaving a wall of gray rocks in its wake. It was a sight I knew all too well.

Right there, in the center of Yankee Stadium, a monstrous flume was being born. It was larger than any flume I'd ever seen. The mouth had to be thirty yards wide.

"Quite the show," came a voice to the rear of the helicopter. It was the red-shirt dado. My antenna went up. Until then, none of the red shirts had spoken. What was different about this one?

I should have guessed. The guard lowered his machine gun, raised his arms, and transformed. Yes, it was Saint Dane. I didn't react. Nothing surprised me anymore. I was floating through a dream. The demon casually strolled across the cabin and sat down on the far side, making himself comfortable.

"Don't bother staring at *me*, Pendragon," he declared. "The show has only begun."

What did that mean? I looked back down to see the spinning star was so deep within the flume, it was no more than a pin spot of light. It had burrowed into the depths of infinity. A moment later its light winked out. It was quickly replaced by another type of light. A familiar one. From deep down inside the vertical tunnel, a faint glow appeared. The new flume was coming to life.

Seeing the tunnel activate made me realize what this was all leading to. The demonstration at the conclave the night before was prelude. This was the main event. Whatever happened to Mark and Courtney and the other poor victims was about to be repeated here . . . times seventy thousand.

I was about to witness the Bronx Massacre.

Saint Dane didn't even bother to watch. He sat straight,

with his arms folded across his chest. "I thought it was quite accommodating of the Foundation to provide us with the opportunity to make this bold statement."

"What statement?" I spat. "That the Ravinians are mass murderers?"

"The people of Earth made their choice, Pendragon," Saint Dane said with finality. "They have accepted the Ravinians' philosophy. Still, there are doubters. The events here today will prove the power of the Ravinians is absolute."

"You mean you'll create such fear that nobody would dare oppose them."

"Yes," Saint Dane declared. "We'll then move on to other territories and repeat the process."

The smoke surrounding the flume began to whirl, creating a tornado-like effect around the mouth of the tunnel. The light from down below grew brighter.

"Fear is such an effective tool, don't you think?" Saint Dane remarked. "It certainly worked to fill that stadium with thousands of people for this demonstration. Though I suppose the lion's share of credit belongs to the professor here."

Professor Gastigian finally stirred. He had been lying on the deck of the helicopter since being thrown inside. I thought he had been too frightened to move. Not anymore. He sat up slowly, looked at me, and smiled. He actually smiled. It was a totally odd reaction. His cause was lost. His movement crushed. His glorious, peaceful demonstration had come crashing down around him. Yet he sat there looking as if it didn't bother him at all.

I lied before. There were still some things that surprised me.

As he sat on the floor of that helicopter, Professor Haig

Gastigian began to transform. My stomach dropped. The nightmare had gotten worse. Seconds later the professor was gone.

In his place was Nevva Winter.

I fell against the side of the chopper, as if I had been pushed. I had seen many things as a Traveler. None shocked me as much as this.

"Well done, Nevva," Saint Dane said. "You throw quite a party."

Nevva stood up and brushed off her pants. She wore a dark suit, much like Saint Dane's. Her dark hair was as perfect as always.

"Thank you," she replied. "It really is gratifying when a plan is realized with such perfection."

"I never doubted it," Saint Dane replied.

I was spinning out of control. Any sense of reality was long gone. I needed to grab on to something solid or I'd go out of my mind.

"H-How long?" I croaked.

"How long was I Professor Gastigian?" Nevva asked. "About a year. Long enough to use his network to arrange this rally."

"This was all a setup?" I gasped. "All the speeches against the Ravinians, all the protests, all the interviews—it was just to get these people to trust you so you could lure them here?"

Nevva smiled innocently and nodded.

Saint Dane had done many horrible things. He set tribes against one another. Races against one another. Even criminals against one another. This was the single most heinous act yet. He and Nevva Winter had arranged a cold-blooded mass murder, the likes of which never had been seen anywhere in Halla. Calling them monsters would be a compliment. Together, they were the physical embodiment of evil. I couldn't look at her. I couldn't look at either of them. I turned back toward the window to see the mouth of the flume was glowing. Through the light, I saw the faint hints of the sparkling tunnel walls that had turned to crystal.

It was beginning to pull.

The people felt it. This giant, impossible hole in the center of the field was drawing them toward the edge. It wasn't dramatic, but it was relentless. The people didn't realize what was happening at first. They grabbed on to railings; they hugged each other; they clawed at the ground—all to keep from being pulled into the swirling smoke and light. I was grateful for the sounds of the helicopter rotors. It meant I couldn't hear their screams.

"Nevva, my love!" Naymeer exclaimed.

The old man stepped out of the cockpit. He went right to Nevva with his arms open, as if greeting a long-lost daughter. Or long-lost nanny. Nevva had raised him on First Earth. "This could not have gone better. I trust you weren't jostled too roughly."

"Not a bit, Alexander. Congratulations."

"To us all!" Naymeer declared.

My back was to the fuselage wall. I think I would have fallen over without that support. My heart raced. I was breathing so hard I was hyperventilating. Below us, thousands of people were being pulled to their deaths, and the people up here were chitchatting casually like old chums. I looked sideways out the window to see people being pulled along the grass, digging their hands in, desperately trying to stop themselves. They were going to lose. I saw people tumbling down from the upper decks, falling into the crowd below. Other people hung on to railings, dangling dangerously over the side, as the insistent force kept pulling at them.

Naymeer hurried to the window near me and looked below. He frowned. "Isn't this over yet?" he grumbled impatiently. "I should be at the United Nations by now. Or the White House. Or anywhere with a camera where I can speak to the world. How long will this take?"

The guy was talking about the terror below as if it were nothing more than a minor annoyance.

"Soon enough, Alexander," Nevva said with a chuckle. "You always were such an impatient boy."

"Alexander," Naymeer repeated thoughtfully. "Such a common name. Perhaps I should be knighted. How does Sir Alexander strike you?"

"If that's what you want, that's what you'll have," Saint Dane assured him. "You deserve nothing less."

Naymeer smiled, satisfied. He glanced down again and exclaimed, "Look! It's like they're being pulled down the drain of a sink. It looks quite silly actually."

That's when I snapped.

In that one instant, my swirl of confusion and shock and horror grew focused. It became rage. Everything that had happened in the previous few fateful minutes flashed through my head in fast forward. The sad faces of the people below, the UN announcement, Saint Dane munching popcorn, the predatory helicopters, the red shirts, the fear, the panic, the looks on the faces of so many people who'd had no idea that they were being lured into a trap, Naymeer's ring, the new, monstrous flume, Nevva.

Nevva Winter.

Maybe above all, I remembered the violent death of my

friend Alder. It all came back to me in a blistering barrage of images that ended on the smug face of Alexander Naymeer. The founder of Ravinia. The face of the horror. The mass murderer. It's hard to describe the anger I felt, but I'll try.

I lunged at Naymeer. It was the last thing he expected. I grabbed him by the throat with both hands. I could have squeezed the life out of him right there, but that would have been too easy.

"Pendragon!" Nevva shouted with genuine surprise.

I locked looks with Naymeer. His face was turning red. He couldn't speak. Hands crushing your windpipe will have that effect. I saw the terror in his eyes. I liked it.

"Pendragon, no!" Nevva screamed. "There are other choices."

I don't know why Nevva bothered talking. After all that she had done, did she actually think I would believe anything she had to say? There was only one thing on my mind. Revenge. I wanted to kill Naymeer. A guy who had so little regard for life simply didn't deserve to live. I pulled the horrid little man over to the door of the helicopter. With one foot I lifted the handle, released the door lock, and kicked it open. Wind filled the craft along with the thunderous noise of the rotors. Naymeer struggled futilely. He wasn't strong enough to fight me. I was being driven by insanity. I would not be denied. I forced him to look out the door, over the edge. Below us, the people were grasping at one another in one last desperate attempt to keep from being sucked into the flume.

"Look!" I screamed at him. "Is this your glorious future? Is this what the people of the world have to look forward to? Mass execution of those who don't fit your ideal?"

He closed his eyes. He didn't want to see it. I wouldn't accept that. He had to know.

"I said, 'Look!'" I bellowed. "This is your paradise. This is your Utopia."

"Bravo, Pendragon," Saint Dane said. He walked to the center of the helicopter and stood with his hands behind his back. He didn't make a move to stop me. "I knew there was another side to you. My only surprise is that it took so long to surface."

"Don't come near me," I shouted to the demon, and pushed Naymeer farther over the edge.

"I don't intend to," Saint Dane said calmly. "This is your show now."

"Bring him back in, Bobby," Nevva said with what actually sounded like compassion. I was way beyond hearing it. I tightened my grip on Naymeer's neck. He moved his eyes to look down. I don't think he cared about seeing what was happening with the flume. He was afraid of falling.

"By the way, Pendragon, did you know that the Traveler from Third Earth is dead?" Saint Dane asked. "Patrick was his name, I believe. He was killed by Ravinian guardians on Third Earth. Alder from Denduron lies dead below us. Mark and Courtney are gone as well. You've lost so many friends in such a short time. It's a shame, really. Now the man responsible is in your grasp. His fate is in your hands. Literally. Will he live to rule Earth? Or pay for their lives with his own? The decision is all yours."

I heard Saint Dane but couldn't take my eyes off Naymeer. He really was the guy responsible. He was a Traveler. He used that as a tool to gain power. It didn't matter that he was being influenced by Saint Dane. The choices were his.

He chose to create Ravinia. He chose to condemn half the population of Earth. He chose to execute thousands. He chose to kill my friends.

"It's not hard to kill," Saint Dane said in a low growl. "When it's justified."

The helicopter was hovering directly over the flume. In a matter of seconds people would start falling in.

"Bobby, listen to me," Nevva pleaded. "This isn't you. It doesn't have to be this way."

If I had been in my right mind, I might actually have thought she was being sincere. I wasn't. Her words had no meaning. Second Earth was lost. Saint Dane's quest to control Halla had succeeded. I had my hands around the neck of the man he chose to run it all. Through the swirl of emotion and insanity, I had a moment of total clarity. In that instant, I understood that this was inevitable. From the moment I left home with Uncle Press, all that happened had led to this. All the battles for all the territories. All the successes. The defeats. The deaths. The sacrifices. The sadness. The loneliness. I had lost everything. My life. My friends. My home. My family. Where was my family? *Where was my family?*

All of that had been prelude. It had come down to this.

"Don't do it," Nevva begged.

"She's right," Saint Dane added. "Don't do it. Show the same weakness that caused you to hide on Ibara. That is why you failed, Pendragon. You don't have the strength to lead."

I was shaking with anger. For a brief moment I thought I heard the sounds from down below. I heard the screams. I felt their fear. It was the final horror. I couldn't take it anymore. Somebody had to pay.

I shoved Naymeer out of the helicopter.

The man screamed. He plummeted down, headed directly for the flume. Our eyes locked as he fell. I could feel the surprise and terror that gripped him as he plunged to his death. For that brief moment, I embraced revenge. It felt good.

And then Saint Dane laughed.

"Finally!" he declared in triumph.

I spun back to him, holding on to the edge of the doorway, the rush of blood and adrenaline still pounding through me.

"Pendragon, it is now truly over."

I couldn't find the words to ask what that meant. Saint Dane found them for me.

"It all came down to this. *This* was the final test, Pendragon. As I predicted, you have failed."

Those words will haunt me forever.

I glanced down to see the final, excruciating moments of Alexander Naymeer's life. He fell directly into the flume. Out of sight. A moment later, a ball of light and smoke leaped from the flume, shooting straight to the sky. Straight toward us. We were hit with a blinding flash of light and a rush of energy that could only have been powered by some demonic force. The helicopter buffeted wildly. It started spinning out of control. It felt as if we were caught in a tornado. I held on to the helicopter's frame to keep from falling out. Nevva did the same across from me. Saint Dane didn't move. He stood there calmly. Laughing. The pilot no longer controlled the helicopter. We were moving, that much I could tell. But to where? Between the smoke and the bright light outside, I lost all sense of direction. We could have been flying higher, or

people from the stadium . . . and the music of the flume. I couldn't tell whether I was falling or floating. Had I been caught in the power of the flume? There was no reference.

The sounds slowly diminished. The noise of the doomed helicopter blended into the people's screams until it all became white noise. Moments passed. How many? No idea. The white noise slowly faded, leaving only the music of the flume. I no longer thought I would crash into something. I was definitely floating. For the longest time my eyes had been closed, with my arms wrapped around my head. But for how long? Seconds? Years? I had lost all sense of everything.

I slowly dropped my arms and cautiously opened my eyes. What I saw at first made no sense. I was free floating. Alone. The helicopter was gone. Saint Dane and Nevva were nowhere in sight. It seemed as if I were traveling through the flume, but it wasn't the same. Surrounding me were the floating images of Halla. It was a mess of images so dense that I couldn't see through them to the star field beyond. I saw faces I recognized from the different territories. Not individuals, but different races. Batu, Novans, Africans, gars, klees, Asians. It was a swirling sea of a billion faces, all folding in on one another. I heard their voices, too. Nothing specific though. It was more like a random chorus of words, and even song.

I was strangely calm, and more curious than frightened. What did this all mean? Unlike a normal flume trip, I didn't get the sense that I was actually moving. It was more like floating in this sea of faces. Did they see me? Was I just another one of the billion faces? Was this my fate, banished into a limbo of souls? Is this where Naymeer had exiled his enemies?

I saw my first star. Then another. The ghostly faces were

slowly disappearing, as if being blown away on a celestial breeze. The star field beyond was being revealed. Order was returning, yet something was wrong. As the faces melted, I realized I wasn't looking out through the crystal walls of the flume. I was free floating in space. That was impossible. How could I survive that?

A new image was revealed. Many, in fact. They weren't clear at first, because of the many faces that still surrounded me. As the faces disappeared, more detail came clear. They appeared to be long white streaks, like clouds. There were several of them, crisscrossing one another in no particular pattern through the star field. They reminded me of the contrails left by jets as they streak through the sky. There were dozens of them, at all different angles. Some crossed in front of me. Others went past me and on to forever. I was floating through a three-dimensional maze of infinite lines.

As the last of the faces of Halla disappeared, I recognized the streaks for what they were. They weren't clouds. They had substance. They seemed to be made of brilliant, clear crystal. Light from the stars bounced off their multifaceted surfaces, making them sparkle. I knew what I was seeing. I had seen it many times before, though from a different perspective.

I was looking at the highways through Halla. I was seeing the flumes . . . from the outside. All of them. It was a complex maze that seemed to have no beginning and no end. I knew that wasn't the case, of course. The flumes connected the territories of Halla. They were the conduits that allowed us to move between time and space. It was an awesome, humbling sight.

It also raised the question of where I was. I wasn't in a flume, that much was clear. I didn't feel like an astronaut floating in space, either. I know this makes no sense, but it didn't feel as if I were actually there. It was more as if I were imagining what I was seeing, as if it were a vision. There was no physical sensation of any kind. It wasn't as if I were lying down somewhere and dreaming either. I was really there, but I wasn't. I was part of what I was seeing, but I was a ghost. I don't know how else to describe it. I also don't know how long I was there. A minute? An hour? A billion years? It was a calm, almost spiritual feeling of being a part of the continuum of time and space, but not being bound by it. I'm not sure if I liked it or not. It just . . . was.

Then it all fell apart.

The flumes started to glow. Like neon tubes full of charged gas, the crystal flumes lit up. I heard the music return as well. Unlike every previous trip through the flume, where the music was a calming travel companion, this music sounded harsh. Angry. Chaotic. It was muffled, as if the sound were contained inside the flumes. It grew louder. More frantic. The lights grew brighter. So bright I had to squint. The music grew faster, building to something.

That's exactly what was happening. As the music reached its peak, and the glowing flumes grew so bright they nearly caused a complete whiteout in the heavens, a flume exploded. Chunks of crystal material erupted, blasting every which way. It was followed by another explosion. And another. With each new eruption, the sound was released from inside, filling the universe with chaotic debris and discordant music. When a flume exploded, its light went out. Crystal pieces of all sizes scattered through space. Some looked like mile-long chunks, others were tiny, twinkling shards. Pieces flew past me, though I didn't feel them, which added to the impression that I wasn't really there. At least not physically.

I watched in horror as the explosions continued. One after another. Three at a time. A chunk of one flume crashed into another tunnel that was still intact, breaking it in two. It was a dreadful, violent display. I was witnessing the destruction of the highways through Halla. As a final insult, I saw a large chunk of crystal heading directly for me. I didn't know what to do. Was I in danger? Would it blow past me? Or through me? After all, I was a ghost. When the crystal wall was nearly on me, I did the only thing that felt right.

I closed my eyes.

SECOND EARTH

The Conclave of Ravinia was jammed with people. More so than ever before. Every seat was filled with a true believer. Many more had to be turned away at the door. There simply wasn't enough room. Those who arrived late had to be content to sit on the stairs outside the marble structure, and wait for news to come from those who were lucky enough to be allowed inside.

The atmosphere outside the conclave was very different from the last gathering. Though security was provided by red-shirt Ravinian guardians and the New York City police, it wasn't necessary. There were no protesters. Quite the opposite. The streets were empty, except for Ravinians who came for the conclave. Nobody else dared to come within three blocks of the building. The demonstration at Yankee Stadium had served its purpose. The Ravinians had power. The Ravinians were feared.

Yet the mood of the Ravinians wasn't one of celebration. There was tension, both inside and outside the conclave building. Rumors of what had transpired at Yankee Stadium flew across the world. What exactly had happened to the people inside? The only solid fact was that over seventy thousand people entered Yankee Stadium on the evening of March 12, and nobody came out. The television cameras showed helicopters arriving over the stadium, and Alexander Naymeer striding onto the stage. He thrust his hand into the air . . . and that was it. The cameras failed. Every last one. There was no record of what occurred after Naymeer thrust his fist into the air. The broadcast ended. The tapes were clean.

Most Ravinians had their suspicions. Many had witnessed the earlier event at the conclave where twelve nonbelievers were exiled into the flume. Did something similar happen at Yankee Stadium? It was the only logical explanation, save for one minor detail: There was no flume at Yankee Stadium. Not anymore. The earth around the pitcher's mound at the ballpark was scorched. The grass destroyed. It looked as though there had been a fire. That was all. Any sign that a flume had once been there was gone. There were no witnesses. Nobody to describe how an infernal tunnel was blasted into the earth and made to swallow up tens of thousands of people.

The very next month, baseball would return. Soon after, Yankee Stadium would be vacated and turned into a museum. A newer, modern stadium would rise next door, replacing the hallowed site. Eventually the old stadium would be bulldozed, covered up, and forgotten. The mystery would never be solved, because there were no witnesses. What remained was the fear. Fear of Ravinia. It was part fact, part mystique. As horrifying as the unexplained disappearance of seventy thousand people was, it was nothing compared to the fear of what Ravinia was capable of. They would not be challenged again.

It was the turning point. Second Earth was theirs.

There were plenty of rumors about what had happened that spread across the globe. Besides the horrifying mystery that would come to be known as the Bronx Massacre, people wanted to know what had happened to Alexander Naymeer. He hadn't been seen or heard from since those final, dramatic images were broadcast from the stadium. People expected him to make some sort of appearance or announcement, especially in light of the historic vote of confidence given to Ravinia by the United Nations. Yet Naymeer was nowhere to be found. It was with that feeling of uncertainty that the Conclave of Ravinia met. The atmosphere in the room that night was a mixture of relief and dread. Hope and horror. All had gone according to Naymeer's vision. Ravinia was on the threshold of becoming a major force that would dictate the future of the world.

Yet its leader was missing. The Ravinians came to the conclave needing answers.

The room went dark. The Ravinians became quiet. A spotlight hit a podium next to the mouth of the flume. Every last person in that room hoped to see Alexander Naymeer step up to the microphone and speak to them. They desperately hoped to see him. They needed him.

They wouldn't get him. Instead, another man stepped into the light. It was someone the Ravinians were familiar with. Or thought they were. He always seemed to be at Naymeer's side, offering him advice, helping their leader with the challenges of creating a new world. His name was Eugene.

His name was Saint Dane.

His open, kind face served to both calm them and fill them with dread. Why wasn't Naymeer there? This evening Eugene wore a dark suit instead of his trademark Ravinia-red golf shirt. It was another sign that something was wrong. Eugene always had a bright smile. Not tonight. Eugene looked sober. It caused a buzz to ripple through the room. Eugene raised his hand. The crowd quieted in anticipation.

"My friends," Eugene began somberly. "Alexander Naymeer is dead."

A collective gasp and cry went up from the crowd as their worst fear was confirmed.

"Please," he said, his voice amplified through speakers. "Please. Shhh . . ."

He was soon able to quiet the crowd and continue. The only distraction was the occasional sound of someone's uncontrolled weeping.

"Alexander Naymeer was not a young man. We always knew his time with us would not last forever. He was mortal, as are we all. The excitement of recent events proved too much for his all-too-human body. He passed away quietly, painlessly, his lion's heart beating its last on a life well spent."

The weeping continued as reality settled in. People nodded and smiled to one another in support. The idea that the god-who-was-Naymeer was actually human somehow made the man even more accessible. More beloved. In spite of his awe-inspiring greatness, he was one of them. His death catapulted him from leader to legend.

"As disturbing and sad as this news may be," Eugene continued, adding resolve to his voice, "now is not the time for grief. Certainly we should mourn the passing of such a great man, but we should also realize that his passing came at the moment of his greatest triumph."

People nodded. They agreed. They wanted something positive to grab on to.

Saint Dane was all too willing to give it to them.

"Which raises the question, what are we to do now? Should we lick our wounds and stumble in the dark, after all we have achieved? All that *he* has achieved?"

There was a general murmuring. The crowd didn't like that idea.

"Should we forget what brought us here, and lament that without our leader to tell us what to do, we are nothing?"

A few "nos" were called out.

"To turn back now would mean we are no better than the people we disdain. Our future will not be determined by any one person. Our strength is in our common vision. That is what Naymeer taught us. That is what the world expects from us. That is what Halla expects from us."

Excitement was growing. The people were getting worked up. The wailing cries were heard no more.

"To turn back now would be an insult to the memory of Alexander Naymeer, and to our own beliefs and values. His mortal body may be gone, but his spirit lives on in each and every one of us."

Applause broke out.

Eugene smiled. Saint Dane smiled.

"Even now, Ravinians from Second Earth have been sent to Denduron to aid the Bedoowans in their battle against the Lowsee. Military strategists have arrived on Zadaa to help the Rokador plan an insurgency against the powerful yet primitive Batu. The island of Ibara will soon be under siege. Right here at home, the dramatic events that occurred not far from this spot have cemented our power. The people of Second Earth fall into two camps. They either embrace our philosophy, or they fear us and will be marginalized. We are at the forefront of a new world. A new Halla. That is the legacy of Alexander Naymeer. We must not fail him."

The crowd cheered. The promises were all coming true. Their cult of excellence had taken hold and would grow, even without Naymeer.

Eugene held up his hand to quiet the enthusiastic crowd.

"Naymeer foresaw all of this. He anticipated many things, including his own demise. He knew his body would not live forever. That is why he had the foresight to groom an heir to take his place."

The crowd once again gasped in dismay. Eugene pressed on, not wanting the momentum to slow.

"As great as our ship is, we must have direction. Guidance. Experience. We must have youth. There is an individual whom

Alexander Naymeer has tutored in the ways of Halla. Together they traveled to other territories, learning of the customs and idiosyncrasies that make up many different worlds. They have broken bread with leaders from all territories, forging alliances and laying the groundwork for the common good we all so desperately want. This is the person Naymeer put his trust in. This is the person who will guide us. This is the face of a new Second Earth. A new Halla. Fellow Ravinians, I present to you . . . our future."

A spotlight flashed into the flume. Standing there, wearing the dark red robe that was once worn by Alexander Naymeer, was Nevva Winter.

The crowd didn't know how to react. There were confused murmurings rather than cheers. Gasps rather than applause. It didn't bother Nevva. She looked to Eugene.

To Saint Dane.

He gave her a reassuring nod.

Nevva raised her arms as if to embrace the conclave. In an assured voice she announced, "This is not about me. This is not about any one of us. This is about us all. We are the elite. We are the strong. We are the enlightened. We are Ravinia!"

She held up her right hand—the hand with her ring. Light blasted from the stone, activating the flume. The tunnel sparkled, turning instantly to crystal. As Nevva stepped aside, light grew from within, coming forward like a ball of charged energy.

The crowd watched in awe.

The light drew right to the mouth of the flume and formed an image. It was the face of Alexander Naymeer.

People fainted. They fell to their knees. Some cried. Others simply stood in awe, holding their hands out, trying to touch the ghostly image. Naymeer had gone from leader, to legend . . . to god.

"My friends," the disembodied image bellowed with a voice that echoed eerily through the conclave building. "The first territory of Halla is now under your control. You alone will decide its future. Do not mourn my passing. Embrace my spirit. Through Nevva, I will be there for you. I will be there for you all. This is not an end, but a glorious beginning. For you. For Halla. For Ravinia."

The image of Naymeer erupted with light, turning into a three-dimensional star. Nobody flinched. They stood staring, as if the light were the very essence of Naymeer that was sent to embrace them.

Nevva looked to Eugene.

"This is it, isn't it?" she said. "After all this time. It's finally over."

"It *is* over," Saint Dane replied with confidence. "And now we can begin."

JOURNAL #36

(CONTINUED)

SECOND EARTH

I didn't feel an impact. I felt something else. Gravity. My body suddenly felt heavy. I was no longer floating, or whatever it was I was doing. It felt like lying down. Other sensations returned. I felt a chill. Air moved over me. Sound returned too. I heard the moan of a far-off, hollow wind. I didn't think I was hurt. There was no pain. I wondered whether I was dead. Not knowing what being dead felt like, I had no opinion.

Wherever I was, I was lying facedown. I cracked an eye open to see that I was stretched out on bare ground that was covered with a fine, light brown dirt. Or sand. I couldn't tell. I brought my hand to my face and touched it. It was just that. Dirt. I guess that sounds like no big deal, but it was to me. It meant I was someplace solid. Some place real. The question was, where?

I sat up to see . . . nothing. Or almost nothing. A quick three-sixty showed me a whole lot more of nothing. Still, the place felt real. I had the thought that I was in the middle of a desert, with nothing around me for miles. The air was hazy and full of dust particles that hung like fog. I had no depth perception. Could I see for ten miles or ten inches? There was no perspective. I didn't know where I was. I didn't know *when* I was.

It was a lonely place to be.

That's exactly how I felt. Lonely. I was totally, miserably alone. I had lost the battle for Halla. For Second Earth. I had become a killer. Most of the people who meant anything to me were gone. I had failed them all. Saint Dane had done exactly what he said he would do. What he predicted he would do. He had torn the territories of Halla down, so that he could rebuild them and rule the way he saw fit. Halla was now controlled by a dictator.

I sat alone in that grit, not able to move. Not wanting to move. I wouldn't know where to go anyway. I wanted to lie down, close my eyes, and let the swirling sand bury me. I was done. I had no future. There was no future worth having. If I wasn't dead, I wanted to be.

That's when I heard a voice.

At first I thought I was imagining it. It could have been a trick of the wind. It wasn't loud, or distinct in any way. I thought maybe it was someone speaking far away, and the words were being carried to me on the breeze like a whispered memory.

I heard it again. Closer. More distinct. One single word cut through the howl.

"Bobby."

I knew that voice. It was so familiar, but I couldn't grab on to it. It was like the answer drifted on the edge of my consciousness, waiting for me to reach out and grasp it. I looked around and saw nothing but dusty haze. I felt sure I was hearing a ghost.

My eye caught movement. A shadow. Something was out there. I focused on it, desperate to see anything that would tell me I wasn't trapped in an endless limbo. The shadow moved closer. It was a person. Someone was walking toward me. I couldn't find the energy to stand. The shadow walked boldly, confidently, as if it knew exactly where it was going. Whoever it was, whatever it was, it didn't seem like a ghost. It seemed to be wearing some kind of long, open coat that flapped in the breeze.

My heart stopped. I swear. I couldn't breathe. I had finally reached out to the edges of my very being and grabbed hold of the truth. It was impossible. It was beyond reason. The ghost was a man. Or the man was a ghost. He stepped out of the dusty haze and stood over me.

I saw his face. A face I hadn't seen in years. A face I thought for sure I would never see again. But he had made a promise. He said we'd be together again. That was a long time ago. So much had happened. I'd given up hope.

I shouldn't have.

He kept his promise.

Uncle Press always kept his promises.

"Hi, guy," he said casually. "Havin' a rough day?"

He looked exactly as he did the day we left home so long ago. His hair was still longish and a little messy. He still needed a shave. He still wore a brown work shirt and jeans. It really was his long, tan coat I saw flapping around as he walked. He stood over me, looking down with the smile I had missed for so long. There were a million things I wanted to say. Only one came out.

"I'm sorry," I whispered.

"Stand up, Bobby."

I slowly got to my feet and faced my uncle.

"Hey," he said with a crooked smile. "When did you get taller than me?"

I jumped forward and hugged the guy. I couldn't help myself. There was something else I couldn't help doing. I cried. Yeah, I cried. I felt as if I were six again. I think what put me over the edge was touching him. He was real. He wasn't a shadow or an illusion created by my wishful imagination. It really was Uncle Press. We stood that way for I don't know how long. He let me cry. He patted my back. He let me enjoy the feeling of having at least one part of my family back. It felt safe. I think I would have stayed like that forever, if I hadn't heard another voice call to me.

"All right! Enough!" a girl's voice said sarcastically. "You're going to get me crying too, and you do *not* want to go there."

I turned quickly to see a blond girl in blue coveralls and yellow-tinted glasses. She stood with her legs apart and her arms folded across her chest, looking at me like a disapproving parent.

"Hello, Pendragon," Aja Killian said. "What took you so long?"

I stood there, stunned. My mouth opened, but no words came out. A shadow moved toward her from behind, coming forward out of the haze. It was a big guy, who lumbered up behind Aja to give me a small wave. He once again wore the armor of a Bedoowan knight.

"I know you tried to help me," Alder said.

I stood there with my mouth open, unable to think or make sense of what I was seeing.

"A-Are you all right?" I asked my friend. It seemed like such a lame question.

"I am now" was his definite answer.

I turned to Uncle Press and asked, "Is this real?"

Uncle Press shrugged, as if to say, "Yeah, why wouldn't it be?"

My eye caught more movement. There were shadows everywhere. We were surrounded by a ring of phantoms.

"Hello, Bobby," said an elderly woman with long gray hair. "Remember me?"

I nodded numbly. It was Elli Winter. Nevva's mother. The Traveler from Quillan.

"I don't know what to say about my daughter," she said sadly.

"You don't have to say anything," I replied.

"You owe me, Pendragon," came a guy's voice that sounded pretty ticked off.

From out of the haze stepped Siry Remudi, the young bandit. The Traveler from Ibara. "If I knew you were going to bury the flume, I never would have left Ibara!"

"I didn't want to trap you there," I explained.

Siry smiled. "Yeah, I get it. I'll let it go this time, but don't you ever leave me out again."

"I take it you got my note," came another familiar voice. It was Patrick. Alive and well, or whatever it was that we were.

"I did," I answered. "I wish I could have done more with the information."

"You did just fine," Patrick assured me. "Nobody could have done better."

I heard an animal snarl. Under normal circumstances I probably would have jumped. I didn't. A beast on four legs stalked out of the haze, stood up, and walked the rest of the way on two legs. Kasha, the cat from Eelong, joined the circle.

"You made me a promise, Pendragon," the klee growled.

"I did?"

"You said that one day you would bring my ashes back to Eelong. I haven't forgotten."

I nodded.

"Hello, shorty!" came a warm voice that made me smile, and almost start crying again.

Stepping out of the haze, wearing the same dark suit he always wore on First Earth, was Gunny Van Dyke.

"Whoa now!" he exclaimed as he looked me over. "Maybe I can't be calling you 'shorty' no more!"

I ran over and gave him a hug.

"Heck of a thing, Pendragon," he said wistfully. "Heck of a thing."

"Yeah, that's one way of putting it." I sniffed.

He held me out at arm's length and asked, "You all right, son?"

Unbelievable. With all that had happened, Gunny was worried about *me*.

"Getting right real fast," I answered.

He smiled warmly. "Wouldn't expect nothing less."

"Where is he?" I asked him.

Gunny gave me a mock confused look. "Who? Who you talking about?" His eyes twinkled and he smiled slyly. He knew exactly who I was talking about.

"Hobey!" I heard a familiar voice call. "Don't go starting the party without me!"

Running into the circle, out of breath, was Vo Spader. The Traveler from Cloral. Though he looked a little older than the last time I'd seen him, so much about him was the same. His black hair was still long. He wore his black aquaneer's swimskin. He still had that mischievous look in his eye, that said he was ready for whatever adventure was coming his way.

"Haven't missed anything, have I?" he asked me.

"Heck if I know," I answered. "I have no idea what's going on."

"Ahh," Spader scoffed. "You'll get a handle, no worries." He grabbed both of my arms and leaned in to me. In a quiet, sincere voice he said, "I meant what I said, mate. I'm there for you. I'm ready."

I didn't realize how much I missed Spader until that moment. He gave me a hug, then backed away and stood next to Gunny in the wide circle.

I was standing in the center of a ring of Travelers. It's hard to describe my emotions. It was all too much to comprehend.

"Wait," I said to nobody in particular. "We're not all here."

Everyone exchanged looks. Nobody responded. At least nobody in the circle.

"Not yet," came a familiar voice from outside the ring.

A tall, dark form strode confidently into view. She wore the light armor of a Batu warrior. Strapped to her back was the long, wooden cross-stave weapon that had served her so well. Seeing her gave me a surge of confidence like I hadn't felt in a very long time.

The Traveler from Zadaa had arrived.

Loor walked right up to me and stood looking into my eyes. "Why didn't you come for me?" she demanded to know.

"I wanted to protect you" was my answer.

Loor looked surprised. Surprise turned to disbelief. Disbelief turned to intensity. "*You* wanted to protect *me*?" she declared, incredulous.

All I could do was nod dumbly.

Loor leaned in. She got right in my face, nose to nose. "Do not make that mistake again," she ordered . . . and kissed me. Right on the lips. It wasn't exactly the intense, romantic kiss we *almost* shared that incredible, rainy night back in Xhaxhu during the Festival of Azhra, but it was still pretty okay.

Except that I nearly fell over.

Loor backed off, stepped into the circle, put her hands on her hips and declared, "Now we are all here."

We were. Every one of us. Almost. Uncle Press strode into the ring, joining me in the center. I looked to him and quietly asked, "What about Mark and Courtney?"

Uncle Press shook his head and spoke softly. "They're not Travelers, Bobby. I'm sorry."

His explanation made sense, but it didn't make the news sting any less.

Uncle Press stepped away from me and walked around the inside of the circle. As he moved, he looked at each Traveler in turn. Nobody said a word. Nobody dared to. The only sound was the far-off howl of wind and the crunch of Uncle Press's boots on the gritty dirt.

"We've lost," he declared. "The fate of Halla was in our hands. All of our hands. Yet this is where we find ourselves. Beaten. Alone. Outcast."

As painful as this was to hear, nobody turned away from him. Each in turn held his eyes when he approached them.

"None of you asked for this responsibility. None of you know why you were chosen. Why you are Travelers. There was a reason for that. It's time you knew."

My eye caught something in the distance. It was mostly obscured by the haze. For a brief moment the wind pushed the dust around enough for me to catch a glimpse. It was only a shadow, with no detail, but it seemed to be a building. A tall building that came to a point on top. It was on a slight angle, as if it were listing to the side. I still had no perspective to understand how far away it was, or how big it was, but its shape looked vaguely familiar. A small glint of light flashed off what looked like glass windows. Then it was gone, obscured by the haze.

Uncle Press continued his walk around the inside of the circle of Travelers. He made sure to look everyone dead in the eye. Nobody flinched. When he had covered the full loop, he stopped at me.

"Bobby," he said, "I told you a long time ago this would not end until Saint Dane thinks he's won. Do you remember?"

"Remember? I've thought about it every day."

Uncle Press nodded thoughtfully. "Would you say he thinks he's won?"

"Yeah, pretty much" was my answer.

Uncle Press continued to walk. I saw his jaw muscles working. He was clenching his teeth. He was not happy. "I'll tell you all something right here, right now. This is *not* the way things were meant to be." He was angry. In all the time I'd known him, I'd never seen him show that kind of emotion. He wasn't out of control or anything. He was just incredibly intense.

"Pendragon," he barked. He never called me Pendragon. It made me jump. "You've made mistakes. We've *all* made mistakes. My question to you is, are you able to see past them? Or will it end here?"

I didn't answer right away. That was too huge a question to give a quick, flip answer to. It was probably the most important question I had ever been asked in my life. I had to be sure that whatever I said, I meant it. That I believed it. A few short minutes before, I was lying alone in the dust, feeling defeated and alone. Now I stood in the center of a group of people that meant everything in Halla to me. In turn, I looked into the eyes of each one. I needed to draw strength from them. I needed to know I wasn't in this alone.

I looked to Elli Winter, the kindly historian from Quillan who had lost her husband, and then lost her daughter to the temptations of greed and the lure of power.

To Siry Remudi, the young outlaw, who was driven to uncover the truth about Ibara and live up to the high expectations of his father.

To Patrick Mac, the teacher from Third Earth, who struggled through his own insecurity and ultimately gave his life in a failed effort to put Earth back on course.

To Kasha, the hunter klee, who rebelled against her tribe to fight for equality among the races of Eelong.

To Vo Spader, the carefree aquaneer from Cloral, who set out to avenge the death of his father, and had a hand in stopping Saint Dane on three territories.

To Gunny Van Dyke, the soft-spoken hotel worker, whose calm wisdom helped the klee of Eelong to thrive, and who made an impossible, brave choice by letting a tragic moment in history play out the way it was supposed to, in order to save First Earth.

To Aja Killian, the brilliant scientist, who tried in vain to save Veelox, but didn't live long enough to know that the plan she put in motion eventually succeeded hundreds of years in the future.

To Loor, the fearless girl from Zadaa, whose abilities as a

warrior were second to her fierce belief in using her skills to fight for what was right and just.

And finally to Alder, the selfless knight from Denduron, who always put the safety and well-being of others ahead of his own. His loyalty and sincere goodness were perhaps the greatest of any of us.

Then there was me. Bobby Pendragon. The Traveler from Second Earth. The lead Traveler. As much as I didn't want to admit it, the role that the other Travelers played in this battle was secondary to mine. Not that they didn't sacrifice and fight as hard, or harder, than I ever did, but when it came down to it, I was the one on the line. Saint Dane told me more than once that the battle for Halla was really the battle between the two of us. It was probably the only truthful thing he ever said. He said it was all about him and me.

I lost.

As I stood there, looking into the eyes of the Travelers, something happened. For each one of those brief moments, I reconnected with a true friend. Though no words were exchanged, they were each telling me the same thing. They were with me. I truly believed that if I had asked any one of them to follow me through the gates of hell, I'd have to hold them back from going in first.

"Pendragon?" Aja called out.

I turned to her.

"A long time ago I asked you to give me another crack at Saint Dane. You said you'd see what you could do. Remember?"

"I do."

"I'm calling in that promise, Pendragon. Right now. See what you can do."

The other Travelers looked to me, waiting for a response.

Uncle Press called out, "What do you say, Bobby?"

I took one last look around at my friends. The Travelers. Each one of them gave me the same, silent response. They nodded with confidence.

I walked to my uncle and declared, "I say . . . we are *so* not done yet."

Uncle Press smiled. It wasn't dramatic. It wasn't huge. But it was real. Just as quickly, he let it drop and turned to the others.

"All right then," he announced. "Now it's our turn."

He strode out of the circle, walked off, and disappeared into the haze. Where he was going, I didn't know. The Travelers watched him leave, then turned to me as one. They had heard my answer to Uncle Press. They wanted their own.

"He's right," I declared. "I've made mistakes. More than my share. Hopefully, I've learned from them, but I can't guarantee anything. There's only one thing I can promise. I'm taking this to the end. Saint Dane thinks we're already there. I don't. Where it will be . . . when it will be . . . I don't know. But I'm going to be there. Whether he likes it or not, Saint Dane will be there too. He says things have played out the way he planned. Maybe they have. I say we start making plans of our own."

The circle closed. The Travelers drew close and stood together, shoulder to shoulder, facing me. I couldn't have been more proud.

I stood up straight and said, "And so we go."

I walked past them, headed after Uncle Press. The Travelers followed behind me. First Alder, then Loor, then the others. There were eleven of us. Each more different than the next. All with the same mindset.

Things weren't the way they were meant to be.
It was our job to make things right.
We were the soldiers of Halla.
It was time for us to take it back.

END OF JOURNAL #36

To Be Continued . . .